BIND UP YOUR BROKEN HEARTS

Cynthia Mills

Souvenir Historical Books
Cleveland

Other books by Cynthia Mills:

Missing, Believed Killed
Bring the Dead to Life

ISBN: 978-1-4303-0067-0
Published by Souvenir Historical Books through Lulu.com
www.lulu.com

Dedication

To all families who have suffered losses in wars

To the survivors of war,
who carry those memories with them always

To Noreen Beacon Bellamy
1924-2004
A wonderful lady who is sorely missed

And to my Grandmother,
Lottie Kotecki
June 3, 1909 – April 1, 1976
She loved her grandchildren and gave them
many gifts of her heart that remain with them

Acknowledgements

Once again, I have to thank Mike Neibert, computer expert deluxe, for the great cover and his expertise. Jim Grundy gave me the idea for the title when he told me one of his many excellent Great War stories about a Vicar seeking to console his congregation by quoting Isaiah. It seemed appropriate for my story – thank you, Jim!

My dear friends who have encouraged me to keep writing despite the obstacles: Diana Campbell, my proofreader and lifelong friend; Margaret Gallagher, a rock of support and generosity; and Sherri Robertson, who stands by me through thick and thin. I also can't forget those who have told me how much they love the story that began with *Missing, Believed Killed*: Dennis Alstrand, Dr. Louis Barbato, Don Barth, Ginny Billson, Jenny Bowey, Barbara Britt, Margaret Frank, Katy Glenn, Sally Hendricks, Philomena and Dexter Johnson, Sharon Moss, Bonnie Orgovan, Chuck Rippin, Irene Rozakis, Mary Smith, Ann Thompkins and Steve Wright.

My colleagues and friends at Lake Erie College have been so supportive of my work: Maria Bagshaw, Deb and Ric Cattell, Sue Coen, Elisabeth Giedt, Lori Greuber, Jamie Harty, Alista Lineburg, Robin McDermott, Mary Kay McManamon, Michael Norris, Laken Piercy, Nancy Prudic, Lorrie Rowe, Eileen 'Bud' Roberts, Franzi Ruehl, Dale Sheptak, Jason Spotz, John Stewart, Bob Trebar, Joyce and Steve Yachanin, Sue Wovrosh, and many others too numerous to mention here, but you are not forgotten! A very special thank you to Holly Menzie, a wonderful writer and good friend. Her articles and written works have helped so many – including me!

Many thanks to my dear friends in England who have contributed so much to the mosaic of my knowledge about that wonderful country and its history: Ian and Elaine Whitlock and their family, Michelle, Wayne, Tom, and Jack Young, Maurice Johnson, Sue Light, Alie Cameron, Roger Packham, Pat Rodgers, Godfrey Goodman, Brian and Mary Rust, Tom Morgan, Terry Reeves, Avril Williams, Ted Smith, Malcolm Bowey, Mark Davison of the Surrey Mirror, Harold Batchelor, Violet Weatherley – the list could go on, but without their help and input, this trilogy could not have been written.

As always, my family: my sister Laurie, my niece Casey, and my stepmother Judy – thank you.

Verily the Lord has sent me to bring glad tidings

He has sent me to bind up the brokenhearted...

To comfort all who mourn

To place on those who mourn a diadem

Instead of ashes...

To give them oil of gladness in place of mourning

A glorious mantle instead of a listless spirit...

And to open the eyes of those who are bound.

Isaiah 61:1-3

Chapter One

Margery watched as her husband's face was covered with a white sheet and put into the ambulance. Jack, she cried to herself. Jack, what happened here tonight? Her face was an impassive mask, her gaily colored head scarf flapping in the strong wind as she stared at the closed doors of the ambulance.

"Margery?" The familiar voice of Upper Marstone's resident physician, Dr. Mitchell, sounded in her ear as he took her arm gently and steered her out of the path of the ambulance. There was no need for sirens now; Jack was dead. An hour ago she had stood at her front door, waiting for him and wondering why he was so late.

"I'll take you home," Dr. Mitchell said, maintaining his grip on her arm as she walked obediently next to him. She stopped suddenly and looked at him. "Elizabeth," she said, her eyes alarmed. "Where is Elizabeth?" She broke away from his grasp and searched the small throng of people who were looking at her sympathetically. Where was her daughter? Elizabeth had driven her to this spot on the road between their quintessential English village of Upper Marstone and the nearby town of Caterham. The urgency in her voice when she told her mother they had to go to Caterham had sounded so unlike her lively eighteen-year old daughter Margery had been compelled to get in the car. Now Jack was dead.

Elizabeth was talking to a constable who seemed to be interrogating her about what had happened. Elizabeth had been near Jack when he pulled a gun on a stranger hidden in the woods. She had made an attempt to stop him from shooting the man. The man, Margery pondered. In her shock she was sure the man had been Robert, Jack's brother. Robert, her darling who had been lost nearly twenty years earlier in 1916 on the Somme. It must have been her imagination caused by the horror that unfolded before her this night. It could not have been Robert, although she was sure she had looked into his

9

eyes. Those eyes were unmistakable – blue-grey with silver lights in them. Yet under duress the mind can play tricks.

"Mother," Elizabeth said as a light rain began to fall, "Are you all right?" Margery was trying to recall the man in more detail. He wore Robert's buckle ring...

"She's quite a bit in shock, you see," Dr. Mitchell nodded over Margery's head to Elizabeth. "I'm sure you are feeling upset yourself, dear. Can I take you both home?" He looked at Margery's staring, dark eyes. Haunted eyes, he thought. Haunted by what happened to Jack, but something more.

He turned his gaze to Elizabeth, whose slender, graceful frame and grey eyes were unlike either Jack or Margery. Not one to spread rumors, he could only conjecture to himself that Elizabeth Morne was very like her uncle Robert, who had died in the Great War. Of course, in families, genetics can cause traits to emerge in succeeding generations, so it was not totally unusual that she should favor her uncle. Still, the resemblance struck him as they stood on the dark, windswept road.

"I think I should go to hospital to be with Jack," Margery murmured almost to herself. "He may need me and...."

Elizabeth stared at Dr. Mitchell, her own eyes full of tears. There was no need for him to explain to her that Jack was dead. It was obvious she not only knew, but knew there was nothing they could do by going to hospital. "Come on, Mummy," Elizabeth cajoled her nearly-catatonic mother toward Dr. Mitchell's car. "I'll bring our car back. You go with Dr. Mitchell." She pushed her mother gently toward Dr. Mitchell's blue roadster.

"No," Margery said, trying to pull away, "I must see Jack. I have to see Jack. Where have they ..."

"There, there, Margery," Dr. Mitchell said gently, putting her into his car. "I'll see you home. Tomorrow we can sort out the details. Tonight you need to rest." Elizabeth smiled gratefully at him as he motioned for her to get in as well. "Perhaps you should let someone else bring the car back to the house, Elizabeth." Elizabeth shook her head and said, "Daddy loved that car, Dr. Mitchell. I think he would want me to drive it home, not anyone else." She turned away quickly as he started to protest, fighting back her own grief and tears over her father's death.

Margery stared straight ahead as he drove carefully away from the scene. What had happened here tonight? What information he gathered was that Jack Morne had walked several miles from Upper Marstone, ostensibly to meet someone he knew from his past. He had brought a relic of the Great War with him – a German pistol he had taken from a dead officer. This man he was meeting was an enigma, but must have been someone he knew from his days in the Army Service Corps, perhaps someone unstable. Jack had tried to kill the man, but apparently Elizabeth's timely action in trying to wrest the gun from her father had caused the man only a flesh wound in his upper arm. The presence of both an Army doctor in full regalia and a nurse who accompanied this man to hospital proved that this stranger must be an escaped lunatic from one of the many hospitals that still harbored the remnants of those whose minds were destroyed in the War.

What happened to Jack was that the stress of this incident triggered his blood pressure to soar and he had a stroke that killed him outright. As his doctor he had warned Jack repeatedly to relax, to let himself enjoy his wife and daughter and take a holiday. Jack was just about to turn forty-one in November, far too young to be lying under a white sheet in the hospital morgue.

He turned to look at Margery on his left, carefully avoiding a badger that had wandered into the road. That haunted expression on her face seemed dreamy in the darkness. As a girl she had been much sought after by both Morne brothers, and had been engaged to Robert. He seemed to recall that she had married Jack with unseemly haste very quickly after the news had arrived that Robert was missing in action. Although not the prettiest girl in the village, her dark eyes and hair had given her an almost exotic demeanor.

He drove toward the new cottages on Tilburstow Hill, thinking again of Jack and his final actions. The vision of Jack as a boy came to him so strongly he had to swerve to bring the car back on the road. Jack had always been a strange boy, dark, like Margery, but his darkness had an ominous cast to it. So unlike his older brother Robert, whose grey-blue eyes and fairer tones had captured the heart of the young Margery. It didn't surprise him that Jack should die in such a bizarre fashion. The War had produced this effect in him. He had known of Jack's continuing shell-shock symptoms. Margery had briefly mentioned the nightmares Jack had regularly.

Tomorrow he would try to sort things out, but now he had to get Margery home, give her a sedative, and arrange for someone to be there with her and Elizabeth. As strong as Elizabeth appeared, she, too, needed looking after. Margery's sister May had been very ill and would not be able to handle the trauma well. Sally Shepherd seemed the logical choice. She had been Margery's friend since they were girls. Her husband, Billy, had been Robert Morne's dearest friend. Billy had been wounded twice in the War, and also suffered recurrent nightmares. His mind was made up to ring Sally as they pulled up to the house, lights still ablaze as if Jack were inside, waiting for Margery.

Elizabeth pulled up behind them, switching off her headlamps and coming over to the doctor's car. Margery made no move to get out, still sitting with a dreamy, dazed expression on her face. Dr. Mitchell nudged her arm, but she seemed not to notice. Elizabeth appeared at the passenger door, her expression a combination of pain and worry. She tapped lightly and Margery turned to look at her.

"Come on, Mummy," Elizabeth said as she opened the car door and took her mother's arm. "It is far too cold and windy for us to be staying outside." Margery nodded and followed Elizabeth to the house, as if she were her child instead of the other way around. Dr. Mitchell gathered up his bag and went up the front path behind them.

It always amazed him how normal things seemed when such abnormal circumstances had occurred. He had been in many houses where someone had suffered and died, yet the tables, bureaus, and lamps all looked almost arrogant in their normalcy. A savory smell of the dinner Jack would never have met his nostrils as he stepped in from the wind.

"Would you like a cup of tea, Dr. Mitchell?" Elizabeth questioned. "I've just put the kettle on." Her calm demeanor belied the shattered girl beneath.

"No, I think I will tend to your mother first. I don't think she should be alone tonight. Or you either, for that matter. I'd like to ring Sally Shepherd so she can stay."

Elizabeth's composure slipped slightly, but she quickly gathered herself again. "I am fine, Dr. Mitchell. Mummy won't be alone." Her voice cracked as she fought back tears.

"Now look here, Elizabeth," he said, guiding her to the settee next to her mother. He sat down between them, Margery still unresponsive and lost in another world. "I know you are a very strong and capable young lady, but these are unusual circumstances. What happened tonight was tragic," he continued carefully as Elizabeth put her head down and gulped audibly, fighting back tears, "and it would put an old doctor's mind at rest to know that someone was here. I would like to give you both a sedative tonight. It will help you sleep."

"But I don't want to sleep!" Elizabeth said, getting up suddenly, tears shining in her eyes. "My father is dead, my mother is in shock, and..."

"And you need to rest, dear," he said gently, guiding her to a chair. "Let me give you this sedative. Then you can run along to bed. I'll see to your mother until Sally can get here." He pulled out a syringe from his bag. Elizabeth waved it off.

"No, Dr. Mitchell, I do not want a sedative," Elizabeth said. "Save that for Mummy. But I will go to bed. You can ring Sally if you like. Goodnight." She turned her tear-stained face away from him, her woolen plaid skirt swirling quickly after her as she disappeared up the stairs.

The kettle was whistling loudly from the kitchen. Dr. Mitchell checked on Margery, who still sat silently, then headed toward the kitchen. The table was set for three, a cold roast sat on the cooker, and everything seemed cozy and comfortable on this cold, windy night. He turned off the kettle, gasping slightly as he inadvertently caught his own ghostly reflection in the kitchen window.

Sally Shepherd had heard something about an accident, and agreed to come straightaway when Dr. Mitchell rang. He told her he would give her the details when she arrived. Within minutes both Billy and Sally Shepherd stood on the front doorstep, their worried expressions mirrors of one another.

"Where is she?" Sally said, taking off her coat and handing it to Billy. "Is Elizabeth all right? And Jack?"

"Jack is dead," Dr. Mitchell said as Sally stopped in her tracks. "Dead?" she repeated. Billy dropped the coats down and put his arms around his wife. "What happened, Doctor?" Billy asked quietly.

Dr. Mitchell recounted the story, including the man who seemed to be the cause of the tragedy. "Have any idea who he might be, Billy?" Dr. Mitchell queried hopefully. Billy shook his head.

"Let me go to Margery," Sally said as they all went into the neat parlor. The room was light and airy, with pale shades of green, pink and blue on creamy backgrounds. Margery did not acknowledge their presence.

"Hello, Margery, dear," Sally said, sitting down and hugging her. "How are you now?" Margery's pale color and lack of expression frightened her.

"I'd like to give her a sedative so she can sleep tonight," Dr. Mitchell said, again drawing out the syringe. "Elizabeth has already gone to bed, refusing a sedative. She is deeply upset, as is to be expected. She is a strong-willed girl, so I thought it best not to push the issue."

"Of course," Sally said, holding Margery's cold hand. Dr. Mitchell gave Margery the injection and told Sally to take her upstairs.

"She'll be better able to deal with reality in the morning," Dr. Mitchell told Billy once Margery went upstairs. "She'll need someone to lean on. Knowing how long you and Sally have been friends with both of them, I hoped you might be willing to help with the funeral details and other things."

"Yes, of course we will," Billy said, sitting down heavily on the sofa. Dr. Mitchell studied him with a practiced eye. Another man who needed to look after himself better, or he, too, would wind up like Jack. Billy had always been heavily built, but at his age his girth would only hurt him.

"It's this bloke I can't understand," Billy said, his hazel eyes reflecting concern and puzzlement. "Why would anyone want to kill Jack? Or, more like, why would Jack want to kill anyone? It makes no sense whatsoever to me. Jack never said anything about having a problem in the Army with anyone."

"Well, Jack was always very secretive, as we know too well," Dr. Mitchell said, gathering up his hat and coat. "I'll make enquiries, of course. The man is in hospital in Caterham, I believe. A flesh wound of the arm, apparently. If I saw correctly, it seemed he had a seizure right before he was taken away in the ambulance."

"Blimey!" Billy said, walking Dr. Mitchell to the door. "And you said there was an Army doctor there as well? We're nearly twenty years on since the War ended. I didn't think there were that many blokes left in hospital from that War."

"Unfortunately that War caused more horror than any of us can imagine, and it is warehoused in hospitals across the country." Dr. Mitchell smiled sadly at Billy, noticing his obvious limp from the shrapnel wounds he suffered. He opened the door, the wind howling into the room and blowing the curtains askew.

"Goodnight, Billy," he called. "Thank you. I'll see what I can find out about this man in hospital."

"Goodnight, Dr. Mitchell," Billy shouted. He turned around and looked at the house. Jack's house, he thought, but not anymore. "What have you gone and done, Jack?" he asked sadly as he went upstairs to tell Sally he would be going home.

Billy said his goodnights to Sally and Margery, noticing Margery's vacant expression, raising his eyebrows as he left. Sally gave him a wan smile, pulling up a chair next to the bed while Margery rested, her eyes shut and her face pale.

"Sally?" she heard Margery call to her after she had dozed off for a few minutes in the chair. "Sally?" Sally opened her eyes and reached for Margery's outstretched hand.

"Are you all right, Marge?" Sally said, looking into the frightened eyes of her friend.

"Jack? Where is Jack?" Margery's voice rose as she looked around. "Where is he?"

"He's not here right now, Marge," Sally said weakly. What could she say? It was apparent Margery did not remember the night's events and was in a stupor from the sedative. Better to wait and discuss things in the clear light of day.

"Sally," Margery said, trying to sit up. "He was there tonight. I saw him."

"Yes, Marge, Jack was with you tonight," Sally said, trying to get Margery to lie back down and straightening up the blankets.

"Not Jack," Margery said, grabbing Sally's arm. "Robert."

Sally froze at the sound of his name. Robert! Of course, the sedative had no doubt made Margery delirious.

"Perhaps it was someone who looked like Robert," Sally said, smoothing the hair from Margery's face. Margery's eyes seemed unusually bright.

14

"No, Sally," Margery insisted. "It was Robert. I looked into his eyes. I could never mistake his eyes for anyone else's, not ever. No matter how many years have passed, I would know those eyes in a minute." She seemed very convinced of her story. Sally thought it best to go along with her so she would relax and go back to sleep.

"Sometimes we see the people we need to when we are feeling upset," Sally said carefully. "That may be why you thought you saw him. Or perhaps he is more on your mind because of the time of year it is, with his birthday Sunday...."

"No, Sally," Margery persisted. "He had the buckle ring like mine. He was there. He smiled at me and I knew he was there. He was warm and alive. I touched his hand." She fell into the pillow, her eyes rolling back.

Sally stood over her, not sure what to think. The night's events seemed so unreal – Jack dying so suddenly, some strange man attacking him, Margery thinking she saw Robert. She shuddered involuntarily and decided that Margery's calm breathing was enough for her to go downstairs and rest on the sofa.

Elizabeth got up early the next morning, stopping briefly by her parents' room and feeling a stab of grief when she saw her mother lying alone in the bed. It did not seem as if the night's events could really have happened and that her father was gone. She went downstairs and saw Sally Shepherd on the sofa, a crocheted afghan over her. Yes, it was real, or Sally would not be here this morning.

The kitchen seemed cold and strange, the table still set for last night's meal that had never occurred. What were you doing out there with that gun, Daddy? Elizabeth kept thinking about it as she put the kettle on the hob. It was so out of character for her father she could not even fathom what possessed him. He was a quiet man, one to walk away from a fight rather than initiate one. He seemed to be the aggressor in this fray on the road to Caterham. She shook her head and picked up her tea mug, sitting at the table when the door opened.

"Oh, Elizabeth," Sally said, trying to smooth down her ash-blonde hair. "I thought perhaps your mother had got up. She had a restless night. How are you?" Sally's kind blue eyes looked at her as she touched her arm.

"I don't know, really," Elizabeth said, starting to get up to make a cup of tea for Sally, who waved her back and got it herself. "I can't understand what Daddy was doing, and who that man was. Why? Why would he do something so unlike him?" Elizabeth stared straight ahead, her fine features looking ashen in the grey light.

"It is all very odd, I grant you that," Sally said, sitting down with her tea and again putting her hand on Elizabeth's arm. "Billy is going to try and find out who the man is. Perhaps that will shed some light on what happened."

"The only thing I can think of is that this man was threatening to Mummy and me," Elizabeth mused, keeping her gaze on the white china handle on the cabinet. "There would be nothing else that would make Daddy act so. Why would anyone want to harm us?" She put her cup down and continued to stare at the cabinet.

"Elizabeth," Margery said, coming into the kitchen. She had washed and dressed, pulling her hair severely away from her face, enhancing her cut-glass cheekbones, a feature she had given to her daughter. Her dark eyes looked hollow and her somber grey dress did little to give her any sign of life. She went to her daughter and put her arms around her shoulders. Elizabeth gave a little sigh, then began to cry, so loudly that Margery sat down and pulled her into her arms.

"There, darling," Margery said, rocking her back and forth. "There now. You cry, my darling. Mummy is here for you." She continued to rock her daughter gently as Elizabeth wept. Sally went to the stove, putting the kettle on to make Margery a cup of tea. She did not want to intrude on this moment between mother and daughter, this moment of grief at the loss of father and husband.

Margery remained dry-eyed while her daughter wept. She had cared for Jack, but not loved him. It was a simple fact, one Jack well knew. The circumstances of his death were so odd, but Jack had always been odd. He had done things in ways others never understood. Elizabeth had adored him, and he had given all the love he had inside him to his daughter. Margery had not wanted his love; of that he had been certain. In her sadness and confusion over his death, she almost felt a sense of relief that now the charade was over and she would not have to go on acting like Jack's wife. She had always felt like Robert's wife.

She accepted the tea gratefully from Sally as Elizabeth stopped crying and wiped her eyes with a handkerchief proffered by Sally. "Why don't you have a long bath, darling, while I find out what needs to be done next?" Margery smoothed Elizabeth's silky brown hair from her forehead. This morning her face radiated the look of her father, more so because Margery was sure she had seen his face again last night.

Elizabeth went upstairs as Margery drank her tea in silence, only murmuring a few words to Sally in reply as to making the funeral arrangements and contacting the vicar. Her mind went back to last night, that electrifying moment when Robert knelt over his brother's body and looked into her eyes. Was he the ghost that appears to claim the souls of the dead? He

16

had been too warm, too alive. She had touched his hand, and his buckle ring. The exact ring she had on her hand. Unconsciously she touched the ring. Perhaps Sally was right about the time of year. Robert would have been forty-two on Sunday. In 1916 he went missing on September 28th, a few days after his birthday.

"So would you like Billy to do that for you, Marge?" Sally repeated, noticing that Margery's expression had assumed a vague look. Not one of grief, but as if she were far away.

"Sorry?" Margery said, focusing on Sally. "I was thinking of last night."

"It was a horrible experience for both of you," Sally said, taking her hand. "Jack was too young to die like that. Billy is going to find out what he can about the whole thing. What I asked is whether you would like Billy to take care of the arrangements for you. He will, you know."

Margery smiled, the first smile Sally had seen. It was reminiscent of the smile of the girl she knew so long ago, a girl in love. What an odd expression, Sally thought. Perhaps I had better not leave her alone.

"I would appreciate that," Margery said, getting up and putting the cups into the sink. "It would help me greatly. I don't even know where to start. There is so much that is trying to find its way into my mind now. Like this." She pulled out the marriage certificate between her and Robert, a document she had found on the car seat as they sped toward the confrontation on the road to Caterham.

Sally took the certificate and stared at it, then looked at Margery in disbelief. "But you never said you married Robert! Why?" Sally's expression was one of hurt and uncertainty.

Margery turned from the sink and smiled slyly. "It was Jack. Always what Jack wanted. Do you remember when I followed Robert to Folkestone before he went to France? I married him that night Sally, as you can see from the certificate. We went to a room and had one beautiful night together. That night is as clear in my memory as if it were yesterday. Can you guess the rest of the story?"

Sally contemplated the paper as if she thought it would speak to her. The rest of the story? That two months later she married Robert's brother Jack after Robert was said to be 'missing, believed killed,' on the Somme? It had seemed so odd to her at the time, but Margery had offered no explanation. Seven months later Elizabeth was born. 'Early,' Margery's sister May had said. Sally lifted her eyes from the paper and gasped.

"Elizabeth is Robert's daughter," she said blankly. "You were Robert's wife at the time."

"Jack went to Folkestone to find the marriage certificate so I could give Elizabeth Robert's name and claim his pension," Margery said calmly.

"Without it I would have to fend for myself as a single mother with a child. Not the easiest thing to do. When Jack came back from Folkestone, he told me no certificate existed. Apparently he assumed Robert had 'tricked' me into believing we were actually married, in order to have his wicked way with me." She barked out a laugh that echoed around the colorless kitchen, all surfaces appearing grey in the bleak light. "All these years I believed it, too, that we had not been married."

"So Jack offered to marry you?" Sally asked hesitantly, not liking the look on Margery's face.

"Yes," Margery replied. "When he knew about the marriage being legitimate in 1919, he never told me. He just let me keep believing the worst of Robert." Her expression hardened as she peered into the distance, as if looking for Jack to confront him.

"Perhaps he thought it made no difference once you were married to him and knew Robert was not coming back," Sally said helpfully. Jack could do some odd things, but she did not believe he would have hid this information from Margery for any reason other than he thought it was unimportant. It was a flimsy excuse. Sally did not want Margery to become more upset than she was already.

"But Robert has come back," Margery said, sitting down and looking directly into Sally's eyes. "I saw him last night at the crossroads. I saw him, Sally. There was no mistaking him."

Sally had hoped that the trauma of last night would have dissipated in the morning light and that the belief that Margery had seen Robert would have been just a grief-ridden dream. Strangely, Margery did not seem a grief-stricken widow, although Sally knew that she had never loved Jack. It was not until this morning that she had truly understood the façade of marriage that her friend lived every day.

"Look, Marge," Sally said gently. "What happened last night was too unbelievable for any of us to understand. When people are under great strain, they sometimes see what comforts them. I think you thought you saw him."

Margery sighed. Yes, she knew that it was probably true, but for that moment she wanted to believe he was back. The strange thing is that she was sure it was Robert. He looked older and more mature. Would she have been able to conjure that in her mind's eye?

"It now remains for me to tell Elizabeth the truth about who her father is," Margery said, sipping her too-hot tea gingerly. "She'll have to know the truth sooner or later. She obviously saw the marriage certificate. God knows what else Jack kept locked in that drawer." She gazed vacantly as Sally shifted on her chair.

"Don't tell her about Robert," Sally whispered. "Not yet, Marge. She is so upset about Jack. It just doesn't seem the right time to tell her about this."

"Upset about Jack?" Margery exclaimed. "She should have good reason to be upset about Jack and what he has created. I am upset about Jack, too, leaving this issue unresolved. If he were here I think I would..." She clenched her fists as Elizabeth's pale face appeared at the kitchen door.

"Mummy?" Elizabeth questioned, wondering why her mother seemed so angry. "I thought I might go to Daddy's office and make sure everything is locked up tight. When I was there last night everything was in a mess." She lowered her head, not wanting to meet her mother's angry expression.

"Yes, Jack left a mess, he certainly did," Margery said. "But go on if you want to. Just don't move anything at present. There's a lot we need to talk about." She hesitated and caught Sally's warning glance. Sally was right; it was not the time to tell Elizabeth the truth.

"Do you want me to bring any of his things back here?" Elizabeth knew that her mother's anger was normal in the circumstances. What would they do now? She figured she would have to forego University now and get a job. All that paled with the fact that she would never see her father again.

"Why don't you go and make a start on things there?" Sally smiled, trying for brightness but missing by a few degrees. "I'll sort your mother out, and make sure you have a nice lunch waiting for you when you get back." She nodded encouragingly at Elizabeth, who stared at her mother's back.

"Yes, all right," Elizabeth said, furrowing her brow but trying to give Sally a weak smile. "I just don't seem to know what to do. The police said they would like to talk to Mummy and me about what happened. They may be by today as well." She turned quickly, the kitchen door shutting behind her.

"Police?" Margery said. "What can I tell them? That Jack never confided in me? That even though I had known Jack for nearly 25 years I never knew what he was really thinking? I have no explanation for his behavior, or any idea of what he was doing. I am sure the police would be happy to know that I have been living a monstrous lie for nearly twenty years." She began to sob quietly as Sally put her arms around her.

"You did what you had to for Elizabeth," Sally said, trying to comfort her. "And Jack knew that, too. He knew why you married him. Just try to remember some good in him, because there was something good in him. He loved you, Marge, in his own way. He did love Elizabeth as his own daughter. Let's try to get through these next few days, for Elizabeth's sake. Then you can decide what you want to tell her about you and Robert." Margery looked up, thankful to have such a level-headed friend who could help her steer her course through this nightmare.

19

Elizabeth walked down the High Street, noticing the furtive glances from shop windows as she passed by. She held her head up, the cool autumn air playing with her sleek brown page boy cut. Everyone knew about her father, she was sure of that. They probably think he went mad, she smiled dismally to herself. There had to be a good reason for his doing what he did. It centered on that man, the man who was standing in the shadows. When he emerged and knelt down by her father's body, she felt her mother start as she looked at him. There was something almost electrifying between them. Her mother recognized this man and was just not admitting it.

The office door had been shut and locked, most likely by the constable last evening. She pulled out her key and opened the door. All the papers that were on the desk last night seem to have been taken. She rummaged through the desk but could find no trace of the telegram she saw last night. The comfy leather chair, her father's one indulgence in the spartan office surroundings, offered her a refuge as she sat down heavily. "Daddy," she called out plaintively, "I wish you could explain all this to me. I just don't understand." Tears pricked her eyes as she looked at the silly little things she had bought for him on holiday trips: a large conch shell, a glass paperweight with a single rose inside, and a tiny hand-carved dog. He had them on his desk, along with his business paraphernalia. She began to sob softly when she heard a knock on the door.

It was the young constable from last night, nervously holding his hat in his hand as he enquired whether he might ask her some questions. Somehow it seemed out of place for him to be in her father's domain. The house was always Mummy's, but here her father had his own world. Obviously a world she knew little about. It was a world of his own. And his secrets.

The constable nervously questioned her again about the events of last night, going over every detail with her and asking her if she knew of anyone who might want to harm her father. His face was pink and flushed, his strawberry blond hair highlighting his ruddy complexion. Wearily she recounted the story again and assured him she knew of no one who would hurt her father. He had been a pillar of the community, a good husband and a loving father. It made no sense.

"That man who caused all this," Elizabeth asked as he finished his questions and started to leave, "Have they found out who he is? I think if you ask him just what he was doing there you will find your answers."

He shuffled nervously toward the door. "From what I know, Miss, he is isolated on doctor's orders in the Caterham hospital. No one has had a chance to talk to him yet, as he had a seizure and he's not conscious, you see. Wounded in the War, the guv said. In the head. Until he wakes up he can't talk. They won't release his name as yet."

Elizabeth felt like going to the hospital, walking in the room and telling that man to get up and explain why her father was dead. Why did he come here? If he had not, her father would still be alive.

"Thank you, constable," she replied. "If you are going to talk to my mother, would it be possible to wait until after my father's funeral? She is in a very bad state of shock right now. I don't think she saw much of anything." She smiled at him as brilliantly as she could manage. He blushed crimson, clearing his throat in embarrassment.

"Well, I suppose that can wait, if you think it best, Miss," he smiled back at her shyly. He hadn't known such a pretty girl existed in the village before, as she had never mingled much with the village crowd. Posh sort, not the sort he went round with.

"I so appreciate that," Elizabeth said, touching his arm lightly. "I won't forget how kind you have been."

"That's all right, Miss," he smiled again before his expression became serious. "Sorry for your loss. Your Dad was a right nice bloke to me. I used to come here and hang about. He taught me a lot about motors and things." He looked away as he saw Elizabeth's eyes fill with tears. Her composure quickly returned as she saw him out. As he walked down the street, she sighed in relief. Her mother was in no fit state to talk to anyone. Especially if there was any scandal connected to this incident. Her mother knew something of this stranger, of that she was certain. There was something else, too, something she couldn't remember from that night. Something about those papers that were strewn on her father's desk. Was it the telegram? The man's name had been on the telegram, but she couldn't remember what it was. Now it had disappeared.

Margery awoke early on Sunday morning, her heart racing and her memory dull. As she opened her eyes she saw the sun shining directly on the marriage certificate that lay on the bureau. It was illuminated by the rays, the common white paper appearing pearlescent. She stared at it, transfixed by the pattern of light. It was going to be a beautiful autumn morning. In the distance she heard the bells of St. Nicholas ringing in an ecstasy of sound. Today would have been Robert's forty-second birthday.

Her habit on his birthday in past years had been to wait until Jack and Elizabeth left in the morning, then take the sacred box she kept containing Robert's things and press each one to her, remembering the significance of every item. The box now stood open on the bureau, next to the certificate, the contents spilling out after she had opened the box on Friday night. "Happy Birthday, my darling," she whispered, startled by the glorious song of a

21

blackbird near her window, its sound mimicking the whistles Robert had used to call her to him when they were young.

Her feet hit the floor as the memory of Jack and what he had done pulled her back to reality. Robert was long dead now, only these paltry items remaining of the vibrant, beautiful young man she had loved. Jack tried to destroy her love for Robert, but he could never annihilate her memories. If only he had known how much she dwelt in the hallowed places of her love for Robert. She held the marriage certificate to her, looking at her pale, disheveled reflection in the bureau. What would Robert think of me now? These past few days had played so much with her sanity that she had truly believed Robert had come back. Holding the box close to her, she went to the window and threw it open wide, marveling at the soft autumn sunshine reflecting from the golden leaves. The garden appeared enchanted, as if overnight a wizard had come and transformed the trees from green to spun gold. She sighed, clutching the box even more tightly to her and resting her chin on the engraved border. How many years had she held this box to her every September 22, wishing beyond all reality that the box could turn into Robert, that the power of his belongings and her love could resurrect him from that cold, lonely, horrible place known as the Somme. Placing the box on the bed near her pillow, she covered it tenderly, blowing a kiss to it as if it were Robert lazing in bed on a Sunday morning. Opening the bedroom door, she turned once, seeing only the wooden box lying inert on the bed. There would be only the same dull pain of grief, transferred now to Elizabeth's eyes. She peeked in at Elizabeth, sleeping soundly, before she began the same morning tasks she had done for nearly twenty years.

The next few days went by so quickly that Margery and Elizabeth had little time to think about what had happened or the stranger in hospital. Relatives, friends and neighbors came in a constant stream to the house, some to talk about Jack, some to bring meals, and some to comfort. Elizabeth was especially glad when her Aunt May came. Her health had not been good and she was still recuperating from a recent surgery. Auntie May had never been very strong. The shock of Jack's death rendered her useless as a consoler. Her husband, Uncle Harry, had also not been well, and was thinking of selling his motor repair business. Jack had told her repeatedly of how Harry had helped him get started in his business after the War, and what a good businessman he was. Besides, Uncle Harry had always made her laugh. He seemed to openly like Jack more than anyone else, despite her father's often surly ways. Their children, Lily, Nicholas and Alyce, had been good cousins to her, although very much older. Now they were all scattered – Lily was now twenty-five, married with two children and living in Norfolk; Nicholas, her twin, was working as a manager in Manchester; and Alyce, twenty-one, was recently engaged and living in London. Elizabeth fervently wished they were here now.

Her godmother, Rose Henning, also showed up, limping terribly after a fractured hip earlier in the year. Well into her eighties now, Auntie Rose, as Elizabeth called her, insisted on staying alone in her own cottage, although it was difficult for her to manage the house and garden herself. Elizabeth went over often to help her out and just talk about everything in her life. Auntie Rose never pulled any punches with her, always telling her what she thought, whether Elizabeth wanted to hear it or not.

Tuesday morning dawned clear as they prepared for the funeral. At times Elizabeth found herself bursting into tears, as when she found her father's slippers still under the chair in the parlor. Yet her mother was dry-eyed and almost without grief. Perhaps it was the calm before the storm, Elizabeth thought. While she had never seen overt affection between her parents, she had never doubted that they loved one another. Her mother seemed almost relieved by Jack's death. Again the memory of her mother's reaction to the man at the scene made her ponder what secrets her mother held in her heart.

Margery appeared nervous throughout the service and at the graveside, scanning the people who attended and looking out into the distance. Who is she looking for? Elizabeth thought, impatient with her mother's behavior. It is almost as if she is expecting someone. The man from the hospital, perhaps? Her mother had almost become someone she did not know. Auntie May, pale and weak, stood holding Margery's arm firmly, tears falling from her eyes while Margery remained dry-eyed and aloof from the service. Sally and Billy stood to the side, like two rocks of Gibraltar, Elizabeth thought. They were so much a part of her life she thought of them as her family, too.

Wednesday morning began with a visit from Jack's solicitor, who said everything was straightforward in terms of the house and business. Jack had left them very well off. He advised them to sell the business straightaway, even suggesting a buyer. Elizabeth detected a patronizing tone to his advice, as if two women would not be capable of carrying on such an enterprise. She interrupted the solicitor as he drew out the papers and said she would like them to think about it. Margery seemed surprised, but Elizabeth had changed her plans and had decided to wait until next term to go to University. An idea had been forming in her mind, and idea that she thought would make her father proud. She knew something of his business. She had worked with him and done some of his typing, taken orders, and even helped make a sale or two. It was not impossible for her to do this, although she knew her credibility in a male-dominated business would need to be proven. Even though Jack had left them well off, the money would not last forever. The business was solid, booming even, and could expand under the right direction. Uncle Harry

23

could help. She excused herself and decided to go to the office. If Elizabeth could manage to keep the business going on her own for a few weeks, she and her mother could decide the best move. Besides, the nagging feeling about the telegram and the other papers would not leave her. If the police had confiscated her father's papers, she wanted to know about it.

Chapter Two

Billy awoke early, listening to the rain beating down on the roof as he stepped onto the cold floor. Seemed very cold now for September, after such a lovely, warm start to the month. He groaned audibly as Sally shifted to his side of the bed, reaching out and touching the warm spot where he had lain. There was something he had to do this morning, something he knew he had to find out for Jack's sake.

The bathroom floor was even colder than the bedroom, causing him to yelp quietly when his feet hit the floor. He was a big man, once solid but now going to fat. His bleary eyes and the beginnings of jowls on his face stared back at him from the mirror. Never one to be considered handsome, any vestiges of good looks he once had were now long gone. The cold basin seemed reproving as he filled it with hot water and began to wash and shave.

"What are you doing up so early?" he heard Sally's voice behind him, her ash-blonde hair tousled and her eyes sleepy. He smiled at her in spite of his mood. She looked so young, almost like a little doll. The vision of her years before when he first met her, and how he had thought she was rather a dull yet pretty girl made him smile. She glared at him.

"And what is so funny about me this morning?" she questioned, but he just touched her nose with the tip of his shaving brush and kept smiling. She smiled back at him, watching his warm hazel eyes dart in the mirror as he expertly shaved himself. Her arms reached out and she hugged him from behind.

"Steady on, or I'll cut my throat," he chuckled. "Then where would you be, all alone in the world, and with four children to look after?" She giggled and said, "I'd find myself a sugar Daddy. It's all the rage now, you know. I think I might still be fanciable enough, don't you?" He smiled at her in the mirror,

25

thinking yes, indeed, she was still fanciable. Still had her slender figure and her eyes, those lovely bright blue eyes, were as gorgeous as ever.

"Now, go on, get my breakfast, or I won't be responsible for my actions," he said as she scampered out the door with a girlish giggle. Rinsing his shaving brush and finishing with his washing, he trudged back to the bedroom to dress. His leg was hurting terribly this morning, the wounds where the shrapnel had hit him and nearly torn his leg in half throbbing a chorus of pain this cold morning. It was one reason he dreaded the cold, damp weather. It not only made his leg ache, but brought back the memories of the day he was wounded, a day much like today. As he dressed, he stared out the window at the rain and grey skies, a pale light visible in the East. His head was filled with the memory of the mud, slipping, getting up, then running forward amidst the shouts and screams of the wounded. Seconds later, he fell, his leg hanging at an odd angle. The doctors wanted to take it off, but he insisted they leave it. He did not want to return a one-legged hero. Better to not return at all.

He finished dressing, putting on a tie and jacket. If he had to force his way into the hospital, he at least wanted to look like the prosperous businessman he was. Normally he wore old clothes, better to help his customers and make them feel more at ease. His father, Dick, still came down to the shop every day to talk to his old customers about the latest in farm and heavy equipment. Not that there was much farming around this part of Surrey anymore, but Dick Shepherd's reputation as an honest, knowledgeable dealer brought customers from as far as Kent and Sussex. Billy had carried on the tradition, although he winced at himself in the mirror, remembering how he thought he would rather die than spend his life selling farm implements to tight-fisted farmers.

The War had changed all that. Jack Morne had a tough go of it when he came home, trying to find work and finding nothing. Jack had not been wounded, not physically, but they both shared stories of the recurring nightmares about the trenches. Jack seemed to suffer from something – shell shock, Billy thought. While Billy had nightmares, they always centered on the day of his wounding. He turned gingerly on his sore leg. If he hadn't been able to work for his father, he doubted he would have been able to find work either. That is why Jack started his own business. The intense determination Jack showed when he wanted anything proved an asset that made his business a roaring success within a few years.

The sounds of his children, awake and clattering up and down the stairs, made him smile. Everything seemed so normal, as normal as his life had been as a child. Then the War came, and everything changed. So many victims, including his best friend, Jack's brother Robert Morne. Rob had been killed on the slaughter fields of the Somme, as had two other good mates:

Steve Burridge and Bert Porter. They weren't the only victims. Their families and their girls still mourned them. He knew Margery did, even though she had married Rob's brother Jack. When Marge married Jack, Billy couldn't believe it. He had never seen a couple more in love than Rob and Marge. But the War did funny things to people, things he couldn't, or didn't want to, understand.

"Good morning, Daddy," a chorus of voices said as Sally gave him a strange look when she spied his coat and tie. "Morning, all," he smiled, noticing their faces bright and scrubbed. I pray God none of them have to ever endure what we did. It must have been unthinkable for his parents to worry about him and his brother when they were out in France.

"Here's your breakfast," Sally said, then bent and whispered, "What are you up to dressed like that this morning?" She patted his shoulder and told her two daughters, eleven-year old Lydia and nine-year old Jenny, to stop slapping each other and get on with their breakfast before they were late for school. Her seven-year old son, Rupert, named after Billy's brother, was interested in the slapping match and threw a bit of toast at his sisters. Sally looked helplessly at Billy, who knew he had to take action. Only her thirteen-year old son Robert seemed to be making any progress with his breakfast.

"Enough now," Billy bellowed as all four pairs of eyes turned toward him. "Can't your old Dad have a peaceful breakfast before work? Get on with it." They stopped immediately, giggling under their breath, knowing that Daddy's bark was always worse than his bite.

"So where are you going dressed like that?" Sally questioned as she brought him more bacon and sat down with her cup of tea. "Not work, I am guessing."

"I want to go to Caterham," he whispered while the children's voices babbled among themselves. "I'm going to the hospital to see if I can find out who that bloke is that Jack tried to ..." he hesitated, noticing Robert's head turned their way, " you know." She nodded and he continued. "He's got to be someone he knew from the War. If anyone can understand how the War changed a bloke, I can. I just need to know. For Marge's sake, if anyone's."

"You do that, then," she said, feeling nervous. Margery seemed so unlike herself since Jack's death it worried Sally. Perhaps finding out what really happened would alleviate the fears and tensions. If this man meant to harm Margery, or Elizabeth, it was better to know and get it sorted.

"Do you think they will let you talk to him?" Sally whispered, keeping an eye on the children's antics as they gradually finished their breakfast. "I heard in the village that they are keeping him under guard. No one even knows his name."

"Seems he is unconscious, too, Dad told me," Billy said. As if on cue, the back door opened and Dick Shepherd came through.

"Got any tea for Granddad, then?" he shouted, his almost toothless smile lighting up the room as the children squealed.

"Sit down, Dad, I'll get it for you," Sally said, getting up and pouring him a cup. He removed his cap and sat down, waiting to go to the shop with Billy.

"Dad," Billy said, as his father eyed his clothes. "I'm not going to the shop this morning. Would you mind keeping an eye on it while I run an errand?"

Dick Shepherd smiled as he took another sip. "What errand might you be running in that get up?" he chuckled as the children joined in. "If I were you, Sally, I'd wonder what fancy woman he has."

"Oh, go on, Dad," she smiled, hugging Billy's shoulders. "I know what he's up to, so I think I'll let him go. This time, at least."

"He's off to Caterham," Robert said knowingly, then looked at his Dad. "Can you give me a lift to school, Dad? It's raining awfully out there. It would be so much easier than taking the bus." Robert attended the grammar school in Caterham, while the other children went to the village school.

"There are no secrets in this house," Billy shook his head with a grin, then nodded to Robert. "Get your things, then. I'm off in a few minutes."

"Right, Dad," he scrambled from his chair to get his books.

"So what business do you have in Caterham that requires you to look as if you are going to church?" his Dad persisted as Sally refilled his teacup.

"Don't, Dad," Billy said, feeling as young as his own son Rupert in the presence of his father. "It's nothing much. I should be back by early afternoon." Dick lifted an eyebrow, but left it at that. Billy was an open person, not prone to be secretive about anything. When he fell in love with Sally, everyone in the village knew it just by his words and actions.

The road to Caterham was slick and grey with a light fog. Robert chatted about his school activities and things he spotted along the roadway. Billy listened with half an ear. His mind was set on finding out about this man, and putting his questions to rest. It was almost as if Jack were prompting him from his grave to sort it out. He stepped on the accelerator as Robert gave a gleeful shout.

"That's the stuff, Dad!" he cackled. "Real racing speed round the corners." Billy quickly let off the accelerator and pulled up in front of Robert's school.

"Don't get used to being chauffeured," he said severely, but gave his son a broad smile as Robert bounced into the school. He had named him for Robert Morne. He and Rob had attended this same school in Caterham so many years ago. It was where they had first become fast friends.

He drove further on in the grey mist to the hospital, its red bricks the only spot of color in the scene. Before going in he took a few deep breaths, not sure how he would handle this. Whenever there was a fight or a confrontation, Billy had always tried to find the best way out of it. He preferred the motto, 'live and let live,' to demanding his rights or forcing an answer. Now he knew that the next few minutes would test his mettle and his persistence. With a sigh he hauled his bulk from the car and walked quickly to the reception area.

There was no one around, so he walked past the desk and into the hospital itself. Not sure where the stranger would be, he wandered around, trying to look official. Finally he spotted a nursing sister and asked in as authoritative a voice as he could muster where the patient from the accident on the Caterham Road was as he needed to question him. Her deferential answer pointed him to the second floor and a room at the end of the hallway.

With every step Billy felt sure someone would surely stop him and ask, "Where do you think you are going?" When no one did, and Billy nearly reached the door, he hesitated. Should he just boldly walk in and say, "Who are you?" and "What did you want with Jack Morne?" He stood for a few minutes outside the door when it suddenly opened and an older man in a Royal Army Medical Corps uniform walked out. A high ranking officer and no doubt a doctor, Billy thought. He stepped out of his way quickly, inadvertently drawing himself to attention.

Dr. Cyril Gibbons eyed the man who had been hovering outside the door. A reporter, perhaps? A few of them had been here, trying to find out what had happened. Mainly the police kept coming around to question the patient. This was probably yet another detective sergeant determined to get answers from his patient. A patient who was still unconscious, and might possibly never awaken from the shock of everything that had happened.

"Are you looking for someone?" Cyril said wearily. He had little sleep since last week, when all this had happened. He knew he had to get back to his hospital in East Preston, the hospital that was slated to close in a few weeks time. Yet until he knew that his patient was in good hands, he could not leave.

"Well, I, uh," Billy began, nervously running his hand around his collar. "Well, Sir, I wanted to see the patient."

Cyril relaxed slightly, recognizing the signs of a man who had been in the Army at one time. Calling him 'Sir' was a dead giveaway, along with his standing to attention when he saw his uniform.

"And what business do you have with this patient?" Cyril asked, looking directly into the eyes of this man. He did not seem to be a policeman, as their eyes looked wary and full of determination to get answers, even from an unconscious man. This man's eyes were full of questions.

29

"Well, Sir, it's like this," Billy thought, all his resolve to be firm fading away in front of this officer. "My friend was Jack Morne. I know something happened last week when he died, something to do with this man in the room here. His widow and daughter are frightened, wondering who this man is and why he seemed to want to kill Jack. They wonder if he wants to kill them as well, or we all wonder that..well, we..."

Cyril Gibbons was chuckling lightly as Billy tried to explain. Billy was unsure of what exactly would bring on this reaction. As far as he could tell, he could see nothing at all funny in what he said.

"Have you known Jack Morne a long time?" Cyril said, returning to a more serious expression.

"Since we were children," Billy nodded, moving his hat from hand to hand nervously.

"Ah, so a long time family friend," Cyril said. "I suppose we should introduce ourselves. I am Major Cyril Gibbons, Army doctor and long-time physician of this patient." He waited while Billy cleared his throat.

"William Shepherd," he said, extending his hand. "I served with the Queen's."

"I thought as much by your bearing," Cyril said. "Once you learn the drill, it is hard to forget it." He smiled warmly at Billy.

"Do you have time for a cup of tea, Mr. Shepherd?" Cyril asked. "I was just going to have some breakfast."

"I would like to see this man," Billy persisted, but Cyril raised his hand and said, "Once I tell you about him, I am sure you will want to see him. Quite sure. And you shall." Billy looked perplexed as they headed toward the small cafeteria at the other end of the hall.

Cyril noticed Billy's limp, his heart feeling the same pain he often did for victims of that awful War, now nearly twenty years over. A friend of Jack Morne's. No doubt Robert's, too. Well, someone finally had to know the truth as it would all come out soon. This man was not a policemen or reporter. Robert would have to be discharged back to a hospital, possibly near people who knew and loved him. It was time to tell the story.

They settled down and while Cyril ate, Billy told him about growing up in Upper Marstone, the Morne brothers, and his friendship with them. He talked a little of Margery and how she had once been engaged to Robert, but later married Jack after Robert was killed. The easy manner in which he spoke convinced Cyril all the more that here indeed was someone who should know the truth and tell others in the village.

"Mr. Shepherd," he began, wiping his mouth on a napkin. Billy asked him to call him Billy, as everyone did. "Billy, then," he smiled at him. "What I am about to tell you will seem unbelievable, but I assure it is true." Billy's eyes looked almost frightened. Cyril took a sip of tea and continued.

"You want to know who that man is who was on the road to Caterham and met Jack Morne last week?" Billy nodded, his apprehension more obvious. "And you want to know what would possess your friend Jack to take a gun with him and attempt to kill this man? Because that is indeed what he tried to do. It was only the fortunate interference of Jack's daughter that caused this man to suffer only a flesh wound to his arm."

He let that information sink in before continuing. "That man, Billy, the man who now lies behind the door at the end of the hallway, is Robert Morne. Jack's brother Robert."

Cyril fully expected the reaction he got from Billy, who sank back in his chair, mouth open, eyes staring, and uttered only the words, "I don't believe it."

"But it is true," Cyril said, reaching across to pat Billy's hand but also surreptitiously taking his wrist to check his pulse. The way this news hit everyone made Cyril positive about his suspicions that Jack Morne had never told a soul that his brother was still alive.

The pieces of the puzzle were all fitting together now. Billy's chatter about the Morne brothers and the girl they both loved, Margery, confirmed much of his knowledge of Jack Morne and his behavior.

"But how?" Billy said, tears glimmering in his eyes. Robbie alive! It seemed impossible. Impossible that no one could have known all these years. Then it dawned on him. Someone did know. Jack knew.

"He was wounded on the Somme, as you know," Cyril said quietly, still holding Billy's wrist and encouraging him to take another sip of tea. "When he was brought in he had no papers or identity discs. Very bad head wound that rendered him unconscious for a long time. Also wounded in the chest and arm, but those eventually healed. With devoted care he was transferred back to England, eventually winding up in the East Preston Army Hospital for Neurological Cases. There was one nurse who worked with him extensively to bring him back, and eventually succeeded. The problem was that Robert could not remember anything of his past." He stopped, letting this sink in before going on.

"The nurse who worked with him, Louise Whiting, is with him still," he continued. "She has devoted much of her care to him. Without her, I am certain he would have died long ago. It was she who found out his first name in 1917 from the ring he wore. His name was engraved on it. Along with…Margery's."

"The buckle rings!" Billy said, smiling now. "How we gave him what for over wearing that ring! A bloke wearing an engagement ring, we said. But he insisted. Good thing he did, I'd say."

"His surname was not there, so we still did not know who he was," Cyril continued. "After several surgeries, he began to improve, so much so that he eventually recalled his surname. That was in 1926 when we contacted his family."

"Jack," Billy whistled under his breath. "So Jack knew Rob was alive since..."

"1926," Cyril said quietly. "Nine years. Am I right in guessing he has never told anyone?"

"I would think so," Billy said, looking dazed. "But why? I know they didn't get on, but I can't believe he would withhold that information from the people who loved him. His parents, me.."

"He received the letter from the Army on the day of his father's funeral, apparently." Another low whistle from Billy before Cyril continued. "So who else would there be to tell? Except Margery, of course."

"And he wouldn't want to tell her, would he?" Billy said, looking angry. "Because she would have gone straight to Rob without a doubt." Billy put his head in his hands, obviously not as surprised as Cyril thought he might be by Jack's behavior.

"What happened the other night, though," Billy said thoughtfully. "Would Jack really want to kill him? I can't believe that of him, no matter how hard I try. They never really got on. No doubt Jack hoped he would never have to deal with Rob coming back, seeing how badly wounded he was, but kill him? No, I can't believe he meant to do that. Scare him off, maybe. Send him back to hospital. Not kill him."

"That's as may be," Cyril said, patting Billy's arm. "He may have wanted to scare him. He became quite adept at causing seizures in him, you know, at least according to his nurse, Miss Whiting. It kept Robert from coming home, until he took matters into his own hands and left the hospital alone Friday afternoon."

Billy sat back in his chair, then said quietly, "May I see him, Doctor? I won't disturb him, I promise you that. Just let me see him for a few minutes."

"Of course, Billy, but I warn you, he is not conscious." They left the cafeteria, walking to the door where Billy hesitated.

"Robbie," he said quietly under his breath as Cyril turned the handle. The room was dark, a provision to prevent light sources entering that could trigger more seizures. Standing next to the bed was a tall, thin nurse, middle-aged, her brown hair and eyes almost the same color. She looked at him suspiciously as he walked quietly behind Dr. Gibbons.

"How is he?" Cyril asked, looking at the pale face of the patient. Louise nodded and said, "As well as can be expected. Did you find out whether they can get the specialist here today?" Cyril shook his head and said, "I forgot to ask, as I met this gentleman and we talked. This is William Shepherd. This is Nurse Louise Whiting, who has looked after Robert for many years." Billy offered his hand and she shook it, her face still registering suspicion.

"A very old friend of your Robert," Cyril said. "They grew up together and went to the same school together." Billy stood silently behind Dr. Gibbons, sensing that he would not be allowed to move toward the bed until this nurse gave him permission.

"I see," she said, shifting reluctantly. "You do understand, Mr. Shepherd, that he is not conscious? That he has suffered much, especially at the hands of his brother. Now this final insult. He may never awaken from the deep seizures he has experienced." She turned away quickly before she would let him see the tears in her eyes.

"I won't upset him, Sister, that I promise," Billy said, putting his hat on a nearby chair. "I just want to see him briefly, tell him I am here. Does he know about Jack?"

"I don't think he does," Cyril said, furrowing his brow. "We have opted not to say much to him until he regains consciousness. He has made so much progress. It is dire to see him like this again."

Louise beckoned this friend of Robert's to his bedside. Now it would all emerge, she thought. The old friends, the other family members, they would all want to see the miracle man who has been resurrected. He would become a spectacle, a freak in his own village. She wanted to steal away with him and take him to Sussex, where he could live in relative obscurity with her until the end of his days.

He had insisted on coming back here, to find ....yes, to find his Margery. The girl he had once been engaged to and for whom he never stopped pining. Although Louise knew that over the years she had developed strong feelings for him that went beyond his position as a patient, she had never really revealed them to him. When he began to get better and stronger, eventually taking on the role of gardener at the hospital and living in his own cottage, their relationship had deepened. Still the specter of Margery stood between them. Robert had to find Margery and settle his mind and heart. Although Louise worried she would lose him to a dream, she agreed. It was the only way he would ever truly be hers.

Here he laid, a broken man again. Jack had told him Margery had married and moved away from the village. On one point Jack was right – Margery had married. What Jack neglected to tell his brother is that Margery had married him. That is why in nine years Jack had fought so hard to keep Robert away from the village. He was so determined to keep him away he was willing to kill him, as he tried to do several days before.

For one instant Louise had caught a glimpse of a pale, dark-eyed woman standing on the road as the ambulance doors shut to take Robert to hospital. At first she could not place the face. Then she remembered. Robert had drawn that face, over and over again, trying to bring his Margery back to him.

"It's all right to go up close to the bed," Cyril was telling Billy as he walked toward his friend gingerly. "He can probably hear you very well, but may not respond."

Billy walked closer, taking in the pale, thin face of a man he didn't recognize at first. As he came closer, the face began to resemble the boy he once knew. It was indeed Rob. The sense of it overwhelmed him as he let out a gasp and felt his knees buckle.

"There, Mr. Shepherd, do sit down for a moment," Louise said, her heart breaking to see the love and sadness mixed in the face of this friend. Billy sat down heavily, heaving slightly. Louise gave a look to Cyril, tilting her head with concern. Cyril shook his head, indicating that all Billy needed was time to collect himself.

"Robbie?" Billy said gently, searching for the thin hand beneath the sheets. "Robbie? It's Billy, Billy Shepherd, your old mate." He took the hand and was surprised to feel how strong it was. He held it and kept talking to him. Suddenly he felt a hard squeeze of his hand. He turned to the doctor.

"He just squeezed my hand. Hard, too," Billy grinned. "What a grip he has! I thought he would be all soft and mushy, lying in hospital all day." Louise said, "He works as a gardener at the hospital, so he is very fit."

"Ouch!" Billy shouted, then laughed. "I guess he didn't like that bit about 'soft and mushy.'" He turned around and looked at Louise and Cyril.

"When I came here today, I was so certain that I was going to take this man out somehow," Billy said, trying to put some power in his words. "No one could understand why he wanted to kill Jack."

"As you can see, Mr. Shepherd, it was not Robert who wanted to kill anyone," Louise retorted. "It was Jack Morne. Mr. Morne never had good intentions toward his brother. I am sure I understand why now, although I never did before."

Cyril gave her a cautioning look as Billy looked puzzled. "I never thought it of Jack, that he would be so determined to have his way," Billy said. "Not enough to do this, of course. All for Margery. It was always for Margery." He muttered under his breath as he extricated himself from the bedside.

Robert began to cough as Louise deftly pulled the drape, dismissing Billy as he walked to the door.

"Is it all right for me to tell Margery?" Billy said. "I think of all people she ought to know. There's only her and her daughter Elizabeth now left from the family. His parents are dead. Jack was his only sibling."

"Perhaps it would be better coming from you first," Cyril agreed as they shut the door behind them. "It is difficult to say how she would react to his reappearance after all these years. Especially as she married his brother."

"Ah, but everyone knows they were not a love match," Billy nodded to himself. "She always loved Robbie, always. My wife, Sally, is still her best friend. We both knew it to be true. She was good to Jack, to be sure. But she never loved him."

Cyril pondered this and added, "But Robert is much changed, as you can see. It is altogether rather emotional for everyone at the moment. Do as you see fit. If she would like to see him, I would like to speak with her first, so as not to upset either of them too much."

"I'll be careful how I tell her," Billy said, walking down the hallway. "Very careful."

Driving back to Caterham Billy pondered how he would tell Margery. She had always been a very opinionated and feisty girl, so much so that Billy remembered giving Rob a talking to when he had first become involved with her. Despite his fears, Rob and Margery had been true lovers of the heart. Billy had always thought Margery more suited to Jack. When they did marry, they were not unhappy, but there was a hollowness to their marriage that anyone could detect. Even their daughter could not create the warmth between them that should have been there.

The ride back seemed to pass much too soon and he found himself parked in front of the house on Tilburstow Hill Road. He wanted to go home and tell Sally first, but thought that the first person to know should be Margery. If Elizabeth were there, perhaps Margery could send her on an errand. He did not relish trying to explain that Rob was still alive to Margery with Jack's daughter looking on. The rain had dissipated somewhat, but the clouds in the distance still looked threatening. It reminded him again of that morning he went over the top and he shuddered. Going over the top is what put Robbie where he was now, in that hospital bed, unconscious.

The horror and shock of seeing his friend again overcame him. He sat in the car, weeping loudly and cursing a God who would allow so many of his friends to be mutilated or killed. Their names and faces paraded before him: Bert Porter, Stephen Burridge, Robert Collins, Fred Batchelor. All slaughtered in that war, as he thought Rob had been. As the years passed he had studiously tried to avoid thinking of the War and what had happened, even finding excuses to avoid the Remembrance Services at church every November. The memory of Charlie Morne being led out, weeping uncontrollably, by an equally bereft Albert Burridge, haunted his memory. Charlie had been a strict father, but loved his boys more than life itself. Rob's death had destroyed him. It had killed Rob's mother Eliza, who took her own life after remaining inconsolable because of his 'death'.

All in vain, Billy thought, as he wiped his eyes. Rob was still alive. No one had to die because of Rob's death, and now three people had. Would Margery really have given up everything to be with Rob? Although Billy liked the idea of Margery being sensible, he knew that was not one of her strong traits. Jack knew it, too. Jack also knew that the minute he would have told her that Rob was alive, it was the last he would have seen of her. She would have flown to Rob's side, whether he was conscious or unconscious, and lived out her life with him.

Except there was Elizabeth to consider. Billy knew that his sitting in the car was just a way for him to delay what needed to be done. He opened the door, straightened himself out, and walked up the long, winding path to the front door of Jack's house.

Chapter Three

Margery was clearing up the dishes in the kitchen from the solicitor's visit when she heard the front doorbell ring. Elizabeth had just left, taking the car this time because of the rain, to go back to her father's office. Her strange idea of running Jack's business surprised Margery this morning, but she felt too weak and overwhelmed to argue with her daughter who seemed to have become more strong-willed since Jack's death, almost as if to replace him.

Sighing deeply, Margery put down her towel and walked slowly to the door. After the funeral the flow of visitors had turned into a trickle. She was glad, because she wanted to put everything to rest, including Jack. It still bothered her about the circumstances of his death. Perhaps the police were here to question her about the man's identity and why Jack would be brandishing a gun on a dark road.

Billy smiled weakly and said, "Hello, Marge. I wanted to stop in and talk to you for a bit, if I could?" She was surprised to see him, the look registering on her face. He was dressed formally and was acting visibly nervous. It was so unlike the Billy she knew her suspicions were aroused.

"Of course. Come in. Did you think I had changed so much you needed to dress up to come and see me?" Her weak attempt at humor made them both smile slightly, but Margery sensed some pressing concern in Billy. She led him to the kitchen and asked him to sit down.

"Tea?" she asked, and he nodded. He had not taken off his coat. "Make yourself comfortable, Billy," she said, pointing to his coat. "You know Jack and I were never ones to stand on formality."

"Right," Billy said, clearing his throat nervously. Whatever was the matter with him, Margery thought. First of all he should be at work right now. Second, he never dresses up unless absolutely pressed by the circumstances. It was all too odd to contemplate.

Billy watched Margery expertly make two cups of tea and bring them to the table. Her dark eyes seemed like endless black pools in her chalk-white

37

face. This whole episode has caused her damage, he thought as she pushed the milk toward him. She seems to have lost weight in a few short days, her drab grey-green housedress hanging loosely around her hips. She took a sip and stared directly into his face, a look he remembered all too well from their early days when she seemed to intimidate every bloke in the village. Except for Rob. And Jack.

"Well?" she said as he shifted uncomfortably in his chair, bringing his hand up to run it through his thinning, sandy hair. "I know you didn't come here to have a cup of tea, Billy. Is it something to do with Jack? Have you found out something? You know I prefer to have things said straight out to me. No cushioning things with fancy phrases."

Billy cleared his throat again. Yes, he knew that about her, but how do you tell someone that the man she loved and thought was dead for nearly twenty years was alive? He hoped no one else in the world would ever have to be in this position again.

"Marge," he said, his voice husky. "I don't even know how to start. It's, it's…"

"Just tell me," Margery said, gripping his arm. "Has Jack done other things with that gun I don't know about? Just tell me."

"No, Marge, it's not about Jack," he said as she looked at him questioningly, "or Elizabeth. It's about…Robbie."

Margery sat back in her chair at the mention of his name. Yes, she still loved him, loved him with the same passion she felt for him nearly twenty years ago. It never diminished. The vision of it was fading as the years passed, but not the feeling.

"What about Robbie?" she questioned, her eyes burning with a feverish light. "What do you have to tell me about him?"

Billy hesitated, unable to meet her gaze. "It's all so complicated," he began. "It's about Jack, too, really, and what he did. It's about…"

"What about Robbie?" she almost shouted, gripping his arm so tightly he felt she would wrench if off.

"I went to Caterham this morning, which is why I am so dressed up, as you put it," he began softly. "I felt I had to know who this man was who had caused Jack's death, and why. I'm dressed like this so I could get into the hospital with no questions asked, if you know what I mean. No one's been able to see him, you know. Not even the police. He's unconscious and under doctor's care."

Margery maintained her grip and her fixed stare. "Go on," she rasped.

"I talked to his doctor, an Army doctor. Cyril Gibbons, a major." Billy was babbling and Margery knew it. Her tightening on his arm made him go on.

"He told me a story, incredible, really. But it was true." He gulped and said, "The man who Jack went after with the gun was Robbie, Marge. He's alive. It is Robbie in that hospital bed in Caterham." He felt her grip loosen as she sank back in her chair, her face even whiter than before, her eyes looking wild.

"I knew I saw him," she whispered to herself. "I knew it was Robert." Billy seemed confused, but tried to finish the story.

"He was badly wounded on the Somme. A head wound that has made him…different." Billy searched for words that would convey what he saw earlier. "A nurse has looked after him for years, worked with him, until he started remembering things. He couldn't remember his name until nine years ago. It was the buckle ring that allowed them to know his Christian name. Those rings of yours." He glanced at her hand where the ring still rested. She touched it tenderly.

"Nine years?" she said. "But if they knew who he was, why didn't anyone tell us? I don't understand." Billy was silent as the realization dawned on Margery. She stood up grabbing the table for support and turned her gaze on Billy.

"Jack knew he was alive," she murmured to herself. "Was Robert in Sussex? Was he?"

She shook Billy so hard he just nodded yes and added, "East Preston, near Worthing."

"No!" she shouted to herself, then began to laugh. "Oh, no, Jack, this is too much. You lied and cheated and deceived me, but this, this…no Jack, no…"

Billy stood up and took her shaking shoulders in his arms, trying to comfort her. Margery had always been clever. It had not taken her long to understand that Jack had deliberately kept this information from her.

She sat down heavily on the chair, still shaking. Billy waited until she became quiet, then heard her laughing softly.

She looked up at him and said, "Don't you understand, Billy? It is why he kept the marriage certificate from me as well. Jack and I were never married, not as long as Robert was alive." She laughed again, hiccoughing at the end.

"What marriage certificate?" It was now Billy's turn to be baffled. "Yours and Jack's?" Margery looked up at him, her eyes dark and deadly looking.

"Let's have the truth in total today, shall we?" she laughed again. "Yes, Jack was very clever, wasn't he? And I never suspected for an instant. I couldn't see anything but what I wanted to. I devoted my entire life to Elizabeth and her welfare. Do you know why, Billy?"

"She's your daughter and you love her?" Billy said tentatively.

39

"Oh, yes, Billy, she is my daughter. She is also Robert's daughter. I married Robert before he left for France. I followed him to Folkestone, married him, and spent one heavenly, beautiful night of my life in his arms before he left for France. He gave me Elizabeth that night. Did you ever wonder why Jack married me so quickly after Robert was declared missing, believed killed? It was to save my name and reputation, and to give Elizabeth her father's name. It seemed crazy. Jack told me he could find no record of the marriage certificate between Robert and me. I believed him. I believed that Robert and I had not married, that Robert had arranged it to appear that way. It made no matter to me, I loved him and I loved the child he gave me. But Jack thought it would tarnish his image in my eyes. Even when it didn't matter anymore, he withheld the evidence." She reached deep into her apron pocket and threw a document onto the table. "There it is. He must have kept it for years locked away in his office. When he got his gun out so quickly, in his haste he left this on top of the desk. Elizabeth found it."

Billy picked up the marriage certificate between Robert James Morne and Margery Isabella Hill, dated August 24, 1916 in Folkestone. The accompanying letter, addressed to Jack, explained that the certificate had not been filed in a timely fashion and that is why it was not found when Jack first went searching for it in October 1916. The letter was dated 1919. Jack had never told Margery it existed. For years she believed she had never been married to Rob.

"He must have thought it best for some reason." Billy tried to make sense of it, but Margery guffawed at the idea.

"Don't you see, Billy? I was never truly married to Jack. I was always married to Robert. When Jack learned that Robert was alive, he knew that Robert was still my rightful husband. My marriage to Jack was invalid. And our daughter – she is Robert's daughter. Jack would have no place in the scheme of things."

"He loved you, Marge," but she shook off his hand and took out her handkerchief.

"If he loved me, Billy, it was a strange sort of love," she said, wiping her nose. "Because if he truly loved me, he would not have withheld the knowledge that Robert was alive. Never. He did not love me as we think of love. It was more...possession. Possession of something he could never have. Possession of someone's heart even though it still belonged to the one person he could not eradicate. But he tried to, didn't he, last Friday? He did try to kill him." She wept loudly now, only stopping for sharp intakes of breath.

Billy sat overwhelmed. Rob and Margery married. Elizabeth was Rob's daughter. It was all too much for him to understand at the moment.

"Take me to him," Margery said, standing up suddenly. "Take me to the hospital. I have to see him."

"It might not be the best idea at present," Billy cajoled her. "You're very upset. The doctor does not want him to get distressed anymore because he has these seizures and…"

"Take me to him," she said again. "I will deal with the doctor. I will not upset him, not my Robert." She caressed his name on her lips tenderly.

"The doctor wants to talk to you first, of course," Billy said breathlessly as Margery marched to the front door and grabbed her hat, coat and bag from the hook. She stuffed the marriage certificate into her handbag, then quickly scribbled a note to Elizabeth saying she had gone out and would be back shortly.

Billy followed her fast steps to the car, quickly opening the door for her so she could get in safely. He drove slowly and in silence, occasionally catching a glimpse of her sharp nose and cheekbones under her shapeless felt hat. She might scare Robbie to death, he thought to himself. There was no stopping her. He knew that she would have walked to Caterham if he hadn't taken her there.

Margery pondered the last words Jack had said to her, the words taking on a different meaning with the news of Robert being alive. "I promised you if he came back I would step aside," he had said as he lay dying in the road. It was the promise he made to her when they married in 1916. It made no sense to her last Friday amidst the chaos of the whole incident. When she thought she saw Robert, it had seemed to be from the shock of the night's events. Now it all made sense.

No one knew Jack the way she did. Those who talked about what happened still professed shock over Jack Morne, friendly, pleasant Jack Morne, pulling a gun on a man with the intention of killing him. Of course, they conjectured, he must have done it to protect his wife and daughter. Margery smiled grimly to herself. Yes, that is exactly what he did. He wanted to protect his wife and daughter from ever knowing their true husband and father was alive.

Jack had been capable of awful things when he was young – stalking her and Robert when they walked out together, telling her lies about Robert and other women, fanning the flames of any argument she had with Robert. At other times he could show incredible concern and care for her and his brother. She remembered when Robert had been ill and her mother-in-law, who had always despised her, refused to let her see him. Jack had gone out of his way to arrange for her to spend hours alone with Robert in his room, keeping guard and making sure they had not been caught.

He was an enigma. She was not surprised that he had lied for nine years about this. Her memory of his 'business' trips to Sussex fueled her suspicions. For all the trips, he rarely seemed to actually do any business in Sussex. Elizabeth had thought he had another woman. Margery was sure it was not that, but could never put her finger on exactly what it was. Now it was all too clear. Jack had kept her from Robert. But he would not keep her away any longer. No one would.

Chapter Four

Louise Whiting trudged wearily from her temporary home in the nurses' quarters at the Caterham Hospital. She had spent all night in Robert's room, only taking a few hours off this morning to refresh herself. Her uniform had been freshly washed, but still she felt the sense of displacement and disorganization one did when away from home. Except this had been no holiday. She wondered how long they would remain here. It was nearly a week since the incident and death of Jack Morne. Robert still had not fully regained consciousness. Earlier this morning, a friend of Robert's had shown up, someone from his past to pull him back to Upper Marstone.

The raindrops spattered at her feet as she trudged across the open courtyard to the hospital. Cyril said he must get back and attend to closing the East Preston Hospital. Louise knew he had stayed much longer than he anticipated. Both of them had invested so much into Robert's recovery they could not leave him at this juncture. She also had to go back and help with the closing of East Preston. But she could not bring herself to leave her Robert.

Her Robert. Yes, she considered him hers. The fact that the long-lost dream lover Margery was still alive, well, and nearby did not daunt her. Margery had married Robert's brother Jack. How could she explain that to Robert? Surely there could be no good reason for her to have done so, unless she had loved Jack Morne. A large raindrop hit Louise squarely on the cheek, almost a smite from Jack Morne himself. The disappointment Robert would feel could send him reeling backwards again, knowing the woman he kept as his ideal had betrayed him, and with his own brother.

Cyril was talking outside Robert's door with the local neurologist, Dr. Newland. A small, round-faced man, he looked more like a clean-shaven

43

Father Christmas than a doctor. He had examined Robert, but felt that this case was out of his depth.

"I've asked a friend of mine, a fine neurosurgeon, now retired, to stop in and take a look at our patient," he smiled brightly at Louise, his rosy cheeks glowing and his blue eyes twinkling. Louise almost expected him to offer her a Christmas sweet from an unseen pack.

"I really must get back to my own hospital today or tomorrow," Cyril said uneasily. "My Matron, Sister Meade, has been howling down the phone at me to get back as soon as possible as there are so many things that need my signature. I do hate to leave Robert like this, without knowing what is happening and whether he can be transported."

"Where would he go?" Louise interrupted. He could not return to his little gardener's cottage where he had made so much progress. Putting him back into another institution seemed unthinkable. Sister Meade had suggested to Louise that there was only one solution: that Louise should marry Robert and look after him. Louise had inherited a large amount of money, enough so that she would never need to work again in her life. She had been so devoted to her patients, especially Robert, that she kept working. When the staff received word that the neurological Army hospital at East Preston in Sussex was closing down for good, it was necessary that all patients had to be transferred to other facilities or released to their families.

"That is a question that we will answer once we get a good assessment of his condition," Cyril replied. "When did you say this neurosurgeon would arrive?"

"He doesn't live too far from here," Dr. Newland beamed again. "He's the best man for this sort of case. Served as a neurosurgeon during the War, right on the front lines. Knows all there is to know about cases like this." Louise wondered how a neurologist who dealt with dire cases of head injury could look so happy. Happiness was never something she felt comfortable with, although she sought it intensely.

Louise excused herself and went into the darkened room. Robert seemed to be in a deep sleep, breathing evenly and looking like an enchanted prince in a fairy tale. All he needs is his princess to kiss him back to consciousness, Louise thought to herself. She began his morning care, hoping she would hear his voice at any moment. Silence was the only sound.

Time was running out. As she methodically washed, shaved and cared for Robert, as she had down hundreds of times before, she found herself chatting to him aimlessly. It was what she had done with him when he had first been brought into the hospital as a wounded soldier at Etaples.

"So what should we do, Robert?" she said out loud as she carried on her tasks. "We cannot go back to the gardener's cottage, although we both loved it there. The thought of a hospital or nursing home is out of the question. You still need care, but I could manage that. Should we look for another gardener's position?" She smiled at him but saw no response.

She heard voices outside the door once again, then a sharp shaft of light illuminated the room as three figures entered. Cyril and Dr. Newland came in, chatting amiably with a slight figure in a large overcoat. He moved quickly, nodding his head as he seemed to be listening to both his fellow doctors at once about Robert's case.

"This is his fine and dedicated nurse, Sister Whiting," Dr. Newland said, as the consultant stepped forward. Both of them stopped in their tracks, staring at each other.

"This is..uh..Dr. Lewis Warren," Dr. Newland hesitated, noticing the expressions on their faces. "I think they know one another," Cyril smiled as Louise gathered herself together and came forward.

"Louise," Lewis said, his face creasing into a smile. His dark eyes were just as intense as she remembered, but his face had aged, his nearly-black hair peppered with silver. She took his hand and held it, the memory of her first meeting with him as a young girl and his work to save Robert's life at Etaples coming back afresh.

"So Robert brings us together yet again," Lewis commented as he approached the bed. "I hear he had made great progress until this incident last Friday. My guess is this is a temporary setback, but let me have a look at him." He took off his coat and Louise noticed how thin he was, his slight build always belying his vast intellectual abilities.

Lewis commenced to examine Robert thoroughly, asking Cyril and Dr. Newland questions in the same abrupt tone he had always used. Louise had met him while still a schoolgirl, when she sought answers no one could give her about her brother Geoffrey's tragic death at the age of twelve. Geoffrey had suffered a head injury from an accident with a horse. Louise had been blamed for not watching out for Geoffrey. It set her on a path to discover how to help those with head injuries. Years later it brought her to nursing the forgotten of the Great War – those who suffered severe head wounds and were still institutionalized. She had lost her own fiancé in the Great War. This work was how she repaid the debt to those who had suffered and died in that cataclysm.

Seeing Lewis again made her think of her dead fiancé, David Giles. It still haunted her that she had hesitated to marry him until it was too late. Had she loved him? The question plagued her even today. As she looked at Lewis, feelings rose in her, feelings she had denied for years. It had not been allowed for her to have sentiments for him, a married man, yet she knew they were there. She blushed suddenly as he asked for another light to examine Robert's eyes.

"I'm sorry," she said, smoothing her apron and efficiently assisting him. He looked at her briefly, his eyes locked to hers, then he turned to Robert again. He finished his examination and began rolling down his shirtsleeves.

"Now what exactly happened to him?" he asked Cyril as he pulled on his coat. "I think he is suffering a psychological shock as well as a physical one. He seems fine physically. Of course, a great shock would produce a seizure of this magnitude. He has always been susceptible to that, as we know. I think our Robert is trying to make sense of something, and prefers to do it in the privacy of his own mind." He smiled partially and said, "I suggest he be kept quiet for a day or two. You will have to decide what to do with him. Keep talking to him, Louise. Let him know that whatever happened that night it is safe for him to come out again." Louise nodded, knowing that what happened might have been too much for Robert to bear.

Dr. Newland, Cyril and Lewis conferred about Robert for a few minutes, with Lewis prescribing a new medication he thought would control the seizures more effectively. He was sorry to hear what happened and that Robert now had no family, but winked at Louise as he left, saying, "I am sure the indomitable Miss Whiting will find some solution. She always does." He took her hand and asked, "Are you in Caterham long? I would love to meet up and talk about old times, if you are game. What do you say?" He stared at her with the same intensity he had long ago. She held his hand longer than she intended and said, "It depends on what happens here, of course. But yes, it would be nice to have a cup of tea..."

"Or dinner," Lewis interrupted. "Robert is going to be all right, Louise. Of that I am certain. You look tired and worn out. A good dinner is what you need. I am free most nights, since I have retired." She searched his face, wondering about his wife, Constance. Would she want Lewis going out with an old female 'friend'?

"I'll stop by tomorrow to check on our patient," he said as he turned to leave. "So perhaps tomorrow evening? In the meantime, keep him warm and quiet. And do keep talking to him." He winked at her again as he left.

Louise flustered around the bed, wondering what to think. Robert, oh Robert, do wake up, she found herself saying, like a petulant child. It was evident he had been shocked by what he saw and at being shot. His incapacity made her frightened for him. If he did not awaken, then only an institution would be his future.

Cyril pulled on his coat and came toward her. "I have to go back to Sussex, I'm afraid," he said gently. "I hate to leave you alone, but I must. Dr.

Newland will look in on Robert if his condition changes. As to the next step, well....

A knock on the door made them turn as Billy Shepherd put his head in. "Excuse me, Doctor," he said. "I wonder if we might have a word." Dr. Gibbons nodded and went outside. Louise straightened the bedclothes and saw Robert's eyelids flutter lightly. "Robert?" she said. "Open your eyes," she cajoled him. "I know you want to, as I can see you are trying very hard. Please open your eyes." He managed to open them partially and she smiled at him. "Good, very good," she said, putting her hand on his forehead.

The voices in the hall grew louder. This time a woman's voice was dominant. Robert became restless, moving agitatedly from side to side. They must keep their voices down, Louise thought, so went to the door and opened it sharply.

Billy Shepherd stood there with Cyril and a woman, a woman Louise recognized from so many portraits Robert had drawn of her: Margery. She was smaller and sharper than Louise imagined, a rather tired and haggard looking woman of about forty with a still-buxom figure and very sharp features. Her eyes were large, dark and penetrating, full of fire and determination. It was manifest that she would not be stayed from her mission. Louise knew instinctively why she had come: to see Robert.

"Dr. Warren does not want him disturbed," Louise interrupted the fray as Cyril was trying to explain things to the determined Margery. "He is in a precarious state at present, so rest and quiet are what he needs."

Margery turned her full gaze upon Louise, assessing her in an instant. Louise felt naked, all her feelings for Robert now seeming so childish and full of fantasy in the face of the woman who had loved him, and been loved by him. Margery had known him in ways Louise never had. Still, she had broken her trust with Robert by marrying his brother.

"And you are..?" Margery said, not breaking her gaze. Billy shifted uneasily and smiled at Louise sympathetically.

"Nurse Whiting from the Neurological Army Hospital at East Preston," Louise responded, feeling some of her strength come back. This woman will kill him if she sees him now. She has no legal right to see him.

"Well, Nurse Whiting, I would like to see Robert," Margery said. "I have waited many years for this moment, so please don't delay me."

"I'm afraid that is not possible," Louise responded, pulling herself up to her full height which was several inches above Margery.

Margery did not break her gaze. "I insist on seeing him. Now."

"Marge, if it would not be a good idea at this moment, maybe we should go and come back later," Billy tried to intervene. Margery snapped her gaze to him for an instant, then back to Louise.

47

"You have no right to prevent me from entering this room," Margery said. "You are not the doctor or the police. Just a nurse."

"A nurse who had taken care of him for nearly twenty years and knows his condition better than anyone else," Louise retorted hotly, her face flushing. This woman could not be the girl Robert loved. It seemed impossible.

"I'm afraid he is in rather a bad state at present," Cyril attempted to interject. "He was seen by a specialist this morning who feels any more shocks to his system may set him back for a long while."

"I am not a 'shock' to his system," Margery said evenly. "I am his wife."

Louise was stunned by this revelation. "But you cannot be. You are another man's wife."

"Jack?" Margery smiled. "Oh, yes, I was Jack's wife, or so we believed. It was never true. I married Robert first. As long as Robert is alive, he is my husband. See for yourself." She thrust the marriage certificate at Louise, who read it and then handed it to Cyril.

"I believe a wife has the right to see her husband, Doctor. Isn't that true?" Margery asked, her forcefulness subsiding as her shoulders shook slightly.

"Yes," Cyril said as Louise started to protest. "Yes, Mrs. Morne, you have the right to see him. But, please, I caution you to approach him with great care. He has not seen you in many years."

"Of course, Doctor," Margery said, her voice less strident. Louise gave Cyril a look of disbelief as he opened the door and let Margery into the darkened room. Cyril gently squeezed Louise's shoulder as he entered the room behind Margery and Billy.

"Do you think this is a good idea, after what Dr. Warren said?" Louise hissed under her breath. "That woman seems determined to upset him. Is this wise, from a medical standpoint?"

"She would see him one way or the other," Cyril conceded. "She is his wife. How little we really know of our Robert! He was married to his Margery, although he never seemed to recall it. It certainly beggars the question of Jack Morne, doesn't it? He knew all along that he was not legally married to Margery, which explains a lot about what he did last Friday night. So much to lose..." His voice wandered off as they both watched Margery slowly approaching the bed. The princess has arrived to awaken you at last, Louise thought acidly. This princess certainly looked and acted nothing like those in the fairy tales Louise learned as a child.

Chapter Five

Margery's heart was beating so loudly she felt everyone in the room could hear it. Dr. Gibbons and Billy told her that Robert was unconscious, although Billy said he had squeezed his hand. Squeeze my hand, darling, she thought. Just to feel your hand again would be everything to me.

Slowly she approached the still, slight figure in the bed. What if Billy was mistaken, and it wasn't Robert? No, Jack knew it was him. There were so many cases of missing soldiers who had been misidentified by grieving wives and mothers, simply because they could not bear the thought of permanently losing the one they loved. She would know it was him. She could never mistake him for another.

Out of the corner of her eye she saw the looming figure of that nurse Whiting. Almost twenty years she had taken care of him! An odd thing to be so devoted to one patient that long. Did she love him? Her ferocity in protecting him brought to mind her mother-in-law's overprotective attitude when Robert had been ill with pneumonia and she had wanted to visit him. Her mother-in-law thought her presence would 'upset' Robert and cause him to have a relapse. Now this nurse was acting just the same.

She reached the bed, finding it difficult to focus on Robert's features as he lay motionless. The light was dim, ostensibly to protect him from overstimulation that could cause more seizures. Her hand reached out tentatively to touch his face. Her fingers traced the lines of his forehead, his cheekbone, and then his lips. His lips, full and soft, were just as she remembered them. She came closer to the bed, leaning over the rail and looking at his face, long and intently. There was no doubt in her mind – it was Robert, her darling Robbie. Older, certainly, and with a look of someone who has suffered a long illness. Her hands touched his hair, stopping suddenly at the scar behind his left ear. He moved suddenly, then jerked. Louise came forward instantly. Cyril cautioned her to stay back.

Margery smoothed his hair, then bent down and tenderly kissed his forehead, tears falling from her eyes onto his face. Her kisses covered his face, his eyes and his lips gently while she murmured something unintelligible to the others in the room.

Robert opened his eyes, at first not focusing, then seeing a face above him. He closed his eyes, believing this was another dream where he would find Margery again. Then he heard her voice.

"Hello, darling," she said softly, very close to his ear. "My darling, darling Robbie." He looked up into her face and smiled. "Margery," he croaked, bringing his hand to meet hers. "Margery."

"Yes, darling, I'm here," she said, smoothing his hair. "I am here and will never leave you. Never." She kept smiling at him. Billy turned away and blew his nose loudly into his handkerchief.

Robert smiled and began to shake slightly. Alarm showed in his face as Cyril and Louise quickly stepped forward and began to work on him, pulling out tongue blades and filling syringes. Margery stepped away from the violence on the bed, running to Billy's arms as he hurried her out of the room.

Several minutes later Cyril came out and explained Robert's history to Margery. The seizures were uncontrollable at times, especially during great emotional traumas. "It was the reason Nurse Whiting was afraid for you to see him," Cyril said on her behalf. "She has his best interests at heart. He has had a very severe relapse since last week. I am sure you have also been under great strain."

Margery smiled through her tears. "Strain? Oh, Doctor, you have no idea what a strain this has all been. I would not wish this past week on my worst enemy. Except that I have found my Robert again." She sobbed gently against Billy's shoulder.

"When can I take him home?" she asked, her dark eyes shining strangely through her tears. "I want to look after him."

"Very difficult to say at present," Cyril said. "I suspect we may want to talk to the specialist who is on the case, Dr. Warren. No doubt Robert will still need expert nursing care for a time."

"No doubt," Margery nodded sadly. "I want to look after him. I am sure I am capable of looking after the man I love."

"Let's see how he recovers from this episode," Cyril said in a conciliatory manner. "You go home and get some rest. I'll arrange for you to meet with Dr. Warren. He can give you a better idea of what the next steps would be." He excused himself to say goodbye to Louise before leaving for Sussex.

Billy put his arms around Margery, taking her out to the car without a word. It was almost too much to bear, to find her darling at last, only to know he was so injured he could not really respond to her. Of course she thinks she can care for him, he thought as they drove in silence back to Upper Marstone. Only that nurse knows how to care for him. The verdict was clear: Rob would have to be institutionalized for the rest of his life. If he knew Margery, she would not let that happen. He sighed loudly as he thought of the impossibility of their future together as man and wife. Be careful what you wish for, he thought. Her wish had come true, but what now?

Chapter Six

Margery opened the door before the car stopped in front of her house, jumping out and thanking Billy as she turned away from him. Billy thought he should go inside with her, just to make sure she was all right. Her quick exit and her straight back gave him the message to leave her alone.

He watched her move with her determined step to the house, feeling drained by the day's events yet realizing it was only a little past one o'clock. He should get back to the shop and relieve his Dad, but didn't think he could face customers today. With a heavy sigh he decided to go home and have a good meal with Sally. Sally would help him make sense of all this and would also know what Margery would do next.

Margery waited until she heard the car finally pull away, afraid Billy would insist on coming in and fussing over her. There was no reason to fuss now; Robert was back and she would do everything in her power to make him well again. The vision of his violent seizure came back to her in such detail that she had to lean on the doorframe, steadying herself, not only from the memory of the day's events, but also from what her future would be like from now on.

She had sworn to him that she would love him and care for him no matter what happened to him in the War. She would keep that promise. Her exact words came back to her: "It would not matter to me whether you were missing an arm or a leg. I would not care if you lost your sight or your hearing. I would be your limbs, or your eyes, or your ears. Just come back to me." This head wound and the ensuing seizures that had kept him away from her all these years were something entirely different. Tears pricked her eyes as she thought of the cruelty of having him back in such a condition as she saw today.

The front door opened suddenly and Elizabeth stood there, her face so worried as she looked at her mother it made Margery smile.

"Mummy! I was just about to come out to see where you were. You said you went out with Uncle Billy in your note. What has happened? You look awful." She took her mother's arm and gently guided her to the settee, taking off Margery's coat and sitting next to her.

Margery removed her headscarf slowly, looking long into the silvery-grey eyes of her daughter. Eyes just like Robert's, she smiled to herself, and touched Elizabeth's cheek. It was time Elizabeth knew the truth. In retrospect, all these years of keeping it from her seemed silly now. Why had she done it? In deference to Jack and his feelings. Jack had obviously not cared about her feelings when he kept the news of his brother's survival from her.

"I have to talk to you, darling," Margery began, removing her coat just as she heard the kettle whistling. "Go on, dear. Make us some tea. We have a lot to talk about." Elizabeth got up quickly, the sweet scent of lilac soap wafting in the air as she said from the kitchen, "And I have so much to tell you, too, Mummy. I've made some decisions today. I also talked to Uncle Harry about some things, and umm.. well..." She hesitated, but Margery was already lost in her own thoughts of a new life for both of them.

Elizabeth came in with a tea tray, two cream-colored cups decorated with bluebells prominent on the tray. They had belonged to Robert's mother, and were a particular favorite of Elizabeth's, especially when she was feeling sick or insecure. Margery hoped that as she unfolded her story that the comfort the brought would be there for her daughter.

"I was saying I talked to Uncle Harry this morning at the office," Elizabeth said as she poured her mother's tea and handed her a cup. "I've been thinking about the university, and..well, I am not sure I want to go now. There seems to be so much that needs doing here, now that Daddy's gone." She lowered her head and took a sip of too-hot tea, gulping loudly as it went down.

"Darling," Margery said, setting down her cup and taking her daughter's arm. "I don't want you to think you must stay here on my account. So much has changed. Things will be different now. I know Jack would have wanted you to go to university. He was very set on it." Elizabeth looked at her mother, wondering why she had called her father, 'Jack' instead of 'your father.' It seemed an odd phrase to use.

"I'd have to leave by this weekend for the Michaelmas term," Elizabeth said, putting her cup down. "I just don't think I am ready to do that after all that has happened this week. Besides, I've been thinking about things. Uncle Harry said he would help, and..." Margery gripped her arm and looked into her eyes, her gaze softening as Robert's face rose before her in her daughter's features.

"Elizabeth, something happened today, something I never thought would have been possible," she began softly. The tone of her mother's voice was so different it made Elizabeth stop and stare at her mother. There was a strange look on her face, a cross between mystified and dreamy. It was an expression she had never seen before.

"What is it, Mummy?" Elizabeth said, holding her mother's cold hand. She rubbed it absentmindedly as Margery took a deep breath.

"I went to Caterham with Uncle Billy today," she said, struggling with the words. *How do I tell her all this?* It seemed impossible and she wished Robert could be at her side to help her. "Uncle Billy came here this morning to tell me he found out more about the man your father was meeting when he died."

Elizabeth upset her tea cup, spilling tea on her wool tweed skirt and blotting it quickly with her handkerchief. "Never mind, darling," Margery said, taking her hand again. "I can get that out later. You must listen to me. That man was no ordinary man your father was meeting. That man was.." She choked on her words, Elizabeth's expression one of anticipation but something more: suspicion. Margery pulled back her shoulders and carried on.

"You know him, don't you?" Elizabeth asked. "I knew you did. I saw it when he came over and put his hand on Daddy. Is he someone you have known for a long time?" Her defensive air made Margery smile. Elizabeth glowered, not knowing what was so funny in the incident where her father died.

"How do I tell you all this?" Margery said helplessly as Elizabeth tried to pull her hand away. "No, darling, listen to me. Please don't shut your mind to what I am saying. Yes, I know him. I know him very well. And you know him, too, in a way. That man who was coming to see us was not a stranger. He was Jack's brother. He is the man you know as Uncle Rob."

"Rob!" Elizabeth exclaimed. "That was the name on the telegram! I couldn't remember what it was until just now! But how?" She looked at her mother, confusion in her eyes. "Uncle Rob was killed in the War. How could he be coming here?"

Margery kept a tight grip on Elizabeth. *Now the hard part comes out, my darling daughter. Now I must tell you the truth, however painful it will be.*

Margery could feel Elizabeth's eyes on her, waiting for an answer. Although Elizabeth looked so much like Robert, she had many of Margery's personality traits. She didn't suffer fools gladly, she liked things to be told to her with no euphemisms, and she resented being treated like a fragile child who could not comprehend anything. With another deep breath Margery looked straight into her eyes.

"It is time you know the whole story, darling," she said, lightly stroking her daughter's brown hair, a mix between Robert's coloring and her own chestnut shade. "You know I was engaged to Uncle Rob. Auntie Rose told you that. What no one ever told you is how much I loved him, how he was everything to me. When he was killed my whole world ended. September 28, 1916 was the worst day of my life."

"I knew you were going to marry him," Elizabeth said, frightened to see her mother choking up so openly. Emotions had been infrequent in their home. Her father had always been stalwart, only exhibiting a sort of angry-bear impatience at times. Her mother always seemed so placid and yielding. It often made her laugh when people described her mother as quite a feisty and opinionated young woman. She saw no evidence of that, nor of the love she must have felt for her uncle.

"I know, Mummy, but you didn't know he was still alive until now," Elizabeth tried to comfort her, thinking she felt sad for Uncle Rob when he would find out that she loved Jack and had married him.

"That's right, darling, but there is so much more to this," Margery said, turning away from Elizabeth. This will be the hardest part, Margery thought. How to tell her that her entire life has been nothing but a lie.

"I loved Uncle Rob so much that when he was sent to France, I followed him down to Folkestone before he embarked," she said, her head down and her eyes fixed on her hands in her lap. "That night, August 24, 1916, I married him. Do you remember seeing this on Jack's desk? Here it is." She took the marriage certificate from her bag and handed it to Elizabeth, who read it silently without looking up.

"Do you understand what this means?" Margery asked quietly, trying to get Elizabeth to look at her. "It means that I am still married to Uncle Rob. I was never really married to Jack. But that is not all there is to this." She choked again slightly and Elizabeth looked up, her expression wary.

"I spent that night with Robert," she said. "We only had a few hours together before he left. I loved him so and did not want ever to be parted from him, but a few hours were all I could have with him. Except," she hesitated, knowing she had to say it now, "I had something of him with me always. I had you."

Elizabeth's head shot up quickly as she looked directly into her mother's eyes. "What!?" she cried. "Are you telling me that Uncle Rob is my father?"

"Yes, darling," Margery smiled tenderly at her. "Robert is your father. When Jack knew his brother was missing, he offered to find the marriage certificate for me so I could claim Robert's pension for us. It didn't exist, as you can see by the letter. So Jack offered to marry me. I didn't want to. I hoped against hope that Robert would return. Jack said if he ever did he would step aside, but that he would protect and keep us, and make you legitimate. He was certain Robert would not return. I suppose I was, too. There's the horror of it all."

"I just can't believe it," Elizabeth murmured, staring at the marriage certificate and the letter, the writing indecipherable through her tears. She had tried and tried to remember what had seemed so odd to her on Friday night. In her haste she had not comprehended what she was reading. Now it was very clear.

"It is all true, darling," Margery soothed her. "You are Robert's daughter, not Jack's. Jack raised you and loved you as his own child, but he is your uncle. And there is more to all this." She wondered whether she should continue. Elizabeth's too-calm demeanor made her hesitant.

"Jack knew about my marriage since 1919, but insisted on telling me it never happened," she started, watching Elizabeth's downcast expression as she stared at the certificate in her lap. "He also found out that Uncle Rob was alive nine years ago. He never told me. There is only one reason: Jack was not going to give up his wife and daughter to the one man who rightfully belonged here. When Robert was strong enough to come back, Jack could not let him. That is why he was out on that road on Friday night, to make sure Robert would never come back."

"No!" Elizabeth shouted, standing up as the papers fell to the floor. "No! You are saying wicked, horrible things about my father. He loved us and did everything for us. There you sit, disparaging him when all he ever did was love you and try to make you happy. This is how you repay him now. I can't believe anyone could be so cruel."

"Elizabeth," Margery stood up, trying to grab her daughter's arm but she pulled it away. "I am not the one who is cruel. Jack deliberately withheld this information from me. He denied you knowing your own father. He wanted to kill his own brother. And you say I am cruel? I think that is cruelty, to be willing to kill and destroy lives for your own sake."

"Maybe if you had tried to love him more," Elizabeth shouted. "He adored you, yet I could see you didn't love him the way he hoped you would. He would have done anything for you, anything."

"Anything except give me the one person I loved more than anyone else in the world," Margery said. "You didn't know him the way I did, Elizabeth. He could be devious and deceptive in ways no one could understand."

"Perhaps it was the only way he could be," she cried. "I heard some of the stories from Auntie Rose. 'Robbie, Robbie, Robbie,' all the time, and nothing for Daddy. Well, he is still my father in my eyes, and always will be. That man killed him. I will never think differently about him. Never." She started to walk away but Margery was not finished.

"Elizabeth!" she said. "I love 'that man,' as you call him. I am still his wife. Whether you want to accept it or not, he is your father. I want to bring him home where he belongs."

"Two minutes of pleasure in some filthy little bedroom in Folkestone only makes him my father physically," Elizabeth spat at her mother. "Any man could have done the same with you. I know who my father was. He will always be my father in my heart."

Margery reached out and slappèd her daughter, shocked at her own reaction. It had not been two minutes of pleasure in a filthy bedroom. It was an experience that lingered in her heart even now, and brought her this beautiful child who was her life. Of course she knew it would take time for Elizabeth to accept the truth. She had not expected this reaction.

"If you bring him to this house I will leave," Elizabeth said, the stinging red welt on her cheek flaring like a waving flag. "I do not want to meet him, or know him. Or you either, since you seem to have spent your life taking advantage of my father and his kindness just to carry on a tawdry memory in your heart. I am sorry Robert fathered me. I suppose you would not even let a fine man like my father near you." She turned quickly, grabbed her coat, and left the house. Margery could hear the engine of the car revving up as Elizabeth raced down the street.

Margery sat down heavily, unsure of what to do next. Her heart had been so full of hope that Robert would get well and thrive with her loving care, knowing he had a beautiful daughter. Now she had lost not only her daughter, but the possibility that she would ever be able to have the two people she loved most in the world in her arms. She closed her eyes and leaned back against the settee, wishing for an instant that Jack would be here so she could talk to him about what to do. It made her feel odd to think she wanted to talk to Jack. In nearly twenty years of marriage she had relied on him more than she thought.

But Jack was gone and she had to make decisions for herself. Where to start now? It all seemed impossible to even find the beginning.

Chapter Seven

Billy pulled his coat tighter as he stepped out of the car in front of his house. The day seemed colder now than this morning. His house looked as always – serene, welcoming, an oasis from the cares of the world. All he wanted at this point was to go inside and talk to Sally. Sally had always been his rock, the person who seemed able to make sense of a world that often became incomprehensible. He shook his head as he thought that even she would have trouble understanding the events of this morning.

It was after one o'clock, so he knew the children would be back at school. The kitchen door opened, the smells of an appetizing stew greeting his nostrils. Again he sighed, his feelings brimming over as he stepped into the cheerful blue-and-yellow kitchen. So different than the austere look of Margery's kitchen, as if she had denied herself all color and brightness to compensate for losing Robert.

"Sal?" he called, getting no response. He took off his coat and hung it up on the hook in the hallway, noticing Sally's coat and handbag were gone. Where was she? Perhaps Margery had rung up and she had run over there. No, he would have seen her along the way. He turned back slowly toward the kitchen, not sure what to do.

The oak table was scrubbed clean and the dishes sat neatly drying on the rack. The comfort and coziness of it overwhelmed him as he thought of seeing Rob again, impacted by the realization of how injured he was. He sank into the sturdy wooden chair, putting his head into his arms and began to weep loudly.

That damned War. He had tried to forget it for nearly twenty years, but it would not die. Everywhere you went there were reminders: legless men who smiled, but not with their eyes; blind men who walked tentatively with white-tipped canes; the coughs and gasps from men his age as he sat waiting to see the doctor in his surgery. It was an obscene brotherhood. You wore your membership card in your eyes, eyes that no longer showed joy even if their expressions did. He recognized his fellow sufferers by their dead eyes. Did Rob have that look, too? To see Rob, still so slender and youthful looking, shaking uncontrollably from a bullet to his head.... Billy could not contain his weeping. It echoed off the walls of the kitchen, a wailing that he could not restrain.

"Billy!" he heard Sally's voice as she came in the back door. Dropping her shopping bag to the floor, she ran over to him, putting her arms around his shoulders. "Billy, darling! What is it?" She hugged him, the fresh smell of the cold air still clinging to her headscarf and coat as she embraced him.

"Oh, Sal," he said, turning to her and putting his arms around her tiny waist. "Oh, Sal." She ran her hands over his hair softly, holding him while she waited for him to tell her what was wrong. "Is it your Dad?" she asked gently, afraid to set off a fresh batch of wailing.

"No, Dad's fine, as far as I know," Billy said, pulling away from her. "It's Robbie. Robbie Morne."

"Robbie Morne?" Sally asked, puzzled. "Robbie Morne?"

He nodded, then put his face down again, sobbing softly. Sally quickly took off her coat and scarf, going through to hang them up, then put the shopping bag on the table while she waited for Billy to finish. What prompted this? Jack's death, and with it another friend who was part of a generation's slaughter. She knew the men would talk of it among themselves, but not to their families. The nightmares had plagued Billy since she married him, the memories of his time in the trenches and the horrors he experienced. Margery had told her Jack had been much the same.

But why Robbie? First Marge mentioned him, and now Billy. Was this the date he had gone missing so long ago? She watched Billy's strong shoulders quivering as he still kept his head down. Perhaps a bowl of her stew and some fresh slices of bread and butter would help him feel better. Billy loved his food and had never refused a meal.

Quickly she took down a large bowl and plate from her glass-fronted yellow cupboards, and cut two thick slices of bread, slathering them thickly with butter. She put the kettle on, needing a cup of tea as much as she felt Billy did. She served a good portion of the evening stew up in the bowl and carried everything to the table.

"Here, dearest, get this inside you," she said softly, hugging his shoulders. "It will make you feel better." Billy looked up and she smiled tenderly at him, pleased to see he responded. She pushed the bowl in front of him, then the bread. He sat staring at it and then picked off a small corner of the bread and ate it.

"That's right. No doubt you are starving if you haven't had anything to eat since breakfast. That might account for what you are feeling right now about the War." She stood at the cooker, pouring two fragrant cups of tea for them and bringing them to the table.

"No, Sally, it's not that," he said, picking up his spoon and taking a spoonful of the stew. "This morning, when I went out, I found out who that man was in Caterham."

"Oh, yes?" Sally said, watching him carefully. He seemed calm now, making good progress with his stew and the bread. She took another sip of tea.

He looked up, his eyes still full, then said, "The man in hospital, Sal, was Robbie. Robbie."

Sally nearly spilled her tea and said, "Surely not! It can't be!"

"Oh, but it is," Billy said. "I ...I took Marge there. I wanted to come here, but somehow I thought she should know first. I didn't know about her being married to Rob. Or about Elizabeth."

Sally looked into her teacup, then across at Billy. "She told me the other day, after Jack died. But are you sure this man is Robbie?"

"I'm sure," Billy responded, sipping his tea slowly after burning his tongue on the stew. "Very sure. Marge was sure, too."

Sally sat back, remembering what Margery had said about seeing Rob on Friday night. She had attributed it to shock and the sedative. A burst of sunlight illuminated the kitchen like a floodlight as they stared at one another.

"He is profoundly injured," Billy said, his voice cracking as he tried to fight back tears. "Had a terrible head wound from which he has never really recovered. After Marge saw him," he stopped, tears coming from his eyes as he grabbed his handkerchief and mopped his face, "he had a seizure. It was like something I never saw before. He is still so slight. You remember how he was. It nearly threw him out of the bed. And Marge thinks she can take him home." He blew his nose softly and looked at Sally.

"Marge never stopped loving him," Sally said, almost to herself. "That much I know. She would want to bring him home. What of Elizabeth? Does she know?"

Billy shook his head, seemingly lost again in the world of trenches and horrors that Sally was not privy to, no matter how long they were married. She got up slowly and hugged Billy tightly to her, feeling her own emotions welling up. Rob alive! Dear, dear Robbie, the most charming boy in the village. She would have quite fancied him herself if Billy hadn't stolen her heart first. The thought that he was still alive made her sway slightly.

"I'm going to ring Marge right now," Sally said. "The shock of everything must be overwhelming. Will you be all right, sweetheart?" Sally kept her arm around Billy's shoulder as he nodded, staring out the window at the brilliant but cold sunshine.

Chapter Eight

Elizabeth drove toward the village, not sure where she would go. Her tears blinded her so much she found herself going off the road and nearly knocking down some pedestrians crossing the High Street. She drove aimlessly around for nearly an hour before she found herself in Tyler's Green, pulling over suddenly when she hit a grassy hillock on the side of the road.

"Damn!" she said, wondering if she had damaged the car. This part of the road was isolated, Upper Marstone behind her, and Tyler's Green a ways off. She got out, inspecting the car and seeing no damage done, got back in.

Where was she going? She left the house so quickly she hadn't thought about going anywhere, just getting away from her mother. The story of her life now seemed all a complete lie. This man, this uncle she had loved in photographs, this 'war hero', was lying in wait for her father. What had her father said before he died? She had asked him why he was trying to kill this man. He replied, "He is trying to kill me. He's been trying to kill me since we were children." Yet her mother seemed to think it was the opposite. Her head swam as she tried to make sense of what her mother had said. All she could fixate on was that Robert, Uncle Robert, was her father. And he was still her mother's husband.

No, she said, beating on the steering wheel. No, Daddy, I will not let them come in and carry on in your house. It is not right. It never will be, no matter how many legal documents and lies Mummy produces. Not right, not right. She kept beating away, a car slowing down to watch her. They drove off quickly when she glared at them.

Where could she go? It seemed Uncle Billy was in this now, too, so she couldn't go there. Auntie May and Uncle Harry? Auntie May was ill, and besides, she was Mummy's sister, so would naturally take her part. Auntie Rose? Yes, she would go see Auntie Rose. Her godmother would take her in and listen to her. She had always been a shoulder to cry on when Elizabeth felt sad or afraid.

She turned the car back toward the village, driving carefully and feeling a new strength as she came through the village toward the Green. Along Ivy Mill Lane she pulled in front of her godmother's cottage, surprised to see how overgrown it looked, the leaves in brown, sodden piles around the front gate. The once-glossy green shutters were faded against the white stone, and the windows showed a dinginess from lack of cleaning.

Auntie Rose Henning was not her real aunt, but had been a friend of the family for years. She was well into her eighties now, but her mind was as sharp as ever, as was her tongue. Although her mother was a direct speaker, Auntie Rose made it an art. She seemed invincible until last winter, when she had fallen on the ice while shopping and had broken her hip. It had healed slowly, and she had still not recovered sufficiently to carry on the tasks of caring for her cottage and garden. She refused to move or be put in a home. No one dared cross her.

Elizabeth put on the parking brake and sat quietly, watching the leaves swirl around the little garden fence. The roses were still blooming, but many had begun to die and wither, creating a macabre landscape of purplish-black blooms. It almost seemed as if the house was vacant. Elizabeth noticed the curtain move, so gave a little wave and went up to the door.

"Hello, pet," Rose Henning said as she threw open the door, leaning heavily to her left on an ornately carved wooden cane. "What brings you here, and in the motor and all?" She ushered Elizabeth into the cozy parlor and took her coat. The tap-tap of her cane echoed down the hall as she went to the kitchen. "I've got the kettle on, so I'll get you a cup, shall I?" she hollered. Her hip had not healed properly, but there was nothing wrong with her voice.

Elizabeth sat down, looking around the room at all the little memories of Auntie Rose's life. There were pictures of her four children, all grown up grandparents themselves now. She had so many photographs it was hard to know who everyone was. Then her eye caught one she hadn't really noticed before. It was a soldier, a young man with a brilliant smile and dazzling eyes. She knew who it was: Uncle Rob. She got up, not listening to the chatter that Rose kept up as she made the tea. She took the picture from the mantel, staring at it, wanting to tear it from the frame and toss it into the fire. It captivated her, because she could see in his face the reflection of her own.

"What's that you've got there?" Rose said, wheeling a tray in rather than carrying it. There were biscuits and lumpish homemade scones, along with a pot of tea and a hand-knitted tea cosy in a riot of blue, orange and purple, the handiwork of Auntie Rose.

"Nothing," Elizabeth said, quickly putting the photograph back and turning around. "I was just looking at your pictures."

"That's all I've got now, pictures," Rose said, settling herself into a red-flowered chintz covered chair bearing her imprint. She poured the tea and handed it to Elizabeth. "You've been crying, pet. What's the matter?" She took a sip of her tea and waited.

Elizabeth sat down across from Rose on an equally vivid chintz-covered sofa replete with red poppies "It's...it's everything," Elizabeth said, her silvery-grey eyes clouding over. "It's Daddy dying and Mummy and now...well...Mummy..." she choked on her tea. Rose started to get up, but Elizabeth waved her back.

"Is Mummy having a bad time of it?" Rose asked sympathetically. Elizabeth shook her head. "No, Auntie Rose. I am. I want to come and live with you."

"What's brought all this on?" Rose said, suspiciously. "Why do you want to leave your home?"

Elizabeth sat stonily and said, "What do you know about Mummy and Uncle Rob?"

What did she know? Rose asked herself. What did it matter now? Poor dear Robbie was long ago killed. It seemed an odd question. Perhaps with Jack dead things were said that had better been left unsaid.

"There must be a reason for this question, Elizabeth," Rose hedged, wondering what was going on. Could she tell her what she knew about her, and her suspicions about whose child she was? Something had happened that had upset her greatly. With Jack gone, perhaps the truth had come out at last.

"Oh, there is, Auntie Rose," Elizabeth said, looking at her intently. "I need to know all about Mummy, Uncle Rob, and Daddy. Everything."

Rose looked away, staring into the fire as it snapped and popped. It was as if she could find all the memories in the flames and bring them to Elizabeth. How could she tell her what she knew about Jack? She cleared her throat. The silence was interrupted by the mantel clock loudly chiming half past four.

Elizabeth kept staring at her, waiting for answers. Rose took a sip of tea, settled herself more deeply into her chair, and proceeded cautiously in telling Elizabeth what she knew.

"Your mother was very in love with Robert," Rose began, feeling there would be no harm in telling Elizabeth what she already knew. She had often asked Rose about Uncle Rob, and about his being engaged to her mother long ago. "They were a couple who were said to be 'going strong' in the village, if you take my meaning." Elizabeth nodded glumly but said nothing.

"The truth is that Jack also fancied your Mum. The two brothers had a rivalry of sorts for her hand," Rose continued warily, watching Elizabeth's reactions with her every statement. "They had a few rows about it. Eventually your Mum and Uncle Rob became engaged. That ended things for a while. Until the War."

Elizabeth looked up now, her eyes glistening. "And when Uncle Rob was killed, Mummy fell in love with Daddy, didn't she?" Elizabeth wanted to hear someone confirm that her parents had loved one another, and that their marriage was not a charade.

"It was a bit more complicated, I think, pet," Rose said, putting a large slathering of jam on a scone and offering it to Elizabeth. "Go on, darling. This was the last batch of jam I made before I fell. You always loved my jam. Go on." Elizabeth took the scone but left it lying on the plate.

"Complicated how?" she said. She already knew, but she needed to hear the truth from Auntie Rose.

Although the sun was still shining, it filtered through the lace curtains in a weak manner that cast little pools of sun amid the darker tones of the deep blue and red Turkish rug in front of the fireplace. The sun almost seemed to mock the overpowering darkness, as if the truth that was coming out now was represented by the snatches of sunlight. Rose was silent for so long Elizabeth moved her teacup loudly as she set it down on the table.

"Auntie Rose, you have to tell me," Elizabeth said. "I need to know."

"Why?" Rose countered, trying to see her goddaughter's face in the fading light. "What has made you so determined to know what happened long ago when it no longer matters to anyone?"

Elizabeth looked up now, a strange smile on her face. "It matters to Mummy. You do know what happened to Daddy on Friday night?"

Rose shifted in her chair. She wanted to get up and put on a lamp, but Elizabeth's gaze kept her riveted to her chair. "I know he wasn't well, poor lamb. He had an attack, what they used to call...what did they call it?"

"He had a stroke, Auntie Rose," Elizabeth said. "A blood vessel burst in his brain and killed him. The doctor said he didn't look after himself, but I think it was because he let everything overwhelm him. Because there was so much he kept to himself. It killed him."

"Jack was always one for secrets," Rose murmured. The fireplace snapped so loudly when she said that both she and Elizabeth jumped. Rose put her teacup down on the table, looking flustered and nervous.

"I don't think Daddy has come back to haunt you," Elizabeth smiled suddenly. "But I wish he were here. Daddy had a stroke, but there was more to the story than that. There was another man involved. Did you hear that? That man was trying to kill Daddy. Daddy told me so."

Rose hesitated before answering. "I heard that this other man was someone he knew from the Army. He's still in hospital in Caterham. No one seems to know who he is."

"Mummy knows who he is," Elizabeth said. "And so do you."

"Me?" Rose responded. "How would I know who he is? I don't know anyone from the Army, save my grandsons, who came home safe and sound and never had any truck with your father."

Elizabeth got up quickly and went to the mantel, removing the photograph of Robert and bringing it to Rose. "Look at him," she said, "now look at me. What do you see?"

Rose stared at the face of the boy she had loved like her own son. A lovely lad, kind, gentle, charming and dear to her. Crushed in that horrible battlefield known as the Somme. Tears came to her eyes, because she understood that somehow Elizabeth now knew the truth of her paternity.

"Did your mother tell you?" Rose whispered, handing the picture to Elizabeth, who stared at it with a strange expression. "We suspected as much, of course, but no one said it out loud."

"Did you know that Mummy married Uncle Rob as well?" Elizabeth asked angrily. "Oh, yes, Mummy is full of secrets. First she follows him to Folkestone like a lovesick puppy, they marry hurriedly, he fathers me, then off he goes to France, never to return. And who picks up the pieces? Who makes everything all right for Mummy and me? Who marries a woman who never loved him but used him for her own ends? My father. And what do I hear about him? That he was a liar, a deceiver, and a cad. That he lied about everything and ruined lives. How can that be true and how can Mummy be so cruel?"

Elizabeth began to weep again, her sobs so heartrending that Rose got up and sat down next to her on the couch, holding her tightly the way she had when Elizabeth was a child and had fallen down. "There, there, my pet, it is all right, all right," she murmured, brushing the soft brown hair gently away from Elizabeth's face. "People do strange things when they have to. Perhaps you will understand it better if you let me tell you what I know about it all." Elizabeth nodded while Rose began to tell her story.

"Robbie and I worked together at old Mr. Brooke's shop," she recalled, looking over the top of Elizabeth's head to Robert's photograph now sitting on the table in front of them. "He was a lovely boy, very handsome, and quite a catch for the village girls. Your mother decided she wanted him. Whatever your mother decided, she usually got."

Elizabeth was quiet now, listening intently to the story and learning a different side of her mother. Margery had seemed so devoted and passive. It was odd to hear how vigorously she had pursued Uncle Rob.

66

"She asked him to a village dance," Rose recalled. "He was so flattered by that, practically walking on air all afternoon, preening like a peacock around the shop." She smiled as she looked at the grinning boy in the photograph. "From there they became serious, but Jack...well, Jack wanted her, too. He tried to win her heart, but she was smitten with Robert. Jack didn't just try to win her heart. He..he.."

"He what?" Elizabeth said, raising her head and sitting up. Rose offered her a handkerchief while she dabbed her eyes.

"He had some strange ways about him," Rose continued cautiously. "Stalked them wherever they went. Wasn't above creating mischief with your Granddad about them as well. Made Robbie that miserable, I can tell you. He never understood Jack's being so against him."

"Didn't he?" Elizabeth said. "Even from you all I ever hear is how wonderful Robbie was, how charming, how handsome, how everyone loved him. If you were my father, wouldn't you have hated him as well? Then he gets the one girl you love, the one thing you have always wanted."

"That's as may be," Rose retorted. "But it didn't give him the right to try and hurt them both. That's not love, dear. That's something entirely different."

Elizabeth kept her eyes fixed ahead, staring at the last of the fading sunlight through the window. She could understand how miserable her father must have been living in his brother's shadow.

"I didn't know your Mother married Robert," Rose said thoughtfully, her face almost sad as if a secret had been deliberately kept just from her, "but I do remember your Grandmother telling me she had run off at Victoria Station after Robert left for Folkestone. She, of course, thought it must be for reasons I'd rather not say. Your Grandmother, God rest her soul, did not like your mother and thought the very worst of her in any way she could."

"Maybe she was right," Elizabeth muttered. Rose stood up shakily leaning on her cane.

"Now, I'll not have that, as your mother, hard to take as she sometimes was, was devoted to Robert, and a good wife to Jack," she said hotly. "It was hard for her, obviously thinking she was a married woman. Why didn't she tell anyone?"

"Because when Daddy went to get the marriage certificate it didn't exist." Elizabeth said. "He went there to look for it, but it wasn't until 1919 that they found it. By then Daddy and Mummy were already married and had me. There seemed no need for anyone to know, not even Mummy."

"You mean to tell me that Jack never told your mother he found the certificate?" Rose fumed. "Why not? As you said, it would not have mattered then. It would have set her mind at ease to know it was once true."

"Daddy wanted what was best for Mummy," Elizabeth said evenly. "You don't know her now. She is fragile in some ways. Daddy knew that, and tried to protect her from shocks. It was his way with her. Some may see it as him being a liar, but I see it as he loved her so much he just wanted to protect her." She hung her head and Rose asked, "What else did he protect her from?" Elizabeth did not answer right away, then looked at Rose.

"When I went to Daddy's office on Friday night, I saw the drawer he always kept locked wide open," Elizabeth said. "There were papers scattered all around, but two things caught my eye: a telegram stating that someone was coming to Upper Marstone and wanted Daddy to meet him in Caterham, and this marriage certificate. I grabbed the marriage certificate, not really sure what I was seeing. Everything happened so quickly, Daddy with a gun and..."

"With a gun?" Rose almost shouted. "What was he doing with a gun?"

"None of it made sense to me at the time," Elizabeth said. "I sensed Daddy was in trouble somehow. I grabbed the certificate and went to get Mummy. Then we drove to Caterham. I saw Daddy standing in the road, a little way to the side. He was pointing a gun at someone. I was so afraid for Daddy I ran to him, asking him what he was doing. He seemed strange, sweating and unlike I've ever seen him. He told me this man was trying to kill him and always had been. He tried to shoot the gun, but I grabbed his arm. Then he fell backward. I thought he had been shot by the other man. All of a sudden this man was kneeling over Daddy. Mummy came running and also kneeled by Daddy. When she touched the hand of this man, I felt she knew him. They looked at each other for just a second. There was this feeling, the strangest feeling, that they loved each other. I thought I must be in shock, because then the police came and they took the man away in the ambulance. Daddy had shot him in the arm."

She lowered her head as Rose sat back, her thoughts swarming like bees in a hive. "This man," Rose said softly. "Did they find out who he is and what he wanted?"

"Oh, yes, Auntie Rose," Elizabeth said, her expression strange in the darkening room. "Uncle Billy went there today and found out. He took Mummy there, too. Can't you guess who it is?"

"No, child, of course not. I wasn't privy to all your family business, you know," she said impatiently.

"But you knew that I was Uncle Rob's child, didn't you, and that Daddy married Mummy to give her child a name and take care of her?" Elizabeth looked at her with such anguish in her eyes Rose could not speak.

"Jack had good intentions that always went awry somehow," Rose whispered.

68

"Do you remember when Granddad died nine years ago?" Elizabeth looked intently at Rose, who wondered what that had to do with the man in the hospital. "Daddy went to Sussex the next day, 'on business,' he told Mummy. It was not business in the usual sense. It was family business. He found out something that day. To protect Mummy he didn't tell her. Now she knows."

"What does she know, pet?" Rose said, her heart nearly stopping in her chest.

"The man in the hospital, Auntie Rose," Elizabeth said softly. "Is her husband, Robert James Morne. He didn't die on the Somme. He was just injured in the head and has been in hospital all these years. Daddy didn't tell her, probably because Robert is so badly off that it would have broken Mummy's heart. He was only trying to protect her." She threw her arms around Rose, crying once again. Rose knew that she was trying to convince herself that the man she thought of as her father had not deliberately kept his brother away from his family without good reason.

"Listen to me, pet," Rose said, putting Elizabeth's face in her hands. "I'm going to ring your Mother and tell her you are safe with me and will stay here tonight. Then I want you to do something for me."

"What, Auntie Rose?" Elizabeth said, startled by the sound of glass tinkling. Auntie Rose's old grey cat, Catkins, had jumped up on a table behind her, watching as the birds came to the feeder for a final snack before retiring.

"Take me to the hospital in Caterham," she said, her cane tapping loudly as she made her way to the telephone. She turned to Elizabeth with the receiver in her hand. "There's so much high emotion going on here, and so many secrets being uncovered, I think this calls for a calm head and the voice of reason. I want to see him. You should see him, too."

"No," Elizabeth said. "I will take you, but I will not see the man who caused my father's death. I never want to see him. To me he will always be the person who killed my father."

"Darling, you must understand," she said, dialing Margery's number. "He, too, is your father."

Elizabeth looked at the photograph of Robert as she heard Auntie Rose's voice calming her mother over the phone. No, I do not want to know you. I will never accept you as my father, nor as my mother's husband. Nothing in this world will ever change my mind. She closed her eyes, blotting out the picture of the boy whose face was her own.

Chapter Nine

Louise was exhausted. The dark circles under her eyes showed all too obviously as she glanced in the mirror above the basin. Robert was more conscious now, but seemed oblivious to everything going on around him. She had been able to feed him some broth and toast. He said nothing, remaining unresponsive.

Although only early evening, she knew she had to get some sleep and figure out what they were going to do now. He could not stay in hospital much longer. His care now was simply custodial, not medical. Perhaps Lewis could allow him to stay for a while longer while she sorted out where they would go. A nursing home was out of the question. Of course, she had not reckoned on Margery being his wife. Where Robert would eventually go was Margery's decision. Louise's first meeting with the object of Robert's passion made her feel even more anxious about Robert's fate.

He lay so still she checked his breathing once again, knowing the shocks of the past week had taken their toll on his health. Lewis was a godsend. The feelings she had when she saw him again made her remember herself as that young schoolgirl who had been infatuated with the great Dr. Warren. He had saved Robert's life once before in France during the War. Here he was, doing the same thing again. Perhaps tomorrow evening when they had dinner he could suggest some alternatives for Robert, and broach that subject with Margery. Robert could not be cared for at home without someone trained to look after him. Margery could not handle his care alone.

Tucking the sheets around him, she put her hand on his cheek. His cheeks were sunken, but still he was more handsome than any man she had ever known. Her protective instincts toward him brought forth an anger at Margery and her insistence on seeing him, which had caused Robert to have another seizure. If that is how she loves him, Louise thought, he will be dead in a fortnight.

Another commotion in the hallway made Louise wonder just what was going on now. If it was the police again she would send them away with a tongue lashing they would never forget. Robert was quiet now. He did not need another episode like this afternoon.

She drew open the door to find two nurses surrounding a tiny old lady who was waving a huge wooden cane from side to side. "Now, let me through," she stated. "I have business here and I must take care of it." She peered at Louise like a wizened old wren, her grey hair interspersed with fading dyed henna patches. She pointed her cane at Louise.

"You have Robert Morne in there?" she asked, the cane inches from Louise's apron.

"And what is your business here?" Louise asked, straightening her shoulders and staring imperiously at Rose Henning.

"No need to get all la-di-da with me, my girl," Rose continued. "I've known Robbie for years. He'll want to see me. Let me in." She waved the cane again at Louise, who stood fast in front of the door.

Louise waved off the other nurses. This little lady would be easily talked to and did not seem to pose any threat, despite the rather formidable looking cane.

"Your name?" Louise said, wondering if this was an aunt or other relative.

"Rose Henning," she stated proudly. "Worked side by side with that lad. Like a mother to him I was. I just heard he was here from his...well.."

"Yes, his wife," Louise said distastefully, thinking of her former inflated vision of Margery and the shock at seeing the real woman.

"Look here, Sister," Rose said. "I'm an old woman. When I found out about Robbie today, I near thought I would have a heart attack and die. I know he is injured, badly they say. All I want is to see him, just for a second. Would you indulge an elderly lady who is none too well?" She smiled at Louise. Despite the smile, Louise knew this woman was not going to be placated until she saw Robert.

"Just a few minutes, as he is asleep," she said, taking a liking to this feisty old character. Had Robert mentioned her? She seemed to recall someone he worked with who always kept him hopping and made him go out to buy their sticky buns for elevenses. This lady certainly seemed to fit that description.

Rose felt weak in the knees, her cane not seeming to support her. Louise saw her falter and took her arm, helping her to the bedside where she lowered the rail so Rose could see him. Rose gasped, as it was indeed Robert, but much older. She stood quietly, almost praying as she watched his breath come evenly. She put her hand on his hand, then kissed his cheek.

71

He stirred slightly but did not awaken. Rose turned away as Louise lifted the rail and walked her back to the door.

"So what happened to him then?" Rose asked when they left the room. The hall was dim and empty as the day waned.

"He was wounded in the head, chest and arm, and taken to a hospital in Etaples in France." Louise recounted the story she knew by heart.

"Were you there?" Rose asked, eyeing her critically.

Unaccountably Louise blushed, her feelings for Robert always on her sleeve. She cleared her throat and said, "Yes. I was serving with the Queen Alexandra Imperial Military Nursing Service. His head wound rendered him unconscious for a long time. He had also lost his identification in the heat of battle. We didn't know who he was for several years. Only that his name was Robert. Because of the ring he wore." She lowered her head.

"Then nine years ago you found out who he was," Rose said evenly. "How?"

Louise looked at her directly. "He had surgery which made him better, but still his memory was faulty. Then one day he woke up and said, 'Morne.' I thought he was saying good morning, but he told me that was his name. We traced it and his brother came down to see him." She grimaced at the memory of Jack's cruelty to his brother.

"That devil Jack," Rose hissed. "He wouldn't even tell his own daughter." Louise looked at her quizzically. Rose said, "So you don't know about that, do you? Well, you seem to know about Margery being Jack's wife, so you might as well know all of it. Jack and Margery had a daughter, you know."

"Yes, I had heard that," Louise said stiffly, not forgiving Margery in her heart for marrying Jack and bearing his child. Now she waltzes in here to claim Robert as her own after she betrayed him.

"She's outside right now, their daughter," Rose said. "She brought me here. She's that upset, you see. Not only has she found out the truth about her mother and her 'uncle,' but something even more upsetting."

"It has been a trying time for everyone, I can imagine," Louise said sympathetically, feeling compassion for this poor daughter caught in the middle.

"She found out today," Rose said, "that Robert is her father. Not Jack. Margery married Jack so that she could keep her daughter and raise her properly. She never told Elizabeth. More than likely Jack wanted it that way. But Jack knew. I knew. You couldn't mistake those eyes of Robert's. Elizabeth has them, too."

Louise swayed slightly at this news. A daughter! Robert didn't know, she was certain of that. But it was one more thing to bind him tightly to Margery now. The thought of losing him overtook her.

"Are you all right, Sister?" Rose asked solicitously. "There's not a chair around. Use my cane if you need to." She offered the stick to Louise, who waved it away.

"Look, you need a cup of tea and a sit down," Rose said. "Is there a place we can go?"

"Actually, I was just going off duty for my dinner," Louise said. "We could go to the dining room. But you said that Robert's daughter brought you. Why didn't she come in with you? I would think she would like to meet her true father at last."

"Ah, you know so little of this family, I can see that," Rose smiled. "Robbie really must have lost his memory, or you would not even have asked a question like that." She took Louise's arm as they walked to the dining room. A plan was hatching in her mind as Louise talked to the charge sisters and gave her report. This Sister loved Robert, it was as plain as the nose on her face. What a muddle it all was, but a few things she knew: Robert needed the care of a trained and qualified nurse; Elizabeth needed time to sort things out for herself; Margery needed time to be with Robert and to keep her daughter with her; and Rose needed some help herself.

Louise offered to get some dinner for Rose, but she said she wasn't hungry. Louise brought her a large cup of tea along with her own meal. She told Rose of Robert's injuries in great detail, and the strides he had made to regain his memory and be a normal man again. Since Spring he had been the gardener for the Army hospital. Now the hospital was closing within the week.

"So you can see it is a dilemma as to where he will go," Louise said, finishing her mutton. "Sister Meade, my matron, even suggested I marry him so I could care for him." Louise smiled sadly. "Of course, she was joking. He is too ill to be left on his own without medical help nearby, and too well to be put away into a nursing home."

"And Margery taking him home would not be a good thing at present," Rose said almost to herself. "Not only the emotional trauma, of course, but his need for care. Would a nurse be all he needs?"

"Providing he does not endure something like last Friday, a nurse would do," Louise said. "She would need to understand neurological cases and seizures thoroughly. When my father died several years ago, he left me a great deal of money, enough where I need not work again. Sister Meade suggested I start my own nursing home. I have been considering it, of course. That was before I knew about Margery and Robert being married." She sighed in such a heartfelt manner Rose felt moved.

"You know I did not even ask you your name," Rose said brightly. Her idea was taking shape as she watched this Sister talking about Robert.

"Louise," she responded. "Louise Whiting."

"You can see I have a problem with my hip," Rose said, striking while the iron was hot. "I fell down last winter and broke it. It's never healed right, you see. I won't be put out of my own home, but it is hard to look after things. Sometimes I need some nursing care, treatments, massages, that sort of thing. My cottage has three large bedrooms, and the garden, well, it needs work."

"Yes, it is awfully difficult to manage those things after breaking a hip," Louise replied. "Perhaps I could see about getting someone over to help you."

"No, you silly goose, do you hear what I am saying to you?" Rose said impatiently. "You just told me that the hospital where you work is closing. You are out of a job; Robbie is out of a home. No doubt when he gets better he is going to want to stay here in Upper Marstone, isn't he? No doubt you would want to stay, too. You can't stay with him alone, can you? That wouldn't go over well in this village. But he needs looking after. You let me deal with Margery. I can make her see reason on this. She adores her daughter, and doesn't want to lose her. I think it's the best solution."

"Sorry?" Louise said, not comprehending what Rose was saying.

"Oh, everyone is that upset about Robert, but it just needs time, you see," she said, patting Louise's hand. "Miss Whiting, would you consider living with me in my cottage as my nurse, and Robbie's nurse as well? You can both live with me. He can look after the house and garden, and it will be a good place for him to recuperate and decide what he wants to do with his life. Because, it will be his decision, won't it?"

Louise thought about her words. In all the years she had known Robert, it seemed she or the doctors made the decisions for him. Rose Henning was right; he needed to decide for himself what he wanted. He needed to get to know his daughter, to know Margery again, and then make his decisions. She choked on the thought of those eventual decisions, but knew that Rose Henning was offering her a lifeline to remain with Robert a little longer. She smiled shyly, holding out her hand to Rose.

"Mrs. Henning," she said. "I would be happy to accept your offer, if Robert does. As you said, he needs to make his own decisions about his life now. It has been far too long that everyone else has been doing it for him."

"That's right, dear," Rose said, getting up from the table slowly. "I'll stop in and see him tomorrow and tell him what he is going to do. I don't think he'll give me much of an argument."

Louise watched her waddle away, smiling to herself that this tiny woman could be so determined and formidable. The solution she offered seemed ideal, however. It was almost a godsend. It would save him from being sent back into the arms of a woman Louise considered a traitor to the love and trust that Robert had bestowed upon her. Getting up from the table, she went out into the cool night air to the nurses' quarters. In the distance she saw Rose Henning being helped into a car by a slender young lady whose profile looked all too familiar. She looked like a female version of Robert – his daughter Elizabeth. Louise turned away to her room, her eyes full. One more knot in the tie that bound him to Margery. This tie, however, was too strong to overcome by determination alone. Her heart seemed too heavy for her chest as she walked through the darkness to her room.

Chapter Ten

The darkness startled Robert as he awoke, looking around at the unfamiliar surroundings and wondering where he was. It took all his concentration to try and remember, but he was drawing a blank. This was not his cottage, and it was not the Army hospital where he had spent so much time. So where was he? He tried to sit up, wondering if he was dreaming.

"Louise?" he said tentatively, trying to focus his eyes in the dim light. Louise had always been there, almost as if she psychically knew when he needed her. There was no response, so he called out a little louder. The door opened and a young Sister came in, her smile trying to mask the fear in her eyes.

"Did you want something, Mr. Morne?" she said quietly, not coming too close to the bed. "Are you feeling quite well?"

"Where am I?" he said, sitting up and rubbing his head carefully. He tried to move his left arm and winced. "What's the matter with my arm?"

"Don't you remember what happened last Friday evening?" the young nurse said, assisting him to a full sitting position. "Someone attempted to shoot you and you were hit in your left arm." She touched the bandages expertly, checking for drainage and whether they needed changing.

"Shoot me?" he asked quizzically. "Who wanted to shoot me?" She remained quiet as she repinned the bandage.

"I'm not certain of the details, Mr. Morne. I am sure when your regular nurse comes back on duty, she will be able to tell you more." She smiled again, a professional smile with the fear still showing in her eyes. She is afraid of me, he thought. Afraid I am a berserk war veteran who might start having a seizure at any moment.

"Thank you, Sister," he said as pleasantly as he could manage. "I appreciate your assistance. Do you think I might sit up a while? Could I look at a newspaper, perhaps? It is very lonely here like this." He smiled at her and saw her soften a little. "A little light would help as well." He smiled once more, hoping she would not show that fearful look again.

"Yes, I will see what I can find for you," she said, her attitude definitely more sympathetic. "Would you like something to eat as well?"

"That would be splendid," he grinned. "I expect I haven't been eating too much recently. What day is it?"

"Wednesday," she said, turning on the light and bringing a tray table over to him.

"Wednesday," he murmured to himself. "And what is the date?"

She hesitated, the fearful stance returning. He was a wounded war veteran who had gone mad, they all were saying at the nurses' station. A soldier who had lost all his memory from a head wound that made him violent and unpredictable. She had let her guard down when he talked so softly and smiled so nicely. Now he couldn't remember the date.

"September 25th," she said, "and the year is 1935." She didn't know what made her say that in such a sarcastic tone. The words had hurt him immediately after they were said. He didn't seem at all violent to her, but she couldn't be sure. Matron had said to keep her distance as you never knew what the War had done to these men and how they might react after years in hospital.

"Thank you," he said quietly. "Thank you, Sister. I appreciate you taking the time to help me. Do you know when Louise...I mean Sister Whiting will be back on duty?" His expression was so plaintive she felt like going to find this Sister Whiting and bring her back immediately.

"I'm not sure, Mr. Morne, but I will ask. Your dinner will be here soon." She turned quickly to leave the room when she heard his voice again. "One more thing, Sister, if you will bear with me. Where am I?"

"Caterham Cottage Hospital," she replied at the door, her voice having the hurried sound of someone desperately wanting to get away. The door closed suddenly before he even knew she had left.

So that is what I am to everyone, he thought. Something to be feared and avoided. Why did I wind up here? He tried to remember, but all he could recall were fragments of the past few days. Most of them seemed like dreams. Louise had been here looking after him, as she always was. There were other things he remembered. He sank back into the pillows, willing himself to remember exactly what happened and how he came to be here.

What is the last thing he remembered? Friday afternoon in East Preston. He had decided he wanted to come home and visit his brother Jack. It was going to be a surprise because Jack seemed so determined to keep him from coming back to the village where he grew up. He couldn't understand why

Jack was so adamant about keeping him away. When he finally felt strong enough, he decided to go on his own.

Louise, his most devoted nurse and good friend, wanted to go with him, but he felt this was something that he had to sort out for himself. The day had been fair, so he spent the time in the garden until mid-afternoon. Then he changed clothes that he had hidden in a wheelbarrow near the hospital walls, hopped the wall, and took off for the railway station. There he sent his brother a telegram, telling him he was coming home and on what train. He figured once Jack knew it was inevitable, he would accept it.

He nearly burst with joy as the train pulled through the Surrey downs and arrived in Caterham. The station looked so much the same as he remembered he felt unable to leave, looking at the benches and bricks as if they were part of a religious shrine. Walking up the stairs to Station Road he looked around and saw his old employer, the W.C. Brooke Company, now called something else – Ennors. The street looked the same and the memories flooded him so much he thought he should sit down in the station and wait for Jack.

Jack was not there to meet him, not unusual as perhaps he got tied up with his business. It was a fine night, brisk and cool, and the thought of walking the same road he had walked so often as a child and young man was a pleasant prospect. He walked up Station Road, crossing over at the now-closed shops and toward the fountain. All of it was so familiar he could have cried from emotion.

He struck out onto the road to Upper Marstone, past St. John's Church. Once Caterham was behind him, the road got darker, the thickly wooded sides making a canopy that kept moonlight from illuminating his path. An occasional motorcar whizzed by him, one even offering him a ride, but his heart was so full of joy to be home he wanted to enjoy every sensation.

Jack would most likely meet him somewhere along the road, so he kept straight to it, holding Jack's address firmly in his coat pocket. He tried to place where Jack lived, and kept thinking that there were no living quarters in that space where he had his business. It seemed an odd thing that Jack would live there. Perhaps his memory was faulty enough that he could not place the exact location.

About two miles along he saw someone coming toward him. The man was walking strangely, as if he were trying to hide among the trees. Robert tensed, hoping he was not going to encounter some unpleasantness before he saw his home village again. The person was ducking and weaving, so Robert decided to step off the road himself until this person went by. Probably just someone who had too much to drink and was having trouble finding his way in the darkness.

As Robert walked along the side of the road, the person seemed to disappear. All of a sudden his brother Jack appeared before him. The door to his hospital room opened hastily as an older lady with a kerchief came in, putting a tray before him of tasteless, overcooked vegetables, mutton, and watery tapioca pudding. She sat it down hurriedly, saying, "Will you be needing help with that?" and left before he answered.

"Damn," he swore, the thread of memory snapping as he stared at the unappetizing meal before him. "Damn. And it's mutton, too. I hate mutton." He pushed the tray away, closing his eyes and once again tried to recall what happened.

Jack. What did he say? It was all so muddled but he willed himself to remember. Jack said he had come to meet him as Robert had asked in the telegram. Then Jack began talking strangely. It was about Margery. Yes, that was it. That he knew where Margery was and that she....His head ached and he couldn't remember. Then he saw Jack pull a gun on him.

Did Jack shoot him? Why did Jack shoot him? It had something to do with Margery. What had Jack said? "She has two husbands." Then some young girl yelled, "Daddy!" and tried to get the gun away from Jack. If Jack wasn't married, why did this girl call him 'Daddy'? Why did Jack want to shoot him? He was frustrated as always by not remembering the details. It seemed unbelievable that what he remembered could be true.

He remembered kneeling over Jack, then seeing the young girl and a woman. That woman was so like Margery he was sure he had made it up just because he ached to see her again with every bone in his body. He even thought she had been in this hospital room, calling him 'darling,' and kissing him. He had that dream so often it made him smile. He looked in her eyes, kissed her, and she disappeared. There were other voices and people but he could not remember who they were or why they came. But surely if he was in Caterham, he would see someone he knew. Where was Jack? Why hadn't he come to see him at all? Whatever prompted him to act so outrageously it would be forgiven. He knew Jack had not been well. Jack was all he had left now of his family. Nothing would allow him to sever that connection now.

He had to know where Jack was and get out of this hospital. If Louise was here she must know what happened. Everything was a blur after he saw the women and then his brother lying so still. Another seizure came, one severe enough to lay him out until nearly a week later. Damn it, damn it, damn it, he said. Just when I think I can come home, something always seems to stop me in my tracks. Well, I am here now. There is no turning back. Once I get out of this hospital, I am off to Upper Marstone. And I will find out the truth about everything if it is the last thing that I do. He pushed the bedside tray away, climbed over the railing, and looked at himself in the mirror. You,

Robert Morne, are going to confront your brother and get the truth once and for all. You are strong enough and ready to resume your life. He smiled at himself in the mirror, taking a good look at his features. Gaunt is the word for me. When I see Margery again I will look as much the same as I am able to muster. Two husbands? He was still puzzled by Jack's remark, cursing himself that he could not remember the context. She can have one hundred husbands, he thought. It won't stop me from finding her and seeing her one more time.

He turned away from the mirror, putting out the light and climbing back in bed. I have to get out of here. Tomorrow, when Louise comes, I will tell her we have to go to Upper Marstone and have someone tell us the truth. Margery's sister, that would be the person to find. Her name was...he struggled to remember. It was like wood or road or something. Her husband was...Harry, that was it, Harry! Yes, she was named May and her husband was Harry. They had children, too, twins and a little girl. Their names escaped him, but he kept repeating 'Harry and May' to himself, knowing that someone in the village would know who they were. The mantra of their names comforted him as he lay down and drew strength from his new determination to find Margery and to return to the village. Louise would help him. She had never let him down. Even when it would cause her pain, Louise stood by him. If Margery had two husbands and was happy, he would leave her alone, only wishing to see her face once more. It was a promise he had made to Louise. For he knew, no matter how professional Louise was with him and how she cared for him, that Louise loved him. Yet he also knew he would never be able to return her love until he had found his Margery and put his heart to rest.

Chapter Eleven

Thursday morning dawned brightly as Louise got up and had a bath before donning her clean but rather worn-looking uniform once again. She really needed to go back to East Preston and gather her belongings. Robert's cottage would need to be cleared out as well. With a sigh she toweled her hair, combing it out before twisting it tightly into a knot at the back of her head. Dr. Gibbons would be coming back today to meet with Lewis. As today was Thursday, the thought came to her that she had agreed to have dinner with Lewis. What could she say to him after all these years? Surely he would find her very dull indeed, spending her entire adult life taking care of ex-servicemen who were the outcasts of the medical community. She sighed again, putting on her uniform and smoothing it out. It was nearly eight o'clock as she stepped across the courtyard.

The hallways seemed brighter today and she hoped that Robert would have improved enough for her to tell him about the offer to live with Rose Henning. She hesitated, wondering how much he knew about what had happened. Perhaps when he learns about Margery and the fact that he is still her husband, he would not want to do anything but run to her. Her eyes pricked sharply but she drew back her head and walked down the long hallway to his room.

The first thing she saw was the room filled with brilliant sunshine. It took her aback for a moment until her eyes adjusted. Robert was sitting up, his graceful hands tapping on an egg from his breakfast tray. She stood still in the doorway while he grinned at her.

"Good morning, Sister," he said with a lilt in his voice. "We have been neglecting our duty this morning. Here is your patient, up, washed, shaved, and having his breakfast, while you were still dreaming." His smile was almost as radiant as the sunshine in the room and she could not help but grin back at

81

him. Just to see him conscious and none the worse for the traumatic incidents of the past few days made her jubilant.

"What is going on here, Mr. Morne?" she smiled back at him. "Getting other nurses to cater to your every whim, is it?" She came over to the bed, her practiced eye looking at his color, expression, and eye symmetry as she approached.

"I have been told," he said, wincing slightly as he pulled his wounded arm toward him, "that I am in the Caterham Cottage Hospital and that I have been shot. No one will tell me anything else." He looked directly into her eyes as she stood next to the bed. "But you will, won't you? Where's Jack?"

So he didn't remember what happened last Friday night, Louise thought. He seems oblivious to everything that has occurred since he left Sussex. Cautiously she asked him to tell her what he remembered.

"I was walking toward Upper Marstone," he began, stopping to take a bite of toast and egg, "when I saw Jack. He was acting strangely, bobbing and weaving, as if he were trying to hide from me. He..he..." Louise knew that furrowed look very well. Robert was trying to remember and he couldn't.

"Dr. Warren will be here shortly," she said. "Finish your breakfast so he can examine you." He looked at her, almost through her. His eyes seemed particularly penetrating.

"So you are not going to tell me what happened?" he asked, finishing his tea and wiping his hands on a napkin. "I've had some very odd dreams. About Jack. And Margery."

Louise was taking his tray when she heard Margery's name. Her composure slipped as the dishes rattled on the tray.

"Steady on, Louise," Robert said. "They were only dreams. I dreamt she was here in this hospital room. Of course," he smiled to himself, "I used to dream she was in the hospital room in East Preston. In my cottage, too. I suppose there's nothing unusual in that."

"I think Dr. Gibbons is coming back today from East Preston to confer with Dr. Warren," Louise said, putting the tray outside the room.

"I'm not going back now that I am home," he said firmly, folding his arms and wincing again. "I am home now and I intend to stay here and get to the bottom of everything. Jack will have to deal with that, like as not."

"Let's have the doctors look at you first before you make any big plans," she said evenly. "They will be here shortly." She busied herself with tasks and talked to him about the weather and the countryside, deliberately steering the conversation away from Jack, Margery and the past week. Robert attempted to find out more, but she wanted to wait until the doctors saw him to ask what he should be told. To put him back into a coma or worse was unthinkable. The news was so shocking as to put anyone in a coma.

She heard Lewis's voice before he even came into the room and quickly ran to open the door. He was conversing animatedly with Cyril. Her expression must have appeared so different they both stopped and stared at her.

"What is it?" Cyril asked, concerned. "Is Robert all right?"

"He's awake," she whispered, "and asking to know what happened. He doesn't remember anything. Not about Jack, or Margery, or anything that has transpired since Friday. What he has learned was from my replacement last evening. Mercifully she only told him where he was. He wants to know why he has a gunshot wound." Her worried expression had both doctors concerned.

"Would you like me to fill in the details?" Lewis said, concerned for Robert's reactions but also Louise's. He understood her feelings for this man. It was like walking over a minefield.

"I suppose it should really come from me," Cyril said gruffly. "I have been his physician for nearly twenty years. Seems unfair to have you tell him all that has occurred, Lewis. You don't know the entire story, either. He had a visitor, the one and only Margery of the ring. Turns out she is actually his wife."

Lewis whistled low under his breath. "He never remembered that, did he?" He turned to Louise, who shook her head. "But didn't you tell me, Cyril, that this Margery was married to his brother and had a child with him?"

"That is what I thought," Cyril said, looking puzzled as he turned to Louise. Her expression showed she knew more than she was saying.

"My concern is what all the news will do to his health," Louise interrupted. "One shock last Friday and we nearly lost him again. How will he react to learning of his brother's attempt to kill him, Jack's death, the emergence of Margery, finding out he is her husband, and ...." She hesitated as both doctors watched her, "And that he has a daughter? I think having all that news at once might shock me into insensibility myself."

Lewis and Cyril looked at one another. "So the daughter is Robert's!" Cyril said, realizing why Louise was so upset. Once Louise had put all that into one sentence, they knew what they were facing. Louise looked at both of them, wishing they would say he could not be told of anything and had to be taken back to their hospital. A hospital that as of next week would no longer exist.

Why did you have to come here, Robert? Louise thought. We had a life together and could have carried on the same way. It is what Jack wanted, and possibly Margery, too. Now everything was so complicated there seemed no way to untangle it.

"Why don't we examine him first, then decide how to impart all this information?" Lewis suggested. "If he is awake and seems coherent," he looked at Louise who nodded vigorously, "then I suggest we tackle his physical health first, then tell him the basics."

"Right," Cyril agreed, wondering what the basics were. All of the information seemed relevant. How do you deny a man the right to know that he has a wife and daughter? That he rightfully belongs here and should be allowed to go home? He sighed deeply and looked at Lewis, who shook his head and said, "It must be dealt with, of course. The sooner he knows everything the better to see just how he will fare in future." He turned the door handle and entered the room.

"Well, sir, you are looking much better than my last visit," Lewis said brightly as he approached the bed. "How's the head?"

"Not bad," Robert grinned at him. "It's been worse."

"Let's have a look at you," Lewis said, beginning his examination while Cyril stood on the other side of the bed. Louise feared what would happen in the next few minutes. She absentmindedly picked up a tongue blade, holding it close to her chest.

"So what do you think, Doctor?" Robert said, looking first at Lewis and then at Cyril. "Can I get out of here, or must I stay longer? I feel remarkably better today. Even ate a big breakfast. I was hoping my brother might be here so that we could go back to Upper Marstone." The doctors exchanged glances that Robert caught.

"He doesn't want to see me, is that it?" Robert said painfully. "I thought as much, or he would have been here. Well, I am here now, so there is no stopping me from going a few more miles up the road to the village. I could walk it..."

"There are some things you need to know, Robert," Lewis interrupted, his mouth set in a tight line. Louise remembered that expression from St. Bartholomew's Hospital, when he had to tell the families of patients that their loved one would not recover. She stepped closer to him, admiring his bravery and his professionalism. He took Robert's wrist, not only for comfort, but to precipitate a seizure.

Robert looked at both doctors, then his eyes rested on Louise. The look was one of accusation. She could almost hear him pleading, 'Why didn't you tell me?' She turned away from his gaze.

"What do you remember about Friday night?" Cyril began as Robert recounted his story, the ending becoming more fragmented. It was clear he did not remember Jack shooting him.

"Do you want to have the story straight?" Lewis said, watching Robert's eyes with every word. "Because it is not going to be easy to hear it, I guarantee you that. It may send you into another seizure, possibly a fatal one.

84

I don't believe in mincing words. There is much to tell you, most of it shocking."

Robert shifted uncomfortably in his bed, his eyes boring a hole into Louise, who refused to look at him. Shocking? What could be so shocking that he would have a fatal seizure? That Jack disowned him? That the people in the village would not welcome him home? He cleared his throat, looking at the impassive faces of the doctors, trying to discern some idea of this information.

"Go on, then," Robert said quietly. "I have a feeling that most of it has to do with Jack."

"Being his brother you knew him very well," Cyril said, picking up the thread and forging on where Lewis had begun. "This is not easy to tell you, Robert. Your brother...well, he had many secrets. Some of them so distressing he did not tell anyone, especially you. When you came home so unexpectedly, he had to do something to protect those secrets. He had to stop you from coming back to Upper Marstone."

Robert smiled warily. "Secrets? Jack was a great one for secrets. That doesn't surprise me. Please go on." He folded his arms across his chest, almost to gird himself for the next onslaught.

"Your brother Jack shot you," Lewis said, again taking Robert's wrist. "He shot you because if you had come back to Upper Marstone, you would have known that he had kept you away for a reason you would never have believed. We believe he wanted to kill you."

Cyril watched Robert's face drain, then nodded to Lewis. Lewis indicated that Robert's pulse was rapid, but no seizures seemed imminent.

"What was the reason?" Robert asked matter-of-factly. His breath was coming rapidly now. Lewis was glad to see that the seizure medicine he had prescribed seemed to be doing its job.

"You have to know something first," Cyril continued. "Your brother was not in good health. His actions were driven by..well, when he met you on that road, I think he believed he wanted to kill you to keep you away from Upper Marstone. But he couldn't go through with it. The stress of his decision raised his blood pressure to an ungodly high. He suffered a severe stroke. He's dead, Robert."

Robert's head snapped up so quickly Louise took a step closer to the bed, thinking he was beginning a seizure. "Dead?" he repeated. "Jack is dead?" He looked at Louise, who nodded. She saw tears in his eyes and thought how different he was from his brother. He actually cared for him, and felt the pain of that loss, even when he knew Jack had attempted to murder him. She could never forgive Jack and hated to admit she was glad he was dead. The grief-stricken look in Robert's eyes made her feel very small.

85

"Who's taken care of him?" Robert said. "He only had me left, didn't he? I have to get to Upper Marstone." He attempted to get up. Lewis gently pushed him back on his pillows.

"There's more," he said softly. "Much more."

Robert again looked around at the faces. How could there be more than his only brother was dead, his last remaining relative? Their serious expressions told him he did not even know half the story.

"Jack lied about himself," Louise interjected, coming closer to the bed. He had weathered the first onslaught of news; she felt she should be the one to tell him about Margery. "He was married." She watched Robert's face, his questioning look making her rush her words together. "He was married to Margery."

An involuntary gasp from Robert and a slight shake had both doctors on the alert. Robert waved them away. "I'm all right," he said loudly. "All right." He sunk back into the pillows, his eyes closed. "Is she in Upper Marstone?"

"Yes," Cyril said. "She has been here to see you."

"Here," Robert said, sitting up. "Margery was here?"

"You see, you didn't dream it," Louise said bluntly. "She came to see you yesterday. Let me ask you this, Robert. I want you to think very hard about when you went to France in 1916. You embarked from Folkestone, didn't you?"

"Yes," he said hesitantly, looking like a child taking an oral examination who was very unsure of the answers.

"Do you remember anything special about that evening?" Louise was looking at him so intently he felt frightened. Cyril and Lewis remained silent, letting Louise take the lead.

"Think, Robert," she urged him. "Was Margery in Folkestone?" He closed his eyes, a swarm of images flying past him. There was the pub, and that girl, and his mate Arthur saying, "Didn't you say your Granny was a witch? Because you just got your wish." He heard Arthur's voice and saw Margery coming toward him.

"Yes," he said, opening his eyes. "She was there. Why was she there?" He shook his head as if trying to make sense of the image.

"Because, Robert," Louise almost whispered it, "you married her that night. Margery is your wife."

Again the gasp and more pronounced shaking this time. He shook off the doctors and said, "Wife? She is my wife? That is why Jack said she had 'two husbands.' It's all clear now, all clear." His face was very pale and his cheeks sunken. He remained silent for so long the doctors both grabbed his wrist at the same time to check his pulse.

"So that is why he didn't want me to come home," Robert said almost to himself. "Oh, how thick I have been! I should have guessed it, guessed it from the outset." He seemed lost in a world of his own.

"He seems to have never told her about you being alive," Louise continued, determined now to get the whole story out. She knew he would want to run to Upper Marstone and be with Margery. There was so much more he needed to know first.

"And there is one more thing," Cyril said gently, feeling more like an executioner than a doctor. "You have a .." The silver-grey eyes were boring into him and he felt unable to continue.

"There was a young girl last Friday night, do you remember that, Robert?" Louise asked, recognizing the signs that he did remember. "That girl saved your life, really. She tried to take the gun from Jack."

"I remember," he said softly. "She called him 'Daddy.' Was that his daughter?"

"No, Robert," Lewis interjected as he saw Louise faltering, "that was not Jack's daughter. That young lady, the young lady who saved your life, is your daughter."

"Oh, God!" Robert called out. "A daughter! I do remember now, clearly. Margery and I got married but had nowhere to go. We only had a few hours. There was this little room, someone's room.." He hesitated, staring straight ahead at the wall as if he could picture the room there. "We spent a few hours together before I embarked for Boulogne. Those few hours..." He leaned back into the pillows, obviously spent and tired.

"I think we should let him rest now," Lewis said quietly. "But he's come through all the news and no seizures. A very good sign."

"I don't want to rest, Dr. Warren," Robert said firmly, sitting up. "I need to go home. I need to see my wife and daughter. I want to go to Upper Marstone today." He got out of bed and sat with his legs over the edge, pushing the doctors away. Margery his wife! He had to see her, had to go to her now. His legs buckled under him as Cyril and Lewis held him up on each side.

"Not ready to leave just yet," Lewis said firmly as they put Robert back to bed. "No doubt we can arrange for you to see Margery, but you must understand that it may not be as simple as just going back into her life as you are." He stared at Robert, watching his reaction carefully.

"There is that," Robert said quietly. "All those years, those lost years..." His voice faltered as he reluctantly sat back in bed.

"There are others, too," Louise said. "Your friend, Billy Shepherd.."

"Billy!" Robert exclaimed. "Was he here as well?"

Cyril chuckled. "I think he came here to have a punch up with you. It seems he thought that this 'strange' man Jack met wanted to kill him." He shook his head. "It is rather unbelievable for everyone. My advice would be to go slow. It takes time and patience for everyone to come to grips with this situation. No need to make it more difficult by setting everything on its ear. It wouldn't be good for you, either, you know. You still need supervised medical care."

It was said now. Robert's expression was so anguished Louise felt as if she should go and hold him in her arms until the past week disappeared. You can't go home, Robert, not to your Margery or your old life. Now was the time to tell him, and the doctors, of her talk with Mrs. Henning.

"There is a way you can go home and be supervised as well," Louise said, holding her head high. "I can look after you."

"Well, that would be a right pickle, wouldn't it?" Robert snorted. "I'll just have you live with Margery and me so you can look after me. Lovely setup, that is. Proper ménage a trois." He crossed his arms so fiercely his bandage became undone.

Cyril and Lewis were staring at her, wondering what she had in mind. Surely she could not dream of taking Robert away and living with him on her own. No one would countenance that in a village the size of Upper Marstone. Robert was right; the situation would be unendurable if she lived with him and Margery.

"There are other things you still don't know," Louise began as all eyes were on her. "No, nothing as shocking as what you've heard. But think, Robert. Margery has just lost the only husband everyone knew she had. Your daughter must come to terms with knowing you are her father, as well as the loss of the man she thought was her father. I have no doubt Margery would not hesitate to throw convention to the wind," she grimaced. "But there is your daughter to think of. Apparently she is not very happy with all that has happened. She is grieving deeply for Jack."

"Let me talk to her," Robert cried. "I understand she must be grief-stricken, but I can make her see..."

"I'm not so sure of that," Louise interjected. She drew back her shoulders, a gesture Cyril knew from his long acquaintance with her. She has a plan, no doubt about it.

"Of course it will take time for her to know me and accept me, but I am her father," Robert said fiercely. "Surely she can understand that? I would never presume to take Jack's place in her heart. But as her father, I think she could find a place for me, too. A daughter.." He smiled to himself.

"There is a solution, one that will not put Margery in the position of choosing between you and her daughter," Louise continued carefully. "It would allow me to look after you in a seemly manner. You still do need medical care, Robert, as much as you would like to think you do not. Look what happened on Friday."

He hung his head, wondering what plan Louise had concocted. Somehow he always seemed to be the pawn in this game. Not once could he make up his own mind what he wanted to do. It was always someone else's decision. Now once again Louise had taken charge. All he wanted to do was be with Margery again.

"I have a right to live with my wife," he growled. "I have that right."

Louise flushed but carried on. "Yes, of course you do, Robert. But do you know her anymore? It has been nearly twenty years since you have seen her. She has been married to your brother and has raised a child. This is not 1916 any longer. Finding your way back to each other, getting to know each other again, that takes time. Moving in immediately would put much pressure on both of you, especially as your daughter has said she does not want that to happen."

"She doesn't want me there?" Robert cried out again. "But she doesn't even know me!"

"But she will, Robert, she will," Louise soothed him in her usual way. "You must give her time. She needs time to get over her grief and accept what happened without it being thrust upon her. You and Margery need time to get to know one another again. Remember, Robert, you have suffered severe wounds and you, too, are not as you once were." She waited for his reaction, afraid another outburst would set him back again.

He looked up at the doctors, then at Louise. "So what is this plan, then?" he asked. His shoulders sank perceptibly as he bowed to her idea.

"Remember the lady you worked with at the draper's?" she began, warming to the idea and coming nearer the bed. "You told me about her, how she used to make you run all around and get the buns for elevenses."

"Mrs. Henning," he said, half-aloud. "Mrs. Henning."

"That's right, Mrs. Henning," Louise continued, seeing his face soften at the memory. "Well, Mrs. Henning is still with us. A bit the worse for wear, as she broke her hip last year. She needs nursing care and she needs someone to help her with her house and garden. She suggested that you and I have rooms with her. I would serve as nurse for both of you. You could do the gardening and general repairs around the house. She suggested it." She waited until he looked up.

"Is it far from Margery?" he asked, his heart in his throat.

"I don't know, Robert," Louise said, coming over to the bed and taking his hand. "I do know that Mrs. Henning is your daughter's Godmother, and is very close with Margery. It was she who suggested this plan after talking to your

89

daughter and realizing how upset she was by all the news. She was here to see you, too. She cares for you very much. Very, very much."

So close and yet so far, Robert thought. All the years of dreaming of being with Margery again, and now he had the perfect situation: he was her husband. Yet once again fate decreed he could not be with her. It was maddening, utterly maddening, but he knew Mrs. Henning and Louise were right. It would take time to undo all the evil that Jack had wrought.

"All right, then," he said resignedly. "All right. We'll go live with Mrs. Henning, if she knows just what she is getting." He smiled smugly as he recalled her face and her voice. He could not imagine what she was like now. She must be well into her eighties.

"Good," Louise smiled. "I will let her know that we accept her offer. That is, of course," she looked nervously at Lewis and Cyril, "if your doctors agree."

"Do we have a choice here?" Cyril laughed. "I think it sounds an excellent solution. What about you, Lewis?"

"Yes, as it is nearby as well and I can keep an eye on this lad," he smiled.

"There's just one question I have," Robert interrupted. "I have to know."

"What is it?" Louise said, fearful he would change his mind.

"My daughter," he said softly. "What is her name?"

"Elizabeth," Louise replied.

"Elizabeth," Robert sighed. "Elizabeth."

Chapter Twelve

Rose awoke early as she usually did, Catkins purring and crawling over her bedclothes, his desire to have breakfast and his morning stroll the most important things in the world. "All right, all right," Rose grumbled as she reached out and petted his lustrous grey fur. "You just have to be patient with your old Mum. She can't move as quickly as she once did." The room was chilly but the sun was shining as she opened the curtains and looked at her neglected front garden. No doubt if Robbie had retained any of his artistic abilities he would have it looking beautiful in no time.

Elizabeth had not been pleased with the news that Robert and his nurse were coming to live with Rose. All the explanations in the world would not move Elizabeth from her stubborn stance when she did not want something to happen. Rose remembered many temper tantrums where Margery was at her wit's end. Elizabeth was strong-minded. So was Margery, but Margery would not give up either her daughter or her husband, of that she was sure.

She hobbled through the parlor to the kitchen, lighting the stove and putting on the kettle. The back garden was in even worse shape than the front, so Robert would have his work cut out for him. How she had loved that boy! To see Elizabeth reject him so cruelly in favor of Jack seemed ridiculous. Jack had loved Elizabeth and been a good father to her. Rose could not fault him on that, certainly. It wasn't a matter of convincing Elizabeth that Jack had been so evil, it was a matter of showing Elizabeth that Robert had merit and could be the father she no longer had. She methodically began slicing bread for toast, her thoughts racing round and round.

"I can almost hear you thinking up your schemes from here," Elizabeth smiled at her as she came into the kitchen and went to the back door for the milk. Catkins jumped off the table, racing out quickly as the birds scattered in hundreds of directions.

"You come back here, you naughty boy," Rose shouted, waving her ubiquitous cane after him. "You haven't had your breakfast. I don't want you eating any of those birds." She peered outside but there was no sign of her cat.

"Come on, Auntie, it is a little cold this morning. He'll be back soon," Elizabeth cajoled her aunt. "I'll make breakfast for us, if you like."

"So you have forgiven me for my plot, have you?" Rose smiled at her, giving her a kiss on her cheek.

Elizabeth was silent as she went to the small pantry and got two eggs. "There is nothing to forgive. If you want to have him here, I can't stop you. If Mummy wants to take up with him again, I can't stop her. I can only do what I think is right to honor my father's memory." Her face was so solemn Rose had to chuckle.

"Goodness, girl, you sound like someone on one of those wireless programs I've been listening to in the afternoons," she smiled at her again. "No one wants you to think differently about Jack, or love him any less. Don't think your Mother doesn't know what he did for her, because she does. You haven't been in love yet, not truly. And when you are in love, and he is the right one, there will be no other, no matter what. Your mother and Robert were truly in love. No doubt they still will be, if they can surmount all the obstacles. But if they cannot, it is up to them to find it out for themselves. It's not for the likes of us to tell them what they must feel and do." She watched Elizabeth carefully.

"But it would be wrong for him to come and live in my father's house," Elizabeth cried. "It is unseemly, wrong. He doesn't belong there. He doesn't belong in Mummy's arms. That is where my father belongs."

Rose knew that Elizabeth could not be convinced at this point. She also knew that Elizabeth was a kind, intelligent girl. The wound of losing her father was so fresh she could not see anything else. Who could blame her? It had been a traumatic week for everyone. This poor girl was no more than a child. The shocking news she had learned this week was enough to make anyone angry and defensive.

"Yes, it would not be right for him to waltz in and take his place as your mother's husband and your father." Rose nodded, placing several pieces of golden-brown toast in a toast rack and bringing them to the table. Elizabeth watched the eggs boil gently, averting her eyes from Rose. "But he is those things, and everything will have to be sorted. It will take time. I am trying to give everyone that time. After breakfast we have to talk to your mother. I fear she has the same ideas as you in reverse." Elizabeth looked up suddenly from the soothing waves of the boiling water, her expression puzzled at Rose's words.

"Those eggs are more than done now, my girl. Don't just stare at them. Let's have breakfast," Rose said, breaking the tension.

By nine o'clock they had finished their breakfast and found Catkins mewing lightly at the door for his breakfast. After a hasty feeding, they left in the car to go to Margery. Rose felt less confident about tackling her with her plan than she had Elizabeth. Margery had become placid and accepting on the surface, but Rose knew better. The fire of her love for Robert had never stopped burning. To ask her to give him up for some time would not be easy. Rose could see no other way to prevent outright bedlam in their homes and the village.

Margery opened the door quickly when she heard the motor pull up, her worried face full of such pain Rose felt a stab of pity. Poor woman. It seems she was destined to always fall short of having what she wanted. As Elizabeth came up the path Margery held her arms out and cried openly as she embraced her daughter.

"Oh, darling," she said, looking into her face. "I am sorry I sounded so harsh. So sorry. I know how you must be feeling. I have been up all night thinking about everything." Rose came in and could see the dark circles ringing even darker eyes.

"I know, Mummy," Elizabeth said, happy to be back with her mother, but still smarting from all the events. "Auntie Rose wants to talk to you about something."

"Tea?" Margery asked, fearing the worst. She hurried off to the kitchen as Rose settled herself comfortably into the pastel-colored sofa.

Margery came back quickly, carrying a tea tray with three cups and assorted biscuits haphazardly arranged on a plate. Elizabeth had left the room as Rose said, "It's better if we talk alone, Margery. She is still upset by all the events." Margery sat down heavily in a well used chair across from Rose. Jack's chair. She could almost feel him nearby as she sat down.

Rose poured out the tea, her heart aching for Margery. She looks a mess, she thought to herself, not the vibrant woman that Robert loved. Although Robert was injured, he seemed in better health than Margery.

"Here, take this," Rose directed as Margery obeyed. She sipped it and smiled at Rose. "It's all so shocking, isn't it? Robert, my Robert. I can scarcely believe it is all real." Her brow furrowed at the memory of seeing him having a seizure.

"I've been to see him," Rose said, taking a biscuit. Store-bought, but Margery's specialty had always been cakes, not biscuits. Margery's eyebrows shot up. "Did you talk to him?" she asked eagerly.

"He was not in a fit state to talk.to anyone," Rose answered, taking a sip of tea. "The nurse says he is going to get better."

"Yes, that old battleaxe," Margery glowered. "She acted as if she owned him just because she has cared for him all these years. I can only wonder at what sort of care she gave him." She put her cup and saucer down loudly on the table nearby.

"Now, now, Margery, no need to be so jealous," Rose chided her. "She is devoted to him, that's sure. Without her he would be lying out there in France under one of them white stones." Margery winced at the thought and reconciled herself to the fact that he was here, if not totally functional.

"Well, I didn't like her and her bossy ways," Margery said.

"Look who's calling the kettle black!" Rose hooted. "Seems to me Robbie attracts us bossy sorts." She gave her a smile which Margery returned weakly.

"Now listen to me, girl, and listen good," Rose continued. "Robbie needs medical care. There's no doubt about it. You and I do not want to see him put away in some home somewhere, do we?" Margery shook her head, her heart so full of wanting to have him in this room she could almost see him.

"I've got a plan," Rose said. "It's a good one, too, so give me a fair airing of it. The hospital he's been at is closing, so he can't go back there. I want Robbie to live with me for a while."

"With you, Rose?" Margery smiled in disbelief. "But you can't care for him! You need someone to look after you." She sat back in the chair, still looking at Rose in disbelief.

"And that is just what I intend to do," she said. "I'm having Sister Bossy Boots move in, too."

"Are you mad?" Margery nearly shouted. "Why would you have that woman there with him? It is obvious how she feels about him. No, I won't have my darling husband kept away from me and that woman with him day and night."

"So what do you intend to do then?" Rose questioned, her eyes piercing into Margery's. "Bring him here, just as you please, and drive your daughter out? Try to care for his medical needs and get to know him again at the same time? No, you need to give yourself and Elizabeth time to grieve and sort things out. Robbie needs time, too. Louise, that's the Sister's name, knows all this. She is not in competition with you for Robbie."

"So you are on a first name basis with her already?" Margery snorted. "What a little conspiracy has been going on here! Was this Elizabeth's idea?"

"No, it was mine, to save your daughter from any more pain," Rose said, sitting up straight. "Your words to her about Jack were really harsh. Yes, I know what he was like, but you could have spared her. She will never accept Robert if you go headlong into this and bring him here. Personally, I don't think either of one of you is ready for that yet, either. Remember, it has been nearly twenty years."

"Twenty or one hundred wouldn't matter to me," Margery said. "I loved him then and I love him now. All I needed was to see him again in the hospital. I love him." She put her head down, sobbing softly. Rose got up and stood next to the chair.

"It's for the best, dear," she said, putting her arm around her. "It will be like courting again. He has been through hell. So have you."

Margery nodded, defeat evident on her face. Why would something so right be so difficult? She and Robert had loved each other from the minute they met. Their beautiful daughter, the result of their love, would have the parents she rightfully would have had. No one seemed to see it her way. Again it was she who had to make the sacrifices. She was tired of sacrifices: for Jack, for Elizabeth, for everyone she had to ignore when they gave her their reproachful looks because she was not loyal to Robert and married Jack.

"Now, I'll call Elizabeth down. We have a lot to do. First, we'll go off to the hospital," Rose said, bustling toward the hall, giving a shout as Elizabeth appeared at the top of the stairs. "Then, I need you both to help me get the house in order. I can't do it alone, you know." Margery nodded at Elizabeth who gave her a weak smile. A glimmer of hope, Margery thought. "Step lively, you two, we have a lot to do," Rose said, opening the front door wide as she scurried down the walk, her back hunched against the wind. Margery took her coat and turned to Elizabeth.

"Are you all right?" she said, her eyes searching Elizabeth's pale face. Elizabeth nodded, trying to avoid her mother's gaze. "You know what I mean, darling. With this arrangement."

"For the time being it is all anyone can do," Elizabeth said, slipping on her coat. She stepped to the doorway, a smile on her face. "Look at her, Mummy. If the Army ever needed any drill sergeants, she would be the perfect choice."

Rose stood against the car, impatiently tapping her cane on the ground. "No more dilly dallying," she said. "We'd best get on."

"Right, Sergeant," Margery said, shutting the door behind her. Elizabeth giggled and took her arm.

"No one knows more than I how much you hurt, darling," Margery whispered as they walked down the path arm-in-arm. "If anyone can understand the pain of loss, I can. We both need each other now more than ever." She turned her eyes to her daughter's and smiled. "Will you come in and meet him?"

Elizabeth stopped, her face thoughtful but not defiant. "Not yet, Mummy. Does he...does he know about me?"

"I don't know, darling, but he will today," she smiled. "As Jack loved you, so will Robert. In a way you have had two wonderful fathers. And yes," she said, seeing the surprise on Elizabeth's face, "Jack was a wonderful father and he loved you more than anything in this world. Whatever he did, it was done from love for you. I understand that now." They came to the car as Rose pointed her cane at them.

"I thought you would both never make it down that pavement," she huffed. "If we don't get moving we will never get the house in order."

"When will he be coming ...to your house?" Elizabeth asked quietly.

"That's what I intend to find out today," Rose said. "The sooner, the better."

Yes, my darling, the sooner the better, Margery thought as they got into the car. Will I be able to hold you, kiss you, love you? She closed her eyes and leaned against the back seat as they began their journey to Caterham and her future.

Chapter Thirteen

Louise and Cyril had lunch together with Robert in his room, talking about the new plans and how the logistics would be arranged. Lewis left as they sat down to their trays, wanting to consult on a few other patients, but promised he would be back later to pick Louise up so they could go out to dinner. Cyril sensed the tension in Louise, not only because she had made some life-changing decisions, but because of being with Lewis. There had been something between them at one time. What it was he did not know. She had never spoken of it.

This plan to live with this Mrs. Henning left him with an uneasy feeling, as Robert's doctor, but also because he knew of Louise's feelings for Robert. There seemed to be no other solution that he could find short of releasing him to another facility. What would become of Robert then? He knew Louise had been left a good deal of money and would not need to work. The discovery that Robert had a wife and daughter only complicated matters. He watched the easy rapport between Robert and Louise, sensing Louise's desire to hold him to her as long as she could manage. He shook his head as he finished his pudding, feeling that the triangle of Louise, Robert, and Margery would only lead to broken hearts.

Robert was animated but distracted during lunch. It was nothing physical, more an emotional anticipation of what would happen when he left the hospital. They finished their lunches and Louise got up to remove the trays when the door flew open and in walked an elderly lady Cyril could only guess was the notorious Mrs. Henning.

"Robbie!" she shouted as Louise shushed her, but was ignored. "You are awake!"

"Mrs. Henning?" he said hesitantly. "It is you, isn't it?"

"No other," she beamed at him, tapping so rapidly to his chair she nearly fell over. "Oh, darling boy, look at you." Cyril and Louise moved aside as if by

97

a magical force as Robert stared into her face. At first he seemed confused, then he broke out into a grin.

"It really is you," he smiled as she embraced him. "I wasn't sure for a minute, as you haven't changed a bit. I was expecting someone much older." He grinned widely as she let him go and looked at him, tears clouding her vision.

"Now I know it is you as well," she said, looking at Louise. "Butter wouldn't melt, I tell you! Someone else has come to see you, too." She moved aside as Margery stepped into the room, her eyes lighting on the very-conscious man sitting up next to the bed. She felt paralyzed to move toward him. Everything in the room seemed to have become enveloped in a mist and she could only see him, sitting very still in the chair, his smile still evident. For a second her mind shot back to when she first saw him outside Lennox Place. He had been with his father and Jack. It was where she fell in love with him.

"Margery?" he said, his voice as soft as she remembered. He attempted to get up as Louise grabbed his arm to assist him, but he waved her off. "Margery." He began to walk toward her, hesitating with his steps but not his desire to reach her. He kept his eyes fixed on her, his robe tied loosely around his slender frame. In the background she could see only the white veil of this nurse Louise hovering behind him. "Come to me, darling," she said to herself, willing him to come of his own accord. He reached her and looked deeply into her eyes.

"Margery," he repeated, not taking his eyes from hers. She had forgotten how powerful it was to look into the eyes of the man you love and could not look away. All her emotions were tightly in check because she could not believe that he was standing before her. Alive.

"Robbie," she croaked, unable to speak normally. "Robbie, darling." They embraced tightly, her face buried in his neck, recalling immediately his smell to her as if they had just come back from a walk on the Downs years ago. She could hear him murmuring something, but her own tears and emotions eclipsed everything else. She could not let him go for fear she would wake up and he would be gone as he had in so many dreams from the past.

"Come on, darling," he whispered. "Let's sit down and discuss this plan of Mrs. Henning's. All right?" He took her chin and raised it to his, his eyes also wet with tears. She had forgotten that he was taller than Jack and she had a little longer way to look at him. Everything about him felt the same, but his face was different. Older, with creases and lines, but even more beautiful than the boy she once knew.

He put his arm around her and they walked over to the chairs where Mrs. Henning was already seated like a queen on her throne. She was smiling through her tears, her face wet and mottled. "They was always true lovers," she said quietly to Louise. "True lovers."

Louise stood ramrod straight as she watched the couple move toward her, their arms around each other and their heads together. Her heart was racing, bursting nearly, wondering how Robert could forgive this woman her ultimate betrayal of him. He had always seemed so gentle and placid; perhaps it was not the best thing for him.

Cyril noticed her face and indicated they should go outside while the threesome talked about the arrangements. Louise began to leave when Rose said, "Where are you going, then? We need to discuss the arrangements and we need you here as well. And you, too, Doctor. When can he come home with me?"

Cyril had to smile at Rose despite the situation. It was obvious she was not only proud of her plan, but had every intention of being the controlling force in executing it. Poor Robert, he smiled. If he thought Louise was bossy he certainly would be experiencing an even more formidable lady.

"I do think Dr. Warren has the final say on when he should be released," Louise began, using the officious tone she often did when she felt threatened. Cyril again had his doubts that this situation would be anything but a nightmare for her.

"What about him, then?" Rose said, pointing her cane at Cyril. "I thought he was his doctor."

"Actually, I am," he agreed, watching Louise turn to the basin in the corner and begin straightening the items. "He must be officially released from the Army Hospital into someone's care. I suppose," he said, looking at Margery but keeping his eyes on Louise's back, "that would be you, Mrs. Morne. You are in agreement with this living situation?"

Margery could not take her eyes from Robert, holding both his hands in her own, and nodded. "There are ...complications...well, I was told because of his condition he would need medical care," she smiled at Robert. "He seems quite well to me." Louise began to turn around quickly so Cyril jumped in to stave off an eruption.

"He does indeed need medical care," he said firmly. "Dr. Warren and I are in perfect agreement on that. However, since he has managed to work and live somewhat independently, going into a home was not the answer. Given the recent events in your life and..."

"Yes," Margery interjected, noticing the stiffness in Robert's shoulders. What was the matter? He had stopped smiling now and something was bothering him. She touched his arm. Was he angry because she was not bringing him home? Then she would despite all the objections.

99

"I can take him home if that is what he wants," Margery said. Robert's surprised look made her wonder what he was thinking.

"No," he said. "That was Jack's house. Yours and Jack's. I don't want to go there." He leaned back into the chair, staring straight ahead. "I think Mrs. Henning's idea is the best until we can find a place of our own together, just the two of us, alone..."

"What about Elizabeth?" Margery cried as Louise turned around slightly, her interest piqued. "Where will she go?"

Robert looked at her and asked, "Why won't she meet me? From what I understand that is the reason I am going to live with Mrs. Henning in the first place. Propriety, too, of course. It wouldn't do to have me move in with your husband dead so recently." Again he folded his arms and sat back. Margery sat speechless.

"What are you going on about, Robbie?" Rose said. "You know Margery only loved you all these years."

"But married Jack," he whispered. "She married Jack."

Louise definitely turned around now, holding a folded flannel in her hand. Cyril glanced at her. She quickly turned away but he could tell she was sharply tuned to the interchange. Trouble in Paradise already and Robert had not yet left the hospital!

"Robert," Margery said, "please. Please try to understand. I did what I thought I had to. You have to understand."

"I will not live in his house," he said firmly. Louise was amazed at his attitude, something she had never seen in him before. He turned to Margery and looked at her, his eyes blazing with silver the way she remembered they had when he was angry or upset.

"You and I have much to talk about," he said, looking at her levelly. "But not here, in this hospital, with everyone around. There are things I definitely do not understand," he continued, "and I think once I get out of this infernal place and can think again I might be able to understand. Right now I cannot understand anything that has happened or why you married Jack. No matter what reason I come up with, I cannot understand it. Unless..."

"Unless I loved him, is that it?" Margery nearly spat the words out, getting up from the chair and looking down at him. "Is that why you think I married him? Well, Robert, perhaps you have changed far more than I thought you had. If you even could think that was the reason, then your memory must indeed be gone." She got up and walked out of the room quickly, the breeze carrying a scent of lilacs that he remembered.

"Margery," he said weakly. "Margery, wait! Don't leave me alone. Don't leave me." He began to weep uncontrollably as Louise came over and put her arms around him. "There, Robert, let's get you back to bed. It will be all right.

Everything will work out for the best. You'll see." She consoled him as a she would a child, helping him into bed and covering him up. Rose watched the scene, feeling anxious and helpless.

"Louise has always had a way with him," Cyril remarked. "Head injuries react to things in very unpredictable ways. That is why it is still so critical at this emotional time that he have someone with him who knows how to prevent a seizure and keep him steady." Louise remained with Robert, talking to him and fussing over him, checking his vital signs at the same time.

"She treats him like a child," Rose said, watching the scene. "He's become quite petulant. Didn't even let Margery explain why she married Jack. Just made assumptions. Like a little boy." She looked over at him as if she would like to take the cane to him.

"Mrs. Henning," Cyril said gently, "I know it is difficult for you to understand how profoundly injured he is, because he is looking and acting quite normally at present. But I assure you, the 'kid glove' approach is sometimes necessary." He watched Louise bustle as Rose's face softened. "Poor lamb," she said quietly. "Is he prone to outbursts and such?"

"Seizures, mainly, brought on by extreme stress," Cyril said, guiding her gently to the door. "It is critical, absolutely critical, that if he lives with you, you must be aware of his condition. That does not mean he cannot take the truth," he continued, watching her face darken. "It just means that the way it is delivered, and the spirit in which it is delivered, have to take his injury into account."

"Do you think, doctor," she began, looking once more at Robert as they left the room, "that perhaps that nurse..." Her voice trailed off as she shut the door.

"She is very professional with him, Mrs. Henning, I assure you," he said in defense of Louise. "But yes, she is also very fond of him. That may sometimes cause her to rise to the occasion if she thinks he is in danger of becoming emotionally upset. You see, she has seen his progress more than anyone except me. It is remarkable, almost unbelievable. Any little thing that causes him to slip backwards in any way will be strongly counteracted by Miss Whiting. I suppose I have relied on her to do that for me in my absence. Perhaps this has made her relationship with Robert more...personal."

"Yes, I see that," Rose said although Cyril was not sure just what she meant. "What's the worst thing that could happen if he gets too upset?" Her bird-like face looked up at him, her eyes questioning.

"He could die," Cyril put it bluntly. "Or be put back into a coma from which he would not recover. He knows that. So does Louise." Rose tilted her head, her eyes bright.

"You said he can stand the truth," she murmured. "You told him about Jack and his daughter, and he held up. Margery has never been one to mince words. She became quieter with Jack, as if it didn't really matter to her anymore whether she won an argument or made her point. To see her today with Robert...well, in some ways it made my heart glad."

"Glad?" Cyril exclaimed. "Their first meeting ends in tears and anger. I am not sure I would be glad of that."

"Ah, but you didn't know them as a young couple," she smiled, seeing Margery standing in the hallway, her handkerchief over her eyes. "If they carried on like love's first kiss today, I would have thought it was almost unreal. He wants to know about Jack and why she married him. Can you blame him for not wanting to live in his brother's house, where he thinks she was happy with him?" She hooted so loudly a passing nurse nearly dropped her medicine tray. "He'll learn the truth soon enough. There will be a lot of ground to cover before they find their path to love again. And there is the other obstacle that Margery could see immediately."

"What is that, Mrs. Henning?" Cyril said as Margery approached.

"Miss Louise Whiting," Rose replied. "Margery knows Louise loves Robbie. A woman can see these things. While Robbie may not know it, I think he loves her, too. Whether it is the love he felt for Margery, or something else, it's the reason I think that everyone needs to take one of those rests like they do in a football match." She looked puzzled as she searched for the words.

"Half-time?" Cyril supplied, smiling. He had his doubts about Mrs. Henning and her motivations for this arrangement, but found a new respect for her and her judgment. A time out is just what he would have prescribed for everyone concerned, if it were within his power to do so. His heart was still heavy as he saw the anguished look on Margery's face. Nothing was sadder than to see someone whose one dream seemed dashed. He could barely look at her as Mrs. Henning took her arm, adopting much the same attitude as Louise did with Robert. It reminded him of the song, "Two Little Babes in the Woods."

"He'll be ready to come home on Saturday, if you can manage," Cyril said. "I believe Dr. Warren will agree with that assessment. This will give me time to go back to Sussex and process his paperwork."

"What about his things?" Rose asked. "I assume he has some belongings." Margery turned her face up, the agony of thinking she had lost him once again evident.

"Yes, a few things," Cyril concurred. "He was the gardener, you know, at the hospital. He lived on the grounds in his own cottage. I know he has a wireless. He loves that machine." Margery looked up, her eyes more hopeful.

"Can he..can he..? Margery began, Cyril wondering what she wanted.

"Can he what, dear?" Rose prompted. "Sing?"

"Oh, yes, that of course," Margery said, "but is he able to dance? He loved to dance. We won a cup once for being the best tango dancers in Brighton."

Cyril smiled. "Is that right? I don't think he remembered that. I do know he has danced a bit. None of this new sort of thing, of course, with throwing people about and all. A waltz or two-step should be manageable." His expression became serious. "You do know this will all take time, Mrs. Morne? Just give it time."

"Time," Margery repeated dully. "I have given my whole life and now I must wait even longer. I don't understand exactly what happened to him, doctor," she pleaded. "Of course I want to do everything to help him. I am sorry I got so angry with him, but he doesn't understand. He doesn't understand anything of what happened."

"Time, my dear," he said, patting her arm. "He has not changed all that much that he would not be able to understand."

"I am not sure how he is really changed," Margery said. "It frightens me to think he is so different that I would not know him any longer."

"In his heart I think he is much the same," Cyril said. "But now why don't you two go and make preparations for him to come home? I am sure there is much to do."

"Right, doctor's orders," Rose said, turning Margery away from the door where she wanted to linger. "We'll make it a proper homecoming for him." She looked at Cyril sharply and asked, "How will we get his, and Miss Whiting's, things here from Sussex? Will we need a removal van?" He smiled again and said, "Nurses working in Army hospitals do not own much. Robert did not, either. No, a motorcar and a few strapped-on trunks would probably take care of both of their worldly belongings. I suppose I could make the trip again." He exhaled so deeply that Rose interrupted him mid-sigh. "Elizabeth could take us there," she said. "We could take Miss Whiting, as she knows the way. Elizabeth loves to drive, doesn't she, Margery?"

"That is quite a long way for her to go," Margery said cautiously.

"Pish posh," Rose said. "Just nice, straight roads. Right, Doctor?" She winked at him so boldly he found himself nodding in agreement.

"Good," Rose said. "Elizabeth can take us down there tomorrow morning and Robbie can come home on Saturday. Would you tell Miss Whiting we will be here at eight o'clock sharp to fetch her, Doctor?" He nodded as Margery interrupted.

"Saturday is the 28th of September," Margery said, half to herself.

"Yes," Cyril agreed. "We could wait if that is not convenient."

"Oh, no," Margery said. "It is just an odd day for his homecoming, that's all."

103

"Odd?" Cyril asked. "In what way?"

"September 28th was the day he went missing in 1916," Margery replied. "And now it will be the day he is resurrected from the dead." Cyril stared at the two lone figures as they headed down the dark corridor of the hospital, his heart aching for both Robert and Margery, and the arduous road ahead.

Chapter Fourteen

Cyril passed on the message to Louise about the moving arrangements, who agreed somewhat reluctantly to be driven to East Preston in the company of Margery and her daughter. Louise was angry with Margery at her treatment of Robert. He remained in bed, sullen and unresponsive, as she cleared up the room. What sort of wife would she be to him if she treated him this way when he was not even out of the hospital? She could only imagine what his life would be like – a living hell where he might wind up incarcerated in a dark and hopeless rest home.

"Are you going to sulk like that for the rest of the day?" she asked him as brightly as she could manage. He turned over and looked at her, his eyes swollen from the tears, but his face determined and set.

"I am not sulking," he replied. "I am thinking. What a damn mess this all is, isn't it? If she only knew how much I love her, how much the very thought of her kept me alive." He caught Louise's prim look and smiled.

"She always told me I was the romantic one," he said, sitting up. "I suppose that is true. Romantic and probably unrealistic. Jack was there; I wasn't. What else would any normal, healthy woman do?" He shook his head again, not believing his words. "But why Jack? Anyone else but Jack I could understand."

"Perhaps he reminded her of you and she wanted to cling to that memory," Louise offered, not believing it for an instant. He shook his head more vigorously.

"I cannot imagine that Jack would remind her of me in any way, except for a slight physical resemblance," he said. "We were not at all alike, as you knew." He seemed lost in thought and added, "The fact that he even considered killing me is definitely one way we differ." He touched his left arm ruefully, rubbing the bandage.

105

"Robert, you are all right with this move to Mrs. Henning's, aren't you?" she asked him, coming over to the bedside. "I have searched my mind for another solution, one where I could...where you would..."

Robert looked at her and smiled. "Where we could remain together? Yes, I know, Louise. This is a kettle of fish neither of us expected. You must know I have very deep feelings for you." He touched her arm but she withdrew. "I did not remember marrying Margery, although it is clear now. Of course, legally, I am still her husband."

Louise looked at his thoughtful face. Legally? Of course he was just talking out loud, but his admission of 'deep feelings' for her, then his choice of the word 'legally' made Louise wonder what his feelings for Margery were now.

"Yes, legally she is your wife, which is why she has been allowed in here to see you and upset you so," Louise said bluntly. She drew in her breath and asked, "Do you still love her, Robert?"

He hesitated, staring across the room at the sun's reflection in the bureau mirror. "Yes, I think I love her, the Margery I knew. If that Margery is there, I love her still." Again he hesitated before looking directly at Louise. "So much has happened since she and I were young. Here we are now, facing each other as two middle-aged people with so much of life gone already. There is so much to explain. Especially about Jack."

"Yes," Louise agreed. "I do not know how she will explain it. I hope she can." His sad expression whenever he thought of Margery and Jack together broke her heart. How she wanted to take Margery and shake her, make her explain just how she could be so callous.

"Nevertheless, if you are agreed that this is indeed what you want to do and go live with Mrs. Henning," she interrupted his reverie, "then tomorrow morning I must go to East Preston and collect our things. I don't think Dr. Gibbons or Warren will allow you to make that long trip, so I will go alone. I will pack all your things for you."

"There wasn't much," he sighed. "I will miss that cottage. We had lovely times there, didn't we? It is the first time I felt like a whole man again after so many years." He turned his face to the sunshine coming through the window, his profile outlined in silver. She stood still, the moment inviolable until he smiled. "Don't forget my wireless, will you? You know I would miss that."

"That was the first thing on my list," she smiled, glad to see his mood had lightened. He was always so accepting of whatever happened, yet underneath he often went ahead with his own plans. It made her wonder what he was really thinking and feeling as he pondered this new move. "Mrs. Henning volunteered your daughter to drive me back to the hospital."

"Elizabeth is going to take you?" he exclaimed, sitting upright. "Are you sure I cannot make the trip? What would she do if I turned up and said I was going, too?" He looked at her eagerly, obviously unaware of how strong the feelings of the women involved were when it came to him. Elizabeth would not respond well to being coerced into meeting him. Besides, Louise felt she wanted to meet this daughter of Robert and Margery first. If she were anything like her mother, her effect on him would not be beneficial at present.

"Let me do all the necessary things first," Louise soothed him, checking the time and realizing she had to leave to prepare for her evening out with Lewis. "That way things can take their course rather than trying to make things happen the way we want."

"I don't know what I want," Robert said mournfully. "All I ever dreamed about was being with Margery again. Having children, being together, dancing – I suppose I never really thought about the day-to-day reality of being married to someone. Especially after she had been married to someone else for years." He sat back as the door opened and his supper tray arrived. Louise stayed to make sure he was set up, his mind wandering back and forth between excitement and fear about the move.

"I'm off now," she said, making sure he had his newspapers nearby. "I won't see you before I leave in the morning. I will let the nurses know you may need assistance."

"If I am going home Saturday," he replied. "I'd best get used to taking care of myself again. The thought of what Mrs. Henning would say if I don't is enough to get me well enough to be sent back to the front." He grinned at her, but his eyes still reflected the apprehension she saw in him all day. It was the fear that Margery would reject him in the end. For Robert, it would mean the end of his dreams.

"I really do think things will turn out for the best, whatever that may be," Louise said soothingly as she pulled on her coat. "Please don't dwell on it tonight, Robert. It may seem bleak and uncertain now. Once you are out of here and back in the world again, you will see it right."

He smiled weakly, tucking into his meal with a less than enthusiastic appetite. She hated to leave him, wondering again if living with Mrs. Henning would be a good thing for both of them. Perhaps Lewis would have some insights into the situation.

Lewis picked her up around half-past seven that evening, his motorcar freshly waxed and exuding a lingering smell of honey. He looked dapper as always, his eyes seeming to twinkle as he helped her into the motor. They drove out of Caterham for a few minutes until she spotted a sign that said, 'Brockham.'

"Oh, I have never even told Aunt Eleanor and Henry what has been happening," she said, clasping a hand to her mouth. "Here I have been sitting so close to them in Caterham and I didn't even think to ring them." She leaned back in her seat in resignation. Her Aunt Eleanor had practically adopted her when she was fifteen, taking her from her abusive mother after the death of her brother Geoffrey. Eleanor had met and married the village doctor at that time, and they had relocated to Brockham before the War.

"Well, considering the emotional powderkeg, not to mention physical ailments of your patient, that is not surprising," he chuckled. "I did know that Henry and Eleanor lived in Brockham. I must confess that I have been rather lax myself in visiting."

"Have you kept up with them?" Louise asked, surprised. "They never mentioned it in their letters or calls."

"Infrequently," he said, turning away from Brockham and following a narrower, darker road toward Reigate. "So many things have happened in recent years that I lost touch with nearly everyone. In fact," he said, taking a turn toward a village called Leigh, "I really regret not keeping in touch with you. I knew where you were, of course. Eleanor told me. How she hated that you remained so distant. She thought that working constantly with patients like Robert was not good for you." He turned and smiled at her. "Of course, those of us who become invigorated by our topic can never explain it to lay people."

Louise returned his smile, feeling as comfortable with him as she had years ago when she worked for him. In some ways Aunt Eleanor was right; she had devoted so much of her life to her patients she had almost forgotten what it felt like to have a life of her own.

He turned the car down a tree-lined drive, the gravel crunching beneath the tires as an old stone and brick house emerged in the distance. Obviously the house was built in the Elizabethan era, some of the half-timbering showing in the reflected pools that shone from inside. Lights seemed to blaze from every full-length window. Was this a restaurant, tucked away in some small corner of Surrey?

"Welcome to l'Etoile du Arts," he smiled at her while she remained puzzled. "Not to be confused with the Seven Stars Pub in the village. My home."

"Your home?" Louise said, unable to believe that one family lived in such a huge dwelling. "I had no idea I would be meeting others tonight. Look at me! I have been wearing this uniform for a week." She reached up to straighten her hair as he grabbed her wrist.

"There is no one here but me, save the servants," he said. "Very lonely."

"But your wife?" Louise said, seeing his sad expression. The lines on his face and near his eyes seemed more evident than minutes before.

"A very long story," he said, getting out and opening the door for her. "I hope you don't mind me bringing you here. I felt we could talk more easily away from crowds and noise. It is all perfectly respectable," he laughed, seeing her wary look. "I have cooks, maids, and a butler. Very good chaperones they will make."

Louise blushed visibly, muttering something about not being concerned with that at all. What had happened to his wife, Constance? And his children? Her steps on the gravel sounded unearthly as she followed him to the door.

"Good evening, Sir," an elegant gentleman opened the door, taking Lewis's hat and coat. A maid stood shyly near the door, helping Louise with her things.

"Dinner is ready, Sir, if you would care to come through to the dining room," the butler said.

"Yes, thank you, Bales. Would you like a drink first?" Lewis asked Louise.

"No, dinner would be fine," Louise said, unable to contain her curiosity as to how Lewis wound up here sans wife and family. She followed Lewis through the vast entrance hall to a dining room lit only with candles. The solidly built oak table looked as if it had entertained guests from the royal court of Elizabeth I. Louise sat down gingerly, fully aware of how out of place she looked as she gazed at the expensive gold rimmed serving dishes and the cut glass crystal goblets.

Dinner was served, a delicious repast of soup, fish, meat, cheese, and a light sponge pudding. They talked amiably about old times at St. Bartholomew's Hospital in London, where they had both trained and worked. Memories of their colleagues and friends came out in bursts of laughter at some of the incidents.

"Do you remember," Lewis began, taking a sip of wine, "how I left you sitting in front of my office all day on your first day of work? God, how self-involved I was! And there you were, always stalwart and true."

"Then you took me to dinner and brought me home," Louise giggled, the wine going to her head. "Aunt Eleanor was furious, thinking her eighteen-year old niece had already slipped off the rails."

"I could never get you to slip, could I?" Lewis smiled, then looked down. "That is one of the things I admire most about you, Louise. You are loyal and steadfast. One can depend upon you without reservation. You would never let anyone down."

"Not knowingly," Louise said, the mood in the room becoming serious. "Are you living here alone, Lewis?"

He cleared his throat, the candlelight reflecting the wine in his glass as he took a long time to answer. "Yes, Louise. The children are grown, you know. Abigail is married with three fine children. Married a doctor who trained in Edinburgh and took her back there. I go up as often as I can, do some fishing and hiking as well as visit the grandchildren." He leaned back in his chair, smiling at the recollection of his latest visit.

"Brian finished University and is working as an engineer in Manchester," he said. "He has been rumbling about buying his own business and working for himself. Thought he might come back here to Surrey. I think he worries about his old Dad on his own."

"And you have retired as well," Louise said. "Why?"

Lewis shifted in his chair. "It all became political at Bart's. I didn't feel I could treat my patients as I wanted to. I still consult, of course, as I did with Robert. The pace is much slower now."

"And Constance?" she nearly whispered.

"Constance died a year ago," Lewis said quietly. "We had no marriage to speak of for years. She had her friends and interests and I had mine. She became ill and died quite quickly." He reached for the bottle of wine and poured himself another glass.

"I am sorry," Louise said.

"So am I," Lewis agreed. "I miss her being here, you know, her presence. The house was always full of noise and artists and people. Sometimes I hated it, but it became so much a part of my life I got used to it. She even named this house, "Star of the Arts." My youngest daughter, Anne, was quite cut up by Constance's death. She is living in London with some artist friends and studying at the Slade. Hardly ever comes to see me now. I think she believes I have no artistic soul whatsoever." He grinned, his eyes slightly bleary.

"I don't think that is true, Lewis," Louise said softly, surprised to hear how easily his Christian name rolled off her tongue.

"I have spent most of my life in science, delving into people's minds, literally," he said. "To me there is a beauty in the rhythm and patterns of the brain. Nothing seems more beautiful to me than that." His eyes showed him to be reflecting on that thought.

"We are not unalike," Louise said. "I appreciate art and beauty, certainly. How well I remember my mother trying to get me to play the piano. I was an absolute failure at it, no sense of rhythm at all. Even Robert, with all his injuries, can sing and dance far better than I can."

"Yes, Robert," Lewis said. "Odd how he brought us together again, as he did in Etaples. I was stunned when I saw you in that hospital room. Even more so when I saw Robert."

"He has suffered much, you know," Louise said softly. "All this trauma physically, and now emotionally." He watched her before speaking, seeing the look of loss.

"It was inevitable once he began to remember that he would have to go home sometime," Lewis said, taking her hand in his. "You must have known that."

"I suppose so," she said, her voice cracking. "But that Margery. I cannot think that she would take care of him and ..and.."

"Love him?" Lewis said. "I know you love him, Louise. I knew it when I saw you fight for his life in Etaples." He kept holding her hand tightly.

"It is a ridiculous, futile thing," she said, pulling her hand away. "He is married to this woman, for God's sake. There is no changing that. I know it now, but still..."

"If you truly love him, and he you, I suppose that can overcome anything," Lewis said resignedly. "Does that sound artistic? Romantic perhaps. I was never much of a romantic."

"Funny, Robert was just telling me how much of a romantic he is," Louise said. "I've never been romantic, either. Quite straightforward. Even frosty, I suppose."

"Frosty is not a word I would use to describe you," Lewis said. "Shall we retire to the drawing room? Bales has got a nice fire going."

The warm, rich wood shone in the light as Lewis led Louise into the drawing room. Although Louise was not well-versed in art, she could see that the works were modern, yet had a certain style and expertise that caught the lights from the fire and added to the warmth of the room. She settled into a comfortable leather sofa near the fire and was amazed at her own ease as she sat with Lewis in the home he had once shared with Constance.

They spent the rest of the evening talking about their lives, catching up on all the years they had missed. Louise felt alive, even animated, as she discussed patients and their prognoses with Lewis. How romantic, she thought to herself. I have never been happier than when discussing trephinations and shunts! Lewis looked at his watch, seeing it had gone past midnight.

"What will they think of you, Sister?" he smiled. "Look at the hour! I had better get you back to your quarters."

"Yes, I have to be up early as I am going back to East Preston in the morning to collect my things," she said, gathering up her coat and bag. "It will be a relief to wear something other than this uniform."

"I think it is very fetching," he smiled at her. "And a tribute to the one who wears it. Do you know why I chose this village to live in?"

"No," Louise said as they walked to the car, the cool night breeze refreshing them.

"The parish is St. Bartholomew's," he laughed. "I suppose Bart's is where I was happiest. I must have believed that living here he might bestow some special blessing upon my marriage and family."

"And did he?" Louise asked as they pulled down the drive and back onto the dark country road.

"Not until tonight," he said softly as he took her back to Caterham.

Chapter Fifteen

Elizabeth awoke early the next morning, having spent a sleepless night. When Auntie Rose had told her she would be driving to Sussex to collect Robert's things, she balked. She wanted no part of him, yet everyone seemed to conspire to bring her closer to him.

The nurse who looked after him for years was coming, too. What would possess someone to spend their entire life caring for such wounded men? She could not understand. Her picture of this 'Miss Louise Whiting,' as Auntie Rose called her, was one of an old hatchet-faced woman who never smiled.

She sighed, seeing the sky cloudy but not threatening from her bedroom window. Her room overlooked the front garden, where she could see the birds flying amongst the overgrown rosebushes. Her parents had never been much for gardening and it showed. To think that Robert was now a gardener made her realize just how different he must be from her father.

Yet she had shown artistic talents herself when neither of her parents exhibited any. Was that a gift from him? If it was, it was not something she wanted to discuss with him. Ever.

Her mother was already up as she could hear the bath running. It was very early, but they had to fetch Auntie Rose and this Miss Whiting from Caterham, then double back towards Sussex. She loved to drive, loved the feeling of the wind in her hair and the freedom it gave her. She had shared that with her father. He had loved motorcars and driving. When she was just fourteen, he had taught her to drive, a secret she shared with him. "Don't tell your Mother," he would smile at her as she shifted the gears loudly along one of the back roads of Upper Marstone.

Tears came to her eyes again. Daddy, what should I do now? She had withdrawn from University for this term. It was all too much to countenance at present. Would she ever go back? She wasn't sure now, nor was she sure she wanted to pursue running her father's business. When Uncle Harry had come around to look at the books and appointments, it had all seemed far more complicated than she had first thought. Uncle Harry graciously agreed to run it until she and her mother made a decision. It was already booming under his expert guidance.

A soft tap on the door and Margery peeked her head in, her hair wet and her eyes large and dark in her pale face. "Just wanted to see if you were up, darling," she said. "There's still hot water for your bath." She closed the door as Elizabeth did her morning routine. After a good breakfast with little conversation, they left the house to pick up Auntie Rose, who stood waiting at the gate, then proceeded to Caterham.

Miss Whiting was also waiting, her nurse uniform more creased than nurses usually wore, but as she had not had an opportunity to do more than wash it out every night, it didn't surprise Elizabeth. What did surprise her was this lady did not seem to be the battleaxe she pictured. While not beautiful, she had a soft, almost fleshy face. Elizabeth realized she seemed hesitant to look at her.

"This is Miss Louise Whiting," Rose announced loudly as Louise got into the back seat next to Margery. "This is Elizabeth Morne."

Louise was struck with her resemblance to Robert, so much so she let out an involuntary gasp when she looked into her eyes. Elizabeth shook her hand quickly, then turned around and put the car into gear with such ferocity it leaped forward, throwing Rose and her cane up against the dashboard.

"Steady on, dear, I don't want to fly to Sussex," Rose cried out, holding onto the dashboard. "We have plenty of time. No need to rush."

"Sorry, Auntie Rose," she said quietly. "The gear slipped."

Louise sat stiffly in the back seat, feeling her nurse's uniform only added to her sense of being different from everyone else in the car. Margery was within one foot of her. She could sense the tension between them and the divide felt more like one thousand feet. Margery did not look at her, but kept her eyes directly ahead, staring at her daughter as she drove.

Rose was chattering away, trying to ease the tension by talking about village goings on. No one spoke of Robert, or his return to them. Was it in deference to Elizabeth, Louise wondered? Margery did not join in the conversation. Elizabeth only muttered a few words in response.

"How did you come to be working as a nurse in the Army Hospital, Miss Whiting?" Rose said, turning around to look at Louise. Louise had been staring out the window, watching the trees flash by as Elizabeth drove quite skillfully after her faulty start.

"Sorry?" Louise said, turning to Rose. "I'm afraid I was rather lost in the scenery."

"It is lovely along the way," Margery said so quietly Louise was not sure she heard her. "But a long way from Surrey."

Louise looked at her, but Margery just continued to look straight ahead.

"I asked you how you came to work in that Army Hospital," Rose repeated. "Were you there long?"

"Nearly twenty years," Louise replied and noticed Margery tense. "I served in France during the War, then transferred there to work specifically with neurological patients."

"Did you train for that, Miss Whiting?" she heard Elizabeth's voice ask. "It must be very difficult work."

"Please, I would like it much better if everyone called me Louise," Louise said. "If I am to be living in Upper Marstone, I would feel it would be quite formal if I were always called Miss Whiting by those I have come to know."

"Well, if that is the case, you must call me Rose. You already know she is Margery," Rose said pointing to Margery. "Elizabeth does not warrant a title as yet. She is still a child, aren't you, dear?"

"No, Auntie Rose," Elizabeth smiled. "If I were, would I be driving us to Sussex?"

"Well, Miss Morne, if that is what you want, drive on," Rose laughed. Louise and Margery both smiled.

"What about your patients, Louise?" she heard Margery's voice. "The War must have done terrible things to them. Terrible." Louise looked at her, seeing those dark eyes that had haunted her from Robert's drawings.

"Yes, it was terrible in many cases," Louise said. "One of the things I always liked about neurology is that there is hope. If you work with many of the patients, instead of giving up on them, you may be able to help them recover."

"Dr. Gibbons said that you never gave up on Robert," Margery said again. "Was he that badly injured that they thought he would not recover?" Elizabeth had visibly tensed as the conversation turned to Robert.

"I shall never forget when they brought him into the hospital at Etaples," Louise said, lost in the memory of that day. "He had lain out in No Man's Land for several days. One of his friends, who was also severely wounded, was lying atop him. When they brought him in he was pronounced a morbid case," she saw Margery jerk involuntarily, "but I believed otherwise."

"Why?" Rose asked, riveted to her account of how Robert was found. "And why couldn't they identify the poor lamb?"

"He came in without his tunic, identification papers, or identity discs," Louise said, remembering every detail of that day. "He was unconscious and unresponsive. There was no other diagnosis but to pronounce him a morbid case and let him die."

"But you didn't," Margery said.

"No, I didn't," Louise responded. "My brother Geoffrey died when he was twelve after suffering a severe head injury. I held his hand, talked to him, did everything the doctor said. He responded for a while before he died. I always felt that if somehow I had been able to be there with him enough, he would have got better." She almost winced at the painful memory of being sent out of the room by her mother the night her brother died. It still haunted her that she might have saved him.

"What made you think he was not morbid?" Margery asked, her eyes intent on the answer.

"There was something about him, something that seemed…different," Louise began, trying not to betray her feelings to this woman who was his wife. "Although he was unconscious, he didn't seem to be dying. I held his hand and asked him to squeeze mine if he could hear me. He did."

She heard a sharp intake of breath from Elizabeth. Margery reached over and touched her daughter's shoulder lightly. "I know he had other wounds, too. Was he in pain? Did he…suffer?" Margery's eyes were so full of anxiety Louise felt sorry for her.

"He had wounds to his chest, arm and head," Louise said. "A machine gun caught him as well as the sniper's bullet to his head. In normal circumstances I think he would have been uncomfortable, but being unconscious I don't think he realized how injured he was. The wounds healed cleanly and he has no ill effects from them." She felt very much like a nurse giving a report.

"My poor darling," she heard Margery murmur so quietly so that Elizabeth did not hear.

"But that is now in the past," Rose said quickly, trying to lighten the mood. "He must have recovered fairly well to be the gardener at the hospital."

"Yes," Louise said. "He is doing well. It is just the seizures that cause so much trouble. Under most conditions he is fine and functions well. Under extreme circumstances he can suffer as he did last Friday."

Elizabeth swerved slightly and Louise decided that she had said enough. "I think we are almost there. I saw the sign for Worthing as we passed."

"Worthing," Margery repeated. "I wondered why Jack always came here." She sank back and closed her eyes. They made the rest of the trip in silence.

Seeing the familiar gates of the hospital gave Louise a feeling of homecoming, although she quickly saw how empty everything looked. Removal vans stood in the courtyard near the entrance. Dr. Gibbons was standing outside, talking to the removal men. Sister Meade stood behind him, ticking off items on a list.

"Louise!" Cyril said, seeing the car pull up. "I just got off the telephone with Lewis Warren. We had a long discussion about Robert and his care." Margery, Rose and Elizabeth followed.

"So this is the place where he was all these years," Rose said. "And we never knew."

"Jack knew," Margery said quietly. "Jack knew."

Elizabeth looked at her mother, her heart feeling torn in two like a paper rag. Why would her father keep her uncle locked up here? Could it really be because of her mother? It seemed so out of keeping with what she knew of her father that she still found it hard to believe. Yet it appeared Robert was not so badly injured that he could not have come home and been cared for by his family. Except for that one little problem: the marriage certificate. If no one had ever told Mummy, she would not have known, would she? She shook her head violently, trying to dispel the thoughts of lying and deception that she now conjured.

"What is it, dear?" Rose said, taking her arm. "Perhaps that drive was a bit long for you."

"No, I am fine, Auntie Rose," Elizabeth said. "Fine."

"This is Sister Meade," Cyril said, introducing her to the group. "She is head matron here and did much to look after Robert."

"Not as much as Louise, of course," she smiled at them, her face reflecting a healthy glow that almost shone, "but he was such a dear patient we could all not help but care for him."

"This is Robert's wife, Margery," Louise said, watching Sister Meade's face register shock and then a perfunctory smile, "and his daughter, Elizabeth." Elizabeth scowled, again angry that she was being introduced as Robert's daughter when she was Jack's daughter.

"Well, we didn't know," Sister Meade said, almost to herself. She looked first at Louise, then at Cyril. What a turn of events must have happened in Upper Marstone! She shook hands and looked long at Elizabeth. There was no mistaking that Robert was her father.

"Why not have a cup of tea first before you make a start on the packing?" Cyril encouraged. They all looked rather weary. Cyril wondered how Louise fared riding down with Margery and Elizabeth. Her face, as usual, did not register any emotion.

"I think I will go and clear my things first," Louise said. "I am so anxious to have a change of clothing I can barely wait another minute." She smiled slightly as she left them in the dining room.

The hospital was empty of all patients now, the iron beds being dismantled by the removal men. She walked through the ward, touching some of the beds as she remembered the names of the patients she had cared for and

117

yes, loved. Fred, Joe, Bert, John – she would have to find out where they all were now so she could write to them. It made her sad she had not been here to see them off to their new homes. As she looked around her tears came freely.

Her little room looked lonely and pathetic, many of the items of furniture already gone as her belongings had been neatly packed into boxes by some kind soul, probably Sister Meade. She would miss her and hoped they would stay in touch. She looked through the boxes and found a dark green cotton dress and jacket. There was no mirror, so she arranged herself as best she could before folding up her uniform and sealing it into the box. Her name was marked on each box in Sister Meade's neat handwriting. There was nothing left for her in this tiny room that seemed devoid of life.

"I took the liberty of packing your things," Sister Meade said as she re-emerged into the dining room. Cyril handed her a cup of tea and said, "I think you could use this." Sister Meade continued, "We also packed up Robert's things, but please make sure you check. They almost took his wireless, but I told them to leave the cottage for last, as I was not sure what was his and what belonged to the hospital."

"Thank you, Sister," Louise said, the feeling of separation overwhelming her as she looked around at all the boxes and furniture waiting to be removed.

While Cyril talked to Margery, Rose and Elizabeth about Robert and his care, Louise and Sister Meade shared their feelings. "It is very hard," Sister Meade said. "It was especially hard without you here, Louise. The patients asked and asked for you. I understood why you were not here. How is Robert?"

"Doing better physically," Louise replied, having another cup of tea. "But the shock of finding out about Margery and Elizabeth was .."

"It is a shock to me, I can tell you," Sister Meade replied. "No wonder he went on and on about her! His wife after all. Cyril says that he is not to go home with her yet, is that right?"

"It is so complicated," Louise said. "Elizabeth will not accept him and refuses to even meet him. Jack was her father, in her eyes."

"Oh, dear," Sister Meade said. "Poor Robert. That brother of his was a shady character, I always thought. So you think this enforced separation will be the right thing?" She stared at Louise so intently it brought back Louise's memories of being called to the Matron's office at Bart's.

"I don't know," Louise replied truthfully. "It is so hard to say what will happen. Margery and Robert had a row yesterday. Life has gone on for both of them without each other. It will take time."

"No doubt," Sister Meade replied. "And what about you? I know how you feel about him. It must have been shocking to find out she was his wife."

Louise sighed. "Shocking is not the word I would use," she replied. "A volcanic eruption might be more descriptive." She smiled slightly. "I am not ready to let him go yet. He is not ready to let me go, either. We have been joined together for so long it is impossible to separate us yet."

"Yes, I can see that," Sister Meade replied. "He is very dependent on you. I suppose that, like a child who is learning to walk, he must one day let go of your hand."

"And I of his," Louise said, putting down her cup. "I suppose we had best get on with clearing the cottage. Thank you for doing all the packing when I am sure you had a thousand other things to do. Are the other staff gone already?"

"Yes," Sister Meade replied. "Just a few more days and we will be no more." Her eyes grew wet but she quickly regained her composure. "I did make a list for you of all the patients and staff, and their addresses. Including mine, should you care to keep in touch." She handed Louise a piece of paper with neatly typed names and addresses.

"Oh, yes," Louise replied. "My address will be different, of course. Do you know I do not yet know my address in Upper Marstone? I have not even seen this cottage of Rose Henning's. I have been so taken up with Robert and the whole drama of this past week it seemed unimportant as to where I would live. Only what would happen to him."

"I hope one day he realizes what you have done for him," Sister Meade said as they got up from the table. "I know you do not think of it as a sacrifice, but it was. A sacrifice of your life so that he could live." Louise shook her head, but Sister Meade persisted. "It is true, Louise. He lives because you devoted whatever life you could have had – husband, children, a home of your own – to make sure he lived. Now you will give him what is left so that he can live with his wife and daughter at some point."

"If that is what he decides to do," Louise said. "It is not certain."

Sister Meade smiled sadly at Louise. "No, not certain, but most likely," she said as they walked arm in arm to the others. Louise looked up to see all eyes on her. The eyes of those people Robert loved and where he would once again become enveloped in their love for him. She turned away, folding the paper precisely as she put it into her bag.

"I will write," she said, the tears coming again. She had noted that Sister Meade, Angela Meade, as she had written on the paper, was staying in Sussex. Not so far to come to visit, Louise thought. After Robert and Margery sorted out their differences, perhaps she would move back here one day. Without him.

Margery felt oppressed by the red brick exterior and the institutional feel of the hospital. To think that her darling had spent year after year in this bleak place. It nearly broke her heart to think of him here. She would make him understand about Jack. He had to understand. She loved him as much as she did the day they became engaged. Even more, when she thought of how he suffered. Knowing him the way she did, she knew that he must have endured much living every day of his existence in this place.

"Why don't we go to the cottage now?" Cyril suggested. "I believe most things are packed. I am sure Louise will have a thorough search of the place, won't you?" He smiled at her and joined her as they began to walk across the lawn. The flowers that Robert tended so diligently were still in bloom, riots of autumn colors, their reds, golds and purples providing brilliant spots in the gloomy grey day.

"Lewis has agreed to take on Robert's care from now on," Cyril said as he walked with Louise. "It puts my heart to rest. In lesser hands, I would have worried about his level of care. I am retiring at month's end and will be moving back to my hometown of Hucknall. It would have been a long journey to see him regularly."

"Yes," Louise replied. "No one besides you could look after him as well as Lewis. Besides, I think it will do Lewis good."

"I see," Cyril smiled. "He did tell me how he painted a rather lurid picture of himself as a poor widower whose children have deserted him. Not to mention his semi-retirement." He smiled at her again. "He also told me he had not enjoyed himself with anyone so much for years." She blushed profusely. "He will look after Robert until he comes to a decision about his future." He patted her arm as they opened the cottage door.

Margery needed to see where Robert had lived, almost as if she could picture what he would have been like if they had spent these years together as man and wife. They went in, the boxes containing his things stacked neatly with his name, 'Morne,' stenciled lightly on each one. My name, Margery thought. My name and his. The little cottage was so dear she closed her eyes, feeling his presence here and wishing she could turn the clock back and they could have been here together, raising their daughter and not living this nightmare.

His beloved wireless was perched precariously on top of the boxes, not packed neatly, as if it was an afterthought that it would go with the other things. Margery noted the curtains, yellow chintz, still hanging forlornly in the empty space. She wondered if she might ask for them. They would brighten her kitchen and perhaps give Robert a sense of home.

"Those curtains," Margery asked as the removal men came in to take the boxes to the car, accompanied by Elizabeth, "Must they stay?"

Louise looked at them, her heart overflowing with emotion. When Robert had moved here in March, she had made those curtains for him. He always said that they greeted him every morning with sunshine, even if it was raining.

"I don't know," Louise replied. "Did you want them?"

"I thought they might make Robert feel more at home when he ..when he comes to my house," Margery said softly. "They are very nice, so bright and optimistic. My kitchen could use some color."

"Then by all means, take them," Louise said. "I think if they wanted them they would have taken them with the other things. Let's get them down, shall we?" They worked together to pack them up, Louise thinking that no matter what happened, there would always be something of her life with Robert to remind him of their time together.

All the boxes were packed neatly into the boot and strapped along the back as Louise said her last goodbyes to Cyril, Angela Meade, and the hospital she called home since 1916. She watched their figures waving at her, her tears flowing freely as first they, then the cottage, and finally the hospital itself disappeared from view. She fumbled in her bag for a handkerchief when one appeared in front of her.

"Here," Margery said. "This will help."

"Thank you," Louise replied wetly. It was an odd feeling to be sitting here with the wife of the man she loved. It was obvious to her that Margery still loved him and was trying to find her way back to him, back to the place where they had once loved one another and nothing else mattered. Now everything mattered and there seemed no solution to any of the problems.

"Well, that's sorted now," Rose interrupted their reverie. "I don't know about anyone else, but a few biscuits and tea were not enough for me. I say we go into the next village and get ourselves a meal before we head home." She turned around to see both Margery and Louise smiling at one another. Strange, Rose thought, but then they both shared something they loved: Robert.

Chapter Sixteen

Robert found it difficult to sleep, tossing and turning until he got up at the crack of dawn. Today he was going home. Back to Upper Marstone, back to his roots, but it was not really home, was it? Only when he could be with Margery and his daughter would he truly feel he was home again.

Would that ever happen? He got up, stretching and reaching for his watch. The same watch he had since he was nineteen and his Aunts Emma and Mary had given it to him for his birthday. His birthday – yes, he had missed it last Sunday. At his age, he chuckled, it didn't much matter anymore.

It was early, nearly seven o'clock, but he got up and decided to have a good wash and make himself presentable. His shirt and suit coat were lying over the chair. When he picked them up, he saw the ragged holes where the bullet had ripped through the fabric and hit him in the arm. Could he wear them? He wanted to look his best when he finally saw Upper Marstone again.

He washed, shaved and dressed, gingerly sliding his arm into the torn shirt. His reflection in the mirror made him look like a forlorn war veteran who had no home. That is exactly what I am, he thought. I have no home of my own. I am simply living with other people, as I have been doing since 1916. He turned from the mirror, a sense of apprehension overwhelming him.

The door opened suddenly and a young nurse came in with his breakfast tray. "Good morning, Mr. Morne," she said with a surprised air. "I didn't think you would be awake yet."

"Awake and ready to go," he responded in what he hoped would be a cheerful manner. She smiled at him readily, no sign of the fear that seemed to be in all the other nurses' eyes when they came into the room.

"You are going home today," she said, setting up his tray then opening the blinds. "I am sure you are glad of that."

"Very glad," he agreed. "It has been many years since I have seen Upper Marstone."

"I don't think it has changed too much," she said, pouring his tea for him. "Those little sleepy villages don't often change, do they?"

"Not on the surface, maybe," Robert responded. "More goes on beneath than most people would believe."

A knock on the door and then it swung open wide, revealing a young man in his mid-twenties wearing an ill-fitting black suit. His dark hair was slicked back so that the hair oil glistened in the bright sunshine.

"Mr. Morne?" he said, opening the door wider. "I wonder if I might have a word."

The nurse came over and enquired, "May I ask your name?"

"Detective Sgt Monroe, Sister," he said, tipping his hat to her. "I was told the patient is awake and I would like to question him about last Friday." The nurse started to protest but Robert waved his hand.

"It's all right, Sister," he said. "I'll talk to him."

"Thank you, Sir," Monroe said. Robert could almost hear him breathe a sigh of relief. He would not have to go back to his superior and tell him he was still unsuccessful in interviewing the victim.

The nurse looked skeptical but left the room. Monroe hoped she wasn't going to get her bulldog-faced superior and throw him out. He had avoided her by coming up the backstairs.

"What do you want to know?" Robert said, offering tea to Monroe but not finding another cup available. Monroe smiled tentatively, looking at this man who was one of the living dead.

He had done his homework on the whole tragedy, finding out about Robert and John Morne and what may have prompted the incident on Friday night. He didn't want to upset this bloke. He had heard he did not remember things too well after being shot in the head by the Huns in 1916.

"Well," Monroe started, "on Friday afternoon, September 20, you were on your way to Caterham from Worthing, is that correct?" This bloke looked perfectly normal to him. He began to wonder if it was some sort of ruse to keep the police from questioning him. Robert nodded.

"And you sent a telegram to your brother John…"

"Jack," Robert corrected him. "Everyone called him Jack."

"Jack, then," Monroe continued. "You asked him to meet you in Caterham, but he never showed up, so you decided to walk to Upper Marstone."

"Right," Robert said, irritated that this policeman was just re-stating the facts.

"So why did your brother come to meet you armed?" Monroe said, watching as Robert's face paled.

"I have no idea," Robert replied. "Perhaps as he was walking to Caterham, he thought he might need protection. What is the crime rate around here these days?" He smiled in a way that made Monroe wince.

"Not much of a crime rate that would warrant carrying a gun," Monroe responded, clearing his throat. "No, he had a reason. We think he meant to shoot you, Mr. Morne. Why would he want to do that, Sir?" He kept his gaze fixed on Robert's face.

"I don't think he meant to shoot me," Robert said, tapping his egg with such an elegant blow it cracked neatly off at the top. "He was on his way to meet me. It was dark and I was walking along the side of the road where he couldn't see me. It must have surprised him to come upon me that way so he pulled the gun. Then it went off, accidentally, when he was startled by his...daughter." The word choked him but he regained his composure.

"Accidentally?" Monroe raised his eyebrows. "Isn't it true that your brother knew of your existence for the past nine years and never told anyone about you? Why would he do that?" He stared at Robert, looking for any signs of deception.

"I asked him to," Robert said quietly. "You can see that I have suffered terrible seizures and have not been well enough to be released from an Army hospital. I was...ashamed." He lowered his head as Monroe softened. Poor sod, he thought. This brother of his must have wanted to protect him with that gun. Maybe he thought someone was trying to hurt him and accidentally shot at something. Well, it didn't really matter now. That poor blighter of a brother was dead and buried. He could go back and tell his superiors that there was no love triangle, no ominous coverup. Just a bloke trying to protect his poor, wounded mess of a brother.

He doesn't know about Margery and me, Robert thought, seeing that Monroe believed his story. He doesn't know the truth about Elizabeth, or that Jack deliberately hid information from everyone. He believes me. What Jack did will never be told to Elizabeth or Margery.

"We have talked to his daughter. She says all she remembers is he was ill and she tried to grab the gun and it went off," he said as Robert exhaled slowly. Good girl, Elizabeth, he said to himself. No one needs to know. "We haven't talked to his wife as she has been very upset by the incident."

"I am sure she has," Robert concurred, wondering how upset Margery was and if it was because Jack had died. Of course she would be upset; Jack had been her husband for nearly twenty years. Was she upset by what had happened, or because of how she felt about Jack? The thought haunted him that she had fallen in love with Jack, that Jack had finally won the war for her hand.

"Thank you for your time, Mr. Morne," Monroe said as he stood up. "I was a bit nervous about seeing you and all. I heard as you were so badly wounded you might not be able to talk to me." He smiled and shook Robert's hand. "I was too young to be in the War, you know. My uncle was in it. Told me stories about it, too. Pretty awful out there." He kept Robert's hand in his for a second and said, "Thank you for doing what you did. You blokes are all heroes to me. I hope your wounds will not give you any more problems. God bless you."

Robert smiled, not sure how to respond to such an admission from this young policeman. Heroes? He had never felt like a hero and never would. The heroes were all lying in France and Belgium.

Louise stood listening to Robert outside the door. It amazed her to hear Robert talking about Jack, telling a tale that protected him from scandal and enquiry. He loved his brother, despite everything. When she heard him say that he had asked Jack not to tell anyone about him in Upper Marstone, she nearly cried. What a noble man he is, really, and how terribly Jack treated him. There was no reason to protect Jack Morne now. He was dead, far from any prosecution. It was simply his brother's love that put a final halo on a very undeserving Jack Morne.

Louise decided to interrupt, dressed in a blue suit and hat instead of her usual uniform. She looked at Monroe and said authoritatively, "Who are you and what are you doing in this room?"

"Uh..sorry....uh, Mrs. Morne?" he said, assuming this must be Robert's wife. "I'm..."

Robert smiled at Monroe's discomfort and said, "This is Detective Sgt Monroe, Louise, from the Caterham Police. He was asking me about Friday night and what happened, so I told him."

"You should have had permission from his doctor to speak to him," Louise thundered. "He is not a well man and the effects could have been fatal. That would not have gone well with your superiors, would it?" She came closer as Monroe slipped past her and put on his hat.

"Thanks, again," he said, tipping his hat to Robert and closing the door. Robert was laughing so hard Louise was afraid it might trigger a seizure.

"Well, 'Mrs. Morne,' you've put the fear of God into him," he laughed, wiping his eyes. "You look lovely this morning. How was the trip back?"

"You're a wicked lad, Robert," she smiled. "I didn't even have time to correct him when he thought I was your wife." The word came out of her mouth with an air of resignation. Robert looked up, pushing his breakfast tray table away from him.

"I am so eager to leave here I hope we can go now," he said softly. "Did Margery sign all the papers?" She nodded, pulling them out of her bag and showing them to him. "It was sad to see the cottage and the hospital so devoid of life. Everyone was gone already, except Sister Meade and Dr. Gibbons. Everything packed up and ready for the removers. Even our ..your little cottage." He got up and came over to her, putting his arms around her.

"I am glad I didn't go," he said. "I don't think I could have stood it. I thought about 'going home' today, but I don't really have a home, do I? I have a wife, who lives in my brother's house. No home of my own. Not really." She held him tightly as they stood there. "That little cottage was the only real home I had on my own. I can remember when I was very young thinking what it must bel like to have a home of your own. I had just finished a night duty tour with the Ambulance Brigade. We had a huge fire, massive, and I was so knackered when I got home. It was a Sunday morning, beautiful June day. I took a bath and sat in the kitchen, listening to the birds and reading the paper. Everyone was at church, so I had the house to myself. It felt like I had my own home. The cottage made me feel that way on Sunday mornings."

"You will have a home of your own one day," Louise said softly.

"No money except my pension. I doubt I could get a job that would allow me to buy a house," he grumbled.

"There will be a way," she soothed. "You'll see. We both never thought we would ever get to this point, did we? Just a few months ago we didn't think you would ever find Margery again, and you have."

"Yes," he said, pondering her words, "but I wonder just what she really feels for me. It is obvious to me I am much changed," he said, turning to the mirror. "I am not the boy I was in 1916 and she knows it. All that time she was with Jack, too. Jack had his own brand of charm."

"I must say it was a very peculiar brand of charm," Louise said, beginning to pack up his toiletries. "It had no effect on me whatsoever, except a negative one."

He chuckled as he sat down again. "I could certainly see that whenever he visited," he said. "No, I don't mean charm in the usual sense, but he had a way of being...intense, I suppose. So intense you could almost be overwhelmed by him."

Louise turned to him, her heart so heavy but she had to tell him. "I think Margery truly has never loved anyone but you. You must try to see it from a woman's point of view, Robert. Just because she lived with him and married him does not mean she gave her heart to him."

"No?" he questioned. "Then why do it at all?"

"Just think for one moment," she prodded. "Isn't there an obvious reason she might have needed him?"

Robert shook his head, thinking of those days when Jack tried every trick in the book to make Margery his own. He finally succeeded somehow, after

Robert was supposedly dead. What would she have needed Jack for? It made no sense to him, unless she had fallen in love with him.

The door opened and Lewis Warren walked in, beaming from ear to ear. "Well, I have just signed your final papers at the desk, Robert, so you are free to go. Of course, I intend to see you regularly to assess your progress. This does not mean you are 100% cured. The medication you are taking could have side effects and may need adjusting. I think a few visits a week from me would be in order."

Robert noticed that even though Lewis was talking to him, he was watching Louise pack his items into a carryall bag. "Naturally," Robert grinned. "I wasn't planning any long voyages to Jamaica or anything like that. Do you know where we will be living?"

"Not exactly," Lewis smiled, "but since I intend to take you both there now, I am sure I will know shortly."

Louise turned around. "Are you? How very nice. I was planning to ring for a taxi." She smiled at him, a shy, almost girlish smile. She and Lewis glanced at one another then she looked away.

"So, Sir, are you ready?" Lewis said as Robert got up. "You look quite dapper, save for the rents in your coat. I have an excellent tailor who can repair that for you, if you like."

"It feels so strange to think that I have to think about things like clothes and tailors and living like any other man," Robert said as Louise made one additional thorough check of the room before shutting the door. "Everything has been done for me since 1916, when I joined the Army. I don't know how to do anything for myself. A complete babe it seems." Lewis slapped him lightly on the shoulder and said, "It will all come back more quickly than you think, particularly as you are home again and with those you love. Remember, Robert, that love really does seem to be able to surmount the highest obstacles." Lewis glanced again at Louise, who blushed, then nodded in agreement.

"Remember, too, Robert, that I have been living in that world as well," Louise added, again directing her words to Robert but her looks to Lewis. "Wearing this suit today makes me feel quite the imposter. I have lived in a nurse's uniform and nurses' quarters for so long I don't know what it feels like to have a home, or carry on the daily tasks that most women take for granted."

"We shall both be like children," Robert agreed, smiling at the nurses who gave him strange looks. Already they are thinking of him as some sort of freak, Louise thought. She glared at her colleagues, wanting to chide them for treating a severely injured patient as an object for speculation.

"I suppose that makes me your father, then," Lewis laughed as he guided them to his motorcar. "I shall be a stern father, too. You will both have to learn to be out in the world again, no excuses. To live and laugh and ..." He hesitated, his words stumbling, "and love again. Both of you."

Chapter Seventeen

Margery was pacing around the parlor, looking at the clock, then the window. Elizabeth sat quietly, a magazine open on her lap but she was not looking at it. The clock chimed one and Margery jumped.

"Really, Mummy," Elizabeth said, putting the magazine on the table in front of the sofa, "why don't you sit down? Auntie Rose thought it was better if you were not there when he arrived. If you keep pacing, you will only wear out the carpet." She looked at her mother's nervous gestures as she went back and forth across the room.

"I don't feel like sitting here," Margery said. "I..I don't know what I want to do just now." She took the magazine and flipped through it nervously.

"Well, go there, then, if you are going to be like this," Elizabeth said harshly. "I know that is what you want to do."

"Elizabeth, you know I am going to see him again," Margery said, finally sitting down. "I love you so much, my darling. I love Robert, too. Please, sweetheart, please do not make me choose between you."

"I am not making you choose between us," Elizabeth replied. "I am only telling you that I could not live in this house, my father's house, with him. How could you even think of bringing him here so soon after Daddy died?"

"But darling, I am not bringing him here to live," Margery tried to be patient, but she felt like shaking Elizabeth and making her see the truth about what Jack did to them both. It was because of Jack and his lies that Elizabeth was acting this way.

"Apparently he has asked to meet you," Margery said, watching Elizabeth's face. "Auntie Rose said his face lights up when your name is mentioned."

"Why should it?" Elizabeth retorted. "He never even knew I was alive until last week. Now he would like to come in here and claim me as his one and

129

only daughter. After Daddy raised me and fed me and clothed me. Very nice for him, isn't it?"

"Do you know, Elizabeth, that I never thought you could be so deliberately cruel," Margery said as Elizabeth looked up shocked. "Here is a man who has done nothing, nothing at all but give you life. He was hurt so badly he could not even remember his own name. He was kept from his family and from knowing he had a daughter by your 'beloved' father. If you only knew Robert as I do, you would understand what a living hell this must have been for him these past years. You saw that hospital. That was his life."

Elizabeth said nothing, her mother's words stinging her. She was not cruel, just truthful. This man meant nothing to her. Everyone was forcing her to accept him as her father, to allow him to come into their lives and take her father's place. She couldn't let that happen. Her father was all but forgotten now and he had only been dead a week.

"I'm sorry, Mummy," Elizabeth said coldly. "I cannot accept him in my father's place. It is as if Daddy never existed. All I hear from everyone is how happy they are to see Robert again, how happy they are that he is alive. No one grieves for Daddy. No one even mentions him. No one says they miss him. Just me. I miss him. I miss him so much and no one will ever replace him in my life or my heart." She ran upstairs so quickly Margery did not even have time to call out to her.

Margery sighed deeply as she sat on the couch. Every fiber of her being wanted to run out of the house to Rose's cottage to welcome her darling home. He should be walking in the door of this house. The stupidity of this enforced separation rankled her. Yet there seemed no other recourse.

Elizabeth was being petulant and unreasonable, but Margery understood how much Elizabeth missed Jack. Jack adored Elizabeth and did everything for her. From that perspective it did seem harsh to expect Elizabeth to just accept Robert and live happily with him. Elizabeth had never known Robert; everyone else had and had their memories of him. They also had their memories of Jack. Only Elizabeth seemed to have fond memories of him.

She went to the kitchen, thinking of last evening when they arrived at Rose's cottage after their trip. Louise had been delighted with everything and seemed almost human. Margery grimaced. She didn't want her to be human. She wanted her to be an old, dried up spinster who had designs on her darling. Yet Louise had been quite upset yesterday when they left the hospital and the cottage. Margery could not help but be moved.

She stared out her back window in the direction of Ivy Mill Lane. What were they doing now? She had asked to prepare Robert's room, taking such care with his bed. She lay on the bed for a few minutes, putting her own essence on it, wishing that tonight she could curl up with him in that bed.

130

Elizabeth was right about one thing; sleeping with him in Jack's bed would not be possible.

A smile creased her face as she remembered herself as the young girl who used to have such 'wicked thoughts' about her Robbie, wishing he would climb in her window and lie down with her all night. She had been naïve then, but not ignorant. He had not been much more experienced than she when they spent that night in Folkestone. What had happened to him since then? Had there been other women? Was he even capable of lovemaking? Cruelty seemed the word for the day, as it would be beyond cruel if he was not able to make love. She had never once let Jack touch her. She could not. He never complained, but the look in his eyes sometimes frightened her. If he had a mistress she would have been glad. He had seemed determined to torment her all their married life by making her feel guilty about not sleeping with him.

It was imperative that Robert understood how she had lived with Jack. It was strictly an arrangement, an arrangement to give Elizabeth a name and a home. Jack understood that. The cruel fact was that Elizabeth had her real father's legal name. Jack knew that, but like a cat toying with a mouse, he tormented her using her love for her daughter.

"I know why you did it," Margery said out loud in the kitchen, "I just can't understand how you could do it. To me. To Robert's daughter. And to Robert." Would seeing Robert when Jack first knew he was alive have made a difference in her life? From all accounts he had not been able to remember anything. Would he have remembered her? No one would know now. At that point he would have been away from her only ten years. The huge chasm of nineteen years seemed almost too much to surmount.

Lewis drove slowly to Upper Marstone, watching Robert's face as he looked at the High Street when it came into view from the crest of a hill. "Yes, it looks the same," Robert said softly. "We're coming up to the Oxted Road. Salisbury Road is just off there, where I used to live."

"Can we make a slight detour?" Louise asked Lewis, who nodded and turned left onto the road. "It's just up there on the right," Robert said excitedly, as Lewis pulled down the street.

The red brick workmen's cottages all looked the same to Robert. He could not remember which one was his boyhood home. Louise noticed his distress and remembered the address from his Army papers. 1, Merle Terrace, Salisbury Road, Godstone. She looked for that and spotted it at the end of the row.

"Isn't that it, Robert?" she asked as Lewis slowed the car down. Robert stared, remembering how many times he had run along the gap between his house and the slightly more posh ones to the left. That was it; it looked the same now. "Could we stop for a minute?" he asked Lewis. "I just want to have a look at it." Lewis nodded and stopped the car. Robert got out, walking slowly to the front gate, his expression so wistful Louise wished she could turn back the clock and allow him to be the boy he once was.

Curtains were twitching in some of the windows, this strange man standing in front of the gate inspiring curiosity in the neighbors. Robert seemed oblivious, lost in his own thoughts as he stood there, his hand resting lightly on the gate. The front door opened suddenly, a woman coming out and down the path shouting, "Clear off. I don't want any of whatever you're selling. Go on, clear off." She stood there defiantly, obviously unaware of who he was. Robert's surprised look and stiff demeanor had Lewis getting out of the car quickly.

"I'm sorry," Robert was saying, "I didn't mean any harm. I used to live here."

"Well, you don't anymore, so clear off," she shouted at him. Lewis took his arm and steered him back to the car.

"Welcome home," Robert gave a weak smile. "What a homecoming."

"I'm sure it will not be like that everywhere," Louise assured him. "It has been a long time. People are different now. No doubt people like your friend Billy and others will be glad to welcome you home."

"I wonder," Robert said, half to himself. "I wonder if people get used to someone not being here. They get on with their lives, closing the door on that person. No one ever comes back from the dead, do they? No one expects them to. So if someone does..." His voice trailed off, his expression full of yearning for the past.

Lewis drove back to the High Street. Robert pointed out the draper's where he used to work, now with another name over the door. He recognized some of the establishments, but most of them had new names and new owners.

Ivy Mill Lane was familiar to him. "We used to go ice skating at the Pond," he smiled, the rebuke from the woman on the Salisbury Road now lessening as he got closer to Rose's cottage. The little cottage looked more forlorn in the sunshine, the brown leaves carpeting the front garden, the flowers drooping sadly in disarray, and the gate slightly askew on its hinges.

"Well, I can see I will have my work cut out for me," Robert said with a forced cheerfulness. "Look at that state of that garden!" The front door opened and Catkins ran out and directly up to Robert, who got down on his haunches and said, "And who are you? What a lovely boy you are." He petted him as Catkins rolled around and had definitely decided that he had found a new mate.

"Welcome to your new home," Rose came out, nearly running down the path to embrace Robert. "We cleaned the place from top to bottom yesterday. We left the garden for you, dear." He grinned and hugged her as he took his small bag with him into the house.

The cottage smelled of beeswax and lavender, the exact smell he remembered from the house on the Salisbury Road when his mother cleaned. It was so reminiscent of the past he felt lightheaded. Lewis took his arm, helping him into a chair near the crackling fire. Louise had helped finish the cleaning, knowing that for hygienic as well as comfort reasons, the cottage would serve everyone better.

Robert had hoped that Margery would be here, but knew that only Mrs. Henning and her cat were in residence. Catkins jumped up on the chair and crawled into Robert's lap, purring lightly and giving Robert's hand a lick. Rose saw he still wore his buckle ring on his left hand. She could barely take her eyes off him, seeing him in regular clothes. She closed her eyes while he talked, listening to his voice and putting herself back in time when he would talk to the customers in just the same way at the W C Brooke Company.

"Are you all right, Mrs. Henning?" he said, alarmed as she leaned heavily on her cane. Lewis got up from his seat but she waved him off. "Can't an old lady indulge in a few memories? I was just remembering what it was like when we worked for Mr. Brooke."

He smiled. "Yes, I remember a lot about that now. How you always used to make me take care of the customers as your 'feet were pinching something awful." He grinned so boyishly she threw back her head in laughter.

"That's right, and that was just as it should have been," she laughed. "You were a young boy then, and I was an old lady. Don't you think so, doctor? Poor old thing like me had to rest her feet. I had terrible bunions you know."

"Being that I am not a podiatrist, Mrs. Henning," Lewis smiled, "I shall take your word for it."

Louise went into the kitchen with Rose to get some tea and cake. The cake was a delicious looking lemon drizzle. The scent seemed to permeate the entire kitchen as Rose cut thick slices and put them on a serving plate.

"That cake smells wonderful," Louise commented as they put the tray together. "If that is what the local bakery sells I am sure I shall gain two stone in the next month."

"No, that's not from the bakery," Rose murmured absentmindedly. "Would you look at those windows? Just gleaming now, aren't they?" The kitchen sparkled so much Rose blinked her eyes. "The cottage seems like a new home to me. That's Margery's doing. She is an expert housekeeper. Poor dear had no choice really, when she lived with old Mrs. Morne, Robbie's mother. Now that woman kept a house so spotless you would not believe she had two sons."

"What happened to her?" Louise questioned as they finished putting the tray together and started for the parlor.

"Well, don't be telling Robbie this, but everyone knows she was so overwrought by losing her boy that she..well, you understand she was not in her right mind, always been prone to being ill and all..."

"She killed herself?" Louise said, stunned. "Oh, to think if we had only known, perhaps she would still be here for him."

"Elizabeth Morne was a difficult woman," Rose said, stopping at the kitchen door before going into the parlor. "She adored Robbie and treated Jack quite second-class. But she couldn't stand Margery and made her life a misery, both when she was engaged to Robert and after she married Jack. May she rest in peace," she added carefully, not wanting to speak ill of the dead.

"So Elizabeth was named for her grandmother?" Louise asked as Rose nodded. "There is so much I do not know about his past."

"Yes, I imagine that is true," Rose said, as they opened the door, "but I tell you this. He was the dearest boy I ever knew. I loved him like a son. Now that he has no mother, I intend to treat him like a son. Woe betide anyone who causes him any ill will in this village."

"Who would want that?" Louise asked, surprised.

"There are people who don't want to accept things," Rose said as they headed into the parlor. "Why do you think he is living here instead of Moorcroft?"

"Moorcroft?" Louise said, realizing she had become so much a part of this world already that Rose talked to her as if she knew where everything was in the village and who everyone was.

"Where Margery lives," Rose added, smiling as she looked at Robert in the chair, playing with Catkins. "So, Catkins, you've decided to even the score by bonding with this lad here. Boys against girls, is it?"

"He's a lovely cat, aren't you, Mr. Catkins?" Robert smiled at Rose. "How is it he's managed to stay so good-natured living here?" Rose smiled at him indulgently, but Louise again noticed that melancholy look in his eyes.

"Here's some cake, you naughty boy," Rose said, handing him a big slice. "In most circumstances I wouldn't give it to you. Seeing as it was made especially for you, I must."

"Did you make it, Rose?" Louise asked, finding it as delicious as it smelled.

"No, no, I am not much for cake making anymore," Rose said. "No, it was made especially for Robert by the best cake maker in the village."

134

"And who is that then?" Robert asked through a mouthful of cake. "I remember that it used to be Mrs. Collins."

"She's dead and gone now, dear," Rose said sadly. "You know she lost both her boys in the War."

"I knew about David," Robert said, sipping his tea. "Not Bob as well?"

"Very sad," Rose shook her head. "Your friends, Bert Porter and Stephen Burridge went just before..."

"So who is the best cake maker in the entire village, Mrs. Henning?" Lewis interrupted, seeing Robert's face darken at the names of his friends who were killed.

"Oh, yes, that's right. Well, of course Robbie wouldn't know it, but the woman who baked this cake is none other than Margery."

"Margery?" he said, taking another forkful. "I never knew her to bake a cake before. Then again, we were so young..." Again his voice trailed off.

"She's quite a cook and housekeeper now," Rose said, helping herself to another slice of cake. Lewis felt that perhaps talking of Margery and what had become of everyone so soon after Robert arrived was perhaps not in his best interests.

"How about a little tour of the house, Mrs. Henning?" Lewis asked, nodding to Louise imperceptibly.

"A very good idea," Louise chimed in. "Would you like to see your room, Robert? It has a lovely view of the front garden. Well, it will be a lovely view once you get it cleaned up." He followed her down a hallway and she threw open the door. A fairly large room with blue and green patterned wallpaper and large windows, his small bag and trunk sat in the middle of the room, with his wireless on top of the bureau. "There it is!" he smiled. "I couldn't miss my weekly Henry Hall and Jack Jackson broadcasts, could I?"

"I've got a wireless, too," Rose said, not wanting to seem old-fashioned. "I like those women's programs. Have you heard them, Louise?"

"No, I haven't had time." Louise smiled at Lewis.

"Where is your room, Louise?" Robert asked, seeming dazed by the wallpaper.

"She's right next to you," Rose bustled, opening the next door that revealed pink and yellow cabbage roses on a cream-colored background. "A bit much," Rose said to herself. "It was my daughters' room. That wallpaper was all the rage in..."

"1899?" Robbie grinned as she grabbed for his ear.

"Very pretty," Louise said, going over to the window and looking at the disheveled garden. "I like it very much. Perhaps I have old-fashioned tastes." She looked at Robert, then Lewis, who both smiled at her.

135

"Nothing wrong with that," Lewis said, "as long as it doesn't pertain to your interest in neurology."

Rose showed them her room, situated facing the back garden. The bathroom stood between, with the water closet next to it.

"All the modern conveniences, you see," Rose said, nearly sounding like an estate agent trying to sell the cottage. "Lovely views, well, lovely when the garden looks presentable, lots of trees, neighbors not too close – I've always loved this cottage."

"How long have you lived here, Mrs. Henning?" Lewis asked, walking down the hall toward the parlor with her, leaving Louise and Robert behind.

"Forty-seven years," they heard her respond until their chatter became unintelligible.

"Seems very nice here," Louise commented as they stood side by side in the hallway, looking into both their rooms at the same time. "A little old-fashioned in design, but comfortable."

"Yes," Robert said, his attention obviously elsewhere. "Mrs. Henning was always such a kind person, really. Bit rough around the edges at times. If you met some of our customers, you would know why."

"Maternal, I would say," Louise commented. "This won't be forever, Robert. You know that. It is simply a means for everyone to be able to sort things out. You. Margery. Me."

Robert turned his gaze from the windows and looked at Louise. "I had hoped Margery would be here," he said, his voice low. "I know it is all a right mess at present, but ..."

"Come on, you two, Dr. Warren is getting ready to leave," Rose hollered down the hallway. "Goodness, Doctor, I feel as if I have two children in the house once again."

"I am sure it will feel that way at first," Lewis smiled at her. "I know you will do your best to take care of Robert. One thing I ask of you – give him room to find himself as a man. He has so long been in care he may find the transition difficult. He is a very appealing man," he looked down the hall, "and has an effect on the ladies where they seem to want to care for him. But he needs to stand on his own two feet again, little by little. It is the best thing for him."

"He always had that effect on the ladies," Rose nodded, keeping her gaze on the still-empty doorway from the hall, "which is one of the reasons he was hired. I know Louise cossets him. I've seen it. Don't worry about me, Doctor. I know when to cosset and when not to." She smiled broadly at both of them as they appeared in the parlor.

"I'm off now," Lewis said. "I shall ring every day, and stop in every few days, as Louise feels will be necessary."

136

"I wouldn't want you to go out of your way for me, Doctor," Robert said, his brow furrowed.

"No worries," Lewis smiled. "I am just over in Leigh, not too far. At this point I think it would be wise to see how you are getting on independently." Robert hesitated and said, "I am sure the Army will pay you for your services. I'm not sure what papers I need to file and such. Perhaps Louise will do that for me." He looked at her with a confused expression. Rose noticed it, too, and nodded at Lewis. The real world was already impacting him and he was feeling lost.

"Of course I shall," Louise said, walking Lewis to the door and handing him his coat and hat. "I am sure there will be no problems on that score." Rose shook Lewis's hand and said, "You are welcome anytime, Doctor. I don't think this old house has had so much excitement in twenty years."

"Just you look after yourself as well, Mrs. Henning," Lewis chided her as he stepped out into the cool, windy evening. "That hip is nothing to play loose with. Who is your doctor?"

"Dr. Mitchell, the village doctor," she replied. Robert came over to the door. "Dr. Mitchell? The same Dr. Mitchell who was doctor years ago?"

"Yes, the very same," Rose nodded. Robert appeared lost in thought, then said, "He saved my life. Twice. Seems like everyone is always saving my life."

"There must be a reason for that," Lewis smiled, shaking Robert's hand. "Just you take it easy tonight, Robert. Make sure you take that medication, too. I'd advise a quiet start to things. Not too many upsets of any kind at present." He looked at Robert, hoping he understood what he meant.

"Right, doctor," Robert said. "I know Louise will make sure I behave."

"Of that I am quite certain," Lewis grinned as Louise gave him a pained expression. What must these men think of her? She was only doing her job after all.

Robert and Rose went back into the cottage. Louise stood on the doorstep, watching Lewis get into the car. He gave a wave as he pulled off. She felt an unaccountable sense of loss as the car drove away in a cloud of dust.

The sun was just beginning to set over the Downs as she heard the church bells ringing in the distance. This was the place where Robert grew up and lived his entire life before the War. She could hear him now, laughing with Rose Henning, feeling a part of this world again. A world where she didn't belong. And possibly never would.

Lewis seemed more a part of her world now. Yet their friendship was just that: friendship. She loved Robert, loved him more at this moment when it felt she would lose him than she ever had before. What did she feel for Lewis?

Respect, admiration, comradeship – but not love. As she watched the sun setting she couldn't forget the feelings she had for her fiancé David Giles. She hadn't thought she loved him. Later she knew she had, but it was too late. He had been killed on the Somme. The memory of his last moments loomed up at her, his pleading for her to tell him she loved him as he lay dying at her feet, his wounds overwhelming her professional demeanor. Even then she still felt it difficult to say it. She had never told Robert she loved him, but he knew it. Loving Robert seemed so easy, so natural.

"You'll catch your death out here, dear," Rose said kindly, breaking her reverie. "Now the sun's gone down the air is too cold to be standing about."

"Yes," Louise said, drawing her cardigan about her. "I must see to Robert's medication as well."

"I'm just going to warm up some soup for us," Rose said, tapping off to the kitchen. "After that huge tea I think something light would be best."

"Yes," Louise said absentmindedly, her mind still thinking of David. "Something light."

"Whatever are you thinking about?" Rose said, eyeing Louise. "You're woolgathering, dear. His medicine should be in his room."

Robert was sitting in a chair, staring into the fire. He did not even notice Louise as she walked through the parlor to find his medication. His pensive expression, his hand on his chin, made her worry. I know he is thinking about Margery, dwelling on her as he did in hospital. He used to say he only wanted to see her again and his heart would be at rest. He obviously never bargained for finding out she was his wife, and that he had a daughter.

Louise found his medication at the bottom of his sponge bag. He had not yet unpacked. Perhaps she would help him with that in the morning. Lewis wanted him to take it easy until he got adjusted. It was new ground to see how he would fare in this environment and with all the shocks of the past week. Suddenly she felt very responsible for him and his life. It was an overwhelming feeling.

When she came back into the parlor Robert was standing by the mantel, looking at all the pictures that Rose had. He again seemed lost in thought, unaware of Louise. He picked up one particular picture and looked at it for a very long time, putting his hand on the glass as he seemed to trace the features.

"Here we are," Rose said, wheeling in her tray. "I thought it might be nice to have this little meal by the fire, as that wind is starting to blow out there." As if on cue, a gust of wind rattled the windows. Robert seemed not to hear her, transfixed by the photograph in his hand.

"What are you looking at there, Robbie?" Rose asked, pulling the tray nearer the fire. "Those are just my old photographs."

138

He turned around. Louise saw he had two frames in his hand. "This one I remember well," he said softly, holding up a photograph of himself in his Army uniform. Louise put down the pill bottle and came over to look. Although he looked fundamentally the same, there was a youth and freshness about him that had long ago died. The wounds he suffered changed him in ways that might be imperceptible when you saw him in person, but noticeable when compared to the boy in the photograph. She took the photo from him and looked long at it, then at him.

"Quite a difference," he said, almost in a whisper. "I wonder who that boy was."

"It's you, you silly thing," Rose said, ladling out the soup. Rose was not one to capture the nuance of the situation.

"What's the other one you've got there?" Rose said, patting the seat next to her. Robert came over with the photograph in his hand and gave it to Rose.

"That's her, isn't it?" he asked, his eyes looking intently at Rose. Rose nodded, her smile fading as she and Robert looked at the picture.

Louise came over with his medication and looked at the photograph. The girl who looked out at the world had the eyes of her father. Elizabeth.

Chapter Eighteen

The rest of their first night at the cottage was spent sitting around the fire listening to the wireless. After Robert had stared at Elizabeth's picture for a long time, Rose took the photograph from him and switched on the radio. The sounds of dance bands from London filled the room. Rose regaled Louise with tales of Robert's dancing and his forays to London. Robert remained silent, only smiling in affirmation at what Rose recounted.

"I think I will head off to bed," Robert yawned as the chimes from the mantel clock struck ten times. "It's been a long day and I am full knackered."

"You go on, dear," Rose said. "Do you want a bath? You need only let the water run a bit so it gets hot. I told you, all the modern conveniences."

"That would be nice," Robert said, coming over to Rose and kissing her goodnight, as he would his mother. He stooped down and looked at her seated in her chintz throne.

"Thank you for taking me in, Mrs. Henning," he said as she blushed. She mumbled something that they were no longer at Mr. Brooke's so he could call her Rose, but he disappeared down the hallway before she finished her sentence.

Louise and Rose sat up talking for another hour while Robert finished his bath and went to bed. Both of them felt too weary to discuss the future and what it held, so confined themselves to mundane topics of general interest. Rose was happy to have company again in her house. She had been active all day and it did her good, even though her hip was suffering.

"Maybe tomorrow you might help me with the treatments Dr. Mitchell prescribed," Rose said, her limp more pronounced than it had been earlier in the day. "I don't do the massage well myself."

"That was on my agenda," Louise smiled, gently assisting Rose to her room and helping her turn down her bed. "You know I am here in a professional capacity for both you and Robert."

"I hope that isn't all," Rose smiled at her. "I've become quite fond of you already, Sister. I feel as if I've known you for years."

Louise blushed and fussed with the blankets on Rose's bed. "And I you, Rose," she said before saying goodnight and going to her own room.

Robert heard the women talking in the hallway. He sat on the bed, feeling more anxious as the night went on. What would make his mind so unsettled? He felt exhausted but unable to sleep. The wind lightly rattled his window panes, the light from the moon casting an eerie glow over the front garden. The dead plants gave the place a look that reminded him of the battlefields – plants lying askew, mole holes, and dead bushes. He stared outside for a long time, adjusting his sense of direction to where he used to live and to where Margery now lived. How far away was Tilburstow Hill Road? All of his memory had not returned and he found it hard to place the exact location. Somewhere near Bullbeggars Lane, he seemed to think.

How long would it take to walk over there? Ten minutes? Fifteen? What if he showed up at the door? Would she let him in? Would Elizabeth have him thrown out? Elizabeth. He had been stunned by how beautiful she was in her picture. It still shocked him to think that this child of his had grown up not knowing him. She did not want to know him now. He was trying to understand, trying to make sense of everything, but his emotions superseded his intellect. What had Louise said about why Margery married Jack? Of course. It was right in front of his face. Because of Elizabeth. If Margery had no husband, no one to look after her, it must have seemed the right thing to do at the time. He narrowed his eyes in the dim light, watching the wind toss the leaves around in whorls. Jack obviously wasted no time in burying his brother and making his move on Margery. No matter what the motive, he knew Jack. Jack set this up and Jack convinced her it was the right thing to do under the circumstances. Why would she consent to a marriage so soon, when she was already married to him? He shook his head, the inconsistencies going round and round.

Elizabeth thought Jack was her father. That much was obvious from her reaction to his reappearance and her refusal to meet him. So not only had Jack taken Margery from him, but he had taken his daughter as well. He slammed his fist on the window sill, feeling the sting but not caring. Damn you, Jack. No wonder you wanted me dead. No doubt my daughter would have preferred that, too, thanks to you.

It made his blood run cold to remember last Friday night when Jack pulled the gun on him. He lied to the policeman about Jack. Why? All Jack had done was compound his agony by keeping him away from those he loved. He sighed, knowing why he did it. Jack was his brother. He would have tried to help Jack, because something was wrong with him and always had been. The fact that Jack could commit fratricide without a backward glance was proof of that.

He closed the drapes, not wanting to look out at the landscape that reminded him of those 'final' days in the trenches. He remembered them in fragments, always stopping short of when he went over the top. He remembered fixing bayonets but nothing else. Some sensation of flying seemed to linger in his memory.

Turning down the bed, he spotted something attached to the headboard and saw it was a tongue blade. So Louise has already made preparations, he smiled bitterly. The damned seizures! Without them he could go anywhere and do what he wanted. As long as the seizures held him captive, he would need a keeper for the rest of his life.

This new medicine Dr. Warren gave him seemed to be doing the trick. He had not had a seizure since Margery came to visit him earlier in the week. That was four days without one. A very good sign. Maybe he wouldn't need Louise anymore. Not as a keeper, anyway. Then what? He didn't know, but he knew he could not go on without her at present. If ever.

He slipped into the fragrant cotton sheets, feeling the tiredness drain out of him as he stretched. His hand felt something under his pillow, a piece of folded up paper. He withdrew it, unfolding it slowly.

My darling,

There is nothing that I want more at this moment than to be lying beside you in your bed. Since somehow the powers-that-be have deemed we must be apart for a while longer, I wanted you to have something from me to hold close to you tonight.

Robert, my darling, my dearest, I have never loved anyone but you my entire life. Never, ever, has anyone touched my heart again. You must believe me, sweetheart. You are all I ever wanted and ever will. It is hard now for us to be apart, but I vow I will let nothing stand in our way. We have both suffered so much and now it is our turn at happiness, at long last.

I love you, darling.
Margery

Robert held the note close to his face, breathing in the scent of paper and ink and something else: her essence. He was so overwhelmed by the note he sat up, turning it over and over in his hands, holding it to his face, closing his eyes and imagining her next to him. It felt as if he had been catapulted backward in time twenty years and was reading her letters to him in France. What damn stupidity this all was! Just as he had when he had been in the Army, he felt like going off and running to her house, begging her to let him in so they could be together, wrapped in each other's arms all night.

Damn Jack! If Jack had not lied and deceived Margery about his being alive none of this would be happening now. Elizabeth would not stand against him and he could go home and take his rightful place as Margery's husband and Elizabeth's father. "You never stopped spreading your venom, did you?" he asked out loud. "It is still wreaking havoc on my life, and the woman you professed to love so much."

He turned off his light and lay still, listening to the wind rattling the window and moaning low. The moaning sounds reminded him of something, but he couldn't quite place them. Was it the sounds from the hospital in France? Tiredness overtook him and he fell into a fitful sleep, clutching the note tightly to him.

The dream was the type that seems so real you are sure it is happening at that moment. Robert was sitting with his friends, Arthur and Jim, in billets outside a Casualty Clearing Station. He remembered where he was now: Puchevillers. The moaning sounds he thought were the wind were the sounds coming from the tents across the road. He got up and went there, offering to help, and then came back in an instant, covered with blood. There was a roll call and his officer told him to get a new tunic. He seemed drenched in blood, his face, his hair, even his boots, which he tried to protect. His father gave him those boots so he couldn't let anything happen to them.

The next instant they were in the trenches, waiting. Then the call came, 'Fix bayonets!" shouted at top decibel by Sgt. Morrison. Nervously he slipped the bayonet on his Lee-Enfield rifle, hearing the snap of the spring so loudly he thought all the Germans would know their exact location.

Arthur was next to him, nervous, and smiling idiotically. The whistle blew, he clambered up the dirt side of the parapet and saw hell before him. Shell craters the size of lorries, filled with water and dead bodies. The smoke was choking and blinding him. Someone shouted at him to keep direction. Was it Sgt Morrison? He wasn't sure, as the noise deafened him and made him feel insane.

Where was Arthur? And Jim? They had promised each other never to let themselves be left in No Man's Land, no matter the consequences. He couldn't see them in front of him, the smoke blinding him. Somehow he thought he was screaming or shouting. Then he stopped and turned around. There was Arthur, smiling in the same idiotic way. He stepped further ahead and saw someone with a gun pointed at him. He tried to pull the trigger on his rifle but it wouldn't move. He stood, fixed to the spot, as the person came into view and cocked his gun. The gun went off, hitting him in the head. As he flew backwards he saw the face of his murderer. It was Jack, smiling with satisfaction.

He jumped up, trying to run away, screaming, but his legs seemed rooted to the spot. If only he could get up, get away....

"Robert!" Louise called, snapping on the light. "It is all right. You are all right." She put her arms around him and rocked him gently while he kept trying to get away. Rose stood in the doorway, her face deadly pale as she watched the scenario. "Rose, please get me a cool glass of water, would you?" Rose nodded numbly, her long grey plait swinging in a wide arc as she exited the bedroom quickly.

"There, it is all right," Louise said with a practiced voice. Robert had mercifully not been prone to shell shock nightmares, as he could not remember much, if anything, of his experiences in battle. Was this a sign of him getting well? It seemed a high price to pay for his memory.

"Louise," he said weakly, wondering what she was doing in his room at this time of night. "What's happened?"

"Here you are," Rose said, shuffling in and noticing Robert's conscious expression. "Are you all right, dear?"

"You had a nightmare," Louise said calmly, giving him the glass of water. She was examining him carefully for signs of imminent seizure, but none seemed evident.

Robert ran his fingers through his hair, which was sticking up at all angles. "I was back in France," he said softly. "We went over the top. It was horrible, bodies, shell holes, smoke, choking stuff. I was running and looking for Arthur, my mate." Louise nodded, her curiosity piqued. He had not mentioned Arthur or this much information before. His memory was returning with a vengeance.

He sipped the water, the note falling unnoticed onto his lap. Louise picked it up and held it while he continued. "Then someone came forward to shoot me. He held a gun up and shot me. It was..." He was unable to continue.

"Who was it?" Rose asked, her voice quavering. Louise's look cautioned her to let him tell it at his own pace.

"It was Jack," he blurted out. "It was Jack trying to kill me." He sobbed softly as Louise held him more tightly. Rose came over and sat on the bed, her heart breaking for his agony.

"Just lie back down now," Louise said, going to the medicine bottles on the bureau. "I think this will help calm you down and get you to sleep."

"No," Robert said, but Louise protested. "It has been a very strenuous day for us all, Robert. Take the medicine, please." He dutifully took the medicine and lay back down.

"Would you like me to stay with you a while?" Louise asked. "I will if it helps."

"No, I will be all right now," he said tentatively. "So sorry to wake you both up. An awful way to start off my new life." He tried to grin but found it difficult.

"I'll be right next door if you need me," Louise said, tucking up his blankets.

"Thank you," he said, taking her hand. "What would I do without you?" He smiled at her as she and Rose left the room.

"I could use some of that medicine myself," Rose grumbled. "Poor lad. Was it the shell shock, then? I've heard tell of it, but never saw anyone in the middle of it. And to think he dreamed Jack was trying to kill him."

"But he was, Rose," Louise said calmly. "Jack did pull a gun on him, which is why he has that gunshot wound in his arm. Whether he was actually trying to kill him or not we will never know. He did try to keep him away from Upper Marstone. And Margery."

Rose nodded numbly, feeling very old and tired. She hoped that she had made the right decision inviting Robert to live with her. He was different, that was certain, although the ghost of the boy was still in there somewhere. Margery, of course, thought he was the same as he had been. After tonight, she knew he was not. Neither was Margery. What a pickle, she shook her head, saying goodnight again to Louise.

Louise shut the door of her room and leaned against it, trying to make sense of the events. He did remember so much more now. It was so traumatic she wondered if it was a good thing after all. The piece of paper in her hand was crumpled as she unfolded it.

She read Margery's words of love to Robert as if they spelled her own damnation. He must have read it, so again Margery has caused him trauma. If Margery had not married Jack, would things have been different? Louise could not help but think they would have been. As long as Jack Morne figured into the scenario, and he most certainly did, dead or alive, there seemed to be no resolution that would make everyone happy.

"Well, Jack Morne, you have certainly left a legacy of evil, haven't you?" Louise said, looking out the window at the same bleak garden landscape that Robert had viewed. "Your brother knows more than anyone what you have done to him and to the woman he loves. I will never be able to understand how you could be so cruel and selfish. And still it goes on."

She opened her door softly and went to Robert's room to check on him. The medication seemed to be working as he lay sleeping soundly. She took the note and slipped it back into his hand. If Margery felt this way about him, there would only be one course for Robert. If it didn't kill him first.

Chapter Nineteen

The next week went by quickly, Robert feeling reluctant to go out into the village, complaining of headaches from the medication. He was still sleeping fitfully. Rain most of the week kept him indoors, staring for hours out the windows, Catkins on his lap. Louise knew he was contemplating his next moves, feeling the loss of routine of the hospital, where he had a chance to go outside, meet with other patients, and find a sense of comfort.

Despite getting on with Rose better than she had anticipated, Louise felt a loss, too. The hospital had been her life for so long she found it hard to relax, pacing anxiously around, fussing over Robert, and trying to find some interest in daily domestic tasks. Used to a fast and furious pace, the leisurely days of being at home were hard for her to take. She wasn't sick or injured, which were the only times she had ever sat still and read books for pleasure.

Lewis stopped by twice, telling Louise to go easy on Robert. "It is a terribly difficult adjustment for him, especially emotionally," he said. "Obviously the nightmares are causing him great distress. Medicating him more will not make them go away."

"In some ways I think they are a good sign," Louise said earnestly. "He remembers so much more than he did before since he has returned to the village."

"Has Margery rung him?" Lewis asked, watching Louise's face for her reaction.

"No. I think he feels sad about that, too," Louise said, turning to look at Robert sitting near the dining room windows, watching the rain hit the panes. "If he could just get out and work in the garden he might be adjusting better."

"I have been thinking of paying her a visit," Lewis said. "Eventually he will go home to her. She should have more information about his condition. I think she is afraid to make any contact with him for fear of causing another seizure."

"She has made contact with him," Louise said low. "She left a note for him under his pillow the first night. It seems whenever she has any contact with him he has a severe reaction."

"What did the note say?" Lewis said, eyeing the rain warily as he put on his hat and opened the door.

"That she loves him, that she has always loved him, and always will," Louise replied. "It was quite heartrending. Perhaps not what he needed to read on his first night back. I know he wants to see her. I saw him looking outside as if he wanted to escape."

"Perhaps now is the best time to see Margery," Lewis said. "I will head over there and have a talk with her. I think they must be allowed to see each other. He has been here now nearly a week. If I ever saw a man with a more poignant face of misery, I don't know where." He glanced at the forlorn figure near the window. "They must be allowed to see one another for a few hours. Alone."

"Is that wise?" Louise said. "Yes, from a romantic perspective it is, I'm sure, but physically? What if she should upset him so much again he has a seizure? She has no knowledge of how to take care of him."

"Then she will have to learn," Lewis smiled at her, "just as you once did. I can't think of a better teacher than you."

"Me?" Louise replied, shocked. "How do you expect me to teach this woman everything I have learned in my years of nursing training and experience?"

"You don't have to teach her everything," Lewis said. "Just how to care for Robert. There is no one on earth who knows how to care for him better than you."

Louise contemplated his words, feeling reluctant to start the separation process so quickly. "Shouldn't he get a chance to re-adjust to his life here first? See his old friends? Go into the village? It seems a lot to ask him to start mending fences with Margery so early on when he is still so unstable."

Lewis directed her gaze to Robert. "Look at him, Louise. Do you think a walk to the village, or a pint with Billy, will cheer him up? He wants to see Margery. Apparently she wants to see him as well. I know there are problems with the daughter..."

"Elizabeth," Louise murmured, feeling she had an ally in this venture to keep the couple apart a little longer.

"Yes," Lewis said. "Look at me, Louise. You are going to have to let him go sometime. You know that, don't you?"

"Yes," she said so quietly he almost couldn't hear her.

"Then what will you do?" he asked so gently she looked into his eyes. "That is what you are thinking, isn't it? You have spent your whole life devoted to these patients, and this one in particular. When he moves on to the life he should have, where does that leave you? Living here with Rose Henning, becoming her caretaker and pining for Robert?"

"I am not pining for him," Louise said defiantly, but Lewis caught her arm.

"If you ever want your old job back, it is still open," he said softly. "I never filled it again after you left."

"But you are retired," Louise said. "What would I do?"

"Semi-retired," he corrected her. "I still do extensive research."

"Not yet, Lewis," she said, looking at Robert. "Not yet."

"Yes," Lewis said. "Not yet. I think an occasional evening out would not go amiss. Robert will be fine a few hours on his own. He would probably enjoy feeling more like a normal man again. Shall we say Friday evening at seven?" He smiled at her in a way that made her unable to refuse.

"I will see," she said, then added, "All right, but if anything happens..."

"Nothing will happen," Lewis grinned. "He has the great neurosurgeon Dr. Lewis G. Warren looking after him, doesn't he?"

"Yes," she smiled back. "I had forgotten that."

"Oh, you might want to know," he said breezily as he walked down the pavement, "that I was knighted several years ago. So now you know I am someone to be reckoned with and should be treated as such." His grin nearly lit up the pathway as he added, "I am off to see Margery now. Shall I tell her you will be instructing her in the use of a tongue blade?"

"Yes, Sir Lewis," Louise laughed and curtseyed to him. He gave her a wave, as the familiar feelings of anxiety returned to her. She remembered her girlish self, smitten with him, more for his brain and his knowledge than in any physical way. Yet his dark eyes were intriguing and his smile warm. Somehow she had never pictured herself as the object of anyone's affection. Even when Robert had kissed her and they had once made love, she had not felt it from a sense of deep attraction. The feelings emanated more from a sense of caring for him and his wellbeing.

Robert turned and smiled at her, motioning to her to sit down with him. She sensed his loneliness, his feeling of being different. How she worried about him feeling like a man resurrected from the dead. A lonely place to be.

"I've been thinking," Louise began quietly. Mrs. Henning had been on the telephone with her daughter for nearly a half an hour and showed no signs of ending the call. It was a good time to talk to Robert alone.

"What?" he said, his eyes so in contrast to Lewis' dark depths. Whenever she looked at Robert's eyes she always remembered the first moment she had looked into them, when he was an unconscious patient brought into her ward at the Base hospital at Etaples in France. The silvery lights had captured her then. It was hard for her to look at him and think that one day, perhaps very soon, he would no longer be here so she could look into those eyes.

"Lewis has asked me to go out for a meal on Friday night," Louise began. She noticed Robert stiffen slightly, wondering if it was fear of being alone or jealousy. No, she could not imagine he would be jealous. Robert understood how she felt about him. "I thought perhaps you might like to see Margery then."

"See Margery?" he said excitedly. "Has she rung? Does she want to see me?" The desperation in his voice was so obvious she took his hand to calm him down.

"No, but I think it is only because she is not sure how to proceed here," Louise said carefully. "Lewis is going over to talk to her about seeing you. He asked me to talk to her, too. If she is going to be with you, she should at least know the basics of caring for you during a seizure."

His expression darkened, then he nodded resignedly. "I suppose that is reality, isn't it?" he said. "She will have to know the extent of my...limitations."

"I am not sure they are limitations, Robert," Louise soothed. "Just a few differences. If you had come home from the War it would have been just the same. Besides, there is one thing no one can replace."

"What's that?" he said, the misery in his voice at feeling like half a man showing.

"The love you have for each other," she said softly. "You mustn't think of my feelings in this, Robert. You know I care for you very much..."

"And I you," he said, taking her hand in his. "I am not sure about Margery. I don't know." He hung his head.

"I think you are sure of your feeling for her, but not what your future might be," she continued, the words choking in her throat. How she loved him, she thought, but in what way? Would he want her to be here, looking after him and being with him all the time? If he wasn't injured, would he have given her a second look? More importantly, she thought, would I have wanted him if he were not injured? The thought jarred her as she looked at him.

"The only way for all of us to find out our true feelings is to make a start," she continued. "Lewis thinks that you should spend some time alone with Margery. Find out what your feelings are."

"I know her feelings," he said. "But I still don't know some of the answers to my questions."

"Then you must ask her," Louise said, getting up as Rose came in.

"That Ethel can talk a hind leg off a donkey," she said exasperatedly. "On and on about her woes with her children, her husband, the neighbors. Well, I don't know." She sat down heavily, rubbing her hip, in her usual chintz-covered chair that bore her impression.

"Seems to me you were keeping up with her," Robert grinned. "Perhaps the poor donkey now only has front legs."

"You see that?" Rose pointed at him. "He hasn't changed in that respect. Always one for the smarty comment, he was. It's a good thing I indulge you, my boy." Louise detected an almost imperceptible wince in Robert at being called 'boy.' No, he most definitely was no longer a boy.

"In any case," Rose said. "She's asked me to come visit for the weekend. I told her I couldn't do it as..."

"Why not?" Louise asked. "It might do you good."

Rose eyed her suspiciously. "What would the neighbors think of you two all alone in the house? Not proper, that. Not that I mind, of course. But one has to keep up appearances."

"Shall we ask the Vicar to chaperone us, then?" Robert said sarcastically. "For God's sake, Mrs... I mean Rose," he almost spat the words out. "I am a wounded soldier and she is my nurse. If anyone wants to think ill of us then let them bloody well do it." He folded his arms and sat back.

"Now, none of that language," Rose said, shaken by his outburst. "You really have become very temperamental, Robbie." Louise wanted to tell her that he was no longer the shop assistant of eighteen, but a man who had endured horrors she could never comprehend. No wonder he reacted as he did.

"No, I don't want to go," she said firmly. "It's a long ride there and trains are none too comfortable for me anymore." She looked around and added, "They might come and take me out instead, so that's all right."

"We all need a chance to get out," Louise spoke up. "I'm going to have dinner with Lewis on Friday night."

"Oh, yes?' Rose raised her eyebrows. "Well, that will be nice for you, won't it?" She wondered if perhaps she only thought Louise was in love with Robbie. She usually was never wrong about these things. Louise looked at Robert, who nodded slightly. No, that look was still on Louise's face. She and Dr. Warren must only be old friends. Louise's heart belonged to Robbie. It made her smile as she remembered how he had been called the 'village heartthrob' by the ladies. Indeed he had been – a handsome, charming, well-dressed lad he was, too. Quite good looking now as well. Some new clothes wouldn't go amiss on him.

"What are you smiling at, ..R ..Rose," Robert asked, stumbling over her name.

"I was just recalling as how you were considered the 'village heartthrob' long ago," she smiled at him. "He was, you know. Dead charming and had all the ladies at his feet." Louise saw Robert blushing and shaking his head.

"No, no, it's true," Rose continued. "Some of the girls who fancied him would come in and buy nonsense items like ribbons and such, just to get him to wait on them. You always were a looker, my lad. Still are, if you don't mind me saying so."

"I never knew that," he muttered to himself.

"Lewis and I were talking," Louise interrupted. "Perhaps Margery and Robert should have a meeting with one another. Alone."

"Oh, well, that would be nice, but is it..you know?" Rose noticed Robert grimacing and did not continue.

"Lewis seems to feel it will be fine. He would like me to show Margery how to care for Robert in the event of a seizure, which Lewis thinks will occur far less often now that he has this new medication." Rose thought and said, "Maybe you might show me as well. You might like a night out with Dr. Warren again."

"Of course," Louise said. Robert looked pained, thinking of how much inconvenience he was causing everyone. He didn't want Margery to look at him as a cripple. The thought of that made him angry.

"Shall I ring her up?" Rose said, getting up just as the doorbell rang. "Now, who can that be?" She shuffled off to open it, talking to someone for a few minutes and then coming back into the parlor with a young man with a vaguely familiar expression.

"This young man says he is looking for Dr. Warren," Rose said, deferring to Louise as if she was the keeper of Dr. Warren's whereabouts.

"Pardon me for intruding," he said cheerfully. "I've just blown in, as it were, and was looking for him. They told me he was visiting his patient here, so I thought I might catch him up. Looks as if I am a bit late." He smiled, his dark eyes sparkling.

"He was here," Louise said. "But I'm afraid he's left."

"Maybe I can catch him at home, then," the young man replied.

"No," Robert interrupted. "He's gone over to Tilburstow Hill Road, hasn't he, Louise?'

"Yes, that's right," Louise said. "He went to visit Mrs. Morne." Again Robert winced at the mention of her name. She had been known as Mrs. Morne, but not Mrs. Robert Morne. Mrs. Jack Morne.

"She's at 7 Moorcroft Gardens," Rose added. "You can't miss it. Just get back on the High Street and head in the direction of Tandridge."

"Thanks, awfully," the young man said.

"Is this a medical problem?" Louise questioned, wondering who this young man was and why he needed Dr. Warren.

"Oh, no," he laughed, revealing fine teeth. Quite a nice looking young man, Louise thought. Perhaps he is a medical student. "No," he continued. "I've just come back from Manchester unexpectedly. To stay. I don't think he was expecting me quite so soon."

"To stay?" Louise said. "Are you working with Dr. Warren?"

Again the young man laughed. "Not working with him, exactly. I've been meaning to come home for some time now, but I had to finish up my business in Manchester first. So now I am all sorted, and here I am." He looked around at the expectant faces. "Oh, I suppose I should introduce myself." He smiled at their confused expressions. "I am Brian Warren. Lewis Warren's son." He shook hands with them all and then backed toward the door. "I'd best be getting over there. Knowing my father, he is probably home with his feet up already."

"Perhaps not this time," Louise murmured under her breath, feeling quite old as she watched the tall, slender figure go back to his car. She remembered when Lewis married and had his children. The weight of the passing years seemed enormous.

153

Chapter Twenty

Lewis drove slowly toward Tilburstow Hill Road, as much from his trepidation at talking to Margery as from being unsure of where he was. He spotted the new cottages nestled on the hill, seeing a number seven on the gate near the end of the row.

He parked his car in front, hoping Margery would be home and they could talk about the future. As much as giving her an update on Robert and a realistic expectation of his future, he wanted to assess this woman's real feelings for Robert. Was she still thinking of him as the brave young hero of yesteryear? If she was, he felt it fair to both Robert and her to tell her what the reality would be living with him.

He walked up the path, noticing a neglected but once pretty garden. A few zinnias and Michaelmas daisies stood bravely among the leaves and brush. It was Thursday afternoon, so perhaps no one would be home.

The door was opened by a startled Elizabeth. Lewis was certain her look was not only because she had not expected to see him standing there, but a reaction to his own expression when he always saw her. Her resemblance to Robert was so remarkable he wondered how many others in the village had twigged that this girl was Robert's, and not Jack's, child. He had not known Jack Morne. Perhaps the resemblance between the brothers was more marked than Louise had told him.

"My mother is in the kitchen," Elizabeth said nervously. "I am guessing you have come to see her?" He nodded and added, "This is simply a complimentary call to talk to her about Mr. Morne's condition." Elizabeth nodded and ushered him into the parlor, then excused herself to get her mother.

Margery came out, wiping her hands on her apron, her face a mask of anxiety. "Please, Dr. Warren, be seated. I have the kettle on. Or would you prefer coffee?" He answered that either one was fine. The poor woman looked very distraught. He smiled and asked her to sit down.

"Elizabeth," she said, before sitting down. "Would you mind bringing tea for Dr. Warren?" Elizabeth agreed and Margery sat, smoothing her apron over her knees. Her forward posture gave her the look of an animal poised to run.

"I know you are wondering why I am here," he began and she nodded, the tense look around her eyes making deep wrinkles, "but I assure you this is simply to inform you of your husband's condition." He saw the slight relaxation and almost a verification that indeed Robert was her husband.

"I haven't rung or visited," she said very softly. "I was not sure whether I should. Perhaps after our last visit he might have another seizure or I might cause him to be injured in some way."

"No, Mrs. Morne," Lewis said. "That is one reason I am here. I know about the note you left for him."

Margery looked at him, her startled eyes again reminding him of a deer in flight for its life. "I hope it didn't upset him, doctor. I..I wanted him to know how I felt. I wanted him to understand about Jack and me."

Elizabeth came in with the tea tray, arranging things and pouring out cups for Lewis and her mother. She began to leave when Lewis said, "Won't you join us, Miss Morne? This concerns you as well."

Elizabeth turned quickly, ready to protest that she was not interested, when Lewis interrupted.

"Miss Morne, I know your feelings are very strong against Robert. I hope you will at least hear me out. Please, sit down." Something in his manner made her sit next to her mother, her hands folded primly in her lap but her jaw set so firmly Lewis knew he had a difficult task before him.

"Now, Mrs. Morne," he began.

"Please call me Margery," she asked. "And she is Elizabeth." He smiled and said, "Fine, Margery. I want you to know that there is nothing you can do to harm Robert by talking with him. He has long been in hospital. There is a certain readjustment period necessary for any patient who has been incarcerated for so long when they return to the outside world. He is not having an easy time of it, understandably."

"Has he been ill?" Margery said, her eyes worried.

"Not ill," Lewis said. "He is pining. Pining for his old life, pining for his old body, and pining for ...you." Margery blushed and Elizabeth shook her head in protest.

"Please, Elizabeth," Lewis said. "I know this is difficult. Please bear with me. Do you both understand how severely injured he was?" They nodded simultaneously. A good sign, Lewis thought. "He does not need

155

hospital care. But he does need someone who can assist him when he has a seizure. I have been giving him some new medications that seem to be working. He is remembering things so well now he even remembers his war experiences in great detail. I'm afraid they have resulted in nightmares. But he is moving forward at a fast clip."

Margery was looking at him so intently he understood why she had been attractive to both Morne brothers. Her eyes were hypnotic in their gaze, dark and intense. Although Elizabeth had Robert's eyes, she had inherited the look of intensity from her mother.

"Would you like to see him?" Lewis said and Margery nodded. "I think that perhaps if you would like to have him come for an evening, dinner perhaps." He smiled and said, "From the smells emanating from your kitchen I think that would be a treat for him."

"Would he be..all right without his nurse?" Margery asked.

"Ah, now that's just the thing," Lewis said. "I am going to speak plainly here. Do you want him to live with you, as your husband?" Elizabeth looked disgusted but Lewis continued. "If you do, you had better know the facts. It is doubtful he would ever again be able to maintain serious employment. He is very moody, depressed, and his condition makes him angry. He has been used to being cared for, and now finds that as he takes responsibility for himself, it is a hard go. It will not be an easy path for any woman, especially one who loved him when he was healthy. You would be undertaking a lifetime different than you envisioned when you wanted to marry him years ago. Do you understand?"

Margery nodded weakly, the tears beginning to flow as she drew out her handkerchief and wiped her eyes. Elizabeth remained defiant, holding her mother's shoulders and asked, "Why are you telling her this, doctor? It sounds as if you do not want him to come back to her."

"I very much want that for him, Elizabeth," Lewis replied. "But I do not want him to come back here and have your mother unprepared for what she will encounter. He is changed in many ways, in ways that will emerge as she is with him again. I do not want to see him tossed back into the kennel, as it were, like a dog that has been adopted but the family can no longer deal with it. That is why, as his doctor, I want you both to understand that if you choose this path, what you will encounter will not be easy to handle."

"No matter what, I love him," Margery said wetly. "I love him and will take anything from him. Just give him back to me, doctor. Please, give him back to me."

Elizabeth began to get up but Lewis looked at her and said, "Elizabeth, wait. I do understand how you feel very much. I know how difficult this is for you."

"How can you?" Elizabeth snorted. "You didn't know my father. He was a good man, a fine man, no matter what people say. If Mummy wants this man here, so be it. I do not know what I can do about it. But I do not have to stay."

"If you love your mother, Elizabeth, then you will want to help her, because she is going to need all the help she can get," Lewis said sternly. "This is not going to be easy for anyone. She loves you more than anyone in the world and she needs you now."

Elizabeth sat down again, looking from Lewis to her mother, who was weeping softly into her handkerchief. "I do need you, darling, so much," Margery cried. "Please, please, don't make me choose. I have not forgotten what Jack did for us. Remember, darling, he did it because of Robert. Robert was his only brother. Jack wanted to protect the child his brother fathered. There is no one closer to Jack on this earth than Robert. No one." She wiped her eyes and looked at Elizabeth.

Elizabeth looked pensive and less defiant in her belief. Perhaps that was true. Still she felt it difficult to face this man. "Must I see him yet?" she asked meekly. "I do not know if I can stand it right now."

"Whenever you're ready, my dear," Lewis said. "He desperately wants to meet you, of course, but one thing I have learned about Robert. He is very patient and very understanding. Whether he was like that before his injury I do not know. Long years in hospital have made him so."

"He was in the St. John Ambulance Brigade," Margery sobbed. "One woman told me that when she had been ill and nearly unconscious from pain, he knelt next to her and held her hand, talking to her. She said in her delirium she thought she had died and he was an angel." She smiled through her tears as Lewis got up.

"Would you like to ring him up?" he said gently, holding her shoulder as she walked him to the door. "I also think you might like to learn some basic medical procedures to handle seizures. Louise, his nurse as you know, would be happy to teach both of you." He looked directly at Elizabeth who kept her gaze averted.

"Yes, I will ring him and I will do whatever, whatever it takes to bring him home to me," Margery said, more calm now as she put her handkerchief in her pocket.

"Would tomorrow evening be a good time for him to visit?" Lewis asked. "I think if we wait much longer poor old Catkins will lose all his fur. All Robert does is sit in front of the window, petting and petting that cat."

Elizabeth and Margery both smiled at the picture of that, much to Lewis's delight. It would take a long time for Elizabeth, but not as long as he first thought. *It's up to you now, Robert. Cast your charms on your wife and daughter and may God do the rest.*

He waved to them both as he saw Margery heading into the hallway for the telephone. *The game was now afoot.*

Elizabeth heard her mother talking to Auntie Rose as she shut the door. It didn't seem as if Mummy was going to have the opportunity to talk to Robert after all. *There*, she thought, *I've done it. I've actually called him Robert, not 'that man.' Once you dignify someone with his name, you know you are catapulting toward accepting him.*

"He's asleep," she said to Elizabeth. "He's been having headaches and not sleeping well since he started the nightmares." She looked so sad that Elizabeth went up to her and hugged her.

"It will be all right for you, Mummy," she said, looking at her. "I know it will."

"Not if you are unhappy, my darling," Margery cried, brushing a stray strand of hair away from Elizabeth's forehead. "You know you are always first in my heart."

"I know," Elizabeth said turning away. "I know I am, Mummy. I do know how much you have given up for me. There are other places in your heart that I cannot fill. He can."

Margery began weeping again, holding her daughter close to her. "You are an angel, darling," she said. "I know how hard it is for you to understand everything. I would never, never do anything to make you forget Jack and how much you loved him. In one sense, Robert is here for you now, as Jack was there for us when we needed him." She hoped the argument made sense.

"Will he be coming here?" Elizabeth asked.

"I told Auntie Rose that I hoped he would come for dinner tomorrow night around seven," she replied. "Auntie Rose said he has been moping around so much she would be glad to see him get out a bit. You know how blunt she is." Elizabeth nodded, both realizing that Robert's condition precluded him from going out at all on his own.

"I'm...I'm not ready to meet him, Mummy," Elizabeth pleaded. "Not yet. I know he might feel hurt by that. I need to mourn Daddy in my own way."

"Of course, darling," Margery said, looking at her daughter's face and seeing Robert so close to her again. "He will understand. You didn't know him, darling. He was a fine boy. Loving, kind, and understanding. A gentleman and a good man."

Elizabeth nodded, seeing in that description the father she knew, Jack. It sounded as if the brothers might have shared the same traits. Others seemed to feel differently.

"I do feel nervous about being all alone with him this first time," Margery said, hoping Elizabeth might relent. "Not in a girlish way, of course, but because it might be so awkward."

"Why not ask Uncle Billy and Aunt Sally to come over for dinner as well?" Elizabeth suggested. "He would be comfortable with them, wouldn't he?"

"Yes," Margery agreed. "That might make it easier at first. Then he and I can talk after they leave. Yes, that is a good idea, darling. I will call Sally right now." The doorbell rung as Margery ran off to the telephone.

Elizabeth opened the door and saw a young man standing there. He was fairly tall, dark hair and eyes, and a very nice smile. She assumed he was a salesman and stood ready to send him away.

"Is this the Morne residence?" he asked cheerfully.

"Yes," Elizabeth replied. "I'm afraid we are not interested in anything you have to sell today." She began to shut the door but he said, "Wait, please." Elizabeth hesitated and he moved his hat around in his hands.

"I suppose I am not making myself very clear today," he chuckled. "I'm like that, you know. You would think someone who completed an engineering course would be far more organized with his thoughts." He smiled as Elizabeth waited to hear what he wanted, obviously intrigued.

He held out his hand to her. "I'm Brian Warren," he said, smiling broadly now. Elizabeth blushed slightly. He was very handsome and she could tell he liked her as well. "Dr. Warren's son. I was told he was here. No doubt I've missed him again. He moves like a bolt of lightning."

"Again?" Elizabeth smiled.

"I was over at the cottage on Ivy Mill Lane," he answered. "He has a patient there, a Mr. Morne. Who, I assume, is your relative?" He ended the sentence on a questioning note.

"Yes," Elizabeth responded, not saying more.

"Right," he continued. "They sent me over here to look for him. Of course he would be gone already." He ran his fingers through his hair and gave her another dazzling smile.

"So sorry to have bothered you, Miss Morne," he said. "I'll try to catch him up at home. If he is still there when I get there."

Elizabeth smiled and said, "No bother at all, Mr. Warren."

"Oh, Brian, please," he responded as he started down the path. "My father is Doctor Sir Lewis Warren, don't you know. All this 'Dr. Warren' and 'Sir Lewis' formality... Well, I like just plain Brian."

"Very well then, Brian," Elizabeth smiled again. "If that is the case, you must call me Elizabeth."

"A lovely name, Elizabeth," he said. "I shall remember that. And you." He tipped his hat to her as she leaned against the doorframe, watching him drive off in the distance.

"Well, that's all set for tomorrow," Margery came to see what Elizabeth was doing standing in the open doorway. "It's a bit chilly, dear. Close the door. Who was that?"

"That," Elizabeth said, her voice dreamy, "was a very nice young man named Brian Warren. Dr. Warren's son. He was looking for his father."

"Really?" Margery said, her eyebrows raised. "A very nice young man, was he?"

"Very," Elizabeth agreed, walking slowly upstairs with a smile on her face. Margery breathed a sigh of relief. Whoever had sent Brian Warren to the house this afternoon had been an answer to her prayers. This was the first genuine smile that she had seen on Elizabeth's face since Jack died. She had almost forgotten how much it was like Robert's until today. A smile she hoped to see again tomorrow night.

Chapter Twenty-One

Margery awoke on Friday, full of anticipation and dread at the same time. Robert had not rung her back. Perhaps he would not come, although Rose assured her he would most definitely be coming. As she lay in bed, she thought about the first time she went out with him. May 1913 and the village held a dance at the Village Hall. She and her sister May had made her dress and she had been so excited she was near to bursting as the day drew near. She turned over in bed, looking at the box that held all her memories of Robert. She got up and withdrew the carefully dried camellias that she had worn that night. Her dress had been white with a sky-blue sash. The camellias had once been a blushing pink, but now were dry and fragile. Like she and Robert and their love for one another. Could it be rejuvenated again? Her heart was in her throat as she contemplated what to cook for him. Roast chicken. That would be the thing. It was the first meal they had shared together when she had invited him for her eighteenth birthday in 1913. Her sister May had fussed and flurried, but her roast chicken was always spectacular. Robert had enjoyed it enormously. That meal confirmed to her that she was in love with him, although the trials and travails of their love confirmed the old adage that the road to true love is never smooth. It certainly isn't, Margery thought as she got up. This road has almost been destroyed.

Off to the shops first, then preparing the meal and tidying the house. What would she wear? She opened the cupboard and was taken aback by Jack's things still hanging on the left side. She slumped against the mirror, catching a glimpse of herself. Oh, Margery, she thought, you really have gone downhill. Her hair was all askew, her face lined and drawn. What will he think of me when he sees me fully in this light? She turned from Jack's clothes and looked at her paltry selection of dresses. She and Jack had never gone out socially unless absolutely required. Most of her wardrobe consisted of drab housedresses. The one nice dress she had was a somber affair in navy blue. When she held it up to herself, it made her look like a rather severe matron at a women's prison.

There was nothing else but to find a new dress. Her heart was fluttering although it was only a little after eight o'clock in the morning. I have not felt like this in years, she thought, going downstairs. Like a young girl anticipating her lover's arrival. It made her smile to herself as she could almost see the young girl she once was. How she had worried that Robert would change his mind and not show up after all for that village dance. The kitchen was full of sunshine, the new curtains she had brought from the cottage lighting up the entire room with a brilliance that made it warm and inviting. Jack had never cared what she did with the house. She had always kept things in neutral tones, as if any indication of joy in her life was forbidden. These yellow curtains almost symbolized a release from her prison of sadness.

She began to hum as she put on the kettle and began to make breakfast for her and Elizabeth. Perhaps Elizabeth would accompany her to Caterham so she could find a dress. It would be much quicker and easier if they went by motor. She cracked eggs in a bowl, remembering how she had once been so bold as to walk up to Robert on the High Street and ask him to the village dance. Her heart had been in her throat while she waited for what seemed hours for his reply on that fateful day. That nasty Helen Lassiter was so sure Robert would say no she smiled smugly when Margery returned to the knot of girls eagerly awaiting the answer. Margery gave a final beat to the eggs as the vision of Helen's crestfallen face when she heard Robert was going to the dance with Margery emerged.

"What have those eggs done to you, Mummy?" Elizabeth said, still in her nightgown and robe. "You were beating them to a pulp."

"I was just remembering something," Margery replied, smiling at Elizabeth. "Are you going to the office with Uncle Harry today?"

"Why?" Elizabeth asked, bringing the milk in and setting the bottle on the table.

"I thought we might go shopping together," Margery replied. "I wanted to make a roast chicken with all the trimmings. Just as Auntie May does." She poured the eggs into the pan and put bread into the toaster. Elizabeth was getting cups and plates from the cupboard and began to lay the table.

"You don't need me to go with you into the village, do you?" Elizabeth said. "You are only feeding four people. Although sometimes Uncle Billy eats enough for two." They both smiled at each other. Margery's heart sang to see her daughter smile again.

"It isn't getting the food in, really," Margery said, turning the eggs skillfully in the pan. "I wanted to go into Caterham as well. My wardrobe is appalling. I wanted to buy a new dress for tonight."

Elizabeth's brow furrowed slightly. Her mother had never made much effort with her appearance, although she certainly was a striking looking woman. Dull, loose housedresses, oversize coats, bland headscarves – these were the fashion items her mother always wore. It was almost as if she had not wanted to appear attractive for her father.

"You never seemed to feel you needed a new dress before for any reason, except weddings and funerals," Elizabeth countered. "Why not wear the navy dress?"

"It makes me look old and drab," Margery replied, putting toast and eggs onto plates for Elizabeth and herself. Elizabeth made the tea and brought it to the table.

"I know you are doing it for him," Elizabeth said. "You've never seemed to have wanted to do this when Daddy was alive."

"Daddy didn't notice that sort of thing much," Margery said, trying to keep her voice calm. "He was a practical sort of man."

"And Robert is not?" Elizabeth said, the first time his name had come from her lips.

"He was very elegant as a young man," Margery smiled. "Quite handsome and well-dressed. I don't know what he is like now, but I want to look my best."

Elizabeth was silent, wishing Jack was here so she could tell him how much she understood what he must have suffered. Why did you feel you had to marry her, Daddy? If it was just to give me a name, you could have left afterwards and found a woman who truly loved you, who would have had the excited flush to her face that her mother now had. Why?

Elizabeth sighed heavily. "I've rung my friend Lucy and we are going to go out to the cinema tonight and have a bite to eat afterwards, so I won't be here for dinner. Most likely I will be home around midnight." She looked at her mother with a warning look.

"Yes, I am sure the dinner will be well over with by then," Margery flustered, clearing her plate and Elizabeth's and putting them into the sink. She turned and looked at Elizabeth, the sun streaming in through the yellow curtains and casting a golden glow on her daughter's face.

"I understand you need time to adjust before meeting him," Margery said. "You know I would never force you to do anything you do not want to do, darling." She came over and kissed the top of Elizabeth's head. "I love you too much to ever hurt you."

Elizabeth nodded but her heart was in her throat. "All right, Mummy. We'll go off and buy you a new dress in Caterham. Just don't wear anything too bright outside the house. You are still a widow in mourning to the village."

"Yes," Margery replied, having forgotten that the village judged her harshly for years. Any breach of that would make it unbearable to live here. Maybe she and Robert should just run away and start a new life somewhere else. No, she would not run away. She had done nothing wrong. She had been a good wife to Jack and a good member of the community.

While Elizabeth took her bath, Margery rang up her sister May to tell her the news that Robert would be coming to dinner. She wanted to make sure she had the original recipe just perfect so she could make it the same way he enjoyed it at May's house that long ago day in 1913.

"Harry has just gone off this instant," May's weak voice said when she picked up the phone.

"I wasn't calling about that," Margery replied. "Robert is coming to dinner."

She heard May gasp and say, "When?"

"Tonight," Margery answered. "His doctor was here yesterday and said it would be all right, even advisable. Oh, May," she said, her voice choking, "when I told you and Harry he had come back, I know it sounded unbelievable. I sometimes think I am having a very long dream and I am going to wake up again next to Jack and find it gone."

"Is he well enough to do this?" May asked, coughing lightly.

"The doctor says yes," Margery replied. "I will have to look after him, of course, when the time comes for us to be together again and..."

"Harry says Elizabeth is not happy with this arrangement at all," May interrupted. "She knows Robert is her father and poured her heart out to Harry. He did his best, Marge, truly, to tell her about Robert and you. She seems to want to have none of it. What are you going to do about her? She loved Jack deeply. You know that."

"Yes, of course I know that," Margery retorted sharply, feeling remorseful as her sister kept coughing for several minutes before returning to the receiver. "Jack is dead no matter what we do. I have tried to keep my mouth closed about Jack and all the agony he caused."

"But you did agree to marry him, remember?" May responded.

"Yes, May, I know I did," Margery replied. "Now I am sorry. What an awful mess that decision has caused. The things he has done are inexcusable. If I could only turn the clock back I would change everything."

"But you can't so you had better find ways to reconcile your daughter and your husband," May gasped for air. "Besides, it has been a long time apart for you and Robert. You said there is this nurse who cares for him and loves him. What does he feel for her?"

"For his nurse?" Margery asked. "I am sure he is grateful for her help and her assistance, but love her? No, no, I can't imagine he does." They became quiet then Margery added, "Whose side are you on anyway, May? You seem to be as difficult as Elizabeth about all this. I know you loved Robert, too."

"Of course I did, Marge," May replied. "That was a long time ago and much water has gone under the bridge. Look how people can change in twenty years. You have changed, certainly. So has he, and he has been severely injured. Try to be realistic."

"I love him," Margery responded hotly. "I have always loved him and always will, despite every obstacle and objection thrown in front of me."

May chuckled. "Now I feel as if we have both gone back twenty years when you were so adamant he was the man for you."

"He *is* the man for me, and always has been," Margery replied. "You will see."

"Yes, all right then," May replied. "Now what about the roast chicken recipe you wanted?"

They talked a little more until Elizabeth came downstairs fully dressed and ready to go. "Come on, then, Mummy," she said. "You don't want all the best buys to be picked over, do you?" She smiled at her mother but inside she felt like a traitor to her father. If only she could find it in her heart to be happy for her mother. Every time she looked at her mother's face her heart broke. Her mother seemed like a different woman – smiling, happy, somewhat apprehensive. It reminded her of her friends when they met a new lad and were falling in love. The look on her mother's face was exactly the same. It was as if they had changed roles, and she was the mother and her mother now the daughter with her first love.

The morning was spent going from one dress shop to another in Caterham, each one not offering quite what Margery wanted. Elizabeth was exasperated by the fifth shop.

"What are you looking for, Mummy?" she said, seeing the sad look on her mother's face.

"The Fountain of Youth, darling," she replied as they approached another shop. "I suppose I am looking for a dress that will make me look twenty again. Do you think they might have that in there?" Her eyes were so sad that Elizabeth took her arm and said, "They might, Mummy. You are beautiful the way you are. If he doesn't think so, he doesn't deserve you. Remember, too, Mummy, that he is no longer twenty himself."

"But even in the hospital he looked so very handsome," Margery replied, lost in thought. "So very handsome."

"No doubt he thinks you are Greta Garbo, too," Elizabeth smiled. "Come on."

Margery bought a silky emerald green dress that accentuated all her best features. It felt expensive and elegant and made her feel more beautiful than she knew she was.

"Perfect," Elizabeth murmured, wondering who this lady was standing before her. It wasn't just the dress, she knew; it was the power of love. Would she ever look that way and feel that way about someone? The vision of Brian Warren came back to her as he headed down the path. She blushed as they left the shop.

"What are you thinking about, darling?" Margery smiled, looking up at the blue sky and breathing in the fresh air.

"Nothing much," Elizabeth said as they piled their purchases into the motorcar and headed back to Upper Marstone. "Let's do the rest of the shopping."

All afternoon Margery kept up a flurry of activity, cleaning, chopping, stuffing the chicken, peeling potatoes, and making everything as perfect as possible. The house was redolent with the scents of the meal. Margery had even baked a sponge cake garnished with whipping cream, jam and berries. By five o'clock she was satisfied with everything as Elizabeth came into the kitchen.

"That smells so good I am sorry I am going out," Elizabeth said, looking at the cake and reaching out her finger for a bit of cream.

"Not this cake, darling," Margery said. "I will save a piece just for you."

"You had better have your bath, Mummy," Elizabeth said. "If you like, I can do your hair for you."

"Sweetheart, that would be very special to me," Margery said. "Could you keep an eye on the potatoes? And no fingers in the cake!"

Margery fairly skipped upstairs, using all the scented bath salts she had and luxuriating for a long time. Her hair was still long as she had never felt like bobbing it when other girls did. At times it was a nuisance, but it had been one link with the girl she had once been. Robert had loved her hair and it seemed she had not cut it out of deference to him.

She wrapped her robe tightly around herself, amazed at how beautiful the day seemed to her. Two weeks ago Jack had died, but he had died for her long ago. They had gone through the motions of living together as man and wife. They had never been more than two people joined together by a common tragedy. Robert must understand that. She began to comb her wet hair out, hoping Robert could see that her love for him had never diminished.

Elizabeth knocked at the door, seeing the dreamy expression on her mother's face in the mirror. It struck her again how little she really knew about her mother as a person. Auntie Rose and Auntie May often commented on what an opinionated and headstrong girl she had been. Elizabeth had only seen a loving mother who seemed almost invisible. It was as if someone else had emerged from the cocoon that had once been her mother.

"Shall I do that for you, Mummy?" Elizabeth said, her heart softening toward her mother and her love for this man who had long been thought dead. Margery smiled at her daughter in the mirror.

"I didn't hear you come in, darling," she said. "I guess I was lost in thought."

"When I heard the bath draining, I thought you might be ready for your new coiffure," Elizabeth smiled fondly at her mother, leaning her chin on top of her mother's head. They locked eyes for a moment, their intense expressions matching. "So, what shall it be, Madam? A chignon? A French twist? Or a plait?"

"Oh, nothing too exotic, darling. I don't want him to think he has come to the wrong house." They giggled together as Elizabeth took the rich, chestnut-hair and began to style it into the fashion of the Great War, with a modern twist.

"That is beautiful," Margery exclaimed, looking at all sides

"Now, a dash of French perfume, your new dress, and any man would be foolish not to love you." Elizabeth watched her mother spray herself with perfume and slip into the new dress. She was stunning, no doubt about that, and no wonder both Morne brothers were so mad for her. Her father must have been broken-hearted more than anyone knew to not ever be able to have her love.

"Gorgeous, Mummy, just gorgeous," Elizabeth approved. "It is nearly half-six. I had better make a start, as I said I would pick Lucy up and we would go to Croydon tonight."

"All that way for a movie?" Margery said. "Do be careful, darling."

"It seems to me I remember Auntie May telling me you were always going to Croydon to dance," she smiled at her mother's solicitude. "I am eighteen, you know. As old as you were when you met...Robert."

"Yes, darling that's true," Margery said. "I felt much older."

"So do I," Elizabeth laughed.

"I told Billy and Sally to get here at half-six, so they would be here when Robert arrives," Margery said. "It is amazing that I feel just as nervous as I did when I went to the village dance with him all those years ago."

"Don't be nervous, Mummy," Elizabeth said. "Just be yourself and relax. Please." The look on her face made Margery laugh.

"Yes, mother," she laughed. "Quite a role reversal, isn't it?"

"It seems that all everyone wants is for you to be happy," Elizabeth said thoughtfully. "It was all Daddy ever wanted. He got it wrong, didn't he?"

Margery's face darkened. She did not want to think about Jack and his betrayals, tonight of all nights. "Yes, darling, he got it wrong with me. But not with you."

"I'd best be off now," Elizabeth said, grabbing her hat and coat as the doorbell rang.

They both froze, wondering if Robert was early or if it was Billy and Sally. Margery went to the door and Elizabeth heard Billy's bellowing voice greeting her mother. She breathed a sigh of relief; she could not have handled meeting Robert tonight.

"I hardly recognized you," Billy said as he and Sally came in, both staring in amazement at Margery and her transformation.

"Elizabeth did my hair for me," she smiled almost shyly. "It really is quite in mode, isn't it?"

"Hello, dear," Sally said to Elizabeth, holding her at arm's length. "Where are you off to tonight?"

"Croydon," Margery winced. "Such a long way."

"Come on, Marge. We always went to Croydon. Don't you remember?" Billy chortled. "Got up to all sorts of things, we did.."

"Never mind, Billy," Sally smiled. "No need to corrupt Elizabeth's mind."

Sally walked to the door with Elizabeth, holding her arm. "I know how hard this is for you, dear. It is hard for everyone I imagine. You obviously have made your mother very happy today despite how you feel. You are a wonderful daughter and I know how proud your mother and Jack were of you. Robert will be, too." Elizabeth felt very moved but threw back her head.

"Thank you, Aunt Sally," she said. "This is Mummy's night and I hope all goes well for her."

"Oh, me, too, my dear," Sally replied. "Billy and I will do our best to see that it does."

"Good," Elizabeth said. "Mummy is very vulnerable right now."

"Don't worry and have a lovely evening," Sally said, kissing Elizabeth. "Billy and I are here. I must say I am so excited to see Robert again I feel like a schoolgirl myself."

"He was very handsome, Mummy says," Elizabeth said. "I suppose he still is."

"I would think so," Sally laughed. "He was quite a looker. You are very like him."

"Yes," Elizabeth said. "That is what everyone keeps saying." She turned as she stepped out the door saying, "Goodnight. Have a lovely dinner." Margery ran over to hug and kiss her. "Thank you, darling," she whispered. "Thank you for being so understanding."

"I love you, Mummy," Elizabeth said, running down the path.

"No kiss for your old Uncle?" Billy said as Elizabeth came back and gave him a big hug and kiss, theatrical style.

"What will the neighbors think?" he laughed. Despite all the smiles, Elizabeth sensed they were all very tense and nervous about the dinner.

It was nearly ten minutes to seven as she pulled away quickly and turned around to head toward the High Street. A car was approaching slowly, almost as if it were in a funeral procession. She slowed down and saw Dr. Warren and Louise in the front seat. Wondering if something was wrong, she stopped, then saw Robert sitting in the back, adjusting his cuffs. He looked up suddenly and their eyes met. As everyone said, he looked elegant and indeed was as handsome as his photographs had shown him to be. For a few moments they kept their eyes on each other. Elizabeth looked away and pulled quickly down the High Street, tears coming to her eyes. There was no doubt at all that he was her father. One only had to look at the similarity of expression and his eyes to know that she was his child. What would have been so wrong if they had told her the truth? She pondered this as she drove furiously through the High Street, waving recklessly to a puzzled Uncle Harry who only saw the blur of her face as she sped past.

Chapter Twenty-Two

Robert had been more nervous than Catkins the entire day, so much so that Rose made him go out and make a start on the garden before he made her crazy. As the hour drew near, he had a bath, shaved, and laid out his best navy-blue pin-striped suit and silver-blue tie. He had his original silver watch and a pair of silver cufflinks that Louise had given him one year for his birthday. As he looked in the mirror and fussed with his hair for the tenth time, he chuckled to himself. Jack had hated when he did that. It was one of the primary ways in which they were different.

Lewis showed up around six-thirty to pick up Louise and take Robert to Margery's. He whistled in appreciation at both Robert and Louise, who looked very nice in her camel suit. They made arrangements to pick Robert up at eleven o'clock, thinking that four hours would be enough for his first time out. Louise's worried look all the way to Tilburstow Hill Road made Lewis turn and wink at her.

The houses came into view as Lewis slowed down, looking for number seven. He and Louise spotted Elizabeth and watched as she and Robert looked at one another before she drove off. Robert said, "That was Elizabeth, wasn't it?" Louise nodded as they pulled up in front of the house.

"This is it, my boy," Lewis said, feeling much like a father dropping his son off on a first date. "Just enjoy the evening and relax."

"Right," Robert said, stepping out of the car and looking at the long path to the house. He had asked Louise to get him some flowers to take to Margery, a lovely bouquet of autumn-colored flowers tied with a burnt orange ribbon. He turned once and smiled at both of them, his face a mixture of anticipation and fear. Louise felt her heart nearly breaking at leaving him on his own, so forlorn looking as he turned to the gate.

170

"Please, Louise," Lewis said. "He will be fine, I have no doubt. He has had a good dose of his anti-seizure medicine. Four hours will not cause any problems."

"Unless they have a row," Louise said tartly.

"Now I will not have you being with me tonight and thinking of the utterly charming and devastatingly handsome Mr. Morne," he lectured her, suppressing a smile. "It has been long enough that I have been running in competition with him."

"Competition?" Louise said, surprised. "He is our patient. And someone else's husband."

"True," Lewis said. "He is nearly to the door now. Do you want to wait until he goes in?"

"No, it would be better to go now," Louise said, rummaging in her handbag while Lewis pulled away.

Robert stood on the doorstep, his hands cold with fear. What did he think he was doing, trying to act like a normal man? He felt a strange, swimming sensation in his head, partially the result of the new anti-seizure medication, but also a giddiness he could only associate with the feelings he had as an adolescent. For God's sake I am forty-two years old, he said to himself. It didn't decrease the feelings.

He pushed the doorbell, hearing the chimes from deep within the house. Jack's house, he thought, looking around at the disarrayed garden. It was twice the size of the house they grew up in on the Salisbury Road. He must have done all right for himself with his business.

Margery smoothed her dress and hair before she opened the door. It was not a dream after all, she thought, looking at Robert and seeing once again that young man who had once come to fetch her for the village dance. His tailored, pin-striped suit gave him the air of a city barrister, his cuffs perfect and his tie an exact match. He certainly had not lost any of his bandbox qualities.

"Come in, Robert," she said, ushering him in but not taking her eyes from him.

She looked more beautiful to him than he ever remembered, her eyes showing such love he felt overwhelmed and tripped slightly as he came through. "Are you all right?" she said, the worried look on her face making him almost angry. I don't want her to treat me like a cripple, his thoughts flared.

"Fine," he said, trying to smile. "Just tripped coming over the step." He handed her the flowers and said, "These are for you, Margery."

"They're beautiful," she said, taking him through to the parlor. "I have a surprise for you, Robert. Billy and Sally are here as well." Robert looked startled. Did she think she needed to have someone here to protect her? He thought this would be the chance for them to talk together and decide their future. Why did she invite them?

"Rob," Billy said, slowly unearthing himself from the plush chair. "Don't you look the same old Robbie! Not a hair out of place." Robert smiled at him as Billy grasped both his hands and held them, almost staring into Robert's face. What is he looking for? Robert thought angrily. Does he think every time anyone says anything to me I react by having a seizure?

"Oh, Robbie," Sally said, moving from behind Billy's bulk to look at him, her eyes full of tears. "Oh, Robbie." Without another word she threw her arms around him and held him close to her, murmuring his name and then looking into his face. "Robbie, how incredible this all is. To see you again, to know you are with us again, well...."

"There, now, Sal," Billy said, taking her shoulders. "Unhand that poor man, will you?" He grinned at Robert, who felt familiar yet alien at the same time in this house. Jack's house. It kept going round and round in his head that this was Jack's house, where Margery lived as his wife and where Elizabeth grew up as his daughter. Jack was everywhere, in every stick of furniture and every speck of dust. Sally motioned him to sit down in the chair vacated by Billy. They didn't really look all that different, he thought. He remembered both of them, which was something he was afraid he wouldn't be able to do. They began talking aimlessly about the village and their children. Robert asked polite questions about all their children and updates on the business. He felt as if he had been invited to a tea party where he was the guest of honor among total strangers.

Margery came back in with the flowers in the vase, everyone murmuring how lovely they were and how they added to the festivities of the occasion. "What's that I smell for dinner?" Billy said, a slight nervousness appearing on his face. Rob seemed different in a way he couldn't identify. He didn't think he would just jump in and act as he once did. Too many years had passed. There was a synthetic quality about him, something unreal, as if he were just going through the motions of being Rob. Sally noticed it, too, he was sure. Perhaps it was just the medication.

"Would you all like to come through?" Margery asked, leading them into the dining room. "I've made roast chicken and potatoes, peas, fresh bread and butter, and baked a lovely sponge cream cake for dessert." She stood proudly by the table, the food smelling delicious and the table set beautifully. Two tapers were lit and a chilling bottle of wine stood next to her plate.

I should open the wine, Rob thought. Jack would have, no doubt. Was he sitting in Jack's chair? If Jack was her husband, he must have sat at the head of the table, where he now sat. His vision dimmed slightly as the thought that he was becoming Jack made him dizzy.

"Steady on, Rob," Billy said, touching his sleeve. "You all right?"

"Fine, just fine," Robert snarled. "I don't need a keeper, you know."

"Of course not, Robert," Margery said nervously, her smile fading as she passed the potatoes to Billy, who took a generous serving. "We know that you are...."

"Crippled?" he nearly shouted. "Mad? What do you know?" He sat back, his head pounding as everyone looked at him in shock.

"Come on, Robbie," Billy said. "No one thinks that. We are overjoyed that you are back. It is all hard to believe, that's all. Eat up. It's too good to miss." He smiled at Rob and put his hand on his arm.

"That's not the same watch you had all these years, is it?" he said, rushing into a new topic. "How come the RAMC robbers didn't get it?" He grinned at Rob, who seemed to have calmed down and returned the smile.

Margery looked at Sally, her face flushed and they passed a silent understanding between them. Thank God for Billy, Margery thought. He always had the knack of defusing a situation before it got untenable. Robert seemed edgy, but was talking amiably enough with Billy about his watch.

The rest of the meal passed uneventfully as they talked about old times and old memories. It was evident that Robert did not remember everything they talked about, but nodded in agreement or smiled vacantly. Lewis's words came back to her in full force "He is not the boy you once knew." As he sat there trying to keep up with the conversation, she could see the boy was still in there, trying desperately to be the person he once was.

The cake and coffee were served in the parlor as they continued to talk. They steered clear of any mention of Jack or the War, instead talking of old neighbors and people in the village. Robert mainly listened, again the look on his face belying the fact that he did not quite remember. Billy kept them laughing at tales from the farm equipment business until the clock chimed nine.

"Let me help you clear up," Sally said. Margery waved her away.

"No, Sally, don't bother," she said. "I know you two have to get home to your children." She nodded to Billy, who was still regaling a slightly bewildered Rob with another story about someone from their boyhood days.

173

"Come on, Billy," Sally said, handing him his coat. "You will tire Robert out completely with all your talking." She smiled at him and came over to Robert.

"Welcome home, Robbie," she whispered in his ear, hugging him tightly and giving him a kiss. "You were missed more than you know."

He smiled at Sally, remembering her as always being one of the nicest girls in the village. "Thank you, Sally. Thank you." He gave her a kiss on the cheek and hugged her.

"Hardly been home and look at him already, making passes at my wife," Billy grinned. "Same old Robbie."

"Not really, Billy," Robert said, looking serious. "Not really."

"Well, I meant, it's just..." Billy started as Sally took him to the door. "Good night everyone," she said. Billy went over to Rob and took his hands. "Sometimes I didn't believe in God, not since the War," he began, looking into Rob's eyes. "Now I know he exists. Goodnight, mate. Welcome back."

Robert and Margery stood by the door together, watching Billy and Sally go down the path, turning and waving. They could hear their laughter as they got into the car, and watched them drive away in silence.

"Shall we go back into the parlor?" Margery asked, looking at Robert next to her. She wanted to call him darling, wanted to kiss him, but he seemed cold and forbidding. Why? Was it her note? Perhaps he was not feeling well. She knew this was his first time out alone.

He nodded and they went back in, the remains of the coffee and cake sitting on the low table in front of the settee. He seemed to be brooding as he settled himself on the settee instead of the chair, where he had been sitting previously.

"Are you feeling all right?" Margery asked, disturbed by the look on his face.

"Please don't treat me like a patient," he retorted. "I'm fine."

"I'm sorry, Robert," Margery said, stung by his words. "I am not sure what to say. I do not know how your health is normally."

"Don't dwell on it," he nearly spat the words. "Do you think I cannot see how everyone is so very careful when they talk to me? 'Don't say this' or he might have a seizure; 'Don't do this' or he might have a seizure. It makes it damn difficult to feel as if I am like everyone else. Which I am not, of course."

"Yes, you are," Margery said, sitting next to him and taking his hand in hers. "You have been injured and you are not the same as you were in that respect. You are still you. You will always be my Robert."

"And did you say that to Jack as well?" he retorted angrily. "Was he 'your Jack'? I look around in this house and all I can think is, 'This is where Jack and Margery Morne live with their daughter Elizabeth.' That is what others must think, too." He laughed, a growling sort of sound. "Do you know what Jack said to me on that night I tried to come home? 'Ghosts have no place in Upper Marstone.' He was right."

"No, he was not right," Margery said angrily. "You are being totally irrational about this. Yes, I married Jack. I had to, because I was pregnant with your child. There was no other recourse."

"No other recourse but to marry the one person in the world I would never want you to marry?" he scoffed. "That makes no sense to me, even if I have half a brain."

"You do not have half a brain," Margery said, getting up from the settee. "But you are only using half of it if you insist on not understanding everything that happened since you were missing, believed killed."

"You married Jack and let Elizabeth believe he was her father," he said bluntly. "What else is there to know?"

"There is much to know," she said, turning around as she cleared up the plates loudly. He seemed to be shaking slightly. Was he going to have a seizure? She tried to calm herself down. He stood up suddenly, shaking.

"Maybe I don't want to know," he said, nearly knocking over the table as he got up. "Whatever you tell me I will never believe it. You married him and lived with him as his wife. What else could possibly change that?"

"You are being unreasonable, Robert, totally unreasonable," she was shouting now, even though she kept telling herself to remain calm. "I have never known this side of you before. Perhaps that injury of yours has changed you for the worst. No one ever crosses you, do they? That nurse is so devoted to you she would probably let you beat her every night if you wanted to." Robert looked up at her, startled by this accusation. "Oh, yes, I saw how much she loves you. She is like a lovesick cow. Who is it that she loves? This spoiled, selfish boy-man that you are? You are so used to being catered to because of your head injury you refuse to listen to anyone but those who coddle you so you won't have a seizure."

She stomped off to the kitchen, her head aching and her eyes burning with tears. Physically he was the Robert she had once loved, so heartbreakingly beautiful to her she wanted to make love with him in the parlor. The man inside the body was someone else, someone she didn't know. He seemed determined to make her pay for doing what she thought was right for his daughter. No matter how she tried to explain it to him, he would not listen.

175

She heard a thump and ran into the parlor, only to find it empty. Frantically she searched the room, then noticed the front door open. He had slammed it against the wall on his way out. He can't go out there alone and in this state, Margery thought. Oh, God, what have I done?

She pulled on her old cloth coat over the dazzling silk dress that now made her feel foolish and vain. "Robert!" she shouted, not seeing him anywhere along the road. "Robert!" She ran toward the village unable to see him. The road bent at the Bell, where laughter and smoke emanated from the interior. Perhaps he went in there? She ran in, but was met only with blank stares from the villagers.

There was no way to determine where he had gone. She went back to the house and thought it best to phone Louise. If he had a seizure and was ill, she would know what to do. She rang Rose's cottage. Rose told her Louise was out with Dr. Warren. Not wanting to upset Rose, she told her she had wanted to ask a question about Robert's medication as he had a slight headache. No need to worry. Everything was fine. Rose's hearty chuckle as she rang off made Margery's throat tighten. Everything is far from all right, she choked. He may be lying somewhere having a seizure.

She rang Billy and Sally and told them what happened. Alarmed, they told her they would be right over. It seemed like seconds when they arrived at her doorstep. Sally took her into the parlor and sat down with her. Billy stood at the door, his face a mask of confusion and sadness.

"I'll go look for him," he said firmly. "Don't worry, I'll find him." He went off and they heard the tires squealing as he pulled away.

"What has happened?" Sally asked, holding Margery close to her.

"I do not know him anymore," Margery choked out her words. "I don't know him."

She told Sally what happened, jumping every time she heard a car door slam. It was now a little after ten o'clock and no sign of Robert. He had been gone for nearly an hour.

Billy drove aimlessly, trying to figure out where Rob might have gone. Obviously he had not returned to Rose Henning's cottage, as Margery had rung there. Where would he go? Salisbury Road? He couldn't get in, could he? Who knows how Rob thought anymore. He was different, that was certain. Was it his injury or something else? He had seemed nervous and jumpy, the way people are who have something on their minds but haven't said it out loud.

He drove around for ten minutes before it struck him: Diana's Fountain. It was the place where Rob and Margery often went when they were courting. He drove as close as he could, then got out and walked down the winding path to the spring where the lovers of Upper Marstone frequented.

The water was gurgling softly but the night had become very chilly. Billy drew his coat around him, finding the once-easy path difficult to maneuver with his added bulk and years. As he came upon the clearing, he saw Rob sitting on a rock, staring out over the water.

"This is not the place to come to alone, Morne," Billy said, approaching him carefully. "You have to bring a girl. That's the rule."

Rob turned to look at him. "What will they think if you and I are sitting out here together then?" He grinned at Billy, so like he once was Billy was unnerved.

"Unless we want to get arrested, we best get out of here, right?" Rob nodded, taking Billy's extended hand as they climbed back up to the top and went to Billy's car.

They sat together in silence for a few minutes before Rob said, "I was a fool tonight, Billy. She is the most beautiful woman in the world and I love her. Why did I say those things to her? Why?" He put his fist to his forehead, shaking his head.

"We men have a propensity to say stupid things to our women on a regular basis," Billy said. "Just ask Sally. If she kept a record of all the daft things I said to her over the years it would stretch from one end of the village to the next. So join the club." He grinned at Rob who returned it.

"I think what we need, mate, is a couple of pints and a good talk," Billy said. "Hare and Hounds?"

"Right," Rob grinned. "Although I am not supposed to drink too much with the medication."

"Just this once," Billy said. "I'll see you home safely."

Once inside the Hare and Hounds, Billy chose a secluded booth and ensconced Rob inside. No use having people come up to stare at him or ask him questions. Time enough for that later. Tonight he had to talk to Rob about Jack.

"I'll get this round," Billy said after Rob sat down. "You can get the next one."

"Right," Rob said, looking around like a child in a new place. Billy watched him trying to remember. They hardly ever came in here when they were young.

After a quick word with the barman, Billy went over to use the telephone to call Margery.

"He's all right," Billy said, muffling his voice. "We're at the Hare and Hounds having a pint."

"Where was he?" Margery asked.

"Diana's Fountain, just as I suspected," Billy replied. "I'm going to talk to him about Jack, Marge. He needs to know the whole story. Somehow I think coming from me it will be easier to take."

"I don't know, Billy," Margery sobbed. "I think I should be the one to tell him."

"It will be easier and less emotional coming from me," Billy said calmly. "Both of you are so highly charged up right now I don't think you can make sense of what the other is trying to say."

"All right, Billy," Margery said.

"It will be all right, Marge," Billy said before he hung up. "Believe me on this."

"I hope you are right," she sobbed. "I love him so."

"I know I am right," Billy replied. "He loves you. He told me how much he loves you when we were at Diana's Fountain. Which is why I need to sort him out about Jack. Tonight." He replaced the receiver, picked up the pints at the bar, took a deep breath, and headed to the booth to try to explain the most complicated mess he had ever seen.

Chapter Twenty-Three

Lewis caught Louise's eyes as she kept watching Robert until they pulled off the road and headed back toward Caterham. "He will be fine, Louise," Lewis said softly as the road unwound in the gathering darkness.

"I know he will," Louise snuffled. "I suppose I am just afraid she will upset him once again as she has done before. Without me there I don't know what he'll do."

Lewis didn't respond, thinking of how to put this gently. "He will survive. Has it occurred to you, with all your devotion, that perhaps it has stopped his progress?"

Louise swiveled her head quickly. Without looking Lewis could feel the glare of her eyes. "As a professional nurse I would never do anything that would impede my patient's progress. Never." She folded her arms, smarting from the insult to her professionalism and knowledge.

"Not knowingly, of course," Lewis said. "But the latest research on head injuries indicates that it is sometimes necessary to be cruel to be kind. You know that is true of other diseases and injuries. How often have we been accused of administering a medication or treatment where the cure is worse than the disease?" He smiled at her, the flash of his teeth lighting up the dark, country lane on which they were driving.

"I have encouraged him to be independent," Louise retorted. "It was I who suggested to Dr. Gibbons that he take the gardener's position at the hospital. I have accompanied him to concerts, art galleries and other events in Worthing. I helped him buy clothes and get his confidence back before going out into the world. Sometimes he is overwhelmed by it all. Should I just ignore him when he is like that? Let him fall, literally and figuratively? That goes against all my training, Doctor."

"Lewis," Lewis corrected her. "You needn't convince me of your professional judgment, Louise. I know you are the consummate nurse. I

179

just have to add that I think that Robert Morne has become more than a patient to you. That can cloud your judgment when you are trying to help him. Your dislike for Margery does not help."

"I do not dislike Margery," Louise replied. "In fact, she was very friendly when we were in Sussex. I just do not like her effect on Robert. It might kill him if she persists in upsetting him every time they meet. That is why I am so nervous about his seeing her alone tonight."

Lewis turned the car expertly toward Croydon, the road becoming wider and more well-traveled as they passed other cars. They didn't speak for a long time. "At the risk of pulling rank on you, Louise, I want you to remember that I am his doctor. While I respect your opinion of his condition and your assessment of what he can and cannot undertake, I must overrule you on his relationship with Margery. He is much, much stronger than he lets on. You are so close to him that you cannot see him as I do. The new medication has almost controlled his seizures totally. While there is still danger, of course, that under severe duress he might have another incident as he did, I think he will be able to handle things very well. If he wants to, that is."

"Of course he wants to," Louise snapped. "Seeing Margery again is all he has talked of for years."

"Ah, but our dreams often pale in the face of reality. Now he is face-to-face with his dream in the flesh," Lewis said as the lights of Croydon came into view. "The dream Margery is in reality a middle-aged woman with an opinionated, obstructive daughter, a marriage to his brother, and a lot of explaining to do. He is a very severely injured man who will never function fully in society. It is easy, very easy, to go back into the cocoon that you offer him, where you comfort him and cosset him and make everything right in his world."

"You make me sound like his mother," Louise snorted.

"In some ways you function that way," Lewis replied. "What I am seeing is a man-child. He is, for all intents and purposes, still a twenty-three-year old boy whose life stretches before him. You treat him as if he is that boy who was wounded. He still lives there in his mind. Now he is being forced to take his place among other middle-aged war veterans who have been fighting it out, trying to find work, marrying, raising children, and learning the lessons of maturity. He has not. When the going gets tough, he can come to you and you will wipe away his tears, or his seizures, as the case may be."

"It certainly isn't his fault that he has been locked away, unable to function normally," Louise said angrily. "You almost sound as if he is doing this willfully."

"No, no, Louise, of course he is not," Lewis said wearily. "What I am saying is that if you offer him a soft place to land every time he encounters something difficult, he will never leave you." He became quiet and added, "Perhaps that is what you really want."

"All I have ever wanted for Robert James Morne is to see him happy," Louise said, tears welling up in her eyes. "I do not like to see him hurt by the cruel comments and the stares of people who do not understand that he is not a freak, or a corpse come back from the dead, but a full man."

"Then let him be that," Lewis said softly. "Being a full man means he will have to learn how to handle the cruelty, the stares, and the rejections. I believe he was most likely a very sensitive young man, acutely aware of the horrors in the world. No doubt the War has affected him deeply because of his own personality. Protecting him further, Louise, will not help make him happy. He will forever be a prisoner, albeit a prisoner of love and caring."

Louise snuffled into her handkerchief, the realization that Robert was slipping away more quickly than she realized striking her hard. Did Lewis know she loved him?

"I love him, Lewis," she said outright, seeing his hands grip the steering wheel tightly. "I think I loved him that first day I saw him at Etaples. Why, I cannot say. Can anyone say why they love someone? Yes, I know he is severely impaired. Perhaps in some strange way that makes it easier to love him. All my life I have accepted whatever fate has dealt me and never complained. But I will fight to the death to make sure Robert is happy. If Margery is no longer his dream, than I will be there to catch him when he wakes up."

Lewis sighed, the words now said out loud. Louise had been denying her feelings for Robert for so long it had become a grotesque parody as she tried to hide it from everyone.

"All right, Louise," he said in almost a professional tone. "If you want to have a life with a man who in some ways will never stop pining for the boy he was, and therefore will never become the man he should, then carry on. As his doctor, I do not want to see him cease to progress. As a man I do not want to see him become a little boy for the rest of his life."

He pulled up to the restaurant where he had made a reservation, planning for a pleasant night with the woman he loved. Should he tell her that? He had wanted to, but now her admission of love for Robert Morne made him reconsider. More than likely she would see it only as a ploy to detract her from Robert.

"Please, Louise, I know I sounded harsh," Lewis said, turning to her but she refused to look at him. "It is not only for his good that I worry. It is yours as well." He took her hand but she did not respond. "Can we at least be professional and enjoy dinner together? Peace between us?" He smiled as she looked up.

"I apologize, Lewis," she said. "I just thought you should know how I feel about him. Until I see him happy and safe of his own choosing, then I cannot let him go. From my care or my heart."

"Ah, I had forgotten how stubborn you are, Louise," he smiled again. "Well, let us go in and raise a glass to Mr. Morne and his continued good health and improvement."

Despite their earlier conversation, they enjoyed a splendid meal in a stylish, modern restaurant in the center of Croydon. Lewis found himself fascinated by Louise's lack of self-consciousness when talking to him about medical topics and her powerful insights into the profession of neurology. What a mind, he kept thinking as she spoke, but he also found the light in her eyes captivating. A light, she had so thoroughly chastised him earlier, that seemed to burn only for Robert Morne.

"Shall we go back to 'The Warren,' for a drink?" Lewis suggested, using the colloquial name of his house. "It is still too early to fetch Robert. Going to the cinema or elsewhere might make us late."

"All right," Louise replied. "Perhaps you can give me the grand tour of the house."

"With pleasure, my lady," he said, smiling so long at her she blushed.

They were comfortably ensconced in the drawing room, their cut-glass tumblers reflecting the golden flames of the roaring fire. Louise sat primly on the deeply-cushioned sofa, finding that, despite her outburst earlier in the evening, a sense of peace and contentment came over her. The room was large, but not cold and unwelcoming, and the furniture very modern yet cozy.

"Penny for your thoughts?" Lewis smiled. "As if I don't already know. Robert."

"No, actually. I was just thinking how comfortable I feel in this room," Louise replied. "I have become so used to living in one little room and never having a place to call my own that this feels rather nice."

"The entire house is like that," Lewis said, sipping his whisky. "Looks large and imposing. Constance had a way of making things beautiful and comfortable." Louise blanched at the thought of this being Constance's work. Of course, she had been very artistic, a trait Louise sorely lacked. The colorful modern art paintings that surrounded them seemed to remind her of her lack of artistic abilities.

"Did you love her, Lewis?" Louise plunged ahead.

"Did I love her?" he said, staring into the fire. "Yes, in some ways I did, but not the sort of love that transcends all barriers. We were good for one another in some ways. She never understood my work, of course, or my devotion to it and my patients. I never really understood how she could find some of those obnoxious artistic types talented. But we muddled along and had a strong affection for one another."

"But did you love her?" Louise persisted as the door opened.

"Oh, sorry, Dad, I didn't realize you were entertaining anyone." Brian Warren came in, dressed casually in a dark blue jumper and grey flannel trousers, his feet in carpet slippers. "I was just coming in to ...."

"Nip some of my whisky, no doubt," Lewis smiled at him. "Go on, help yourself. Why not come and join us?"

"Lovely. Thanks, Dad." He poured himself a tumbler and asked if anyone wanted a refill. After pouring another glass for his father, Brian sat down on the sofa next to Louise. "I know you, don't I? Have we met?"

Louise smiled at him. "I am the nurse, Louise Whiting, that you met the other day when you were searching for your father. Ivy Mill Lane in Upper Marstone?"

"Oh, right," he grinned. "Then I went over to look for him at the other house, but he had already absconded from there as well. Breaking the land speed record, my Dad." Father and son grinned at one another. "I am glad I went over there, you know. There is a smashing, absolutely smashing girl who lives there. Told me her name was Elizabeth. What a looker she is." He gulped his whisky and looked at the subdued faces around him. "Sorry, have I said something wrong? Is she spoken for?"

"No," Lewis said. "She is just part of the whole incredible mess that Louise and I have been discussing all evening."

"Mess?" Brian asked, looking from face to face, his grin fading. "Is she in some sort of trouble?"

Lewis and Louise filled him in on the details of the story, explaining the triangle between Robert, Jack and Margery, and the repercussions for Elizabeth. Brian listened attentively, asking questions, then sat back and whistled low.

"A mess indeed," he commented. "And that poor bloke! To walk back into your life to find all that out. I'm surprised he hasn't collapsed from it all."

"He's much stronger than he looks," Lewis winked at Louise. "It remains to be seen how things will go. He is having dinner with his wife tonight, after nearly twenty years apart."

"Well, fingers crossed for both of them and best of luck, I say," Brian added. "Did you say that Elizabeth's father... Jack, wasn't it? That he owned a motor repair business in Upper Marstone? Are they keeping the business, do you know?"

Lewis and Louise shook their heads, then Lewis said, "Are you thinking of putting a bid in on that, Brian? I didn't think big motor repairs and fleets were quite what you wanted. More in the aeroplane line, I thought." Brian nodded and said, "There is room for expansion, no doubt. I like motors of all sorts, Dad, you know that. This engineering degree you paid for did not go to waste, at least when it comes to understanding mechanics. This might be a good chance for me to take over a successful business, expand it, and incorporate other areas eventually. I wonder if they are interested in selling it."

"At this point I think it might be a touchy subject with them," Louise advised. "Elizabeth is not coping well with all the shocking news she has received. She refuses to meet Robert, her real father. She was quite devoted to Jack, Robert's brother, and considers him her father, despite what she now knows." She set her lips firmly and looked into the fire.

"Well, that is understandable isn't it, Miss Whiting?" Brian asked. "I mean, here she is, a young girl with a Dad she loves. Then this other man appears, and her mother tells her *he* is her father. I don't know what I would have thought, especially if I loved my Dad." He sipped his whisky. "I don't blame her, really. If everyone is pressing her about accepting him, she will just keep pushing against it." He gulped the rest of his drink down and looked directly at Louise. His gaze was unnerving, as he looked so much like the young Lewis she felt pulled back in time.

"From the mouths of babes," Lewis said, looking at the mantel clock. "I suppose we had better make a start for Upper Marstone and pick up our patient." He thought and said, "Or perhaps I had better stop thinking of him that way, now that he is trying to find his life again."

"Probably I am being romantic," Brian mused. "But if these two people love one another truly, they will find a way to be back together. I still can't help but feel for that poor man, though. Nearly twenty years locked away in hospital, not knowing who you are or that you have a wife and daughter." He whistled again, his expression so pained Louise smiled at him.

"You are a very astute young man and I am so happy to have made your acquaintance," she said, extending her hand as he shook it. "I hope we see each other again."

"Thank you," he replied. "Do you think it would do any harm to pop round there next week just to have a look at the business? I definitely do not want to upset anyone with all that's going on. It sounds just ideal for what I hope to do."

"No, but tread carefully," Lewis advised. "From what I can gather that poor girl believes everyone is trying to forget Jack Morne. She might view selling the business as another way of doing that."

"I shall put on my very best bib and tucker and all the charm I possess," Brian grinned. "No hard sell or anything like that. I did get my charm from mother, you know. She always said that you lacked charm, Dad. Quite to the point and direct." He grinned at his father, but caught Lewis looking at Louise with an admiration and a strange expression on his face. It didn't take Brian long to realize that the expression he was seeing was one that had long been absent from his father's face. It was the look of love.

Chapter Twenty-Four

The Hare and Hounds was full of smoke and murmured voices, the gold fittings around the bar diminished in the dim light. Billy carried the pints back to the hidden corner booth. He not only wanted a quiet, secluded place to talk to Rob, but wanted to avoid the prying eyes and nosy questions of villagers who were running rampant with their gossip about Robert's return from the dead.

At the shop they talked of him being a 'zombie,' as one man put it, or so disfigured he could not show himself in public. They said he had violent outbursts, that he had attacked one of the nurses, and was uncontrollable. That was the reason Jack Morne refused to bring him home to the village, because Robert was not able to resume a normal life. It made Billy's blood boil to listen to the gossip. Until Robert walked down the High Street and showed himself, no one would listen to his denials of these ridiculous stories.

Then there was the more insidious gossip. That Robert had attacked Jack and Jack had fired at him in self-defense. Everyone knew Robert had been engaged to Margery. Now Robert was coming home to demand his rights, pushing Jack out of the way. Billy knew that Jack had been well-liked in the village. He was pleasant, a good businessman, and contributed to the village welfare. He had mellowed, people said, especially after marrying Margery. No one could believe Jack would do what it was said he did a few weeks ago on that road to Caterham.

So it must be Robert. Perhaps Robert was violent, and Jack was only trying to stop him from hurting someone. Those who remembered Robert found it difficult to believe, yet many of them had experienced loved ones who came home from the War seriously damaged by it. Billy himself suffered violent outbursts in his sleep. As one man put it, "Them gentler sorts like Robert Morne turn the most violent when exposed to warfare."

186

Billy could almost hear the village waiting with bated breath to see if Margery and Robert would take up together again, in the face of village disapproval. Little did they know, Billy thought, that Rob and Margery were already married. Still, it would not do for them to act like man and wife so soon after Jack's demise. In the village she was still Jack's wife. And Elizabeth was still Jack's daughter.

"You all right?" Billy said as he pushed the pint to Rob. "Anyone annoy you?"

"No, but I did catch a few looks," Rob replied. "I feel like an escaped criminal."

Billy ran his hands through his hair, then lifted his glass. "Here's to you, mate," he said as Rob hoisted his glass. "It is a long, hard road back. Lots of people don't understand, as you can see already. You have to be tough about it."

"Tough?" Rob laughed. "If there is one thing I am now, Billy, it is tough. These past few weeks have made me so tough I feel as if I could qualify as a training sergeant in the Army." He gulped some bitter and looked at Billy. "What am I going to do? I seem to have the wrong end of the stick about everything. Nothing, nothing is going as I dreamed it would. Do you know I would lie in that damn hospital bed, day after day, dreaming of coming home here, of finding Margery again? I suppose I thought it would all have stopped in 1916. I would be the same person I was, she would be the same, the village would be the same. It was a dream, all right." He took another long draught of beer.

"It's not a dream," Billy said.

"No, it's a bloody nightmare," Rob interrupted. "Tonight, there was nothing I wanted more in the world than to be with Margery. No offense to you and Sally, but she felt she needed someone there as a buffer. She was afraid to be alone with me. Afraid, I sensed it." He looked into his glass.

"We're all afraid, Robbie," Billy began. "It's natural, because we are not medical people and we don't know what to expect. You had a hell of a seizure in hospital when she came to visit. It frightened her out of her skin. She thought she killed you. So tonight she wanted it to be perfect. If you had a seizure, or if she thought she did anything to make you upset, she didn't want to be alone and have you die on her. Try to see it from her point of view."

"That's all everyone keeps telling me," Rob nearly shouted. "Try to see it from everyone else's point of view. Well, what about my point of view? I'm the poor bugger who had half his head blown away and spent years not knowing who the hell he was. I'm the one who has seizures at the

187

drop of the pin that no one seems able to control and it makes the people I love afraid of me. I'm the one whose brother kept him away from his one chance of happiness and then tried to kill me. So, why the bloody hell should I care about everyone else's damn point of view?" He stared at Billy, his eyes sparking. Billy prayed that he would not have a seizure right here.

"All right, all right, keep your voice down," Billy cautioned. "You don't want these nosy parkers coming over here to find out what all the shouting is about, do you?" Rob shook his head. "Now, listen. I need to tell you the story and you have to try to understand. If you don't, then forget about Margery. It's up to you." Rob looked up, his eyes inquisitive but apprehensive.

"Here it is, unvarnished," Billy said after taking a big draught of beer. "Should we have another before I start?"

"Right," Rob nodded, taking out some money. "On me. Please."

Billy got refills and hurried back to the booth. "First of all, no one knew you and Margery were married in Folkestone. Not Sally. Not me. Margery never told anyone. Why? Apparently that is what you and she agreed, because you wanted to break it to your parents yourself once the papers came through. Right? Do you remember that?"

Vaguely, in some part of his brain, it came back to Rob. He knew his mother would have hit the ceiling when she heard about what he had done in Folkestone. He remembered telling Margery to send him copies of the papers when she got them, so he could inform his commanding officer and make it official. Then he was going to tackle his parents.

"Yes," Rob said hesitantly.

"So Marge comes home, with her secret marriage, and tells no one. Not until after she married Jack, anyway. Then she told her sister May, and swore her to secrecy. May didn't even tell her husband."

"May?" Rob asked. "Does she still live in the village? Their name was…"

"Cross," Billy said impatiently. "May and Harry Cross. They still live in the same cottage where Marge lived then."

"By the church," Rob smiled.

"Right," Billy said, eager to go on while he had the steam. "Then everything seemed to happen at once. You know Jack had been conscripted into the Army Service Corps. He was off on training when all this happened. Marge apparently began to suspect she was going to have a baby, and kept waiting for the marriage certificate to appear in the post so she could finally tell the world about your marriage, especially as her condition would start to become obvious. Then your Dad came over one night in early October. Right around this time." Rob shivered involuntarily.

"They got the telegram that you were missing," Billy said. "He went over to tell Marge, because he thought she should know. He loved Marge, you know. Doted on Elizabeth." Rob put his head down, staring into the white foamy bubbles in his glass.

"Why didn't she get the marriage certificate in the post?" Rob said.

"Well, that was a mystery she couldn't understand," Billy continued. "She couldn't go to Folkestone to look on her own, and didn't know where to write. Things were looking pretty desperate at this point for her. Then Jack came home on embarkation leave."

Rob drew in his breath sharply. "I can just guess what happened," he said bitterly.

"Give it a fair listen," Billy scolded. "You wanted to hear it out, so listen."

Rob became quiet and motioned Billy to continue. "They were commiserating over you," Billy said. "Marge refused to give you up for dead. She wanted to believe that you were only wounded, or a prisoner. Turns out she was right," Billy mused. "Still, at that time, no one had any definite information. Then she told Jack she was pregnant with your child. Jack offered to go to Folkestone to find the certificate and bring it back with him. He said he would explain to your parents and make sure Margery was all right."

Rob shifted in his seat. Is that what Jack told everyone? He couldn't believe it and it showed on his face.

"He did do that, Robbie," Billy said. "He wanted to help Margery. And you."

"Go on," Rob growled, not convinced of his brother's largesse.

Billy took a long sip of bitter and continued. "The bloke at the Registration Office could find no record of your marriage. None. He took Jack's name and address and said he would forward it if anything came up. It was this bloke who suggested that maybe you had duped Margery into sleeping with you by saying you were married."

"The dirty bugger," Rob swore. "What did he know about it?" He clenched his fists.

"Well, lots of soldiers were not as honorable as you, Mr. Morne, if you take my meaning," Billy said. "How would this bloke know you weren't like that lot?"

Rob nodded, seeing the sordid story unfold before him. "So Jack came home empty-handed and Margery believed we were not married, right?"

"Wrong," Billy said. "Margery always believed you were married, but somehow the proof was lost. She could not claim your pension or anything else. Jack was afraid of what would happen to her. She would be thrown out of her job, she would be made an outcast in the village, and what would become of her and her child? She could not rely on your parents, especially your mother. Jack knew, too, how much your mother disliked Marge. She probably would have said it was not your child." He waited until all this sunk in, watching as Rob obviously was back in time in his mind.

"So Jack offered to marry her, on the condition that if you returned, he would step aside for you," Billy rushed the words together, afraid of the reaction. "I think he believed, as I would have, that you would not come back. You know what it was like out there, Rob. No one came back. Not usually. Jack even went and looked through the corpses at Thiepval because your Dad asked him to find you." Rob looked shocked, his face registering anguish. What a thing to ask Jack to do! For a second his heart softened toward his brother and the horrifying task he endured.

"So Jack did what he thought was the only thing he could do," Billy said carefully. "He asked Marge to marry him, to give her and your child legitimacy and your name. Apparently she refused him, over and over, until her condition was becoming so apparent and she could not refuse any longer. She did it for Elizabeth, Rob. For her future."

"But she did marry him, and he was her husband," Rob said, his face a mask of anger and sadness. "She must have felt something for him. Otherwise, why not leave him after the marriage?"

Billy waited before responding. "She always was fond of him in a 'stray dog' sort of way, Robbie. You know that. But it was not love. Never."

Rob looked at him. "I still find it hard to believe that she could live with him as his wife for nearly twenty years and not feel something beyond a 'stray dog' feeling for him."

Billy laughed harshly. "You're just determined to be thick about this, aren't you? Well, ask Sally, then. You know women discuss their intimate details with one another. And do you know what? Marge never slept with him. That's right, never. You were the only one she ever wanted. She told Jack that straight out when she married him. He agreed to all her terms."

"Why didn't she tell Elizabeth I was her father?" Rob asked, the anguish increasing in his voice.

"Why?" Billy said. "It was almost a concession to Jack, as he adored Elizabeth. She was everything to him and the only person in his life who loved him for himself. Think about that, Rob. You were always the one everyone loved. No one loved Jack. Elizabeth did. How could Margery

190

deny him that? She believed you were dead then. It wouldn't have made a difference. She never told any of us until recently. We all suspected you were her father. Just look at her." Rob nodded, the vision of Elizabeth's face as she passed him in the car earlier in the evening still strong. "Besides, Margery wanted to protect Jack from appearing the cuckold, even though almost everyone knew it."

"He loved her that much that he would endure that," Rob murmured.

"He was obsessed with her, Rob," Billy continued. "I know what he did in keeping your existence secret was wrong. He was afraid, because he knew what Marge would do. Run to you, never looking back, and taking what he now thought of as his daughter with her. He would lose everything. He always felt that you got the best, and he got nothing. It made him almost...mad, I guess."

"I still can't believe he could do that," Rob said, shaking his head. "Even though I understand what drove him, it seems incredible that my own brother could hate me that much that he would want to kill me to keep me away."

"He had a lot of secrets," Billy said. "But I believe he did not intend to kill you that night. He suffered from horrible shell shock, did you know that? Nightmares, used to keep Marge awake. I have them, too. Now I understand you have them as well."

"Yes," Rob replied dully. "Maybe it was better when I couldn't remember anything."

"Maybe in that respect, but there is everything before you now," Billy brightened. "It won't be easy, you know. A lot of years have passed since you and Marge were together. She loves you, Rob, and has never stopped."

"How did she find out we were married?" Rob asked.

Billy hesitated. He hated to add fuel to the fire now that it had been somewhat quenched by his heartrending appeal on behalf of Jack. You're a right bastard, Jack, he thought, but I promised Rob the truth and I have to tell him.

"That bloke in Folkestone kept Jack's address," Billy let out his breath. "One day he found your marriage certificate, just as Marge said. He posted it to Jack. Only Jack figured why bother telling Marge now when it was all in the past? He hated bringing you up, always saying he was only trying to protect Marge from getting upset."

"Sounds like Jack," Rob muttered.

"Kept it locked away in a drawer in his office," Billy continued. "That night he came after you, he left the drawer open. Elizabeth found it and gave it to Marge."

191

"That's just what the bastard would do," Rob shouted, Billy motioning him to keep his voice down. "He knew I was still Margery's husband as long as I was alive. As long as I was alive." His voice dropped off and he stared dully at the dark red upholstery across from him.

"Jack was always...well, he had the wrong end of the stick about a lot of things in this world," Billy eased the conversation back to a normal tone. "He wanted to be you. He thought he could become you if he married Marge and took your child as his own. Then when you turned up, pretty badly wounded and not able to remember, he figured it was best for everyone if you got care. It seemed logical to Jack, and it worked in his favor. Apparently the problems began when you wanted to come home. Then you did."

"Quite a surprise for our Jack, wasn't it?" Rob smiled sardonically. His expression turned sad and he said, "All the years I knew Jack I could never unlock what was in his mind. He could be kind, even loving, then in an instant turn around and want to ruin your life. I never understood him and I wonder if anyone else did. You seem to have sympathy for him."

"The War changed him," Billy said thoughtfully. "I suppose when he figured you were dead and gone and he no longer had to compete with you, he relaxed a bit. Harry, Marge's brother-in-law, helped him start his business and he worked damn hard to make it a success. He did everything for Marge and Elizabeth. All the while he could have married another woman, one who would have loved him properly the way any man wants, and have children of his own. But he stuck with her. Maybe he hoped she would one day realize how much he loved her and would find she loved him. She never did and it broke his heart. Then you turn up again and it must have cracked his sanity somehow. He became short-tempered, sick, anxious. There was something about him we couldn't understand, something indefinable, but it haunted him."

"He did call me a ghost," Rob smiled. "Ghosts have no place in Upper Marstone. That's what he said to me before he fired the gun."

"For Marge's sake, try to understand," Billy said.

"What about Elizabeth?" Rob said. "Now, in a sense, I have become Jack, haven't I? All those years he thought he had to become me to make Margery happy. Now I have to become him to make Elizabeth happy. She won't accept me, Billy. She won't even meet me." He hung his head, tracing initials carved into the wooden table.

"She loved Jack," Billy said softly. "He was a good father, Rob. He did everything for her and she adored him, that's true. That doesn't mean she won't one day meet you and love you, too. Marge is so angry with Jack for what he has done: hiding the marriage certificate from her, not telling her you were still alive, trying to kill you – well, Elizabeth sees herself as the one person who still loves him and does not want him to rot in hell. To accept you would be a betrayal of her love for Jack."

"If that's how she feels then she will never accept me," Rob said sorrowfully. "Now I think I know how Jack felt. When you want something so badly and you cannot find any way to attain it through no fault of your own." He looked at Billy. "I suppose there is no way to make her accept me, is there? No way to make her understand that I would do anything to be the father she wants. Not to replace Jack. I could never do that. I understand that. If she could just grant me a few minutes, a few minutes to see her and meet her."

"We had better get on now," Billy said, trying not to look at Rob's pleading face. "It's nearly time for the final call."

"Will you at least ask her for me?" Rob begged as they stepped out into the biting air.

"You know I will, Robbie," Billy said. "I can't guarantee any results."

"Right," Rob smiled. "But it is a start."

Chapter Twenty-Five

The ride back to Upper Marstone was mainly a silent one for Lewis and Louise, punctuated by references to Brian and his desire to buy Jack's business. As they approached the house on Tilburstow Hill Road, Louise remarked on how many lights seemed to be lit in the Morne house.

"I'll go fetch Robert," Lewis said. Louise sensed something wasn't right. "I'll come with you," she said, quickly getting out of the car. She had been so attuned to Robert she sensed that something had happened. It was just as she feared.

The door flew open after the first ring of the doorbell. "Oh, Dr. Warren," Margery sighed in relief. "Please come in." Louise trailed behind, both women giving each other the semblance of a smile in greeting.

She introduced Sally to Louise and Lewis and then said, "Robert went out with Billy. A drink for old times sake, you know, at the Hare and Hounds. He said he would take him home. We didn't know where to reach you so you wouldn't have to make the trip here."

"We would have had to come back to Upper Marstone in any case," Louise replied, noticing Sally giving her a concentrated look. "Was everything all right this evening?" Louise noticed the cake plates and half-filled coffee cups still sitting on the low table.

"Everything was fine," Sally got up, taking Margery's arm and smiling brightly. "It was so lovely to see Robert again I was over the moon. Are you the doctor who saved his life?" She smiled again at Lewis, who returned it sheepishly.

"Well, I may have assisted, but it is really Louise who is responsible," he replied. "She refused to give up on him even when Matron had. What was her name, Louise?" Louise had been looking at Margery, noticing her tear-stained face and blotchy cheeks. Something had happened here

194

tonight, no doubt about it. She would ask Robert when she got back to the cottage.

"Sister Jennett," Louise replied crisply, not taking her eyes from Margery. If every time Robert and Margery met it ended like this, it would be better to stop it now, before their hearts got broken again.

"Was Robert all right when he left here with Billy?" Louise interrupted Sally as she was asking questions about Robert's condition.

"Y..Yes," Sally stammered. "Billy thought it might be a good idea to take him back to their old haunts, you know. Rather like helping him to come back to part of his old life." Margery choked quietly and turned away.

"We'd best be going, then," Lewis said, taking Louise's arm. She had fixed her gaze on Margery and seemed reluctant to let it go until she drove every last detail of the evening from her. He shepherded her to the door and said their goodnights.

"That woman is going to kill him, I have no doubt of that," Louise said as she sat in the car, her lips set so firmly they seemed made of iron. "This façade cannot continue. They are trying to recapture the past and they cannot. She should let him go."

"Love is not so simple as that," Lewis responded. "It is early days yet."

"It will be late days for him if this is what he endures at every visit," Louise said angrily. "What could possibly happen between them that inspires this reaction?"

"That is not for either of us to know at this time," Lewis said, pulling up in front of the cottage. Billy's car was there, so Louise knew Robert was home.

"Don't go rolling in about it now," Lewis cautioned. "Putting him between two worlds will not help him. Can you please try to have some patience with the process, Louise? You of all people know how long it takes for those with head injuries to recuperate. Be patient with him and Margery. If it is not to be, then it will not be. You can't hurry it up because you want to take him home and be with him." She got out, looking at Lewis and feeling very confused, not only by her feelings, but the feelings of Margery and Robert. Wasn't love supposed to conquer all? Couldn't they see their way to each other? If not, then perhaps the love was no longer there. That is how she saw it. Waiting for it to reappear seemed silly. It was there or it wasn't.

Billy was just coming out when Louise came up the walk. Lewis waved at him and said, "Hello. I hear you and Robert had a few pints together tonight. How'd he manage it?"

"A bit wobbly on his pins, but not too bad," Billy grinned nervously, flinching under the steely stare of Louise. "He's not drunk, though. He knows he has to be a good boy and watch his drinking with his medications."

"It's a good thing he was sensible about it," Louise said, sweeping past him and going into the cottage. The door slammed and Billy raised his eyebrows. "Is she angry with me, Doctor? I promise I didn't take him out to get him drunk. I took him out to..to talk to him."

"It was pretty obvious to Louise something went on tonight at Margery's," Lewis said. "Did he have a seizure?"

"Not a seizure, really," Billy replied. "More like an outburst. He is having a difficult time with the fact that Margery was married to Jack. I think I sorted him out on that one, but it hurts him. And not seeing his daughter. That is killing him, pardon the pun," Billy added quickly. "He seems sort of irrational at times."

"It's been a shock for him these past few weeks," Lewis replied, starting his engine. "I just told Louise we have to be patient. I hope Margery will be, too."

"Oh, she will be, doctor," Billy replied. "She loves him so much that nothing will stand in her way to being with him again. She is not sure he feels the same, though."

"Why is that?" Lewis asked, turning on his headlamps.

"That nurse," Billy answered, cocking his thumb toward the cottage. "She wonders if he has feelings for her. He seems so devoted to her. In some ways she is like his wife."

Lewis nodded. "I suppose when one depends on someone for his life it can form a symbiotic relationship that is hard to break. He has relied on Louise for almost everything. There is nothing she has not done for him, nothing. Being that intimate with someone's body and soul probably gives the impression of a romantic relationship. It may even feel that way to the participants." He stopped, not wanting to denigrate Louise's feelings for Robert, but wondering how accurate they were by his description.

"They had a bit of an argie-bargie tonight and he went off on his own," Billy said. "I knew where he might be, so I went to find him and tried to sort him out. Not sure if it worked. I am trying to talk to him the way I always did. Being injured and all, maybe I ought not do that to him."

"No, Billy, that is exactly what you ought to do," Lewis said, shifting into gear. "That is exactly what he needs to begin to find his way back to this world again. Goodnight."

"Goodnight, doctor," Billy said, waving at the taillights. He shook his head, glad to know he had done the right thing even though it had felt very strange indeed.

Louise came in and noticed that everything was quiet. Only Catkins mewed loudly and begged to go out. "No, Catkins, you are in for the night," she said firmly, wondering if she should talk to Robert about what happened. His light was out, almost a signal to her that he did not want to talk to her. What had happened? She was dying to know, but even Rose was in bed and seemed unaware of the night's events. Should she check on him? For the first time she felt reluctant to knock and enter his room, the way she had for years. He no longer seemed like her patient, but a man, a separate human being with a past and a life of his own. Lewis's words echoed in her ears: Time to let him go, Louise. Not to that woman, she thought. Not to the woman who has killed one husband and may destroy another. I didn't save his life so that it could be wantonly destroyed by a selfish woman who has no understanding of the heart and soul of this man as he is now. He is not the same, dear Margery, she said to herself as she got ready for bed. He is different and needs a different sort of woman to look after him. As she climbed into bed she resigned herself to their continuing relationship. In her heart, she knew that if this sort of incident continued, they would both know they could not make a go of it. It would be hard for Robert, but as always, she would be there to catch him when he fell. She snuggled into her blankets, content to let things take their course. After all, she said, I have waited nearly twenty years for him. I can wait a little longer.

Chapter Twenty-Six

Rain fell incessantly for nearly a week after the incident. Robert and Margery did not contact one another, both afraid to make the first move and so stayed apart once again. Their self-doubts about one another plagued them so much that every time one of them picked up the telephone, the thoughts came fast and furious, causing them to put the receiver down before completing the call.

Louise decided not to mention the incident unless Robert did. He was morosely silent, again brooding as he watched the rain come down on an unfinished garden. Wandering from room to room, he listened to the wireless and jumped whenever the telephone rang. Billy rang up, asking Rob to go out again, but Rob refused. Even Lewis's visit did little to cheer Rob up. Louise thought she might have to plan some sort of outing or event so he could get out of the cottage, away from himself and his dark thoughts.

Margery was acting much the same, brooding and not even being inclined to go out to the shops, sending Elizabeth instead. When Elizabeth had returned that night, she almost expected to see 'radiant Robert' ensconced on the sofa, or worse, in her mother's bed. Her mother had already been in bed when she came in, something she never did, as she always waited up for her. Elizabeth knew things had not gone well. Her mother refused to speak of that night and talked around it.

As much as Elizabeth thought she would be happy to see Robert fading out of favor, her mother's depression and lack of vitality made her anxious. The light had once again been extinguished in her eyes, making her seem much the dull, lifeless woman she had been before. Elizabeth had never noticed that about her mother until Robert had come back into her life. He had fired her up, made her beautiful and excited and joyful. Now she was as drab as the grey rain pelting on the windows.

"I'm going to the office to work with Uncle Harry today," Elizabeth said on Thursday morning. It was nearly a week since the dinner. How much longer could her mother go on like this? "Do you want to come with me and do the shopping? I can take you in the motor and run you back here. It is pouring down out there." She looked at her mother intently as she sipped her tea.

"No, darling, you go on," Margery responded, folding up her tea towel and laying it on the counter. Even the bright, cheerful yellow curtains did nothing to dispel the gloom in the kitchen. "I have a shopping list if you would stop for me." She turned to pick up the list as Elizabeth came over and took her arm.

"Why don't you just ring him already, Mummy?" Elizabeth said, peering into her face. "I don't know what happened, but for God's sake, this can't go on." Margery looked stunned and said, "What, dear? You mean ring Robert?"

"Yes, I mean ring Robert," Elizabeth said. "If you keep moping like this I don't know what I shall do."

"He's the one who walked out," Margery said, nearly to herself. "He should be the one to ring. It is what men should do."

"And when did that stop you?" Elizabeth grinned. "Didn't you ask him to the village dance after all? He must be the sort who lets women do the asking."

Margery looked at Elizabeth and said, "You don't know him at all. Why say that? He is just...just...a daydreamer. He doesn't always catch the signals."

"So throw him a smoke signal via telephone already," Elizabeth said exasperated. "I hate doing the shopping. All those old, gossipy ladies asking about my dear, resurrected 'uncle.' Ha! If they only knew the truth."

"They will one day," Margery murmured. "I hope they will one day."

"I'm off to the office now," Elizabeth said, going into the hall for her coat. "Poor old Uncle Harry is really looking tired. I thought if I help him out, he will really look tired!" She tried to get a smile from her mother. Only one person could do that: radiant Robert. She rather liked her nickname for him. When she had seen him in the car for those few seconds last Friday, it was evident he still retained that special look, even if he had been battered in ways very few people had to endure.

Elizabeth decided to walk, as the rain was beginning to clear and she could see little glimmers of sunshine outlining the high-peaked clouds. It wasn't very far, really, but she had avoided the walk because the last time she did it had been the night her father died. Deliberately she crossed the street and walked on the other side to dispel the feeling of déjà vu.

Uncle Harry was there, talking on the telephone and grinning at her as she came in. A quick look at the post to decide which enquiries could be dealt with by her and which would have to have Uncle Harry's expertise. There were letters to be typed and bills to be sent out. She hung up her coat and started organizing the pile, putting the most difficult letters and bills first.

Uncle Harry was still on the phone when the door opened and Brian Warren walked in, hat in hand and smiling diffidently. Elizabeth was surprised to see him, and surprised to feel her heart jump slightly when he grinned at her. What could he want here? Perhaps he thought they were a motorcar repair business.

"Hello again," he said, extending his hand. "Brian Warren – do you remember me from the other day?" She nodded her head and smiled back at him. "What can we do for you, Mr. Warren?"

"Didn't I tell you to call me Brian?" he teased. "And, if I recall, you are Elizabeth."

Her cheeks colored slightly but she smiled and answered, "That's right. My Uncle is on the phone if you want to do business with him."

"Well, I have come for that, in a way," he said, seating himself on the side of her desk as she began to resume her typing. "I..I know what's happened with your father," he said, Elizabeth's shoulders tightening as she kept typing. "I don't want to sound impertinent...well, ..."

"May I help you, young man?" Harry's voice boomed over the office. He was looking at Brian's familiar attitude toward his niece with a gimlet eye.

"Yes, sir," Brian said, standing up smartly and extending his hand. "I met Miss Morne a few days ago and was just chatting with her until you were free."

"He has some business he wants to discuss," Elizabeth said to her uncle, not missing a beat with her typing.

"Do you have a fleet of lorries that need repair?" Harry asked, eyeing him carefully. "Because that is mostly what we do here."

Brian shuddered involuntarily, saying, "Brian Warren," as he shook Harry's hand.

"This is my uncle, Harry Cross," Elizabeth said, turning away from her typewriter. "He is helping us keep the business going for the time being."

"Yes, I heard from my father, Dr. Lewis Warren, what happened," Brian said.

"It was a bad business," Harry said, keeping a careful eye on Elizabeth's back as she continued typing. "A bad business." He motioned to Brian. "Why don't we discuss your query at my desk?" He pulled Brian over, noticing he was reluctant to take his eyes off Elizabeth.

Harry settled in and motioned Brian to a chair. "What can we do for you?"

"This business was owned by your brother-in-law?" Brian's voice lifted, as if he wasn't sure of his facts. "Elizabeth's father?"

"Jack Morne," Harry said. "Yes, he was Elizabeth's father."

"The reason for my visit," Brian said, drawing himself up to his full height in the chair, "is because I am a mechanical engineer by trade, and have been looking for a business venture for myself. I have the capital, you know. My mother left me a packet. Instead of spending it on wild women and drink in London, I wanted to invest it into a business that I thought had room for expansion." He noticed Harry's suppressed grin at the mention of wild women and drink. Not a bad chap, really. Just looking out for his niece's welfare.

"It really isn't for me to say, you know," Harry said. "I'm not the owner."

"Right," Brian said, appearing confused.

"She's the owner," Harry grinned, pointing at Elizabeth. "She and her mother. You'll have to deal with them in this. I can only advise, as I do now. Even though it appears I am her boss, she is actually my boss. Isn't that right, Miss Morne? I am working for you, aren't I?" Elizabeth turned and smiled at him.

"That's right, Mr. Cross, so you had better get on with it and make sure this man has what he needs." She turned around again, her brown hair swinging as she did so. Brian stared at her back until Harry cleared his throat.

"Sorry," Brian said. "I suppose what I need to know is whether you think she and her mother will want to sell the business? It will be hard on them to run it alone, I should think. Unless, of course, you are staying on?"

"I was just enjoying my retirement after selling out my own business last year," Harry said. "My wife has not been well. She's Elizabeth's mother's sister, you know. We were hoping to spend more time on the coast, where the climate is warmer." He looked at the clearing skies that still threatened rain, as if he wanted to be there already.

"Do you think I should talk to Elizabeth about this?" Brian asked, not wanting to alienate this young lady he found so fascinating. "I would also talk to her mother, of course." He hesitated for a moment and said, "I do

201

understand that things are very jumbled at the moment. My father is Robert Morne's doctor."

"Rob's doctor?" Harry's face lit up. "I have been hoping to see Rob again, as has my wife, May. How we loved that boy! Although I suspect he is a long way from a boy now." His expression turned pensive. "Seems that every time we hope to see him, Marge tells us there is some delay."

"My father doesn't make me privy to all the details," Brian said. "I do know that Elizabeth is dead set against meeting the man who is her.."

"Father," Harry said bluntly. "We suspected, but Marge only told my wife after she married Jack. Even I didn't know. Of course, Marge would have no other from the day she met Rob. Jack, well, Jack got a raw deal in some ways, but in other ways he was his own worst enemy. One thing we know, though. He loved Elizabeth as his own daughter. She is very sensitive about Jack, no doubt."

"So talking about selling the business at this time might not be a good idea?" Brian questioned nervously. "I would not want to put a foot wrong with her."

"Yes, I can see that, my boy," Harry grinned, getting up. "Why not take her for a cup of tea and discuss things? Broach the idea. She is desperate to keep the company going as a tribute to her father. You might want to remember that when you are talking to her." He put his finger next to his nose and smiled.

"It must be awfully difficult for her to find out about her fathers," Brian said, looking at the slender back and neat figure at the typewriter. "I met her real father, Robert, the other day. She looks very like him."

"She could use a friend right now," Harry said, putting his arm around Brian's shoulders. "My sister-in-law Margery is caught up in her own world and trying to make sense of everything. Now Jack is gone and Elizabeth is lost, especially as her godmother has now invited Robert to live with her."

"I would be delighted to be her friend, if she'll have me," Brian said as they walked over to Elizabeth. "I lost my mother not long ago. I know how it feels"

"Good lad," Harry smiled. "Well, young lady," he said, as Elizabeth stopped typing and turned around. "This gentleman needs to discuss business with the owner. That's you. So I suggest you to run along to Curd's Tea Rooms and do so. I will keep an eye on the shop while you are away." He grinned broadly at both of them.

"What sort of business?" Elizabeth asked suspiciously, smiling at Brian in spite of herself. "I thought you handled the business end of things, Uncle Harry."

"No, no, he needs to talk to you," Harry said, pulling her up from her chair. "This has to do with things I am not in charge of."

"Such as?" Elizabeth countered as Harry handed her hat and coat to her.

"Go to Curd's and find out," he smiled, kissing her cheek lightly. "Off you go."

Brian motioned her to his motorcar parked in front, but Elizabeth waved it off. "It is a lovely day now," she said, looking at the sky. "It is not far down the High Street. Why don't we walk?"

"A splendid idea," Brian agreed as they began to walk past the little shops and establishments along the way. On their left a stone wall ran around a large house that had once been the manor house in the village. Soon they arrived at Curd's Tea Rooms that had been in the village for nearly fifty years. The net curtains were sparkling white in the morning sunshine, the windows shining. Autumn flowers bloomed from the window boxes, riots of reds, yellows, golds and purples. Brian found he liked Upper Marstone and it made him more favorably inclined to want to make an offer for the business.

They settled in, Brian ordering scones, clotted cream, and jam along with his tea. He and Elizabeth talked about the weather and Upper Marstone while they awaited their order, Elizabeth telling him of her childhood here, gazing out the window whenever she mentioned Jack.

"Sometimes I find it hard to believe he is gone," she said suddenly as Brian slathered cream on his scone. "The church is over there, just beyond the trees. Whenever I think he is lying there, I cannot believe it." She choked and rummaged for her handkerchief. Brian took her hand across the table.

"When my mother died," he began. "I thought I would never get over it. She was so young, really, and always so modern and beautiful. For a while I hated my father. Why hadn't he seen she was so ill? He is a doctor, after all. Mother was always the sort to keep things like that to herself, throwing parties and dressing up until the very end. That is what she loved and that is how I try to remember her." He became quiet as Elizabeth squeezed his hand gently, her expression sympathetic. He looked up with a wan smile.

"You know what has happened since he died?" Elizabeth said, wiping her eyes. "You know about my mother, and Robert, and what they are saying about my father?"

"I know that Robert is your real father," Brian said gently. "I could see it when I met you. Not knowing your father Jack, I thought they might look alike."

"No, not really," Elizabeth said, reaching in her bag again. "This is my father." She handed Brian a photograph of a dark looking man, slightly smiling, his arm around Elizabeth. Although a resemblance to Robert was there, he could see that Elizabeth was definitely not Jack's child.

"A good looking man," he said after gazing at the picture for a long time. "I know you loved him very much."

"Yes," Elizabeth responded. "I feel as if I am the only one who did now. For years I knew my parents had an odd sort of marriage. Oh, they tried to hide it, always being very pleasant to one another. My mother didn't seem real at times, as if she were going through the motions of living but not actually doing so. My father seemed angry for no reason and sometimes it scared me. It was never directed at me. Sometimes I felt his anger was directed at my mother, although I could not understand why."

"Was it because of Robert?" Brian asked, stirring his tea.

"I suppose it must have been," Elizabeth said. "I didn't know anything really. I knew Mummy had been engaged to Robert at one time. I thought she fell in love with Daddy when Robert was killed. Apparently I was very wrong." She stared into her teacup as if she thought the answer to all her problems would be found there.

"But you didn't come here to hear my tales of woe," Elizabeth said, straightening up. "What was it you wanted to discuss?"

Brian felt blank for a moment. Sitting and listening to her had felt so natural he almost forgot why he had come to Upper Marstone. "Oh, yes," he said. "Well, I have been thinking." He looked into her eyes, feeling speechless as he stared into them.

"Yes?" she prodded him. "Thinking about what?"

"Your father's business," he said, drawing his eyes away. "Your Uncle told me you would like to keep it running. I think that is an excellent idea. But I also think you need a partner. It seems your uncle is not really desirous of returning to full-time work."

Elizabeth bit her lip and looked at him. "I know. I swore to Daddy that I would not let his business go down. I think he loved that business almost as much as he loved me. Maybe even more." She giggled slightly, thinking of the comparison. Brian smiled dreamily at her, realizing he didn't care what she said just as long as he could sit here with her.

"My mother left me very well off when she died," Brian said, pulling himself back to the task at hand. "I've wanted to find a business I could invest in, even run, and this seems a tremendous opportunity. That is, of course, if you are thinking of selling up?" He hated to say it, seeing Elizabeth's furrowed brow.

"I don't know," she replied. "I would have to ask Mummy, of course. I am sure she would say yes, as she has never been much interested in Daddy's business. Somehow I hate to think it would no longer have his name on it."

"Why not?" Brian said. "I would be honored to have the Morne name stay on it."

"Would you?" Elizabeth brightened. "I was supposed to go to University a few weeks ago before all this happened. I wanted to study art history, perhaps work in one of the big art galleries in London. I love art, really. I've always loved to draw and paint, although I am not much good at it."

"Maybe you would show me some of your work one day," Brian said. "My mother was a great patron of the arts. I grew up with artists of all sorts in the house, so I think I have an eye for it. No talent, unfortunately. Much more prosaic, I expect. Engineering type of mind, drafting, that sort of thing."

"I am totally lost with that sort of thing. Daddy was amazing with all things technical," Elizabeth added. "He was a wonderful mechanic, too. He loved motorcars, always loved them. He taught me to drive when I was just fourteen, you know."

"Are you going off to University next term, then?" Brian asked, a sinking feeling in his heart.

"I don't know now," Elizabeth said. "I still feel so stunned by Daddy's death and what people are saying about him. And Mummy. She is an absolute emotional wreck right now. As long as she cannot get together with 'radiant Robert,' she is completely useless." She frowned and took a scone from Brian's plate.

"Radiant Robert?" he laughed. "Is that what you call him?"

"What else can I call him?" Elizabeth asked. "Daddy? Father? No, I could never think of him as that."

"Aren't you a little curious as to what he is like?" Brian pressed. "I would be to meet the man who was my real father. I don't think it would be an insult to your Dad. They were brothers, after all."

"Yes," Elizabeth said, looking directly into his eyes with a gaze that made him gulp. "You do know what happened that night, don't you? They say my father tried to kill Robert. I was there, Brian." She choked again, looking down at the crumbly scone on her plate.

"What happened?" Brian said, taking her hand again. "Please tell me."

"Please do not think ill of my father," Elizabeth pleaded. "I am not sure why he did what he did. For my mother, I think. Because when I see my mother and she talks of Robert, it is clear, so very clear, that she has only ever loved him. Never my father, not once. I think my father lost his sanity when he thought that Robert was coming back here. I think he did try to kill him."

Brian breathed out heavily but kept his hand on Elizabeth's. "But he didn't kill him, did he?" he asked gently.

"No," Elizabeth said, wiping her eyes again. "Because I stopped him. I grabbed his arm as the gun went off and it only hit Robert in the arm. I saved my real father's life, but it killed the only father I knew." The tears flowed down her face so freely he took his fingers and wiped them away. Other patrons were looking, their tongues wagging so much Brian could almost hear them clicking.

"You didn't kill him," Brian whispered, his heart breaking for her. "You saved him from doing something that would have hurt everyone far more than it has. It was a desperate action he took. Who knows what he really intended? He was obviously ill and perhaps his judgment was impaired by that." He proffered that explanation to her, desperately trying to sound like his father, even adopting his authoritative tone.

"Do you really think so?" Elizabeth asked, her expression hopeful. "I could never believe that Daddy would deliberately hurt anyone, especially his own brother. He was a gentle man, really, although I think he could do things that were not always seen as the right thing. He had his reasons, not always evident to other people. I think I understood him better than anyone else. It grieves me so to see my mother turned against him now."

"Your mother is hurt, too," Brian said quietly. "She feels betrayed and angry by what Jack did. My father and Louise Whiting, the nurse, told me the entire story. It is tragic, truly tragic, for everyone. There is hope for happiness now, you know. Even for you."

"Happiness?" Elizabeth said. "I don't think my life will ever be happy. Will my father come back again? He never can. Will my life ever be the same again? Never. That is what would make me happy, Brian."

"No, your life will never be the same again," Brian agreed. "But it can be wonderful in many ways. Do you think your father would want you to grieve and weep for him? It doesn't sound as if he was that sort of man. He wanted you to be happy, and he wanted your mother to be happy. Why he did the things he did we will never know. My guess is that he would want whatever would make you both happiest now." She nodded as he kept holding her hand.

"I wish I could put it all to rest in my mind. I keep thinking he died so unloved by everyone," Elizabeth said. "My grandfather, Charlie, was the only person in the world who seemed to love my father. My grandmother was cold to him, my mother did her best but obviously always loved

Robert, and other people never took the time to know him. Only my grandfather. And me."

"But what a wonderful thing that was for him," Brian said enthusiastically. "He had a daughter who loved him and he knew that. There may be another person who loved him as well."

"Who?" Elizabeth asked, taking a dainty bit of scone and popping it into her mouth.

"His brother," Brian said. Elizabeth looked up and stopped chewing her scone.

"No," Elizabeth said, shaking her head. "Daddy never spoke of there being a strong brotherly bond between them."

"That was only your father's opinion," Brian continued. "I know it would be hard for you, Elizabeth, but why not at least meet Robert and talk to him?"

She shook her head again, taking a sip of tea. "Why is it that everyone is so determined to have me meet this man? I know he is my father, but only in the biological sense. I don't know him at all, really. I'm not sure I want to." She set her mouth firmly. Very stubborn, Brian thought, but she has a heart.

"If you loved your father, then his brother would be the closest thing on earth to him, wouldn't he?" Brian pressed. "Even though he knew full well you were Robert's daughter, he loved you as his own child. He did go to see Robert when he was in hospital. There must have been some sort of bond there, Elizabeth. One perhaps your father would like you to continue."

Elizabeth was very quiet then asked, "Why should you care whether I meet Robert or not, Brian? It is of no importance to you."

Brian smiled slowly. "But you are wrong, Elizabeth. It is of great importance to me."

"Why?" Elizabeth questioned him again. "Have you met Robert and he has set you up to this? I know he wants to meet me. Everyone keeps pushing me and pushing me, telling me how wonderful he was. The past tense, you notice. He made Mummy very upset the other night. I think my father may have known more about him than we like to think. That may have prompted him to do what he did. I suppose I am..frightened of him."

Brian nodded. "I hadn't thought about that. I think my father would be very reluctant to let him back into society if he were violent or dangerous. I think he is a very lonely man who has been desperate for love and companionship, but has only experienced hospitals and isolation. I have to say, I have great pity for the man. He was so young when all this happened to him. My age, really." He stirred his tea vigorously.

Elizabeth was quiet. She hadn't thought about Robert being Brian's age, and she being almost her mother's age when their lives were destroyed. How would she feel if this happened to Brian? Her head was spinning as she found herself trying to walk in the shoes of her mother, father, uncle, and grandparents.

"I think I had better be getting back to the office now," Elizabeth said, standing up. "I will talk to Mummy about your offer for the business and see what she says. Perhaps you might like to come to tea on Sunday afternoon, if you are not too busy?"

"I would be delighted," Brian grinned from ear to ear. Elizabeth liked his grin and his kind manner. He had spent the majority of time listening to her lament her fate. All the while he had let her talk, made her feel better, and asked for nothing in return. It was as if he understood her father better than she did. He was right; her father would not have wanted her to be miserable and unhappy.

They walked back to the office, Elizabeth accepting the offer of his arm. It felt quite comfortable to be walking with him along the High Street. If he wanted to buy the business and run it, she would be happy. It was far more work than she had anticipated. Uncle Harry, while very patient and long-suffering, was tired and eager to get back to her Auntie May. Brian said he would keep her father's name on the business, so that everyone would know that she was proud of him, no matter what anyone else thought or believed about him. She wished she had known Jack better, wished she had asked him more about his childhood and what it had been like for him in the Army. He had terrible, heart-wrenching nightmares. As a little girl she remembered being awakened by his shouts of terror and her mother coming in to tell her everything was fine, Daddy was only having bad dreams. Talking to Robert would probably help her understand him better. Maybe.

Chapter Twenty-Seven

Mid-October stayed dry and sunny, allowing Robert to go outside and make great headway in the garden. He got up early and spent the entire day out there alone with his thoughts. Louise worried about him, missing his conversation. There was something on his mind. When Lewis visited, he talked to him at length, but neither one of them revealed the content of their dialogue.

Louise felt restless, especially as she had been meaning to call her Aunt Eleanor, but always found a reason to avoid it. It pained her, as Aunt Eleanor had been everything to her. In recent years, her disapproval for what she saw as Louise 'throwing her life away in a dark, damp hospital in Sussex,' had made Louise avoid seeing her. She never understood Louise's devotion to her patients, especially to one patient. What would she think now, living nearby in someone else's home, simply to care for this patient? And he was a married man as well.

Louise sighed, watching Robert working in the garden, oblivious to people who walked by but did not speak to him. Their open-mouthed stares as they saw him outside infuriated her, but she refrained from saying anything. Lewis's words that she cosseted and protected him like a mother rankled her, because she knew he was right. Part mother, part sister, and part nurse – that is what she was to Robert. 'Mother' was the first word she used in the description.

What did she want? She knew his body more intimately than many wives knew their husbands. She had washed him, groomed him, dressed him, and shaved him more times than she could count. Changing his dressings, cleaning up his bed when he was incontinent, nothing had been too much for her. Now he stood, lean and strong, in the garden sunlight. She had fought with her feelings, but could not deny that when she saw Robert anywhere, in any situation, her feelings could only be described as love. No other man had ever made her feel that way. Not dear David Giles, the boy she was engaged to marry, and not Lewis. She gulped when she thought about Lewis. There was something tense about her relationship with Lewis. With Robert it felt gentle and easy.

Or it had. Robert's brooding moods and shutting her out made her angry. He no longer needed her as a nurse. Rose really didn't need her, either. Perhaps she should think of going back to Brockham until she figured out what she wanted to do.

"Louise?" she heard Rose call from the kitchen. "I'm just not up to going into the village today, dear. Would you be a dear lamb and do the shopping for me?" Her perky expression had faded in the shadow of Robert's quiet, morose moods since his last meeting with Margery. "My hip is hurting something awful this morning. I think it best if I just put my feet up for a while. Robert is here if I need anything."

"All right," Louise replied. "Have you got the list?" Rose nodded, toddling over to give her a ragged scrap of paper with scrawled words and her shopping bags before sitting down heavily in the chair, her feet propped on a little tapestry stool. Louise had not noticed how old Rose looked until today. This arrangement had strained them all beyond recognition.

"It's a lovely day, dear, so enjoy your walk," Rose attempted to sound cheerful, but her voice was full of anxiety.

"Where are you off to, then?" Robert gave her a wan smile as she emerged into the bright October sunshine. His speech had become more like those of the villagers since he had come home.

"I'm doing the shopping for Rose," Louise replied. "I shan't be gone too long. Would you like to come with me?"

Robert lowered his head and answered, "No, not yet. I don't think I have the nerve to walk down the High Street, trying to explain myself over and over to everyone."

"You will have to do it one day if you intend to live here, Robert," Louise barked. "You can't just stay locked away in this cottage forever."

"I have no intention of doing that," Robert replied testily. "I just don't feel like doing that today." He turned his back on her and continued raking.

Louise bit her lip, wondering how she had come so far from him in such a short time. Her bossy ways had never seemed to irritate him before. He always took her in good stride, even gently teasing her about her manner. She never remembered him being angry or upset when she spoke to him before.

Rose watched until Louise was out of sight then tapped on the window. Robert looked up, nodded, then came into the house. "You better ring her now while Louise is out," she said. "Not that she'd stop you from seeing Margery again. The doctor would sort her out."

"No one sorts her out," Robert said wearily. "She is a wonderful woman, Rose, but she worries about me so much that I sometimes feel as if I cannot breathe." Rose nodded and said, "She cares for you so much, Robbie. I know no one likes feeling grateful for a lifetime, but she has been there to help you come back to life."

"I know, Rose," he said softly. "Oh, how I know that." He went to the telephone to ring Margery. He had to try again with Margery, but not in Jack's house. Here, in this cottage. Perhaps he would feel less defensive if he could be on neutral ground. He picked up the receiver and dialed her number, holding his breath and hoping Elizabeth would not answer this time.

Lewis drove carefully around the winding roads toward Upper Marstone. Earlier in the week he had talked to Robert about trying again with Margery. He encouraged him to do so, assuring him that the medication was working and that he was in no danger of seizures. It had been nearly two weeks since the incident with Margery. Robert had not had a seizure since he had been in hospital.

Was there another reason Lewis encouraged Robert to see Margery again? Of course he wanted Robert to assimilate back into a normal life as quickly as possible. As his doctor he had his best interests at heart, and seeing him sinking into a depression was not good for him. Inherently there was more to it. As long as Robert hesitated, Louise had hope. If Louise had hope for a life with Robert, she would never think of having a life with him.

He swerved the car slightly as he saw Louise's straight back going into the greengrocer's near the bakery. Robert told him that he felt unable to call Margery with Louise there. No doubt Rose had concocted some reason to send Louise to the shops so Robert could make his call. He smiled at the perspicacity of Rose Henning. She seemed to have a sixth sense about everyone, even if they tried desperately to hide their true feelings.

He pulled up in front of the cottage, the brisk October day feeling refreshing as he stepped from the car. Robert was in the garden, clearing up some brush and piling it up near the front fence. He gave Lewis a wave, a smile on his face. Lewis could see why Louise thought him so

211

handsome. Despite his fearful injuries, he looked better than most healthy men half his age.

"This garden is really coming on, Robert," Lewis said, opening the gate. "Have you painted those shutters as well?"

"Did that yesterday," Robert said proudly. "The garden was starting to look so nice the shutters looked awfully shabby. Rose had a tin of paint, unopened, so I used it. I like that green color, too. Adds a nice, warm look to the place." He stepped back to admire his handiwork, shielding his eyes from the sun.

"I saw Louise on the High Street," Lewis said. "Did you make your call to Margery?"

Robert grinned broadly. "Yes," he said. "She seemed so reticent to come at first, but she is coming. This Saturday evening. I told her I was doing the cooking, so if she refused to come, I'd understand." His smile was brilliant and his mood buoyant. It was as if the real man who had lain dormant inside the patient was coming out at last, with a sense of humor and romance revealed.

"Then I expect that I shall have to organize a dinner party for this Saturday evening," Lewis said, grinning back at him. "I will stop and see Margery after I leave today, to put her mind at ease should anything happen. Which," he looked at the worried expression on Robert's face, "I do not anticipate. That medication is working wonderfully well, better than I expected."

"It is like being freed from chains," Robert said, shaking his head in wonder. "Every day I wondered how and when a seizure would happen again. Now I don't think much about it. Sometimes I have headaches," he said, that fleeting worried look returning, "but they are not much bother."

"Does the local doctor live nearby?" Lewis asked.

"Well, if it is still Dr. Mitchell, then he lives in one of the cottages along the Green," Rob pointed down the lane toward the village. "About a three or four minute walk from here."

"Good," Lewis said. "I will put him on alert, just in case Margery needs any help immediately until I can get here. I am not trying to put the wind up, as we used to say in the Army," Lewis shared a grin with Rob, "but it is best to be prepared. Because, as I told Margery, you both have to realize what you are facing. You will always need medical care and medication."

"That's just the thing," Rob said, leaning on his rake, the sun hitting his face. "When I saw Margery last time, I wanted to be as I was. I knew I wasn't, but kept trying so hard to be the same person I was in 1916."

"None of us is the same person we were in 1916, whether we were injured or not," Lewis added.

"Right," Rob continued. "And I think she was trying to do the same thing. It was so...artificial, you understand? One thing she and I always had was the ability to be open and honest with one another, to accept one another, warts and all. Figuratively speaking, that is." He smiled again. Lewis had never seen him so lively.

"This time I am not putting on fancy clothes and trying to pretend I am something I am not," he said. "If I am not what she wants, she will have to tell me straight out." His brow furrowed. "I hope to God she wants me as I am. She is all that I want, all I have ever wanted."

"And Louise?" Lewis barely spoke her name. "What about her?"

"I love Louise as well," Rob said, shaking his head slightly as he thought of the dilemma before him. "It is different than what I feel for Margery. Louise is a wonderful woman, kind, self-sacrificing, and intelligent. Where would I be without her? Six feet under, that's where." He began to rake, the problem not solved in his mind.

"Then you must tell her quite openly how you feel about her," Lewis said. "She will cling to the hope that one day you will come back to her, even if you go to live with Margery. Because she loves you, Robert. She told me so a few weeks ago. She wants you to be happy. With her."

Rob looked uncomfortable. "I don't know how she can say she loves me," he stammered. "She doesn't really know me, not the person I am. She knows the patient, the wounded soldier. The more I become who I am, the more she fights against it. We've barely spoken the last week or so. You see, I feel I don't need a nurse anymore. I think it leaves her feeling lost as to what to say to me."

"You're very astute, my friend," Lewis said, putting a hand on his shoulder. "I think Louise has devoted herself to her work so she did not have to reveal herself to anyone. I remember that young girl I met, a girl so grief-stricken over her brother's death she was inconsolable. I thought she was lovely, fascinating, but much too young for me. I never forgot her. She is an enigma, and does not readily reveal what is inside her."

"I know," Robert replied. "So many times she would not tell me anything of her life. I got the impression it was not a happy one."

"Quite true," Lewis replied. "Another reason I think she devotes herself to making other people's lives happy. Or tries to."

"Tries to," Robert repeated. "At times, I think she devoted herself to me because she thinks I am her brother returned to life. Do you think so?"

"I'm a neurosurgeon, not a psychiatrist," Lewis smiled. "It is possible she may have some identification with that, as you would have been approximately the same age as Geoffrey. Ah, here she comes. Wish me

213

luck. I am going to tell her she is coming to dinner on Saturday night. My son Brian has invited a young lady as well."

"That will be quite nice then," Robert approved as Louise slowed her pace to stare at both of them standing in the garden.

"It's your daughter Brian has invited," Lewis whispered to Robert, whose head swiveled quickly. "No worries. Brian is very trustworthy and Louise and I will be there to chaperone. You're acting like a father already." Rob relaxed, a sense of protectiveness and paternity coming over him.

"Are we holding a garden soiree this afternoon?" Louise said, looking from Robert to Lewis. "Or have you taken up gardening as a hobby, Lewis?"

"Just checking on my hardworking patient, who has been painting shutters, I hear," Lewis smiled. "I was just on my way, actually, but wanted to tell you that you are expected for dinner on Saturday evening. My home. Brian has invited a young lady to dine with us and I do not want to be on my own. Might scare her from ever coming back again." He and Rob were grinning like two silly schoolboys.

"What is going on?" Louise said, trying not to smile back. Robert came forward and said, "My, we are rude. Let us help you with the shopping." He took the bags from her and started toward the house. Rose opened the door, shouting, "Hello, Lewis! Would you like a cup of tea?"

"No, Rose," he said, "but I would like you to come to dinner at my home on Saturday night. Would you do me the great honor?"

"Are you chatting me up?" she toddled out, wrapping her cardigan around her as Robert went into the house. "What a Jack the lad you are, and who would ever have thought it?" She winked at him as Louise stood bewildered. Why did he invite Rose? Why not Robert?

"I'm afraid it is a bit more prosaic than that, alas," Lewis grinned. "Your goddaughter Elizabeth is coming to dinner as my son Brian's guest. I thought you might like to see her, and that you would put her at ease."

"Your son and my goddaughter?" She laughed, shaking her head. "That's lovely, isn't it, Louise? Your son's not half good looking, too. Elizabeth has got good taste." Louise stood openmouthed in the garden. Why did she have this feeling that this 'dinner' was a fait accompli?

"And what about Robert?" Louise interrupted. "Do we leave him all on his own because his daughter is being so stubborn about meeting him?" Lewis and Rose became quiet.

"Robert has other plans," Lewis said quietly.

"Margery again," Louise murmured.

"Yes, Margery again," Lewis said. "She is his wife. You have to accept that they will try to be together until they are certain of their feelings."

"If he is alone with her..." Louise began.

"He will not have a seizure," Lewis interjected. "He has not had a seizure since he was in hospital, nearly a month ago. Dr. Mitchell is right on the Green and can get here in minutes. I am just off to Margery's now to show her how to take care of him should anything happen."

"So, what is the point of me being here at all then?" Louise said, going toward the house. "I see I am no longer needed here. Perhaps I should go."

"Will you try to see reason?" Lewis said. "You wear your nurse's uniform like a suit of armor, keeping everyone and everything away. Can't you see that Robert needs you, and Rose needs you, and...I need you?"

"Robert does not need me," Louise replied, ignoring the rest of his statement. "Robert has what he wants now. He does not need a caretaker any longer. Certainly not an old spinster nurse who stands in his way." She went into the house quickly, leaving the door open.

"Robbie's broken her heart, that's sure," Rose said quietly. "I don't even think he knows how she feels."

"Oh, he knows," Lewis said, looking sadly at the open door. "He knows but he doesn't know what to do about it. I think he wants to talk to her alone. Care to hop in and accompany me to Margery's?" Rose looked longingly at the front door but concurred.

"That poor girl," Rose shook her head. "She told me a lot about herself. How her mother was that wicked to her, and her brother dying and all. There was a boy once, too, a soldier..."

"David Gordon Giles," Lewis said as they pulled out toward Margery's. "He was a lieutenant in the 10th Worcesters. Wounded and died in front of her when she was serving at the front."

"She said his name was David," Rose said sadly. "Then comes Robbie, and that's the end of the story."

"I hope not, Rose," Lewis said. "Why anyone would find such a prickly, frustrating, aggravating woman attractive I don't know. But I do."

Rose smiled at him. "Because you and I know she is not really like that. I've become quite fond of her, really. There is a soft, kind side to her hidden beneath that starchy exterior. I could see from the first day that she adores Robbie. Not that women didn't, you understand. That's the thing with him, you see. He doesn't want to be adored. He wants to be loved. Margery loves him."

"Warts and all," Lewis chuckled as Rose looked at him quizzically.

215

"He's got no warts that I can see," Rose said. "Still quite a looker he is, despite what he has gone through."

"Just a figure of speech, Rose," Lewis said as they pulled up to Margery's house.

"I wonder what we'll find when we get back," Rose said as she got out of the car."Could be carnage with those two. Robbie is tougher than he looks."

"I am beginning to find out how tough he is," Lewis said as they went up the winding path to the front door.

Chapter Twenty-Eight

There's nothing for me now but to go home to Brockham, Louise thought as she put the shopping bags in the kitchen. Robert was nowhere in sight as she put away all the shopping first, not wanting it to spoil. At least in Brockham I will not have people constantly trying to tell me what I should do with my life. Aunt Eleanor knows better than that.

She came out of the kitchen and saw Robert standing in the parlor, waiting for her. "I hope the vegetables survived in there," he smiled but it quickly faded as he saw Louise's angry expression. "Come and sit down, Louise. We need to talk."

"I have nothing to say, Robert," Louise said, standing with her arms tightly folded. "You have made your decision. There seems to be no need for me to be here any longer. You can manage very well without a nurse. So can Rose."

"Yes, that is probably true," Robert cajoled. "I don't want to talk about retaining your professional nursing services, Louise. I want to talk about us."

"Us?" Louise said incredulously. "What 'us' is there? You are my patient, pure and simple. All I have ever been to you is your nurse. Now that is over and you must get on with your life. And I with mine."

"What are you going to do with your life?" Robert asked, coming toward her but her stance was as forbidding as a stone wall. He stopped halfway, his gaze fixed on her. She could not look at him. His eyes and the way he looked at her had been her downfall in the first place. How did she ever let her professional ethics go so much that she allowed herself to fall in love with him? It was wrong and now she had to pay the price.

"It doesn't matter," Louise said. "I will go back to my aunt in Brockham. I will find work. Perhaps I may start that nursing home that Sister Meade suggested after all." She looked at the wall behind him as she spoke.

217

"That's not what you want, is it?" Robert said. "Please, Louise, please come and sit down for a few minutes and talk to me. I think we both need a drink. Rose keeps a nice bottle of Scottish whisky hidden next to the fireplace. I don't think she would begrudge us a little nip." He smiled at her and gestured for her to sit down. She remained standing.

"I do not want a drink," Louise said testily. "I don't understand what you think this little talk will do."

"Don't you?" Robert asked, pouring tumblers of whisky for both of them. "What do friends do when they have a disagreement, then? I think they talk about it and try to understand one another."

"We are not friends," Louise choked as Robert tried to hand her the tumbler. She grabbed it and he took her arm, guiding her to Rose's worn chair.

"So all these years that we have shared were simply a nurse-patient relationship?" he asked. "I beg to differ, Louise. That is not what they were to me. We have shared so much together. We have laughed and cried and even...made love." She blushed crimson at the memory of the one night she spent in his arms. "That hardly constitutes just a professional relationship to me."

"That was a mistake," she said, taking a gulp of whisky and coughing furiously as it burned her throat. "I should never have allowed myself to become personally familiar with you. Never. It was wrong."

"If you hadn't, I'd be dead now," Robert said calmly. "I would have been just another wounded soldier who would have been left to die. You wouldn't let me die, would you?" He came closer, his eyes burning into her. "Because you cared about me. I owe you my life, Louise. I can never repay you for that. Neither can Margery."

The mention of that name made Louise look straight into his eyes. All the dreams she had that they would live out their days together in the cottage at the hospital were gone. Those eyes now belonged to someone else. While they were still soft and full of love, it was not the love of a man for a woman. It was the love of friendship.

"Louise," he nearly whispered, coming to her and kneeling by the chair. "Please look at me, Louise. I know your feelings for me, but...well..." He hesitated, searching for the words with that familiar furrow to his brow that indicated he could not remember. She hesitated to reach out and touch his forehead, soothing away those lines that caused him so much distress.

"The boy you thought you loved is not the man I am," he said carefully, as if he were reciting in class. "What we both love in one another is something based on only knowing some things about each other. When I

218

came home here, I started to become more of the person I had once been. To be honest, I don't think you like me very much."

"That's absurd," Louise said, taking another gulp of whisky. "Of course I like you. I have always liked you. You are not so much different than you have been."

"Then why have you changed towards me?" he pressed. "Margery and I have always believed in being open and direct with one another. I am going to be that way with you now. When I was wounded and needed you, you loved me. Now, I am not in need of you as a nurse, and it makes you unhappy." He scratched his head and said, "And I thought it would make you happy to see me so well. It has caused you nothing but pain."

"Pain?" Louise said. "I wouldn't go so far as that, Robert. I knew you did not have feelings for me as you do for Margery. I suppose I thought that she might reject you and I would be there for you. Because I understand your limitations and what has happened to you."

"She is beginning to understand, too," he smiled so sweetly she could not look at him. "She understands how much you have given me, including love. We are both so grateful for everything."

"I do not want your gratitude," Louise shouted. "I wanted to take care of you and have a life with you. Now it is just, "Put the old cow out to pasture, isn't it?"

"Oh, no, Louise, no," Robert said, grabbing her hands as she tried to turn away from him. "You are wrong, so wrong. What we have together is so special that nothing can ever change that. I love you, Louise. You are so dear to me I could not imagine going on in life without you. I cannot love you the way you should be loved by a man. I cannot give you my heart when it is already taken."

"Very well, Robert," Louise said. "I think it is best that I go, then. There seems no earthly reason for me to stay here now. I imagine you will be going to live with Margery very soon anyway."

"Not very likely," Robert said darkly. "There is still Elizabeth to consider."

"She will come around in time," Louise said. "It is you and Margery that count now."

"And you," Robert said firmly. "I want you in my new life as well, Louise. Do you understand that? As my friend, as someone who has endured with me through my darkest times, and as someone who means more to me than just about anyone else in my life."

"Please do not go on, Robert," Louise said, the tears falling from her eyes. "I cannot bear to listen to this."

"But you have to listen to it, because I mean it," he said, standing up and looking down at her. "I am not discarding you in favor of Margery, although you may feel I am. Margery is my life, my heart. She has been from the moment I met her. Things are difficult for us now. There is nothing I would not do to be with her again. Nothing." He looked at Catkins who jumped up on the windowsill to watch the birds flying by.

"I know that, Robert," Louise said, standing up. "I have known that from the minute you remembered her. I hoped she was happily married and you would just see her briefly and return to me, your heart free. I can see that even if that had been the case, you would not have walked away." She brushed a few stray tears from her eyes. "I knew this was coming. Lewis has been saying things to that effect for the past few weeks as well."

"He is not just saying them on my behalf," Robert smiled slyly.

"I don't understand," Louise said, walking down the hall toward her room. She had to pack and get out of this house for a while. Brockham always made her comfortable. She needed that now.

"He is saying it on his behalf as well," Robert said. "If you can see me through different eyes now, you should take another look at Lewis as well."

"No, I don't think that is true," Louise said. "Lewis and I are old friends and colleagues, nothing more."

"Perhaps you feel that way," Robert said, following her down the hallway and watching as she started to pack her things. "Are you really going then?"

"Yes," she said, pulling out her paltry wardrobe. She caught a glimpse of herself in the mirror, Robert reflected behind her. When did she get so old? Her brown hair had wisps of grey threading through it, her figure was almost non-existent, and her features seemed to have grown, showing a nose that appeared almost bulbous and her teeth more prominent. She stopped and stared at herself, feeling a poor substitute for the still-lovely Margery.

"What is it?" Robert asked, noticing her expression.

"I'm just getting old, that's all," Louise said. "It seems that I have aged twenty years in the past month. Perhaps I need a long rest. Maybe even a holiday."

"You are not getting old," Robert replied, resting his hands on her shoulders. "You are beautiful. Your heart is generous, your passion for helping makes you more beautiful than all the mannequins put together."

"That is sweet to say, but not true," Louise said. "You must have been quite the charmer, as Rose said. You are always saying very nice but untrue things."

"I don't think they're untrue," he protested. "I mean them."

"Yes, I am sure you do," Louise smiled wanly.

"And the next thing that you will say is, "There's a good boy," Robert grumbled. "Louise," he began. "I know your life has been terrible in some ways. I know that you lost your brother when he was so young. I think that maybe you thought I could become him, bring him back to life, so to speak." He waited for her response. She kept packing, not answering him straightaway.

"Geoffrey was my life then," Louise said, folding up her plain cotton nightgowns and packing them neatly into the case. "When he died, I thought my world ended. It did, really. Then you lay there, so like him. Not physically, but something about you. You were almost the same age, you had a spark in your eyes. I suppose I did think that you were my brother come back again. I was determined not to lose you, Robert. Determined no matter what."

"I'm not Geoffrey," Robert said. "And he cannot come back. There is no reason why I cannot be close to you as he was. Like a brother, a brother who is here for you and loves you and would do anything, anything for you. You know I will."

She turned to him, her eyes glistening. "Do you know what is funny, Robert? All these years I have done everything for you. It is what makes me happy and comfortable. Now here you stand, offering to do anything for me. It feels odd, because I have spent my life doing for everyone else."

"Then it is time that you let others do things for you," Robert said, putting his arms around her and kissing her tenderly on the cheek. "Not only me. Lewis. Rose. I hope Margery as well."

"I must ring for a taxi," Louise said, shutting her bag. He grabbed her arm.

"This is not goodbye," he said. "I know where Brockham is, you know." He grinned as she shook her head.

"I am sure you do," she smiled back at him, touching his cheek tenderly.

Chapter Twenty-Nine

Lewis spotted the taxi with Louise in it as he and Rose drove back to the cottage. "Now what has happened?" he said aloud as Rose turned to him.

"What?" she said, cocking her head and staring at her cottage.

"That taxi," Lewis said. "Louise was in it."

"What!?" Rose said. "What has Robbie said to her? Oh, I had a feeling there would be mayhem." She barely waited for the car to stop before jumping out. "Robert!" she shouted. "Robert! Where are you, my boy?"

Lewis followed, wondering what Robert had said to make Louise leave. He trusted that Robert would use discretion and kindness in telling her how he felt, but perhaps his injury had posed problems with the delivery. He could hear Rose tearing a strip off him as he approached, probably reminiscent of how she treated him at the draper's shop.

"Steady on, Rose," Robert said, holding up his hands. "I didn't do anything."

"Well you must have done something to have her go off like that," Rose said, pointing to Louise's now empty bedroom. "She's packed up. Gone off. To Brockham, Robbie says."

"Back to her Aunt Eleanor," Lewis mused. "What happened, Rob?"

Rob explained, his nervousness becoming pronounced as Rose kept her eyes fixed on him. "She made up her mind to go home before I said a word," Robert said. "I did talk to her, told her the truth of things. I tried to be kind about it. I never wanted to hurt her."

"While drinking, I see," Rose said, picking up the tumblers still half full of whisky.

"Sorry," Robert smiled at her. "She was very upset. I thought it might calm her down."

"I will go over and see her later," Lewis said. "As for you, Rob, you look a bit weary. You should probably go down for a nap. All this stress might cause the medication to be less effective."

"Not to mention the effects of the good whisky he drank," Rose chided.

Lewis and Rob exchanged looks. Did he tell her how I feel about her? Lewis wondered. He had not expected Louise to run away. He had really underestimated her feelings for Rob.

"Let me know how she is, will you?" Rob asked as Lewis stepped out the front door. "It was the hardest thing I have ever had to do in my life. Worse than going over the top."

"I will let you know how she is," Lewis said. "I'll be here to pick you up on Saturday, Rose. Around half-six."

"I'll be ready," Rose said, waving at him. "Just make sure you bring Louise with you."

"That is exactly my intention," Lewis smiled as he drove away.

No word came from Louise that evening as Robert and Rose sat by the fire. Rose kept asking him for all the details of what he said and how he said it. Exasperated, he told her that he had only spoken the truth.

"Well, the truth to a lady who loves you may not be what she wants to hear," Rose said, picking up her knitting.

"Then what was I supposed to do?" Robert asked. "Lie to her? Tell her I loved her when I love Margery? I do love her, Rose. Like a sister, really. Not the way I love Margery."

"It's just a bad muddle all around," Rose said, her needles clicking furiously. "I grew quite fond of Louise. I liked having her here. I miss her." Her needles hesitated when she said that, then started up again at a breakneck pace.

"I miss her, too, more than she would ever know," Robert said. "You know Lewis loves her, don't you?"

"Well, of course I do, silly," Rose retorted. "I may be old but I am not deaf and blind. It is so plain anyone can see it."

"Except Louise," Rob responded. "She doesn't see it."

"That's because she only has eyes for you," Rose said tartly.

"Is that my fault?" Rob said. "I didn't encourage her. Not really. We just have been together for so long I suppose we almost felt it would be inevitable that we would be together. I never wanted to hurt her and I think I have done a lot of damage. When I came back here I never expected all this to happen. Not in my wildest dreams would I have ever believed Margery was my wife." He sat back, staring into the fire.

"I can see Louise is not the woman for you," Rose said. "I think we need to wake her up to the fact that Lewis loves her. He seems reticent to tell her."

"Now, Rose, don't go messing about where you shouldn't," Robert cautioned.

"Oh, no, I know how to do these things," she kept knitting. "I did it all the time at Brooke's. I suppose you didn't notice."

"Can't say that I did," Rob smiled. "But I have no doubt you did it."

"Just a word in the ear, you see," she pointed to her ear with her needles. "That's usually all that is required." She smiled to herself, thinking of what she would have to say in plain language to Miss Louise Whiting on Saturday evening.

Louise arrived at Brockham late in the afternoon, the house looking much the same. When had she last come home? Must have been last Christmas when she came for a short visit. Henry and Eleanor had looked as spry as ever, traveling, being involved in the village, and having friends over often. Louise felt dowdy and out-of-place in their lives, so only stayed as long as was polite and went back to the hospital to celebrate Christmas with the men who had become more of a family to her than her own.

She paid the taxi driver, who brought her trunk and suitcases to the door, doffing his cap after she gave him an overly large tip. While she had a key to the house, she felt that under the circumstances it was better to use the doorbell. They may not want me to stay, she thought ruefully. Perhaps I should have rung first.

It was late afternoon and the sun had diminished enough to make the wind chilly. She pulled on the old-fashioned doorbell and waited for response. It seemed that no one was home when the door opened a crack.

"Miss Louise!" Maisie threw open the door, her scrawny frame looking even more shrunken than Louise's last memory of her. Her once dark hair was silvery-grey now, but her eyes were as bright as they had always been, and full of curiosity and suspicion.

"Are you planning a long visit?" she said, eyeing the trunk and suitcases. "It might have been kinder to ring me and let me know, so's I could have your room all ready for you." She stooped to pick up the suitcases but Louise stopped her.

"No, Maisie, I'll do that," Louise said, bringing first the suitcases, then pushing the trunk into the hallway. She stood up, dusting herself off and smiling at Maisie. "It is good to be home. I am sorry I didn't let you know I was coming. It was very sudden."

"I thought you knew the hospital was closing," Maisie eyed her warily. "So how's come you didn't know when the final day was? That doesn't sound like a good way to run a hospital to me." She turned toward the kitchen and said, "Still, it's the Army, isn't it? Look what a muck they made of the War. They say there might be another one, too, if we don't watch out for that little Charlie Chaplin in Germany." Louise followed her to the kitchen, feeling like the schoolgirl she once was when Maisie whipped up magical meals from nothing and made her feel so at home.

"Sit down and I'll make you some tea," she said, going to the hob and putting on the kettle. "Are you hungry? You are so thin it frightens me. Do they feed you in them Army hospitals?"

"Yes, Maisie," Louise smiled in spite of herself. "You have been saying that to me now for thirty years."

"Well, you don't get no fatter, that's certain," she said. "I didn't make a meal tonight as your Aunt and Dr. Henry have gone up to London. Theatre and dinner, so they will probably be late coming in. I was just going to make myself something and listen to the wireless. Shall I make you something?"

"Yes, please, Maisie," Louise said, taking off her hat and coat and sitting down in the kitchen. "Can I help you?"

"Yes, by sitting there and telling me why you've been crying," Maisie said, looking into the icebox and pulling out assorted items.

"Crying?" Louise said, startled. "No, no, Maisie, it was just the wind whipping my eyes and they were watering."

Maisie turned and faced Louise. "Now listen here, Louise. I've known you since you were a young girl. You're strong and can almost be like an iceberg if the mood takes you. So I know when you've been crying. And you have been." She began to beat eggs furiously in a patterned creamware bowl.

"It is just leaving the hospital, I suppose," Louise began tentatively. She felt she could not tell Maisie, or even Aunt Eleanor, about her heartbreak and humiliation at the hands of Robert Morne. She sighed loudly, thinking of Robert in the cottage with Rose, sitting by the fire. Her eyes filled up with tears again.

"I suppose it takes all kinds to make a world," Maisie said, pouring the eggy batter into a frying pan and adding meat and vegetables. Omelets, Louise thought, feeling very hungry. Rose was a decent cook, but nothing compared to Maisie's abilities in the kitchen. "I can't see as how you could spend your entire life hidden away in that hospital with all those mental patients, taking care of them day in and day out. It would be enough to make me barmy, I can tell you." She flipped the omelet to reveal the golden brown underside. The smell was intoxicating.

"First of all, Maisie, I was not 'hidden away,' Louise said huffily. "I was free to come and go and even attend outings with the patients. Second, they are not 'mental patients.' They are neurological patients."

"What's the difference?" Maisie said, flipping the golden omelet onto a plate and cutting it in half. She added freshly buttered toast and tomatoes. "These tomatoes are the last from the garden," she said, putting the brimming plate in front of Louise. "I'll get the tea."

They were silent as they ate together, Louise feeling more ravenous than she had felt in years. Yes, she thought to herself, it was the right thing to come home. Robert and Rose will be fine. Besides, how long would Robert remain there now, if he and Margery were meeting once again. The thought of him living the rest of his life with Margery made her choke. Maisie got up and clapped her on the back. "There, dear, you were gulping it down so quickly I thought that might happen." Louise took a drink of too hot tea then recovered herself.

"In answer to your question," Louise said, taking the last heavenly forkful of her omelet, "mental patients are suffering from an inability to function in society due to their own delusions, hallucinations, or behaviors. Neurological patients have had an injury or wound to the brain or skull. They may also exhibit these sorts of behaviors, but they come from their injuries, not another cause."

"But they act the same," Maisie said, sipping her tea. "If it walks like a duck and quacks like a duck...."

"No, Maisie," Louise corrected her. "Many of the patients I dealt with could recover fully with medication and treatment. They can go back into society and resume their lives."

"Those lads who have been there for over twenty years would find it hard going out there now," Maisie said, picking up the plates and carrying them to the sink. "I've got rice pudding. Do you want some?"

"Yes, please," Louise said, feeling very much like a little girl instead of a forty-five year old woman. Forty-five, she thought, as the reality of her age struck her. Forty-five and sitting in her aunt's kitchen like a little girl who had a bad time at a party.

Maisie set out two huge bowls of rice pudding and a jug of cream. "For rice pudding?" Louise questioned and Maisie smiled, revealing most of her teeth were missing.

"Why not, dear?" she said. "At my age you take your fun where you can get it."

"At my age, too," Louise agreed, pouring a little cream over the already-creamy pudding.

"Your age?" Maisie cackled. "How old are you now?"

"Forty-five this past May," Louise said wearily. "I feel every year of it tonight."

"Forty-five," Maisie whispered. "Not so old really. You could still find a husband. Your Aunt knows everyone in the village, practically in the County. Lots of nice men out there."

"I'm not looking for a husband, Maisie," Louise retorted. "I just wanted to come home and rest for a while before I took on a new position."

"Why do you drive yourself so hard, dear?" Maisie said, pouring out fresh cups of tea for both of them. "I mean, I've never seen anyone so devoted to working herself to death. What fun have you had? Not even when you was with that young man, what was his name?"

"David Giles," Louise said, his face appearing before her as if in a picture.

"I know he was killed," Maisie said, her jaw firm. "That War was something that never should have happened. Killed so many beautiful boys, it did."

"And wounded so many beautiful boys for life," Louise responded. "The repercussions go on and on. It was terribly difficult to find new places for some of them. Some are going home. Hopefully they will be all right. Others are...finding the adjustment difficult."

"You just work, work, work," Maisie said. "You know what I think?" She looked directly into Louise's startled eyes. "I think you work to forget. To forget that mother of yours, God rest her soul. To forget what happened to your poor brother. Thirty years ago now, isn't it? And to forget about David Giles. I still recall him as clear as if it were yesterday. Coppery hair and lovely blue eyes he had."

"Yes," Louise choked, again the picture appearing before her. Why was Maisie going on about David? David had been dead since 1916, right before Robert Morne came into her life and stayed. "I love my work, Maisie. It never feels like work to me. I have had to carry on my life, regardless of what mother, Geoffrey or David meant to me. And I have."

"But it's no kind of life for a young girl," Maisie persisted. "And now look at you. You're forty-five and got nothing to show for it." She leaned back into her chair, sipping her tea.

"I have much to show for it," Louise said angrily. "A woman's place is not always in the home, you know. Just because I am not married and do not have children does not mean I have 'nothing to show' for my life, as you put it. Look at you, Maisie. You are not married and have no children. Would you say you have nothing to show for your life?"

A strange smile played around Maisie's lips. "That's what I am trying to tell you, Louise. I am seventy-four years old. No children, no husband. I live here on the goodwill of your Aunt and that wonderful Dr. Henry. God blessed the day she married him, I can tell you, because he is a saint and has made her happier than she ever thought possible. He feels the same. And what I recall is that she was much like you. Didn't want anything to do with marriage or being tied down, just liked working and traveling and being her own woman. Well, she still is that, believe me. Gets involved in all sorts of business and helping solve mysterious goings on around the county, and brings me into it as well. Oh, I could tell you stories about how she spends her time, but let's leave that for now. But she has love, too. We all need it." Maisie got up and switched on the wireless, turning the hot water on full blast while she added soap powder, making a mountain of suds.

"So you regret not marrying?" Louise asked. "Was there someone?"

"There was once, to be sure," Maisie said. "I was a young girl serving in a big house in London. Just a skivvy, you know, but the footman was the handsomest boy I'd ever seen. We started to see one another, on the sly, you see. He got sacked when he tried to come up to my room to bring me flowers for my birthday." She turned away from Louise, her face wrinkling so Louise knew she was crying.

"What was his name?" Louise said, getting up and taking the tea towel to dry the dishes.

"Teddy," Maisie barely croaked. "Teddy Harte. I never knew what happened to him, as he wasn't allowed to come near the house. I couldn't go out on my own, you see. He begged me to come with him when he was leaving, but I was so young and frightened that I said no."

"Do you wish now that you had?" Louise asked, seeing a different side to Maisie than she ever knew.

"Yes, I do," Maisie said firmly. "There's no good going on about it now. It's all in the past and he is probably long dead by now." She drained the sink and wiped the counters with her dish cloth. She turned to Louise and added, "I just want to tell you that if you find that love, grab it with both hands and don't let it go. Or you will wind up like me. Like me." She turned back, hung the dish cloth on the tap, and started toward the little parlor off the kitchen. "It's Thursday night," she said cheerily. "The Jack Jackson Orchestra is broadcasting from the Dorchester." She flipped the light off, leaving Louise standing in the dark in the kitchen, tea towel in hand. She barely noticed as her thoughts revolved around the circumstances of the past few days. She wanted to grab Robert and cling to him, but he had made it clear where his affections lay. She stood stock still in the dark, her mind revolving pictures of David, Robert, Geoffrey and Lewis. Lewis? His face appeared before her as clearly as the others, but even more so. "Silly goose," she chided herself. "After a wife like Lady Constance, what would Lewis want with you?"

She hung up the tea towel and decided to join Maisie for a while before going up to her room alone. After all, she said to herself, Maisie has not had such a bad life after all.

Chapter Thirty

Aunt Eleanor and Henry were not aware Louise was back until the next morning, when she appeared at the breakfast table. "Good morning, everyone," she said, walking in and taking her usual place at the table where she had sat for years.

"Oh, my word," Aunt Eleanor cried. "When did you blow in?"

"Hello, my dear," Henry said, getting up and giving her a kiss. "How nice to see you. We didn't know you were coming. Although, of course, I had heard you were in the area."

"Yes," Eleanor said, tapping her egg sharply with her knife. "We had heard, but not from you."

"Oh, Aunt Eleanor, I have been meaning to ring," Louise said, again feeling like a naughty child. "Everything has become so complicated lately."

"That was a bad business over in Caterham a few weeks ago," Henry continued slowly. "A bad business. One of your patients, apparently."

"Lewis has been talking to you, hasn't he?" Louise asked, looking at both their impassive faces.

"Well, someone has to tell us what you are up to, don't they?" Eleanor said, tapping the egg again. "You barely write and never ring us. You could be dead down there in Sussex. Then when we heard you were involved with that terrible incident outside Caterham, well, we felt sure you would let us know you were all right." She coughed lightly.

"I'm sorry, Aunt Eleanor," Louise got up from her chair and put her arms around her aunt. "I am an awful niece, and I realize it. It is just that everything is so...difficult at present."

"Lewis told us you were living in Upper Marstone with an old lady and one of your patients," Henry said, looking up at her through glasses that seemed thicker than the last time she remembered. They both have aged so and I never noticed, Louise thought. Aunt Eleanor's silver hair was upswept, but her face, although bright and active, was lined and careworn. Henry looked older and greyer, too. She had neglected them in favor of her patients. She flushed with guilt thinking how old they were and perhaps it was too late now to make amends.

"Yes," Louise replied as Maisie came in and put her breakfast before her. She gave Louise a wink.

"For heaven's sake, Louise, you could have rung to let us know," Eleanor said, putting her spoon down with disgust. "So very close, and we don't even know it. It was one of the neighbors who heard about the incident. Naturally, Henry saw Lewis and asked him. It seems this patient is special to you. Is that right?"

Special, Louise thought. He will always be special to me. He was everything to me. But I am no longer anything to him. She drew in a deep breath and smiled.

"They are all special to me," Louise replied.

"Then why stay over there, when you could have come here?" Eleanor persisted. Henry shot her a warning glance. She looked down at her breakfast, furiously picking the shell off her egg.

"I thought he needed more constant care," Louise said. "With all the patients being transferred, some to their homes, his transition seemed...delicate."

"Why is that?" Henry said, helping himself to more toast. "Lewis said this patient was severely wounded in the head. Was this the same man you have been working with since Etaples?"

Louise flushed again. "Yes, and he has made remarkable progress. His seizures are nearly controlled now. It was just the incidents of the past few weeks that made me feel I needed to be nearby. It was all so hectic. I am so sorry I didn't ring, Aunt Eleanor. Time got away from me."

"We are just glad you came to visit," Henry added. "I'd like to talk to Lewis about this man. I have been looking at new seizure medications for my patients."

"I am sure you can," Louise nodded, not adding more. She remembered she was supposed to have dinner with him on Saturday. Henry's words sunk into her consciousness. "Visit? I have come to stay, for a while. If you'll have me, of course."

Eleanor and Henry exchanged glances. "Of course, dear. You know this is always your home," Eleanor said. "I thought you wanted to be with your patient."

"No, no, he is doing fine on his own," Louise said, staring at her plate. She looked up as she could feel their eyes on her. "It was a very complicated situation. He came home and found out he was married and had a daughter. He never remembered that."

"Very complicated," Henry agreed. "Wasn't his brother married to this lady as well?"

Louise felt her eyes brimming as she stared at her plate. "Yes," she murmured. "As I said, very complicated."

"It must have been shocking for his wife, thinking he was dead all these years," Eleanor said. "What did she say?"

"I don't really know," Louise said, getting up hastily. "It has nothing to do with me now. Nothing." She ran out of the room.

"I think a little talk with Lewis might clear things up here," Henry said, getting up and laying his napkin on the table. "There's more to this than meets the eye."

"She loved him," Eleanor said simply, wiping her mouth daintily on her napkin. "Anyone can see that. And now he has come home to find he has a wife and child. Don't you remember her talking about him so much over the years? Robert, that's his name. Robert."

"Oh, yes, the boy who couldn't remember anything at all," Henry mused. "She didn't like his brother. I do remember her going on about how she didn't trust him. Seems as if she had good reason to feel that way."

"Why, dear?" Eleanor said, coming over to him to straighten his tie.

"Just what I heard at the hospital in Caterham, and from my well-informed patients, of course." He smiled at her as she tapped his nose playfully.

"I told you not to listen to their gossip," she said breezily. "What did they say?"

"Apparently," he continued, still smiling at her, "this brother went stalking Robert as he was coming home to Upper Marstone. Intended to kill him. Seems he did not want him back because he knew that Robert was still married to his wife. A bad business, like I said. He did manage to pop off a shot and wing him in the arm. As if the man hadn't suffered enough already." He put on his hat and kissed Eleanor. "Go easy on Louise, darling," he said softly. "I think things will turn out fine in the end. It is just the getting there that can be so difficult."

"Are you going to tell Lewis she is here?" Eleanor asked.

"He already knows it," Henry winked. "He rang me early this morning to enquire after her and to remind her that she is coming to dinner at his house on Saturday evening."

"Really?" Eleanor said, smiling. "Really."

"Don't start planning the wedding yet," Henry wagged his finger at her. "You know how stubborn Louise is when she gets an idea in her head. It seems she is quite convinced that the man she loves is her patient, Robert Morne."

"Really," Eleanor said, downcast.

"Yes, really, dear," he smiled. "Just don't go interfering in things at this point as you love to do all over this county. Lewis said he may stop by later on after he has done his rounds. Let him make the next move."

"I wasn't planning on interfering," Eleanor said testily. "Whatever made you say such a thing, Henry?"

"Because I saw that look in your eyes," Henry laughed. "I've seen that look too many times over the years not to know what it means." He kissed her on her nose and left, the chill breeze blowing through the hall, refreshing yet carrying the portent of winter.

Eleanor went upstairs, knocked on Louise's door, and came in. "Have you unpacked already?" Eleanor said, looking at the tidy room and Louise seated at her desk, pen and paper before her. She had been staring out the window, watching the leaves dance around the garden. Some of the trees were already bare. Like her life, she thought.

"I didn't have much," Louise answered as Eleanor went to the cupboard and looked at the drab, dark suits and dresses Louise had brought with her, along with her nurses uniforms. A few plain hats were lying in an open hatbox on the floor near the cupboard, the colors so dull and muted they looked like dead animals after a hunting party.

"Oh dear, Louise," Eleanor said. "Aside from this dark green suit," she pulled it out and held it up, "your wardrobe is in dire need of revision. What about shopping with me today in Croydon? We can find some lovely things to brighten you up." She sat down on Louise's bed and looked at her.

"I really don't need 'brightening up,' as you put it, Aunt Eleanor," Louise said, tucking a stray hair behind her ear. "I am only staying until I find another nursing position. Nurses do not need to be brightening up the atmosphere like mannequins. When I don't wear my uniform, these clothes suit me very well."

Eleanor sighed heavily, then got up and came over to the desk. "What will you wear to Lewis's dinner party tomorrow night? You need a dinner dress, something subtle yet attractive. You do look lovely in green. It brings out the little hint of green in your eyes."

Louise turned to Eleanor, smiling sadly. "Please, Aunt Eleanor. I am no longer fifteen years old and in need of making myself attractive. I am not going to Lewis's dinner party, or any dinner parties for that matter.

Don't you understand that I have no desire for that sort of life? All I have ever done is take care of patients, devote myself to them. I don't even know how to make small talk at insipid dinner parties. It would be a disaster, certainly. I am feeling quite bad enough about myself right now. I certainly do not need to feel worse." She organized the papers on her desk, sitting with her ramrod-straight back that reminded Eleanor of herself.

"Of course, dear," Eleanor soothed. "But this is Lewis's party, not someone you don't know. Do you think Lewis would want you to make insipid small talk at his table? I hardly think so. He is very much counting on you to come, dear."

"He's told you that, has he?" Louise retorted.

"No, he told Henry, actually," Eleanor replied, sensing Louise's anger.

"Why does everyone seem to be hellbent on running my life?" She got up and walked to the window, her arms folded across her chest. "Everything was fine, perfectly fine, until Robert took it into his head to come home to Upper Marstone and upset everything. If he hadn't done that, we would be settled in somewhere now. I would be happy."

"Were you really happy, darling?" Eleanor came over, putting her arm around Louise's shoulder. "Happy with a man who could never love you fully because his heart belonged to someone else? Happy with a man who saw you as his nurse and companion, but not his wife?"

"Yes," Louise said, tears in her eyes. "I was happy. Happy to see him every morning over tea, happy to talk to him at lunch, happy to share his meals and his wireless and his conversation. It made my day to see his smile in the morning."

"Now that he is well enough to be on his own, do you think you would still feel that way about him?" Eleanor questioned, looking over the garden and the highlighted grey clouds.

"I don't know," Louise admitted. "But I wanted to find out. Perhaps we would have been no more to each other than nurse and patient as time went on."

"Apparently he no longer needs a nurse," Eleanor said steadily. "So where would that have left you?"

"I would have hoped it would have left me as his wife," Louise said openly. "He and I agreed to marry, without actually saying it to one another, after he saw Margery again. We both believed she was married to someone else and settled in her life. He did not want to disrupt that, he just wanted to see her again. It has gone all wrong. For me." She wiped her eyes.

"Margery is his wife," Eleanor said softly.

"Yes, but it is not only that," Louise said. "It is the fact that he loves her, Aunt Eleanor, and she him. He told me so, as kindly and charmingly as only he is able to manage. I am like a sister to him, he said. A sister." She dabbed her nose with her handkerchief.

"Perhaps it is the best thing, dear," Eleanor said gently. "You don't realize what it would be like to live with a man as his wife, and know he always has his heart with another. It would never be right. It is not what I would wish for you." She touched Louise's cheek softly.

"This is what Jack Morne must have felt," Louise said quietly. "Living with a woman who never loved you. Margery always held that place in her heart for Robert."

"And it was hell for Jack, no doubt," Eleanor said.

"So much so that he attempted to kill his brother to protect what he had," Louise said sadly. "It makes me wonder just how far people will go."

"It would have been wiser for him to let her go," Eleanor said. "It is a great sacrifice to let one you love go, Louise. You are no stranger to sacrifice. There is one more thing that you must do. Let him go, Louise. Let him go, because you will not be able to love anyone else if you don't."

"I am trying, Aunt Eleanor," Louise said, tears flowing down her cheeks. "I feel he is so much a part of me and the fabric of my life that I cannot just forget him. I think of him every moment, wondering what he is doing, what he is thinking. After nearly twenty years I just cannot wish him away, can I?"

"No," Eleanor responded. "Look around you, darling. There are other things for you. You have been so consumed in Robert's recovery and life you have completely obliterated your own. Now it is here, staring you in the face, and you have to live it." She hugged Louise tightly as Louise cried on her shoulder.

"I have no life other than my nursing and my patients," Louise cried. "Someone told me that long ago but I refused to believe it. I do now. There is nothing for me, nothing."

"Nonsense," Eleanor said sharply. "Did I ever tell you about Herbert?" Louise looked at her, shaking her head.

"Well," Eleanor began, bringing Louise over to the bed and sitting down next to her. "It isn't something I'm proud of, but I am going to tell you anyway." Louise perked up her ears, wondering what this confession might be.

"Herbert was one of my employers," Eleanor said, smoothing her russet colored dress self-consciously. "I was governess to his children. Terrible little brats they were, too." She smiled at Louise, who was listening intently. "Herbert and I had a great attraction for one another," she continued, looking at her folded hands. Louise saw how gnarled they looked, obviously arthritic and probably painful. "We...we began an affair," she said, looking up and staring at the wallpaper.

"An affair?" Louise questioned.

"Yes," Eleanor said, looking at her. "He was a married man, but I didn't care. His wife could not possibly love him as I did. Every morning my heart sang when he would come downstairs and say, 'Good morning, Miss Bancroft.' I lived for that, the fleeting moments in my room or meeting him on my afternoon off for a clandestine meal and a few hours in a room somewhere." Louise was silent, looking at Aunt Eleanor in surprise.

"Oh, don't look quite so shocked, Louise," Eleanor chided. "I was headstrong, too, like your mother."

"It wasn't a moral judgment, Aunt Eleanor," Louise said. "It was simply my surprise at your story."

"Yes, of course, dear," Eleanor said, patting her hand. "I know you have probably seen more of the world, and men's bodies, than I ever have."

"Not in quite the same way, though," Louise giggled and Eleanor joined in.

"So what happened with Herbert?" Louise asked.

"Well, I was smitten, absolutely smitten with him. We made plans to run away together. He would leave his wife, a dull, lifeless creature I thought, and we would be happy forever. Except, of course, he didn't mean it. It was wonderful for him while it lasted, but it wasn't love. I, of course, was sure he was the one and only man I would ever love."

"What happened?" Louise asked, intrigued.

"His wife called me in one day and dismissed me," Eleanor said, almost laughing. "She said they were going to India and would no longer need my services. I, of course, was desperate. I said I would be perfectly happy to go to India as well. 'There will be no need for that, Miss Bancroft,' she said in such a haughty, condescending manner I can still hear her voice today."

"What did Herbert say to all this?" Louise asked.

"Herbert? Well, it was Herbert's idea to have his wife dismiss me, you see," Eleanor said. "He could not extricate himself from the situation and she gave him an ultimatum when she found out about us. He had no money of his own to speak of and she held the purse strings. It was a simple decision for him." She hung her head, the pain still there.

"The cad," Louise said, angry enough to find this Herbert and give him a good thrashing. "He used you."

"Oh, no, dear, don't you see?" Eleanor said, looking into Louise's eyes. "I loved him, or thought I did. No one could speak ill of him to me. It took me years, years to see that I really hadn't loved him. When I met Henry, at first I didn't see how I could love him. I always compared him to Herbert and what I felt for Herbert. Then I saw the light. What I felt for Herbert was a mixture of passion, lust, excitement, adventure and attraction. Love can have those elements, certainly, and often does. But true love is something more. It is gentle, and kind, and fine. I tried to hold on to Herbert for years. I followed his doings in the newspapers. When they came back from India, I made sure I saw him. I still felt a strong feeling for him, almost a need to be part of his existence. Eventually I realized there was nothing there. It felt empty and horrible. Which is why I kept trying to fill the void."

"You think I am now trying to fill the void by not letting him go?" Louise asked.

"Yes," Eleanor said. "Robert was your life. His care and recovery were your life. Now it is gone, as Herbert was. What do you replace it with? You weep, you lament, you hope he will come to his senses. But it is you, Louise, who must come to her senses. Because as long as you keep him burning in your heart, you will never be able to see anything else for the smoke."

"Thank you for telling me about Herbert, Aunt Eleanor," Louise said, her heart aching for her aunt. "Does Henry know about him?"

"Oh, yes," Eleanor laughed. "I told him long ago. Do you know why?"

"No," Louise said.

"I once called him Herbert at the breakfast table," she laughed again. "He said there must be someone in your past. I was horrified to think that I could still even think about Herbert. Henry had someone once, too. Life does go on, Louise. You will see, darling."

"I suppose there is nothing else I can do," Louise said sadly, getting up and returning to her desk.

"Are you sure you won't go shopping with me?" Eleanor said.

"No," Louise responded. "I want to get some letters off with the second post today."

"All right, darling," Eleanor said, kissing her cheek. "Open your eyes and your heart to a magnificent life ahead of you. If I hadn't, I would not have had these nearly thirty wonderful years with Henry."

Louise wrote letters well into the afternoon when the sun came out and illuminated the garden. Every time the phone rang she hoped Maisie would shout her that it was Robert on the phone. The calls were never for her. Would he have forgotten her already, so consumed in Margery he cared for nothing else? The story of Herbert and her Aunt played out in her mind. No matter how logical she tried to be in her thinking, her thoughts centered on Robert.

The garden looked so lovely she decided to take a walk around it to clear her mind. Maisie asked if she wanted tea, but she said no, she would rather be out a while and then have tea. Maisie said she was going to have a little lie down before getting on with the evening meal.

The cool breeze hit Louise squarely in the face, reminding her of Etaples when the wind would blow across the dunes. A brisk day like this was the last time she saw David alive and well. She took the pin he had given her for an engagement gift out of the box and put it into her coat pocket, like a talisman that could call up the dead. Finding a little bench near the pergolas in the back of the garden, she sat down and drew out the pin, the emeralds reflecting the sunshine as brilliantly as they had on that afternoon when he had given her the pin.

She was so engrossed in staring at the emeralds that she didn't hear Lewis coming across the garden. He was standing next to her when she looked up, her hand hiding the pin.

"As a doctor I should scold you for sitting out here in this cold breeze and damp garden," he said, smiling as he sat next to her. "I've just been to see our patient. A sad case."

"Is something the matter?" Louise said, so startled she dropped the pin on the ground. Lewis picked it up.

"From that boy, David Giles, wasn't it?" Lewis said, turning the beautiful piece of jewelry around in his hands.

"My engagement gift from him," Louise said. "What of Robert?"

"He is despondent about what happened yesterday," Lewis said, looking into Louise's eyes. "Really despondent. He feels you will never speak to him again and that he has caused an irreparable rift in your relationship. Nothing I said could convince him otherwise."

"Is he well otherwise?" Louise asked, looking so deeply into Lewis's eyes he felt he wanted to kiss her.

"Absolutely topping, as Brian would say," Lewis smiled, looking away. "Healthiest specimen of manhood I have seen. Lean, wiry, strong. No seizures. Just all of what transpired between you two yesterday has made him very depressed."

"There is nothing I can do about that," Louise said huffily. "He said what he had to and I must accept it. So must he."

"I didn't say he changed his mind about what he said," Lewis replied. "Just that he feels he has lost your friendship and yes, your love. It makes him mortally unhappy."

Louise did not answer right away. Lost my love? No, she would always love him. It was fairer to leave him alone to get on with his own life.

"Robert Morne's happiness is no longer my concern," Louise said, crossing her arms tightly. "That is now up to his wife, isn't it? She has been trained, by you, as I recall, to look after him properly. There seemed no reason for me to remain."

Lewis chuckled. "Do you know, Louise, that you are the most frustrating, obstructive woman I have ever met? You deliberately obscure the issue by returning to that professional Bart's nursing school graduate whenever something hits too close to home. Well, please listen to me." He turned her toward him and she did not flinch from his gaze. "Robert loves you, damn it," Lewis began. "Yes, it is not the sort of love he has for Margery, certainly. But it is love. And love, no matter what form, means something. His love for you is as important to him as your love for him. He is heartbroken, too, over this. Love is not always in the package you design, Louise."

"I did not design a love package with Robert," Louise retorted.

"There you go again, deliberately misunderstanding me," Lewis said, exasperated. "All I am saying, Louise, is that Robert loves you. Your Aunt and Henry love you. Maisie loves you. Rose loves you. And..and I love you, Louise."

"You?" Louise said. "You love me?"

"There, it's been said," Lewis said firmly. "Take it as you like. From the first moment I met you I loved you. You were nothing but a schoolgirl. Yet there it is."

"What about Constance?" Louise asked, looking at him intently. "Surely you loved her?"

"Just as I was saying, Louise, there are many forms of love," Lewis said. "I did love Constance, in my fashion. Was I in love with Constance? We were too different, worlds apart. She never understood my passions, nor I hers." He lowered his head, watching the leaves play beneath his feet.

Louise felt stunned by this admission. Lady Constance had been beautiful, wealthy, desirable, and good for Lewis's career. She gave him three wonderful children and the entrée into society that had helped both his career and his research funds. Louise could never give him anything except a.... What had he called her? "A frustrating, obstructive woman." That was what she was, plain and simple. No match for Lady Constance.

"Constance had everything to give you," Louise interjected. "You seemed...happy." Her memory came back to her of a nervous, agitated Lewis whenever he returned from visiting Constance's family in Worcester.

"We often make decisions based on what we think we should do, or who we think we should love," Lewis continued. "She was good for my career, I'll grant you that. Very good indeed. But you would have been better."

"Me?" Louise cried. "How can you say that, Lewis? That is utterly ridiculous and you know it."

"Not at all ridiculous, Louise," Lewis said. "I believe my work would have thrived no matter what I did, because it is important and groundbreaking research. Constance's connections and money did help me find funds. But the results would have proven themselves. With you at my side, it would have happened regardless of whether I had married an aristocrat or not."

"She was so beautiful and talented," Louise said softly. "I am nothing like her. Nothing at all."

"Look at me, Louise," Lewis said. "Yes, Constance was beautiful and talented and an outstanding patron of the arts. And you are beautiful and talented and intelligent and have given life to so many patients they don't even know how much you have given them. But I do. And Robert does."

The mention of Robert's name made her turn her head away from him. "I know I can never replace Robert Morne in your affections," Lewis said so low she could barely hear him, "and I won't try. I used to think I had to compete with David Giles," he chuckled. "He had such an easy way with you. I am not an easy person, Louise, as you know. I lack the charm and grace of Robert, or the easy manner of David. They are the sort of men I wish I could be, able to talk to women, charm them, woo them, and marry them. Perhaps that is why I married Constance. It was easy. She wanted to marry me because she wanted to live in London. No charm required."

"I am sure there was more to it than that, Lewis," Louise said, touching his arm. She had never thought of Lewis as a man lacking in anything. Yet here he was, confessing to her that Robert Morne had what he coveted.

"No, I don't think there was, Louise," he said, getting up from the bench. "My heart had been taken long ago by a very serious, brutally inquisitive schoolgirl who demanded to know what happened to her brother. I suppose I thought you felt the same, although you never said or indicated it in any way. There, you see," he smiled sadly, "I have no ability at all to understand women."

Louise smiled at him but said nothing. What a pair they were! It seemed that they both felt the same about relating to the world and the opposite sex. Because of their ways, they had never told each other their true feelings. What did she feel for Lewis? Right now she felt so muddled she did not think she could possibly know. Who did she love? Had it been David after all? Or Robert? Or all along had it been Lewis?

"Forgive me for going on about all this," Lewis said, standing in front of her. "When I saw you out here alone, I knew you were thinking about Robert. I suppose you will always think of him and there is nothing I can do to change that. My loss." He smiled wanly at her.

"Are you still having your dinner party tomorrow evening, Lewis?" Louise asked.

"Yes," Lewis said tentatively, his eyes showing a ray of hope. "You are still coming, aren't you? Please don't say no. There will only be three others besides us, and you know all of them already – Brian, Elizabeth Morne, and Rose."

"I will be there," Louise smiled. "I will look forward to it."

"Then I will count the hours until tomorrow evening," he smiled back then turned serious. "I do understand how you feel about Robert, Louise. I want you to know that I would never try to make you feel any differently about him. He is a part of who you are, and you are part of him. That will never change. He understands that, too."

"Yes, Lewis," Louise said, walking him to his motorcar. "He has too long been a part of me to forget him."

"Nor will I forget him," he said. "Especially as you never know what the future holds." He took Louise's hand in his, kissing it gently. "I will be here to pick you up around six," he said, his eyes dark and shining.

"I shall be waiting," she said, watching as his car pulled away.

Maisie stood behind the curtain in the front window, watching Louise and Lewis talk before he left. When he kissed her hand, Maisie smiled to herself. "I knew it," she said. "I felt it in my old bones."

Chapter Thirty-One

Robert awoke early Saturday morning, listening to the birds chirping near his window. The weather must still be fair, he thought, running his fingers through his hair. He stopped at the large scar over his left ear, feeling the keloid structure underneath his fingers. This one thing represented all that had happened with the result that he was alone in Rose Henning's cottage. Something so small yet so deadly.

He had the dreams again, horrible, frightening dreams. Shapeless forms that stalked him, always turning into Jack. A sweating, smiling Jack, who fired a gun at his head. "Jack," Robert whispered out loud, "Jack. Why?" He got up, looking out the window at the neatly trimmed and tended garden, ready to take the icy rains of winter. There was more he wanted to do before the sleet and snow began to fall, but he was pleased with his progress.

Catkins meowed at him when he stepped into the hall. "Good morning, mate," he said, reaching down to scratch his ears. "What are you up to this morning?" Catkins went to Louise's door and mewed. Tentatively Robert opened the door, seeing it still empty. Lewis had told him she was fine and settled with her aunt and uncle in Brockham. It was an untenable situation, Robert knew, but he missed her and wished she had not gone. The thought that he might see her there vanished when he opened the door.

He washed and dressed, deciding he was going to walk into the village to shop for his dinner with Margery. He wanted the entire event to be done completely by him. The snapping October breeze caught him unawares as he began to walk slowly to the village. Curtains in windows along Ivy Mill Lane twitched as he passed by, his cap low on his head, but he kept looking straight ahead. He was determined not to be afraid. What was there to be afraid of anyway? These were people he had known all his life. If they feared him he hoped he would put their minds at rest by showing himself.

A door opened as he walked past the Green and Dr. Mitchell stepped out, looking at him closely. A flicker of recognition registered. Robert could tell that the Doctor was uncertain whether he was actually seeing someone he remembered or it was just his mind playing tricks.

"Hello, Dr. Mitchell," Robert said, stepping closer to him. "Robert Morne. I know you have heard I am back from the dead. Wonderful what modern medicine can do nowadays, isn't it?" He smiled broadly at the doctor, who returned it.

"Robert," he said, coming down the steps and taking both Robert's hands in his. "My God, you look well for someone who has been dead all these years! How are you, my boy?" He studied him with a look Robert had come to know from years of being examined by doctors.

"Very well, Dr. Mitchell," Robert answered. "I've been staying with Rose Henning. You remember I used to work with her at the W.C. Brooke Company."

"Yes, yes indeed," he nodded vigorously. "Rose has not been too well herself. The nurse is there now..."

"She has gone," Robert said, "but I know we can manage. I've been working hard on her cottage, doing the gardening and all. I did gardening at the Army Hospital, when I was well enough."

"Quite amazing," Dr. Mitchell said, still looking at him as a practitioner. "I am sorry about your brother. He wouldn't listen to me, you know. His blood pressure was sky high. He always did what he wanted to, never mind doctor's orders."

"Yes, Jack was like that," Robert replied, his arm throbbing as if the memory of that night would not recede. "It was all such a mixup, you know."

"He never told us you were still alive in that hospital," Dr. Mitchell continued. "I can't understand that."

"I..I asked him to," Robert replied. "I was not always as you see me today, Doctor. I was very bad for a long time. I thought it would be easier not to come back until I was well. At times it was dodgy whether I would get better or not. Jack was just doing as I asked him to." He stared straight at Dr. Mitchell without flinching.

"He certainly kept the secret, even from Margery," Dr. Mitchell said, his eyeglasses glittering in the sunlight. "Have you seen her? And their daughter?"

"Yes," Robert said. "Margery hasn't changed much."

"Well, I suppose not," Dr. Mitchell shook his head. "It has been hard for her, of course. I am sure you can offer her some comfort. Jack was much too young to die."

"Yes," Robert said again. "Much too young."

"I must get on now. I have to say I am delighted you are back," Dr. Mitchell said, walking off in the opposite direction. "If you need anything, please be sure to ring."

"I will, Doctor," he shouted, seeing a small group of people near the horse pond on the Green. They were watching him intently. It's as if they think I am going to run across the street and stab them with a bayonet. He put on another smile and waved at them. First one, then another, waved back at him.

By the time Robert got to the High Street he was being heralded as living proof that modern medicine could work miracles. While not elaborating, Robert told something of his years in hospital and his wounds. He did not want to embellish, careful to tell of Jack's devotion to him and making sure everyone knew that Jack had been under strict orders to keep things confidential about his being alive. Jack had only brought the gun to show him and it had gone off accidentally when Jack fell with his stroke. People nodded sympathetically, some staring at him in ways that made him uncomfortable. He gritted his teeth at some of the inane questions, the almost incessant need to touch him and feel that he was really alive. He bore it all gracefully, even receiving hugs from women he barely recognized but knew they had once been his customers at the draper's shop. Nearly two hours had passed and he had not yet finished his shopping. Everyone wanted to fill him in on the news of the past twenty years – who everyone married, who had died in the War, who was no longer living in Upper Marstone, and who all the children belonged to that surrounded him as if he were a theatre star instead of a returned soldier.

It was exhausting and he felt tired enough to sit down in the middle of the pavement. He finally finished up his shopping at the butcher's, buying four lovely pork chops that he would prepare especially for Margery. When he saw her again tonight there would be no mistakes this time. He loved her and she had to know that they were meant to be together.

He shook a few more hands as he left the butcher's and found himself wandering down the Bay Pond Path. The peaceful quiet gave him time to gather his thoughts. While the cold seemed to whip around him, it was so beautiful he sat on a bench and just stared across the water, where his old house on the Salisbury Road stood. This is where he and Margery had walked the first time they went out together. They went to the village dance. She had asked him to go that long-ago spring day in 1913. He remembered being flattered that she asked and Jack's reaction. He shook his head.

"I didn't understand anything, Jack," Robert said out loud, a few ducks startled by the sound of his voice. "I never understood how deeply you felt for Margery. She is remarkable, isn't she? I can't say as I blame you for wanting to keep her for yourself. But she never belonged to you, Jack. Never." He threw a stone across the water, watching it skip as it did when he was a child.

He got up and continued down the path toward St. Nicholas Church. The sky had become threatening, but the rain still seemed a long way off so he carried on. The school came into view on his right. Through the nearly leafless trees he saw the spire of the Church.

He stood across the road for a few minutes, gazing at the place where he had spent so much time as a boy. He had been in the choir almost as soon as he could sing. Sunday school and confirmation and all the services raced back to him as he stood there, reeling back in time so quickly he found himself slightly unbalanced. Not a seizure. The symptoms were more from his emotions than his injury.

He crossed the road, climbed the steps and sat in the lychgate. His hands ran over the wood, his eyes filling with tears. Dad made this gate. He kept his fingers running over and over the wooden frame, knowing almost every stroke of his father's work. The tears ran down his cheeks. Dad and Mum are here now. So is Jack.

He picked up his bags and saw a gleaming stone war memorial to his right. The names nearly shouted at him, his boyhood friends now reduced to these carved letters on the memorial. Someone had left flowers and a poppy wreath, something that the British Legion had begun using. Kneeling down, he read the names out loud, stopping when he came to the names of those he remembered vividly: Stephen Burridge. Steve, a wag and a prankster. The vision of Steve teasing him about his engagement ring came back so strongly he felt as if Steve were standing beside him. The churchyard was empty.

Albert Porter. Bert. The memory of visiting Bert after he had been wounded came back afresh, so much so that once again he wobbled as he knelt there. Bert's injuries were so severe it seemed impossible he could have survived the trip back from France. Margery sent him a letter telling him Bert had died. Bert's presence was so strong it was as if he were just inches away.

Then he saw another name: Robert J. Morne. His name. Still on the Memorial as Jack had told him that fateful night. He looked at it, the disconnection between being Robert Morne and seeing the name of this

245

dead hero so intense he had to close his eyes. "Maybe I should not be here," he said out loud. "Maybe I should be with Bert and Steve. It was meant to be." He ran his hands over the names, the chill wind driving through him. A waste, he thought, looking at the names. A bloody waste of life.

I should be getting back now, Robert said to himself, but decided to walk around the churchyard and find Jack's and his parents' graves. Where would they be? He walked down the path behind the church, looking at the graves, seeing names he remembered. All dead now, he thought. I should be with them. Yet here I am, a walking dead man, floating around the churchyard. He saw a fairly new grave and walked to it, knowing somehow it was Jack's.

The trees showered him with golden and russet colored leaves as he approached slowly. The new stone had not settled, yet the name was clear: John Charles Morne, 1894-1935. Jack. Here Jack lay, too young to die, as Dr. Mitchell said. He looked to the side and saw his parents' graves: Elizabeth Ann Morne, 1859-1923 and Charles John Morne, 1867-1926. Again he knelt down, his heart heavy. Here was all that was left of his family. It seemed ironic and sad that he had been the first one to die, yet here he stood, looking at the cold stones that represented them. His sobs came out, loud, choking, anguished, as he knelt down, crying and talking to his parents and brother. The wind increased and the rain seemed more imminent, but he didn't care. This should be his grave. Not Jack's.

Elizabeth came down the path with some marigolds she had picked from their overgrown garden, salvaging what she could to bring to her father. She pulled her coat around her as the wind increased. I won't stay long today, Daddy. You wouldn't want me to catch cold. As she approached the graves she was startled to see someone kneeling in front of her father's grave. Who came to mourn him? In all her visits she had never seen any flowers or any evidence that anyone else visited him.

She came closer, not wanting to interrupt the man's reverie. He had his cap pulled low yet there was something familiar about him. He seemed not to be aware she was near. She walked closer to him, the leaves crunching beneath her feet. He looked up and she saw it was Robert.

It was too late to turn and run without looking a fool so she said, "Hello. I have come to leave my father some flowers." Her overemphasis on the words 'my father' made him wince. It was such a pained expression she was sorry she had said it.

"Yes," Robert said, standing up and moving aside. "I didn't know I was going to come here or I would have brought some as well."

"He liked marigolds," Elizabeth said, kneeling down and putting the marigolds in the little vase at his stone. "He didn't like to garden, though. Neither does Mummy."

Robert stood silently, looking at the beautiful young girl who was his child. He wanted to embrace her, hold her, tell her he loved her, but he stood mutely by as she finished arranging the flowers artistically.

"There," she said, standing up and wiping off her hands. "Those look nice." She turned to Robert and said, "It was inevitable that we meet one day, Robert. May I call you Robert?" She offered her hand to him and said, "And you know I am Elizabeth."

"Yes," he said, looking seriously at her as if trying to memorize her features. They were so like his it was uncanny.

"I loved Daddy," she said, looking down at the stone and touching it tenderly. "I loved him more than anyone, really. They never told me, you know. About you being my real father."

Robert took a deep breath. "I never knew, either, Elizabeth. If I had, I would have been here."

"I know," she said, looking at him with tears in her eyes. "If you were anything like Daddy, I know you would have been."

"I hope that I can be like him," Robert said softly. "He obviously did a wonderful job raising you. Must have got it from our Dad." He pointed to Charlie's grave, the tears misting in his eyes.

"I adored Granddad," Elizabeth said, touching that gravestone. "I didn't know Granny as well. She died when I was little. They said she died from grief. Over you."

Robert gulped, his eyes filled with tears. "She was a wonderful mother to me," he said, the tears coming down his cheeks. "Both of them were wonderful parents. I don't think I really appreciated them when I was just a boy." He searched for his handkerchief futilely. Elizabeth offered him hers.

"Thank you," he smiled. "Thank you for talking to me, Elizabeth. I know this must be harder for you than anyone else. I will never do anything to hurt you or make you sad. Rest assured of that. Never."

She smiled at him, so much like his own smile he looked surprised. "I know, Robert. I understand. Perhaps one day you will tell me about Daddy. What he was like as a little boy, what you did together. I would like to hear about him. No one seems to remember much about him."

"Any time, Elizabeth," Robert said eagerly. "Any time you want to talk to me, I will be waiting."

Elizabeth leaned over and kissed him lightly on the cheek. "Then I hope we will see each other one day soon." She turned and walked up the path, Robert watching her until he could see her no longer.

He picked up his shopping and stood there quietly, still trying to take in what had just occurred. Again he felt a strange feeling that his family was present with him, standing and watching Elizabeth walk away.

"Thank you, Jack," he whispered to his brother's grave. "Thank you for that."

Chapter Thirty-Two

Elizabeth walked home, her thoughts swirling so fast she found it difficult to keep up with them. She had met her real father. It seemed almost planned, yet she knew that no one knew where she was going when she left the house. The surprised look on Robert's face also confirmed that he had come there of his own accord.

Whether she wanted to believe it or not, she could not help but think that Jack had something to do with it. Oh, believing in ghosts and divine interventions was not something she usually subscribed to, but this seemed different. "Did you want me to meet your brother, Daddy?" she whispered to herself as she crossed the street near the old pub, the Bell.

There was so much that had happened in a month's time that she felt as if she had lived an entire lifetime since then. Who was that carefree young girl whose biggest excitement was planning to go to University? She was gone, dissolved in the morass of all that had happened. Her father dead, her mother married to another, her real father the man she thought was her uncle – she almost wanted to grab her head to hold in all the thoughts.

There was Brian Warren, too, of course. When she first saw him smile at her a few weeks ago, she was left with an odd feeling that he was someone she would know for the rest of her life. She had heard the old wives' tales about seeing someone and knowing that was the person you were going to marry. Did Mummy feel that way about Robert? Brian had not indicated that he was interested in anything more than seeing her again. The dinner tonight was not an actual date where they could be alone and talk. Still, it was a start. And Margery had agreed to sell him the business if he was still interested, so she would talk to him about that later on as well.

"Is that you, darling?" Margery called from the kitchen. "I wondered where you had got to. We both have to be getting ready for tonight." She smiled at Elizabeth, noticing the odd look on her face. "Are you quite all right, sweetheart? You look rather pale."

"Oh, yes," Elizabeth said, hanging up her coat and hat. "Fine."

"Where were you?" Margery said from the kitchen. Elizabeth came in, noticing how the addition of the yellow curtains had brightened the whole atmosphere of the room. "I didn't hear you go out."

"I went to the churchyard," Elizabeth said, sitting down, her hands folded in front of her. "The last of the marigolds were in the garden. I thought Daddy might like them."

"I am sure he did," Margery said, sitting next to her. "Did something else happen? Did someone bother you?" She put her hand on Elizabeth's brow.

"When I walked toward Daddy's grave there was someone else there today," Elizabeth said, keeping her eyes fixed on her folded hands. "Someone was kneeling by his stone. I couldn't imagine who would be mourning Daddy. No one else has ever come since he died, except me." Margery flushed, detecting the admonition in Elizabeth's voice.

"Who was it?" Margery said, concerned. Who would be there to mourn Jack?

"I thought perhaps it was someone he worked for, someone who had business with him," Elizabeth said. "But it wasn't. The man was crying, too." She stopped and looked up at her mother. "It was Robert, Mummy."

Margery sat back in her chair, the shock so evident on her face Elizabeth knew that she had not put Robert up to this. "Robert!" she exclaimed. "What...what did you do, darling?" Her concern was obviously not only for her daughter.

"I couldn't very well run away from him. Although if I had known who he was earlier I might have turned around," Elizabeth said frankly. "He had his cap pulled down low, so I couldn't see his face. Not until he looked up at me when I stood next to him. By that time it was too late to leave."

Margery nodded numbly, afraid once again that whatever happened would put a wedge in her being with Robert again. Elizabeth noticed her fear and smiled at her.

"He was very nice, Mummy," she began, gulping audibly. "I..I talked to him for a little while about Daddy and Granddad. He was crying, saying that he had never appreciated his parents when he was young. He seemed so heartbroken, especially about Daddy."

"He would be, darling," Margery said quietly. "Through everything, he loved his brother. And I know Jack loved him."

"But Daddy did try to kill him, Mummy," Elizabeth said, a look of confusion in her eyes. "It is so hard for me to understand why he did that." She looked intently at her mother, as if the answer would be there. "When I looked into Robert's eyes, I saw they were kind and warm. I didn't want to think that of him, Mummy. I wanted to think he deserved Daddy's wrath. That there had to be a good reason Daddy wanted to kill him. I couldn't see it in him, Mummy. Do you know what I saw? I saw Daddy in him, Daddy's face. I saw how they were brothers. I saw that he loved Daddy, despite what happened. And I knew his heart was broken to bits." She lowered her head, trying to wipe away surreptitious tears.

"Do you know what I heard when I ran to the village a while ago?" Margery said softly. "I heard that Robert had been there, doing the shopping for tonight's meal." She smiled, thinking of Robert especially picking out each item for their reunion. "People were asking him very personal questions about what happened that night, and why Jack never told them he was still alive." Elizabeth tensed, feeling sorry that now the truth would come out and her father would be vilified.

"Robert said he had asked Jack to keep it a secret from everyone, including me, because he was not well enough to come home, and didn't know if he ever would be able to again," Margery said as Elizabeth looked up at her, her eyes registering surprise. "He also said Jack brought the gun along to show him and it went off when Jack fell and had his stroke. He laughed off any idea that Jack would ever want to hurt him, becoming quite upset with those who would think that about his brother." Elizabeth still maintained the shocked look on her face.

"He said that when he knows what happened?" Elizabeth murmured. "It's not true, though, is it?"

"He loved Jack," Margery said. "I know that. It broke his heart to see how difficult it was to make Jack understand that he was loved. By his brother. By me. By many people. Jack had a difficult time believing he was lovable, so almost went the other way to ensure he would not be. There is no denying, Elizabeth, he did some terrible things to Robert and me. Not telling me about Robert being alive is one of them. Not telling me about my marriage being valid is another. I do understand why. In some ways I understood Jack, if nothing more."

"He was such a wonderful father to me," Elizabeth cried. "It just makes me almost mad to think he was two different people."

"Because you loved him without reservation, darling," Margery said, brushing Elizabeth's hair behind her ear. "You were the only person in the world who had no preconceived notions about him. He didn't have to make you love him; you just loved him. Jack thought the only way people would love him is if he had something to hold over them. I understand full well why he never told me about Robert."

"Because you would have gone to him and left Daddy?" Elizabeth asked.

"Yes," Margery replied. "Because I would have gone to him *and* taken you with me. You can see he had so much to lose. He had everything to lose. It drove him to this final episode with Robert. Robert understood Jack, better than anyone except Granddad, I think. Jack got twisted up when it came to love. It was black or white for Jack. Love never is black or white, darling. It is many, many shades of grey. Because I loved Robert Jack felt I could not love him. I did love him, but not the way I loved Robert. He couldn't accept that, and tried everything in his power to make me love him. Even before Robert and I became engaged he tried. It never worked. I have always loved Robert from the first day I met him." She smiled at her daughter sadly.

"Poor Daddy," Elizabeth murmured. "He was so handsome and successful and could have been loved as well. It seems wrong somehow." She shook her head.

"I should blame myself for agreeing to marry him," Margery said quietly. "You were right, Elizabeth. I should not have married him at all feeling as I did. I was scared and alone. I wanted you to have a home and your grandparents with you. Jack was the closest thing to Robert on this earth. It seemed so right at the time." She took out her handkerchief and dabbed her eyes.

"It was right, Mummy," Elizabeth said, holding her mother's wrist. "You thought Robert was dead. You only wanted the best for me, and you gave me the best. You gave me my father. I am grateful for that."

"Darling, you are an angel," Margery murmured.

"You cannot help how you feel when you fall in love, can you?" Elizabeth asked. "If you knew Robert was 'the one' when you met him, you could not deny that. Did you know he was the one you would marry when you first met him, the very first time?"

Margery smiled, her mind back to that day in 1912 at Lennox Place when Robert had come to repair the kitchen door with his father and Jack. One look and she knew he was 'the one,' as Elizabeth put it. "Yes, darling," she answered. "I knew it the minute I looked into his eyes." She hesitated and added, "I know it now as well."

"Then Mummy," Elizabeth said, getting up from the chair, "you must not let him go again. I want you to be happy, Mummy. If he makes you happy, then you must be with him."

Margery was silent, then asked, "Darling, I know how you feel about having him here. He understands, too, which is why he is living with Auntie Rose."

"Yes," Elizabeth said. "I think it is difficult to make sense of it all. I want you to know that after meeting him today, I knew he loved Daddy and you. There was something so sad in his eyes, too," she murmured. "So sad it broke my heart to look into them. It seems to me he has spent so much time away from everyone that he was desperate for love and affection." She put her hand on her mother's shoulder. Margery reached up and took it, holding it firmly.

"I won't do anything without consulting you first, darling," she said. "But you have made me very happy today. No doubt you have made your f...Robert happy as well."

"While I cannot call him Dad," Elizabeth said, "I do acknowledge he is my father. I suppose there are many children, too many, who are not born from love. I suppose I am lucky that I was." She patted her mother's hand and left the room.

Oh, Robert, Margery thought to herself. She is our child, our beautiful child. It did seem odd that he had been at the graves when Elizabeth was, as if someone had pushed him to go there. It was obviously a last minute decision on his part. What prompted it, she wondered? She would have to ask him tonight when she saw him.

The hour was getting late and she wanted to make sure she was ready in time to go. She tidied up the kitchen, smiling to herself as she thought of him doing the shopping. Was he doing the cooking as well? She never knew he could cook. Then again, nearly twenty years had slipped by and he could have learned many new skills since then. What had he done all those years in hospital? She leaned on the sink, her heart aching to think of him being locked up there, with only the nurses for company. The nurses. The vision of Louise Whiting came to her mind, and her almost proprietary attitude to her Robbie. Of course she would think that way about him. Now that Elizabeth had at least broken the ice with Robert and seemed more in favor of their relationship, there seemed to be only one last obstacle to her happiness. Sister Louise Whiting.

Chapter Thirty-Three

All the households from Brockham to Leigh to Upper Marstone were in a flurry as six o'clock approached. Margery and Elizabeth were running back and forth, trying on dresses, asking for opinions, and helping each other do their hair.

"I never look sophisticated, no matter what I wear," Elizabeth groaned as she saw her pink dress reflected in the mirror. "I mean, mother, pink? I look like a little girl going to a birthday party! I wanted something slinky, gorgeous, and silvery. What do I have? A pink party dress! All I need is a lolly to go with it!" She frowned at her reflection.

"It is very pretty on you, darling," Margery said, slipping on a plain cotton dress adorned with tiny rosebuds. "Oh, mother, you are not going like that, are you?" Elizabeth asked, her face shocked.

"Yes, darling, I am," Margery said firmly. "Robbie..I mean, Robert and I decided not to have any pretensions tonight. No suits for him; no dressing up for me. We are going to present ourselves in a simple and unadorned way. So when I get back home tonight everything might be off." She giggled but the nervousness in the sound betrayed the fact that she felt perhaps she was too old and dowdy now to rekindle the passion in his heart.

"That's right, Mummy," Elizabeth said, twirling around and thinking perhaps the pink was subtle enough to look sophisticated in dim light. "You want someone to love you for yourself."

"A good lesson to remember, darling," she said. "When will Brian be here to fetch you?"

"Half-six, he said," Elizabeth replied. "Do I really look all right?" She turned around and Margery smiled at her. "Absolutely ravishing, darling. Do you think you might just do my hair a bit? It does look rather scraggly like this."

254

Rose also was fussing. She had pulled out an old-fashioned black, beaded bombazine dress and put paste diamond hairpins in her hair. Robert whistled when she came into the room.

"Pardon me," he whistled as he saw her. "I didn't know I was in the presence of the Duchess of Ivy Mill Lane." He grinned widely as she came toward him, the beads flying in all directions.

"That's enough from you," she said. "I've not had any reason to go out to dinner in years and this is the only dress I had. Got it special from Wilfred. It was quite the thing."

"In 1910," Robert laughed and she waved her cane at him.

"1910 or now, it is a classic," she said, coming over to him. "You just mind your dinner and don't burn down the house getting carried away, if you know what I mean. No hanky panky. No..."

"We are married, you know," Robert smiled. "But I shall be as good as I can be."

"Hmm," Rose murmured. "That makes me more nervous."

"This means a lot to me, Rose," he said, coming over and putting his arms around her. "You have given me so much. Now you are letting me have the house to myself tonight. I don't know how to thank you for everything. I know you would rather be home with your feet up."

"Go on with you," she said, pushing him away. "You'd better keep an eye on those pork chops. Pork chops go all dry if you fry them too long. Dry and tough. You don't want her eating that, do you?" He pulled away and beamed at her. "Don't stand there grinning like a monkey. Check those potatoes you put on the boil."

"Yes, Sergeant," he said, turning to the kitchen. Rose straightened her beads and pulled her handkerchief from her ample bosom, her eyes tearing. He was always such a dear, sweet boy. It overwhelmed her so much that when he came back in she hurriedly put back her handkerchief and waved her cane at him again.

"Just you go see if Lewis is here for me yet," she said. "Go on."

Robert opened the door, seeing a car coming down the road, followed by another. Of all nights, he prayed, no company tonight. Tonight I just want to be with Margery.

He recognized Lewis's car and said, "He's here, Rose. Don't stay out too late and no hanky panky." He wagged his finger at her and gave her a kiss.

"You're a silly lad," she said, flustered. "Who'd bother having any hanky panky with the likes of me?"

"There are lots of rapacious old men out there," he laughed.

"Ra what?" she said. "Silly lad." She toddled down the walk as Lewis came out to meet her. "Ah! What a vision you are, Rose," he smiled and waved at Robert. "I am enchanted."

"Now don't you start as well," she said, getting into the car with his assistance. The other car pulled up behind, waving to Lewis before stopping. All three people got out – Margery, Elizabeth and a young man Robert recognized as Brian Warren.

"They wanted to stop for a moment," Margery said, coming in. "Just to say hello."

Robert's eyes were moist as he saw Elizabeth come up the walk. Her arm was loosely holding Brian's. "I wanted you to meet Brian, Robert," Elizabeth said.

"Hello, Mr. Morne," Brian said, shaking Robert's hand. "I know we met briefly a few weeks ago, but I thought it might be nice to reacquaint myself. I brought your wife here and Elizabeth asked me to stop."

"Would you like to come in?" Robert said, his eyes having a hard time staying off Elizabeth's face. He felt Margery behind him, her hand on his arm. It nearly made him swoon from the familiarity of it.

"No, we have to be off to his father's for dinner," Elizabeth smiled. "I just thought it would be nice to stop."

"I am so happy you did, Elizabeth," Robert smiled at her, his eyes feeling misty. She recognized the symptoms and tugged on Brian's arm. "We'd best be getting on now, Brian. We'll be back to get you later, Mummy. About midnight?" Margery nodded. Five and a half hours. Five and a half hours alone with Robert at last.

He shut the door and turned around to look at her. "This is me as I am now," Margery smiled at him. "Not very fancy, I'm afraid." She looked at him, standing in shirtsleeves and braces, the way he had looked when they went to the Downs together and would lie in the grass holding one another. To her eyes he seemed little different than that boy he had been.

They kept their eyes on each other for an eternity before she turned from him and said, "Now don't tell me you not only did the shopping, but have cooked the meal as well?"

"Of course," he smiled, taking her to the dining room. The table was set for two, Rose's best china and sparkling crystal adorning the two settings. Two tall ivory tapers cast a mellow glow from their flames. A fresh bouquet of autumn flowers was arranged in a vase, the gold, red and orange colors almost like flames leaping from the tabletop. She drew in her breath sharply.

"Like it?" he said, coming behind her. "Rose has a nice garden. The roses were particularly beautiful at this time of year. The colors turn so brilliant, don't they?" She nodded, still unable to speak.

"Would you like the wireless on?" he said from the kitchen. She heard him drop something and utter a 'damn.' "Are you all right in there?" she shouted to him. "I don't need to be waited on like Lady Muck, you know."

"Oh," he smiled, coming in with a saucepan lid in his hand. "You mean you are *not* Lady Muck? I thought *she* was coming to dinner tonight. Begone, you imposter!" She started giggling like a schoolgirl and he joined in laughing with her.

"Do let me help, Robert," Margery said. "I am so used to being in the kitchen I feel quite useless standing about like this."

"Then you shall just have to get used to it," he said, coming from the kitchen. "Are you ready to eat, my lady?"

"Yes," she said, following him to the dining room. He put down two steaming bowls of vegetable soup. "Made it myself," he said proudly. "Used to do that at the hospital."

"I don't recall you being such a good cook, Robert," she said cautiously. "Did you learn that in hospital?"

"No," he said, seating her and then going into the parlor to turn on the wireless. The sounds of dance band music played low in the background as he returned. "When I went to live in the cottage, I started making things for myself. Things I was familiar with, you know, like pork chops or sausages and mash. Then I had a bumper crop of vegetables last year, so I learned to make soup. I've become a dab hand at cooking, really. See what you think of it."

Margery took a sip and remarked how good it was. "Not quite so nice as when you grow the vegetables yourself," he said, smiling. "But not too bad."

"It's delicious," she said. "You'll have to do the cooking from now on."

"Right," he said, his face disturbed. "You mean from when we are able to live together again, whenever that might be." He removed a bottle of white wine from a cooler at the side of the table. "A present from Lewis Warren," he said, pouring her a glass, then himself. "Plonk, we called it in the Army. Of course, this is nothing like plonk." He took a sniff and sighed. "That's the real thing. Should we have a toast?"

"Yes," she said, picking up her glass. "Will you let me give it?"

"If you like," he smiled. "Go on, then."

She cleared her throat. "To Robert and Margery. Joined together in love and never to be parted."

His eyes misted over as he held her gaze. "Joined together in love and never to be parted. I remember that now. I remember the shop and the man who did the engraving."

"The ring has been on my hand since that day," Margery nearly whispered.

"On mine as well," he said. "Louise told me that because of my ring she was able to learn my name. My Christian name, anyway." He took a few spoonfuls of soup. "There were these two RAMC blokes who figured I was done for, so they thought a gold ring like mine would fetch something. They couldn't get it off my finger, though, as it had swelled up so much. So they were talking about breaking my finger to get at it. Louise was behind the drape with the next patient. She heard the whole thing and gave them hell. No wonder they ran." He chuckled but noticed Margery had become quiet.

"Something wrong with the soup?" he enquired nervously.

"No, Robert, the soup is wonderful." She stared at the colorful mélange of vegetables in her bowl. "I was just wondering about Louise. How did she come to stay at the hospital all those years? Don't Army nurses get transferred?" She took another spoonful, poising it before her while waiting for his answer.

"She's not a proper Army nurse now, although she was," he replied, finishing the remainder of his soup. "She was with the Queen Alexandra Nurses when she first came out to France. Reserves, I think. After the War she resigned, but opted to stay on with the hospital in Sussex. A lot of them did that, not wanting that Army life, but liking the patients and the work. I am grateful she did decide to stay on."

Margery finished her soup and looked at him thoughtfully. "I want you to be honest with me, Robert," she hesitated and drew back her shoulders. "You know the truth now about Jack and me, thanks to Billy. I need to know about you. And Louise."

"Louise and me?" he said, smiling. "There's nothing to know, really. She was my nurse and became a good friend. Without her I would be dead, surely. She was very devoted to my care."

"Why?" Margery questioned. "Why would anyone be so devoted unless..."

"She loved me?" Robert said, looking directly at Margery. "I won't lie to you, Margery. I think she believes she loved me. At one point, when I thought I would never find you, it occurred to me that I might want to be with her for the rest of my life. I do love her, you know. Not the way I love you. She is a friend and a protector and a fighter. She is intelligent and can be really funny and kind and gives too much of herself to others.

There is much about her I admire. But do I love her as I love you? Would I be here with you tonight if I did?" He reached across the table and took her hand.

"I suppose in twenty years much has passed," Margery smiled at him. "I wondered if your heart perhaps might find someone else to be more...more what you would want. I am no longer young, Robert. I am not the girl I was."

"Take a good look at me," Robert responded. "I am not young, or even intact as I was twenty years ago. You are getting no bargain, Mrs. Morne. No bargain at all in your choice of husband."

"There is no one else, is there, Robert?" Margery asked. "You are sure about Louise? Because she loves you. I could see that when we went to Sussex to clear out the cottage. She loves you as fiercely as I do. I don't think she would just walk away without a fight for you. Do I blame her? No. Does she know you better than I do? I wonder if she does."

He got up and collected the empty soup bowls. "She knows me better in some ways," he replied. "But not my soul, not the true man I am and have always been. That has been very clear this week especially. You do know she went back to live with her aunt and uncle in Brockham? I told her how I felt about you. It was an awful scene and I know I hurt her deeply. Never, never did I intend that. I totally underestimated how she felt about me. All along she has encouraged me to find you again. I don't think I quite understood." He looked at Margery helplessly.

"There are some things that haven't changed," Margery said. "Like your inability to see the effect you have on women." He looked so wounded she smiled. "Seriously, Robert, you never seemed to be aware of that even when we were going out. You mean to tell me that you never knew how Louise felt about you?"

"She's very good at hiding it," he said, going into the kitchen. "When I thought I would never see you again, because Jack told me you had moved away from Upper Marstone and were happily married..."

"Ha!" Margery shouted back to him from the dining room. "What a web Jack wove, didn't he?"

"Yes," Robert said, coming back in with two plates replete with golden fried pork chops, boiled parsley potatoes, and fresh green peas, "but I believed him. I believed everything he told me. I had no reason not to. He told the truth, sort of, didn't he? He just left out the most critical information."

Margery murmured her appreciation of the meal as she took her first bite. "You have become a gourmet chef, haven't you?" she smiled at him. "This is utterly delicious."

"Thank you, Ma'am," he said, nodding to her. "Just simple pork chops. I made them for Jack the last time he came to see me."

"He was very upset," Margery nodded. "Did you have a row?"

"Oh, yes," Robert said, taking a forkful of potato. "About you. I told him I was determined to find you, to see you one more time. He tried talking me into marrying Louise and forgetting about you. Then it got ugly, he left, I had a seizure." He moved from one point to another matter of factly.

"What did he say to you?" Margery said angrily, her eyes blazing. "What?"

"It doesn't matter now, does it, Margery?" he said quietly. "He's dead and can't hurt us anymore."

They ate the rest of the meal silently, the pall of Jack and what he had done still hanging over them. Robert got up to remove the plates, and came back with lemon pudding and cream.

"Did you make this as well?" Margery asked, wanting to dispel the gloom that their conversation about Jack had brought about.

"Well, honestly speaking, Rose actually made most of it," he replied, smiling gently at her. "I helped, though."

"It is as nice as the rest of the meal," Margery said, digging into the creamy yellow mixture. "And I am glad we are talking about Jack and Louise and our lives, because I was so afraid we would go on as we did last time, pretending things are the same. They aren't, are they?"

Robert was thoughtful before he answered. "No, they are not the same. I suppose if we had been parted and married others, or had other affairs, and then came back together, it would be much the same thing. I will confess," he held his hand up, "as I want no secrets from you ever again, that I did think I loved Louise. I did think I would marry her after I saw you again, safely married to some rich bloke, living in a grand house and raising children. I knew I would never intrude on your happiness. I had this vision of myself, standing at your gate, watching you send the kiddies off to school, and wondering who that poor, old soldier was. Perhaps you would have thrown me a shilling or something. Then I figured I would come home, happy that you were happy, and marry Louise so she could look after me the rest of my life." He took a spoonful of pudding.

"Somehow I don't see you as being the sort of man who could settle for being looked after for the rest of your life," Margery said, finishing her pudding. Robert noticed her glass was empty and poured more wine. "You need more than that. So do I."

"And Jack could never give you what you needed?" Robert said inquisitively, wanting to hear her tell him what Billy had told him.

"Never," Margery said firmly, holding the cut glass crystal glass up so that the candle flame reflected in all the facets. "Jack was good to Elizabeth and me. He was not a bad husband and he was an excellent father. He never mistreated me or made me miserable. Do you know what I couldn't bear, though?"

"What?" Robert asked, not sure he wanted to hear the answer.

"The look in his eyes," Margery said. "That combination of sadness and anger that he always had when he looked at me. You know I never slept with him, don't you?" Robert nodded, feeling glad but also sad that Jack never had that love from a woman, especially the woman he adored.

"Do you know what I used to do?" she smiled sadly. "I used to go to our room, put on my nightgown, and say, 'Now tonight I will sleep with him. It is the least I can do because he has done so much for Elizabeth and me. He loves me, he is handsome, he is Robert's brother.' As soon as I mentioned your name it became impossible for me to even think of sleeping with Jack. So I would sit there in my nightgown, desperately trying to convince myself that you were dead and he was my husband and it was his due. Then Jack would come into the room and get into bed, giving me that look again. I would sit there until he was asleep. Then I would go to sleep." She stared at her wine glass, mesmerized by the reflections of light.

"He must have loved you so much," Robert said quietly, "to be able to do that for you. Amazing, really."

"He was a stoic in some ways," Margery said. "But he was also stubborn and determined. It almost became a game to him when I would capitulate at last and admit I no longer loved you. That is what it came down to in the end. I only made love with one man in my lifetime. You."

Robert flushed slightly then looked at her. "I don't deserve you, Margery. I don't."

"If you slept with another woman, Robert, it makes no matter to me," Margery said. "I understand men are different that way."

"No!" Robert said. "Only once after you. Only once. It was with Louise."

"Louise?" Margery said. "I would never have thought it of her."

"It was after Jack left and I had that seizure the last time I saw him," Robert continued, his nerves on edge thinking he would lose Margery. She seemed interested but not upset. "He said some terrible things to me that day. That I was not a normal man, that I was a pathetic cripple." He hung his head trying to fight the tears. "When Louise came with Dr. Gibbons, I was shattered. She stayed with me at Dr. Gibbons' behest. I asked her to lie down with me. I told her I would never be a normal man

261

again and didn't even think I could remember how to make love. It went on from there." He was afraid to look up at Margery, afraid she would think him a cad.

"Jack," was all she said. "How could he have said those things to you? I cannot understand. So cruel and uncalled for, as if he wanted to kill you."

"He did," Robert said. "I think he did when I was coming home here."

"Elizabeth said that today, too," Margery replied. She looked at him tenderly. "She was so pleased to meet you today, although she admitted she would not have if she had known it was you. There are still things in her heart that will take time to heal, you know, but she has given us her blessing, in her own way. It was her idea to come to the door to see you tonight and introduce you to Brian Warren."

"She likes him, does she?" Robert said, getting his equilibrium back after his confession.

"Very much," Margery smiled. "She asked me if I knew you were 'the one' when I first met you. All very convoluted but I knew she was thinking of Brian."

"And did you know?" he grinned.

"I did indeed," she laughed. "It was the day you, Jack and your Dad came to Lennox Place. That awful Alf Lawton had tried to molest me and your Dad sorted him out. Do you remember I bit Alf on the arm?"

"That's right," Robert laughed. "Well deserved, too, I'd say." He was quiet and said, "Do you know that ever since I have come back to Upper Marstone I have remembered so much more than I did in hospital? All the little stories and people. Trying to remember when I was there always seemed like a game of chance. I would have dreams where the memory was like a will o' the wisp and just as I thought I would catch it, phhfft." He blew out one of the tapers. "I couldn't even remember my own name for nine years. Louise saw our names in the ring so called me 'Robert.' It was a dream I had about Dad. He said, "Your name is Morne, son. Don't forget it. So I clung so hard to the memory I still had it when I woke up."

"I hate to think of you being there all those years when you could have been here," Margery cried. "It just makes my blood boil to think Jack kept us apart and the things he said to you."

"If I think about it I will probably go mad," Robert said quietly. "Perhaps when Dad died it made Jack go mad. What happened to Dad?"

The memory of that day was clear in Margery's mind. "He had a heart attack and died very peacefully in his shed. He tried to find you for years, Robert. Went to all sorts of hospitals, but never succeeded, obviously. I found him that morning. He and I were very fond of each other." Her eyes misted over as she stared into the remaining candle flame.

"And Mum?" Robert asked. "Elizabeth said she died of grief."

"I suppose she did," Margery said. "It was too much medicine, Robert. Whether it was deliberate or not we don't know. She never got over you being killed. The sad part is all this was in vain, as you were still alive. Why couldn't they identify you? I suppose I don't understand."

"I lost my identity discs," he said plainly. "When I was wounded, my tunic was in shreds and my papers were lost. So there I was, unconscious and unable to tell them who I was."

"Quite horrible," Margery said. "Were you in pain?"

"I don't remember a thing, truthfully," Robert said. "You know what I would like? I would like us to start afresh together from tonight. My parents are dead, my brother is dead, and life is very different. We have to start our life together again anew." He looked at her eagerly.

"Yes, we do," she said. "But we also need to know what happened to each other so we can understand one another fully. I always felt that no matter what, I understood you, because I knew what your life had been like, what your parents were like, and how you lived. There is so much about you I don't know now, and I want to." She took his hand in hers, running her fingers over the ring he still wore.

"Agreed," he said, putting his right hand on hers. "No secrets now."

"No secrets," she smiled.

"Shall we retire to the parlor for coffee?" he said. "There's a nice fire going. I would like to hear about Elizabeth if you would indulge me."

"My pleasure," Margery said. "How did you know that was my favorite topic?"

"I thought I was your favorite topic," he frowned, his eyes twinkling.

"You might be," Margery smiled at him. "You just might be."

Robert made coffee, his clanking in the kitchen almost sounding familiar to Margery as she sat back on the old, comfortable sofa. The music was soothing and the wine had made her feel very relaxed. She looked around the cottage, noticing how comfortable yet spacious it was. This is exactly the sort of house I always wanted, she thought. Jack had chosen the house on Tilburstow Hill Road. It came back to her how quickly he decided to move after one visit to Sussex in 1926. The coincidence was obvious; it was right after he knew Robert was still alive. She closed her eyes, fighting back her anger at Jack. Robert was right; they had to start afresh from tonight if they were ever going to make their life together work.

"Here we are," Robert said, putting the tray down and pouring out a cup. "It occurs to me, Margery, that I don't even know how you like your coffee. I don't think we ever had coffee together before, did we?"

"No, I suppose not," Margery said. "There is so much we haven't yet done, isn't there? Holidays together, seaside visits..."

"To Sidmouth?" he said eagerly. "I suppose my family is still there?"

"Your aunts are both gone now, too," Margery said sadly. "It grieved them so when you were missing. Auntie Emma died of influenza in 1925 and Auntie Mary went back to Sidmouth and died not long after your father. So many deaths in so short a time." She sipped her coffee, its rich flavor filling her senses.

The clock struck half past eight while they sat and talked about twenty years of their lives and their memories. As the time went on Margery felt as if he had never really been away at all, the ease of talking and being with one another coming back so quickly. She was telling him about their friend Milly who had left the village when he said, "Listen to that! They must be playing the old tunes tonight. Do you remember that one?"

"That's our song," Margery said softly. "'Meet Me Tonight in Dreamland.' I have never forgotten it."

"Neither have I," Robert said. "Would you have this dance with me, Mrs. Morne?" He bowed slightly before her and held out his hand.

"I would be honored, Mr. Morne," she replied, taking his hand and putting her other hand on his shoulder.

They swayed to the music at first, moving tentatively around the room as they felt the rhythm of each other as they had done long ago. Their movements coincided as they artfully dodged the tables and lamps around the parlor, moving more confidently. It was as if they had never stopped dancing together, their movements so perfectly coincided.

Robert held her close, then closer, his cheek next to hers as they moved around the room. The motion made him dizzy. It was not a seizure, but her closeness to him. His fingers moved through her hair, undoing the pins. He moved his lips to her cheek, then her mouth, kissing her first gently, then with more passion. Her response was immediate and they stopped dancing, locked into an embrace that made them one person.

She took his braces in her hands, taking them down quickly, then unbuttoned his shirt while his fingers did the same with her dress. Her lips burned on his neck, then his chest, as she covered him with kisses. He steered her down the hall to his room, their hunger for each other so intense they could not let go of each other even as they navigated the hallway. Their lips were joined together as they tumbled into the room and onto his bed, leaving their clothes at the doorway and around the room.

They made love furiously, passionately, not stopping for breath until they had worn themselves out with their fury. They lay next to one another in the darkness, the light from the crescent moon shining in the window, illuminating their white bodies with a silver glow. Margery turned to him, putting her arms around him and her head to his chest. Her face rested on the jagged, smooth scar that cut across his left side, near to his heart. Her fingers outlined it, touching it so tenderly as he lay still, his eyes closed. She lifted herself up, kissing every inch of the scar, then the old scars on his arms, and the most recent one that was still healing. She kissed that one fiercely, knowing that if Elizabeth had not been there, she would not be lying here tonight with Robert.

She climbed on top of him, gently moving over him and bending toward him to take his head in her hands. He came up to meet her, groaning with surprise and pleasure as she made love to him, her hands running over and over the raised scar on the left side of his head. It was almost as if she thought that their passion and pleasure would erase the years that had escaped them and the scars that marred his body.

Again they lay together, hands clasped, bodies warm with each other. In Folkestone she had not been as bold as she was tonight, but tonight her passion dictated her behavior. No other man had been to her what Robert was, and no other man would ever be again. She clasped him fiercely to her and saw his eyes full of tears.

"You have not forgotten anything, my darling," she whispered to him, thinking he looked unreal in the silver light from the window. "Will you do something for me?"

"Anything," he choked out, his emotions running so high he was unable to speak.

"Pinch me," she said. "Go on. Pinch me hard."

He came up on one elbow, wondering what new naughtiness she had in mind. "Why?" he asked her, not sure exactly what to say.

"I've had this dream before, but never in such detail," Margery smiled wickedly. "I know it can't be real, that you cannot be here and we have not just spent several hours doing things we could never repeat in polite company."

"Then you'd best pinch me as well," he smiled back at her, "because I've had the same dream many times myself. Just mind where you pinch!" They spent another half hour wrapped up in one another when the parlor clock struck half past eleven.

"Like Folkestone," Margery said, sitting up. "You had to leave me at half past eleven to get to the ship. It is just the same. Oh, Robbie, I am afraid. So afraid this is all a dream and once again it is half past eleven and we will part and I will never see you again." She began to sob quietly as he took her in his arms and held her tightly to his chest.

"It is not a dream, darling. I will be here tomorrow, and the next day, and the next," he said, brushing her cheek with his hand. "What a damn irritation you have to leave now! Do you remember how vexing it was when we had to sneak around the same way when we were engaged? For God's sake we are grown adults and married as well. What the hell are we playing at?"

"I don't know, darling," she said, kissing his chest again and moving up to his neck. "I don't know. What are we doing?"

"What you are doing has got to stop," he said in a mock stern voice. "Rose warned me not to get up to any hanky-panky, as she put it. If she finds us like this, I'll be out on the street." He could not stop himself from kissing both her breasts passionately before she took his head in her hands again. "It is nearly quarter to twelve," she whispered. "I have to get dressed, darling. I have to." He leaned back, letting her go as he watched her every move. She quickly dressed and tried to straighten her hair when they heard a car drive up.

"Quickly, darling," she said urgently, "you had better get something on." She stared at him as he jumped up, smiling at how beautiful he looked to her. Just like the boy she once knew so long ago in Folkestone. It didn't seem possible that he was forty-two years old and she forty. *We can't turn back the hands of time,* she thought to herself, *but it felt as if we did tonight.*

It amazed her how quickly he was dressed and presentable, smoothing out the bed and smiling at her in the darkness. "I expect we should go sit in the parlor and try and look respectable," he chuckled as they headed back and sat down just as the door opened.

"Come in," they heard Rose's voice. "I can put the kettle on." They heard her beads rattling before she stepped into the parlor. "Well, very cozy," she said as Robert and Margery both smiled at her innocently. Catkins was sitting in Robert's lap, purring, his eyes closed in bliss.

"Are you ready, Mummy?" Elizabeth looked carefully at her mother, hoping all had gone well. The strange expression on her mother's face was hard to read, but she did not think it was the sign of a disaster. She looked at Brian, who smiled at her. Robert and Margery were standing up, looking at one another, their looks full of such love it was tangible to the others in the room. He took her chin and kissed her tenderly, and she responded. "Goodnight, my love," he whispered in her ear. "It won't be long before we are together always. Remember. 'Joined together in love and never to be parted."

"Never," she whispered in his ear, holding his hand as Brian brought her coat over.

Margery was silent on the ride home. Her expression was so dreamy Elizabeth had to smile at Brian, who nodded. "Mummy," Elizabeth finally said, trying to suppress her own smile, "did you have a nice time? Was everything nice?"

"Nice?" Margery smiled like the Mona Lisa. "Nice? Everything was wonderful, darling. He's quite a good cook, you know. He's always been good at everything he ever turned his hand to. Everything." She returned to her dreamy smile as Brian raised his eyebrows.

Margery went into the house first and Elizabeth said she would be in shortly. The dinner party had been very pleasant. She found herself catching Brian's eye and smiling more often than not. He winked, raised his eyebrows, and gave her little signals, especially when Auntie Rose was expounding on some topic. It was as if they shared some delicious little secrets together.

"Your mother seems very pleased with the evening," Brian said as they watched Margery nearly float to the front door. "He seems a right nice chap, doesn't he?"

"He is my father's brother," Elizabeth said, feeling a sharp stab of betrayal come back to her.

"Of course," Brian added quickly. "I just meant he seems very nice. It is obvious your mother is very much in love with him still."

"I have never seen Mummy like this," Elizabeth admitted. "She is transformed, don't you think?"

"I do," Brian said quietly. "Love has enormous transformative powers."

"It must to have my mother look like that," Elizabeth said, looking at the open front door. "She didn't even close the door."

"Elizabeth," Brian said and she turned to look at him. He looked at her and said, "I hope you might go out with me some evening. Perhaps to the cinema. Or we might go up to London if you like."

"Yes, Brian, I would like that very much," Elizabeth said, feeling suddenly very young and vulnerable.

"I had such a great time with you tonight," he kept on talking. "Your Auntie Rose can go on a bit, can't she? What a smashing old thing she is, though. She even made Louise laugh, and I daresay Louise is not all that happy."

"Because of Robert?" Elizabeth said. "I could tell she loves him, too. What a muddle for Mummy and her."

"And poor Robert, caught in the middle," Brian said.

"Yes, I suppose he can't help it if he is attractive to women," Elizabeth said. "I can see that he is. Charming, too."

"If I may say so, I believe his daughter inherited some of the Morne charm." He took her chin and kissed her tenderly. She stepped back and looked at the ground.

"I'm sorry," Brian said. "I should have asked you first."

"Oh, no, Brian," she said, looking at him. "It was quite all right." She ran up the path and into the house, turning before closing the door to wave.

"Mr. Morne, you have a lovely daughter," he smiled as he drove back to Leigh.

Chapter Thirty-Four

It was after midnight when Louise opened the front door of the imposing house in Brockham. Aunt Eleanor had left a little golden lamp burning in the front window, but otherwise all was quiet.

She slipped in, turned off the light, and went up to her room. The shoes that Aunt Eleanor had given her to wear were a little small, so she removed them first and sat down on the bed, thinking about the night's events.

Aunt Eleanor could not allow her to go to this party without a new dress, so when she had come home from her shopping in Croydon on Friday, she came into Louise's room, a large box in her hands.

"Now, before you say anything," she began, handing the box to Louise, "consider it an early Christmas gift." Louise opened the box and pulled out a shimmering, sea-green cocktail length dress, the silky overlay adding sophistication to the simple dress with a dropped waist.

"Oh, no, Aunt Eleanor," Louise cried. "I told you I didn't need a new dress. It is only this one evening out."

"You don't know if it is only this one evening," Aunt Eleanor said, taking the dress out and holding it up for Louise's inspection. "I knew it was you when I saw it. Look how it plays so beautifully with your skin and the green in your eyes." Louise got up and went to the bureau, holding it up to her.

"I took one of your old dresses along for size, so I am sure it will fit," Eleanor said. "You can wear this lovely cream colored satin cloak I have as well. And shoes to match. You will be a picture, dear."

"I feel as if I am going to Buckingham Palace, not Lewis Warren's," Louise said dryly.

"Never mind," Eleanor replied. "It will do you a world of good to dress up for once."

269

All day Saturday Louise was nervous, not only about the dinner party, but about Robert. How would things go for him this evening? She could not keep her mind off the evening's events for both of them. It seemed that they had reached a watershed in their relationship and tonight's events would prove in what direction they would go.

Aunt Eleanor enjoyed doing Louise's hair, combing out the long, brown tresses and pinning them up with decorative pins. "Now a little makeup," she said. Louise protested.

"Not that, Aunt Eleanor," she said, "I'll look like a London streetwalker."

"Not the way I do it," Eleanor insisted. "Just a little powder, rouge and lipstick. That's all. There." Eleanor's face looked pensive. "It needs something. Where is the emerald pin David gave you for your engagement?" Louise searched around the dressing table, knowing she had the pin recently. Where had she left it?

"Well, we don't have time to be looking as Lewis will be here any moment. What about this pin?" She picked up a lovely antique gold pin with green stones. A gift from Robert for her birthday. Eleanor pinned it to her dress. "Yes. Just perfect now."

Louise stared at herself in the mirror, the transformation from plain working nurse to lady remarkable. Eleanor beamed behind her chair. "You are really so very pretty, Louise," Eleanor said. "You look wonderful."

Louise frowned slightly but could not help but think the dress and hairstyle made a difference. She wished that she could call a taxi and go to Rose's cottage, surprising Robert. What would he think of her? Would he find her beautiful, more beautiful than Margery? She sighed so deeply Eleanor was concerned.

"What, dear?" she said. "I've got the cape here."

"Do you know what this reminds me of, Aunt Eleanor?" Louise said. "It reminds me of how I felt when mother would fuss and worry I would never marry."

"Listen to me," Eleanor said sharply. "Whatever you want to do is your own choice, Louise. I would never treat you the way your mother did. I respect your judgment to live your life your own way. But," she added, "I want you to enjoy life, too, not be hard at work all the time. There are so many wonderful things in life, you know, besides work."

"I do know that, Aunt Eleanor," Louise said. "You are one of them." The doorbell rang as Eleanor ran off, waving her hand at Louise and her comments. Louise took one full twirl in her mirror, watching the silky fabric embrace her. It was a lovely dress, no doubt. Aunt Eleanor always had exquisite taste.

Lewis stood there in evening dress, looking elegant and handsome. When he saw Louise his eyes lit up in appreciation. "If I may say so, Louise, you look splendid," he said as Eleanor helped her on with the cape. "Absolutely splendid."

"Thank you," Louise replied. "Aunt Eleanor picked out the dress."

"With Louise in mind, of course," Eleanor said, giving Lewis a quick kiss on the cheek. "Have a lovely evening. I won't wait up." She smiled at them both.

Rose was waving wildly from the front seat of the car. "You cannot believe how excited Rose is to see you again," Lewis said as they came toward the car. "She has been talking my ear off about you and how much she misses you all the way from Upper Marstone."

"Hello, dear," Rose nearly shouted as Louise entered the back seat. "I couldn't wait to see you again. I miss you so much." She turned in her seat as Lewis got in and started off for Leigh. "What a beautiful dress! I'd have hardly recognized you tonight. You look lovely."

"Thank you, Rose," Louise said, starting to feel a bit more comfortable with her new-found image as a beauty queen. The thought made her smile. As they carried on toward Leigh her thoughts went to the little cottage in Upper Marstone. Was Margery there already? Was everything all right? If only she could see Robert again.

"Isn't that right, dear?" Rose said, interrupting her reverie.

"I'm sorry, Rose," Louise said. "I was miles away." Rose huffed but Lewis said, "It is a beautiful evening and I think we will all have a splendid time tonight."

"I am looking forward to it," Rose said. "I never go out anymore, you know."

"Your dress is a vision," Lewis said, turning and winking at Louise, who looked at Rose's bead-bedecked dress and smiled in agreement.

The house was lit like a birthday cake as they arrived. Elizabeth and Brian had not yet come back from Upper Marstone, so they settled in and had a drink in the drawing room. Soon they heard the sounds of the couple. Louise noticed Elizabeth looking very young and vulnerable, Robert's features shouting at Louise as she walked in.

"Hello, Louise," Brian said. "I must say you look smashing, doesn't she, Elizabeth? Really smashing."

"If everyone keeps this up I shall have to register myself in the Miss London competition," she laughed.

Dinner was served and they spent a lovely few hours enjoying a marvelous meal, talking and getting to know one another. Lewis sat at the head of the table, Louise to his right and Rose to his left. Brian kept Rose entertained, and Elizabeth sat next to Louise. It did not escape Louise's attention that Brian and Elizabeth had become very friendly, as their smiles and signals during the meal were evident. They seemed right for each other. If Brian was like his father, Elizabeth was a lucky girl.

At times Louise found it difficult to keep her eyes of Robert's daughter. She had memorized every feature of his face, every line, every lift of his smile. Elizabeth had all his mannerisms, which surprised Louise as Elizabeth had never known him. Perhaps Jack was more like Robert than she believed.

"That is a lovely pin, Louise," Elizabeth said, looking at the jewelry. "It is just the sort of pin I love. Very artistically designed yet subtle, too."

"Yes," Louise said, fingering it nervously. "It was a birthday gift."

"It goes so well with your dress," Elizabeth added. Louise kept fingering the pin, thinking of the day Robert gave it to her last May. All of a sudden she felt the pin snap, the little green gems falling in all directions.

"Oh, no!" Elizabeth said. "Oh, I am so sorry."

"It wasn't your fault, Elizabeth," Louise said, stunned at the pin's sudden break. "I should not have been fiddling with it so."

"Not your emeralds?" Lewis said as they got down on the floor to hunt for the stones.

"No," Louise replied. "This was the pin Robert gave me for my birthday last year."

"Ah," Lewis said. "Here are most of the stones. Did you find any others, Brian?"

"A few, Dad," Brian replied. "If we find the rest we'll make sure you get them back, Louise."

"No need," Louise said. "I think it is broken beyond repair." Her eyes looked sad. The pin seemed to hold all the hopes and dreams she had for a life with Robert. The clock said half-past nine. Perhaps he and Margery had decided to brook convention and be together no matter what now.

They retired to the drawing room for a few more drinks and conversation. Rose dozed off in a comfortable chair, her snoring interrupting the talk. "She is so tired," Louise said kindly. "Perhaps you had better make an early start back to Upper Marstone."

"I am under strict orders from Rose not to get her home before midnight," Lewis laughed. "Perhaps she will turn into a pumpkin or something."

"Oh, no, Dr. Warren," Elizabeth replied. "Cinderella turned from a princess back to her old self in rags. No one turned into a pumpkin."

"Well, I have been told that I do not have much imagination," he chuckled. "Fairy tales were never my favorite reading material. Louise's either, I remember. Do you know she read all my back issues of *Brain* magazine when she was a schoolgirl? Her Aunt Eleanor used to lament that her choice of bedtime reading material was frightening their maid." Louise smiled wryly.

"I wish I were interested in something so exciting," Elizabeth said. "I like art, but I am not much good at it. So I was going to study art history."

"Your father is an excellent artist," Louise said, without realizing what she had said.

"Yes," Elizabeth smiled. "I met him this morning, you know."

"Met him?" Louise cried. "How wonderful!"

"It was an accident, of course," Elizabeth continued, as if trying to extricate herself from a difficult position. "He was visiting the family's graves and I was going there to..."

"And he was there, was he?" Brian interrupted, seeing Elizabeth on the verge of tears. "He's a topping fellow. I met him again tonight. Hard to believe he endured so much."

"He did indeed," Lewis said, carefully watching Louise's expression. "Seriously wounded, but he pulled through. You can thank this lady here for that. A marvel, that is what you are, Louise."

"I knew he had the potential to survive," Louise said flatly. "I did what any nurse would have done."

"Thank you," Elizabeth said, her eyes glittering. "You have made my mother the happiest woman in the world. You have no idea what a changed woman she is."

As the time drew near to go, Brian agreed to take Rose and Elizabeth home. "That way you are not double backing, Dad," Brian smiled and winked at his father. "Brockham is straight the opposite direction nearly."

"Thanks, son," Lewis said. "That will make things easier."

Rose was slightly confused when she awoke but was finally hustled off to the car and farewells were said. "Another drink, Louise?" Lewis asked. She shook her head.

"I think I should be going as well, Lewis," Louise replied. "It is getting close to midnight. And no," she laughed, "I will not turn into a pumpkin or anything else when the clock strikes twelve."

"What you have turned into tonight is a beautiful, fine lady," he smiled at her. "I really quite like the nursing uniforms, too, of course. But tonight...well...you really were sensational."

"It's just a dress, Lewis," she said tartly. "Underneath I am the same dowdy woman I was before."

273

"Why do you always say that?" Lewis questioned her, taking her shoulders. "You are a very beautiful woman in a unique way. I have always thought so." She turned her head from him.

"I think I am ready to go home, Lewis," she said softly, gathering up the cape. "It has been a long day. I hope everything went all right for Robert and Margery tonight."

"No emergency phone calls, so I can only guess they did," he said, grabbing his coat and hat as they went into the cold night air.

They drove silently, each with their own thoughts. As they took the turn off for Brockham, Lewis said, "Louise. I know you are thinking of Robert tonight. I know you will probably always be thinking of him in some way. Do you think you really, truly love him, to the exclusion of anyone else?"

"That's rather a moot question, Lewis," Louise replied. "He doesn't love me. He loves Margery. We are friends. A 'sister to him,' he said." She leaned back in her seat.

"Can you ever see your way to thinking of anyone else?" Lewis said.

"Thinking of anyone else?" Louise replied. "In what way? Do you mean, loving anyone else?"

"Yes," Lewis replied hesitantly as they pulled closer to her house. "I also mean marrying someone else."

"I don't think I am the marrying sort, Lewis," Louise replied. "In fact, I think I would be a terrible wife. It was different with Robert. He needed care. I suppose I would have been more a nurse than wife."

"His expectation of what he wanted from a wife might have been far different," Lewis replied. "Perhaps a nurse was not what he wanted, but a woman who would love him for himself. A woman he could understand."

"Margery, I suppose," she said resignedly.

"Louise," Lewis said as he pulled up and stopped the car in front of her darkened house, the little gold lamp shining in the window in welcome. "You must know how I feel about you." She turned to him, her eyes looking frightened and vulnerable in the darkness. "I...I love you, Louise. I have loved you from the first day I saw you in my office so long ago. What a fool I was not to wait until you grew up and marry you then! Louise," he hesitated, seeing her frightened expression. "I'm not very articulate at this. I want you to be my wife. Will you marry me?"

Louise said nothing, just sat staring straight ahead, her thoughts coming so fast and furious she could not contain them. Marry Lewis! With her heart still torn between Robert and David Giles, what could she say? Did she love him? Right now she didn't think she even knew what love was.

"I don't know, Lewis," she said softly. "I don't know what I want to do at present. Getting married is a big step."

"Yes," he said, chastened. "Yes, it is a big step, but if two people care for one another... You do care for me, don't you, Louise?" She looked at him, his face so eager for a response, the expectation of a negative reply vivid on his face.

"Tonight I don't know what I feel, Lewis," Louise said. "Let me sleep on my decision. I feel as if my head is in a muddle right now. Perhaps it was the wine."

"I shall await your answer as soon as you know your own heart," he said, taking her hand and kissing it. "May I kiss you, Louise?" She nodded, feeling the warmth of his lips against hers, the memory of both David's and Robert's kisses fresh in her mind. Did she love Lewis? She was fond of him and cared for him. To her mind it sounded like the same old record she had played before. It was always too late when she came to the realization that the person she loved was no longer there. Yes, she thought, I loved you once, Lewis. Perhaps I still do.

"Goodnight, Lewis," she said, getting out of the car and waving him off. "I can see myself in."

"I will await your answer, Louise," Lewis said, smiling at her.

She went into the house, closing the door as the car pulled away. She leaned on the doorframe, her heart heavy and light at the same time.

Chapter Thirty-Five

As November began, the cold winds blew from the north and scuttled most of Robert's gardening episodes. He and Margery had been seeing each other like a courting couple, finding a joy in renewing their relationship by doing some of the things they had done when they were young. Robert still felt odd being at Jack's house. As they had done in times past, they walked in the Downs, even finding the old cave where they had once been together.

Elizabeth watched her mother grow happier each day, finding her reluctance to let Robert move back in butting directly with her loyalty to her father. While she and Robert were cordial, even friendly, she still kept up her reserve with him. Every time she felt like relenting and bringing him into her heart, the vision of Jack's sad face appeared before her. Brian had been taking her out, even a lovely night on the town in London, with dancing at the Café de Paris, a place she had only dreamed of going to when she was a schoolgirl.

Brian had also begun the paperwork to buy the business. It was an exceedingly slow process. He was spending more time with Uncle Harry, learning what he needed to while the transfer dragged on. Elizabeth went to the office every day, ostensibly to do the secretarial work. Her heart leapt when she would be greeted at the door by Brian and his friendly, "Good morning, Boss." She and Brian often went to lunch at Elizabeth's house, with Margery pleased to prepare a good meal. She had become very fond of Brian in a short time, smiling at Elizabeth and giving her surreptitious winks whenever Brian was around.

Louise had not yet given Lewis an answer, although weeks had passed. Robert had phoned to enquire after her. Maisie was under strict orders to say she was out. To hear his voice again would be too much for Louise to bear. As long as she kept him in her heart, it seemed she could never give her heart to Lewis. Eleanor was exasperated with her, but kept her silence. Henry was talking to Lewis every day. Louise knew from the questions she was asked each morning at breakfast as to how she felt about Lewis.

One morning near Jack's birthday in November Harry and Brian were working on a big contract when Harry said to Elizabeth, "I almost forgot to tell you. Auntie May wants to throw a big party for everyone. Part of that is because we want to go away for the winter," he said, shuddering in a mock way, "and she wants to see everyone gathered round the old fireside."

"Is she well enough?" Elizabeth questioned.

"Oh, your mother will help out, I'm sure, and Lily and Alyce," Harry nodded, referring to his two grown daughters.

"I can help, too," Elizabeth said, "although I am not much good at cooking or anything like that."

"We'll appoint you chief decorator, then," Harry smiled. "Make the tables look nice. We were thinking of letting the village hall. Invite everyone you know. In fact, so many people want to see Robbie again it seemed the best solution. Everyone brings a covered dish or cake, we all wind up the victrola, and have a right good time."

"The victrola?" Elizabeth and Brian said together, laughing.

"What do you call them nowadays? Record players, that's it," Harry laughed. "I almost said gramophone instead."

"Oh, Uncle Harry, it is nearly 1936," Elizabeth groaned.

"Auntie May is absolutely stuck on this idea. She has already enlisted her cadre of friends to help." He smiled, then became serious. "Do you think Robbie, I mean, Robert, would be all right with this idea?"

"You'll have to ask Mummy," Elizabeth said, turning to the typewriter. "Probably Brian's father, too."

"We'll just have to invite Brian's father, then," Harry smiled. "This village needs a party to pep it up."

The plans went ahead for the party, May handling all the arrangements. The day dawned near the end of November, cold rain and sleet falling. Everyone got to the hall early to decorate the tables, lay out the plates, and arrange the food in hot and cold chafing dishes.

The guests began to arrive by seven o'clock, the music from the record player flooding the brightly lit hall with dance music. Robert and Margery arrived together, holding each other's hands bravely. "I hope we don't run into too many people who give us a hard time," he said, dressed in his pin-stripes and she in her green silk once again.

277

"Who cares what anyone thinks?" she smiled, holding his hand tighter. "They thought ill of me when I married Jack. Now they can think ill of me when I am with you. I never seem to have anyone think well of me, do I?" He grinned and said, "I do."

Their fears were unfounded, with the exception of a few gossipy older ladies who stood off to the side, pointing and whispering at them. "Tonight we should tell everyone we are married," Margery said. "I'll explain it so as not to cast blame on Jack."

"Right," Robert grinned. "Then they won't think we are living in sin, or behaving sinfully, or what have you."

May had aged greatly, but her joy at the success of the party and seeing her sister so happy again made her feel much better than she had. Robert was stunned to see Lily, Nicholas, and Alyce, all so little when he last saw them, grown up and even having children of their own. He sat next to May, she holding his hands as Margery talked to Lily about the newest addition to her family.

"Are you happy, Robert?" she asked, running her hands over his again and again. "I still cannot believe this is all real."

"You're not going to ask me to pinch you, are you, May?" he laughed. "Margery asked me that the first night we were alone together." He looked at her, his eyes so loving May nearly cried.

"No, naughty boy, but I would like to know when you and Marge will live together again," she asked. "You are married after all. Elizabeth has seemed to be less resistant since she met that handsome young man over there." She pointed in the direction of Brian Warren, who was showing some older ladies the latest dance steps and laughing loudly.

"It's not just that, May," Robert said seriously. Harry's voice boomed out over the crowd as he announced a raffle drawing coming up soon. "I...I have no form of employment. All I know how to do is garden, really. How could we have a home together? My pension isn't much."

"Jack left Margery well enough off," May said. "And he left her the house, too."

"That's just it," Robert said. "I can't live in the house where she lived with Jack. Every time I am there I think of her with him and ..."

"You know she never loved anyone but you, Robert," May said, squeezing his arm. "You know I would not lie to you about that."

"I do understand that, May," Robert replied, watching Harry dancing on a table while he called out the winning raffle numbers. "At first I thought the village would not accept us being together after she had been married to Jack all these years. And Elizabeth, of course. They would think it awkward that Jack's daughter..."

May laughed. "Oh, dear, Robert. Everyone guessed she was really your daughter. It shows on her face, her movements, everything. Margery told me right after she married Jack, because I couldn't understand why she did it. But she swore me to eternal secrecy. Now it feels as if everything has come right round again, doesn't it? If you and Margery want to live together now as man and wife, I doubt you would find too much opposition in this village." She saw one of the old ladies against the wall glaring at her and Robert. "Just a few old biddies, perhaps." She looked at him, her face a little wrinkled and her skin pale. "Somehow I think things will sort themselves out. You'll see." She patted his arm and said, "I had better go rescue Harry. He is getting a tad too exuberant there and will probably fall down and break his neck. Then I shall never see the coast." She gave him a wink and smiled.

"You're awfully serious, darling," Margery said, coming and slipping her arm in his. "What was May saying to you?"

"Nothing," he smiled. "Just telling me how much you love me."

"Good," Margery said. "Shall we tell everyone our news?" She stood up, Robert shyly by her side.

"Attention, attention!" Harry shouted like a costermonger on the London streets. "Margery would like to say something to everyone."

"Thank you, Harry," Margery bowed to him. "Many of you know that long ago Robert and I were engaged." There was a murmur in the crowd and heads nodded. "What most of you did not know is that Robert and I were actually married." There was a gasp from everyone. Margery continued on, holding tightly to Robert's arm. "When Robert was declared missing, believed killed, I married Jack. It seemed for such a long time our marriage certificate went missing as well, but eventually it was found. Robert did not remember what had happened to him and was in hospital for a long time. Now that he has recovered, he has come back to me." She turned and smiled at him. His head swam and it felt as if he would have a seizure. God, please not here, he thought. He willed himself to smile and spotted Lewis Warren with Louise on his arm. She looked stunning in her cocktail dress. And happy, Robert thought. She looks happy. He smiled and cleared his throat.

"I know you are all wondering how I could forget such a lovely lady as this," he said, smiling at Margery. "I want to thank the one person who brought me back from the dead with her devotion and belief that I would survive. My dear friend and nurse, Miss Louise Whiting."

The crowd looked around at Louise who seemed embarrassed. Lewis took up the applause followed by a thundering crash of clapping. When the noise subsided, Robert continued. "I am so happy to be here tonight with the woman I love, the friends I care for, and in the village I missed with all my heart." He looked around at all the faces so dear to him. "I want to take just a moment to remember my friends who are not here tonight. Those friends of mine who were not as lucky as I and did not come back from the War." He lowered his head and everyone in the room did likewise. There were some stifled sobs. After a few minutes he looked up again. "Thank you for making me welcome again in my home village. God bless you." He turned quickly, his eyes misting with tears.

"Are you all right, darling?" Margery asked, putting her hand on his back.

"I was just thinking of the names on the Memorial," he said, taking out his handkerchief and wiping his eyes quickly. "Stephen. And Bert. I feel as if I am lucky to be here. I need to understand why they are not here and I am."

"You may never know why, darling," Margery whispered in his ear. "You are here and there must be a reason."

"Yes," he said, smiling at her. "Yes, you're right." Margery knew that even though he said the words, something was planted in his heart that he would need to harvest.

The party went on for hours, everyone having a wonderful time. Robert came to Louise, his eyes appreciative of her new look. "Louise," he said, taking both her hands in his and kissing her cheek. "Pardon me for saying it, but what a stunner you are!" She smiled as Margery came over and took his arm.

"Should I be jealous?" she teased him, then took Louise's hand in hers. "Louise. Louise, never, never can I thank you for what you have done for me. You are the most blessed angel who has every lived, truly. My life...my heart...." She choked on her words.

"Please," Louise said. "This is your party and the start of your new life together. Don't cry. To see him so happy and well has always been my dream."

"I don't know how you can be so giving and selfless," Margery said, regaining her composure. "All those years taking care of him!"

"You would have done the same," Louise said evenly. They exchanged glances, the understanding that their love for this man was the driving force behind his standing and talking to Lewis.

"Congratulations, Louise," Robert said, his eyes a mix of sadness and joy. "Lewis just told me the news. Said your answer was a lovely birthday gift for him last Tuesday."

"The news?" Margery said, looking at their faces.

"Lewis and I are going to be married," Louise said, smiling. "He asked me several weeks ago and I wasn't sure I would be a very good wife. Too long having my own way. Isn't that right, Robert?"

"I never thought that, Louise. Never." Robert replied.

"That's all mythology anyway about being a good wife," Margery said wickedly.

"Is it?" Robert grinned. "Well, perhaps I should file for divorce then."

"You just see how far out the door you get, Mr. Morne," Margery laughed, her head resting lightly on Robert's shoulder. "I am never letting you go again."

"Quite right," Louise smiled at him sadly. "Once you let him go, he will never return." She and Lewis walked away, Robert watching their figures recede. He heard Rose whoop as they told her the news of their engagement. Margery looked at him, her fingers touching his cheek.

"I know you loved her, darling," she said quietly. "I hope she will always remain part of our life for as long as we live."

"We may be related for all that," he pointed quickly to Brian and Elizabeth dancing cheek to cheek near the record player.

"You may be right," Margery said. "Care to join them?"

"What sort of music is that?" he laughed, but whirled her around.

"Swing music, they call it," Margery giggled. "Here, darling, let me take you through the steps."

By ten o'clock the party showed no signs of stopping. It seemed that Margery was talking to every woman in the village. Robert sat down near the punch table. Billy came over and joined him.

"A few of us lads were thinking we would head over to the White Hart for a pint or two," Billy whispered. "Care to join us?" Rob nodded as he, Billy, Lewis, Brian and Harry sneaked out. The biting wind caught them all full in the face.

"Hasn't changed a bit," Rob said as they piled in, ordering their pints. They found a booth and sat down.

"That was a damn nice touch, Robbie," Billy said, 'remembering our friends."

"I was at the War Memorial," Rob said. "When I looked at their names I could see them all so clearly. When I looked at the crowd tonight I wanted to see them there." He looked into his glass. "In some ways I feel guilty about being here and they are not."

"It was just the luck of the draw, Robert," Lewis said, taking a drink. "The wholesale carnage wasn't very particular."

"I think it contributed to Jack's ...condition," Rob said softly. "He had nightmares, didn't he, Billy?"

"Awful ones," Billy agreed. "It never leaves you. You were out there, weren't you, Lewis?"

"I was," Lewis said. "Trying to patch up head wounds that would never recover. There were days when I felt I should just as well go down the row and shoot them all outright. It would have been more merciful." They all sat silently. Harry tried to lighten the mood by saying, "I escaped only because of flat feet. Even I worried once conscription came in, but thankfully the Army had the good sense to leave me at home." He swigged his pint down and stood up to get another.

"I want to go back," Rob said, everyone looking at him. "I want to go back to France and see where this all happened. I saw this in the newspaper on Remembrance Day." He pulled out a clipping showing the Thiepval Memorial. "There are nearly 73,000 names on there. 73,000. Mine is on there, too." He folded up the newspaper and put it into his pocket. "I feel I have to go back there one more time."

No one said anything. Billy broke the silence, "I'd go with you, Rob, but I can't leave at present." Lewis said he was also unable to go. Harry said that he and May were busy packing up for Dorset. Brian was silent and said, "I'll go with you, Mr. Morne. If you'll have me. I can do the driving, as it is easier to navigate that way than buses and such." Rob looked up, surprised.

"That would be a fine idea, Brian," Lewis agreed. "Brian is an expert driver, Robert. At least, in my presence."

Brian grimaced and said, "And a fair mechanic, too, should we get stuck. At present I am free until the full transfer of the business is in my hands. Of course, I would have to ask 'the Boss.'"

"The Boss?" Rob questioned.

"That's what he calls Elizabeth," Harry chimed in, chuckling.

"By all means, ask the boss," Robert grinned. "She had better say yes, or I shall speak to her mother about it."

"When would you like to go, Mr. Morne?" Brian questioned.

"As soon as possible, Brian," Robert answered, feeling an urgency to see the places that had made him what he was today. "But please, one thing."

"Yes, Mr. Morne?" Brian questioned.

"Call me Robert," he smiled, taking the last draught of beer. "I feel like my old man when you call me Mr. Morne."

"Right," Brian grinned at him. "Now off to tackle the Boss." They tottered back to the village hall, seeing the frantic looks on the faces of their women wondering what had become of them.

Brian found Elizabeth among a group of male admirers, talking and laughing animatedly. She is not yet over her father's death, he thought, seeing the sad look hidden in her eyes. She is coming along slowly toward happiness again. I hope I can be part of that happiness one day. "I need to talk to you for a moment," he said, pulling her away amidst cries of protests.

"What is it?" she queried, looking worried.

"I just offered to accompany Robert to see the old battlefields in France," he said quickly. "He feels he has to go back there. I can understand that. But I knew I had to ask the Boss first. Is it all right with you?"

"On one condition," she said severely.

"What is that, Ma'am?" he suppressed his laughter at her young face trying to look stern.

"That you take me with you," she said. "I think I need to see these places, too. The places that destroyed both my fathers in some way." Her face was so thoughtful he hoped she might reconsider.

"It's pretty primitive out there still," he hesitated. "Not exactly like staying at the Ritz."

"I am much tougher than I look," she argued. "Besides, I think it is important for me to see these places for myself. So, unless you take me, you cannot go and I shall have you sacked."

"All right, all right," he held up his hands in mock surrender. "If you're game. It will just be you, Robert and me."

"I know that," she giggled. "Who better than my own father to protect me from the likes of you?"

"Right," he said. "I'll tell him. We want to go soon."

"I'm ready whenever you like," she said as he went to find Robert and tell him.

When Margery heard the news she insisted she wanted to go, too. "I think I need to do this alone, just on my own," Robert pleaded. "Then why is Elizabeth going?" Margery asked.

"She asked to go," Robert said. "She wouldn't let Brian off work unless she went."

"Well," Margery said. "I don't understand, but..."

"It will let me be with her," he said. "It will let me get to know her."

"You and your buttery and beguiling ways," Margery smiled. "Go then, find out what you need to. Just make sure you come home to me, darling. Don't leave your soul there." Her worried look made him take her face in his hands.

283

"I will be back, soul intact," he said softly. "It is the last thing I need to do to let go of what happened to me. From there it is just our new life, together." He kissed her gently to a smattering of applause from the remains of the partygoers. They both blushed, their hands entwined. Margery saw the darkness in his soul, a darkness formed on the battlefields and grown in the incubators of the hospitals. If this trip was what was needed to root it out, then he had to go.

Elizabeth came over, holding her mother's hand while Robert shook hands with the villagers. "I want to go with him, Mummy," she said. "I want to know what happened to Robert and forged the person he is today. And I feel that Daddy wants me to go, to understand him and why he did the things he did."

"Yes, darling," Margery said quietly. "I want to know, too."

"I think," Elizabeth said evenly, holding her mother's hand even tighter, "that it is the way that I will learn to love....my father."

"Darling," Margery said, hugging Elizabeth tightly. "Darling." Her tears fell on Elizabeth's neck, hot and wet, but Elizabeth kept her eyes fixed on the man who was her father.

Chapter Thirty-Six

The decision was made to leave early Monday morning. Although they all hoped for good weather, they were aware that late November in northern France could be a cold, muddy, icy rain affair. Lewis thought perhaps Brian should bring chains for his tires. Brian scoffed at that.

"We'll not be in Switzerland, Dad," he said, checking and rechecking his tires, extra water containers, oil, and petrol tins in the boot. There was a huge basket of sandwiches, fruits, cakes, and flasks of tea and hot soup, packed and sitting in the back seat. Piles of warm blankets and every imaginable item for a comfortable trip were put into the car continually by the servants until Brian stopped the housekeeper from adding another blanket.

"Stop, please," he laughed. "If I carry any more cargo I will not be able to take my passengers." Lewis stood solemnly on the steps, the grey, threatening skies not making him any more optimistic about the trip. He had a wooden box in his hands and came over to Brian.

"Not you, too, Dad?" Brian asked, smiling. "What is this? Dueling pistols in case I run afoul of some French pater familias?"

"No, it is something rather more serious," Lewis said, watching Brian's smile fading. "You are not only doing something I think would be better left until Spring," he glanced at the skies, "but I hope Robert's emotional state is fully ready to encounter the former site of his wounding. It will be a very trying time for him. He may find himself less able to handle things and there is a definite possibility of seizures. Here are four glass syringes, already filled with doses of his medication. I've also included tongue blades and a bottle of oral medication, in case he forgets it. He feels well now and thinks he is completely cured, but he needs medication. You will have to see to it that he takes it. If he needs an injection during a seizure,

285

it is up to you to do it." He handed the box to a stunned but brave-faced Brian.

"Right, Dad," he said, opening the box and looking at the items. "I'll look after him, don't worry. We've got reservations for one night at a hotel in Boulogne and two nights in Albert. I'm sharing with him. Elizabeth has an adjoining room. I'll be responsible for him. You can be sure of that." His expression was so frightened under his bravado Lewis had to smile.

"My God, I must have painted a morbid picture here," Lewis said, slapping his son on the back. "It is merely a precaution. I would have preferred to be going with him, but can't at present. What's this?" Henry Eaton pulled up into the courtyard, Louise running out of the car toward Brian and Lewis.

"Oh, I am so glad I didn't miss you," she said breathlessly. Henry followed more slowly behind her and muttered a quiet 'good morning.' He, too, glanced at the rain-sodden clouds above and said, "Rain any minute now, Lewis, wouldn't you say?" Lewis stared at Louise. Surely she was not going to go at last minute? He clenched his teeth, hoping her feelings for Robert and his care had not overridden her good sense to let him find himself again.

"Louise," Lewis began, but she interrupted him.

"Brian," Louise said, looking at him so intently he felt as if he were naked on an examination table. "Would you do something for me on your trip? I don't know if I will ever go back there again." Henry heard a soft exhalation of breath from Lewis. So he thought she was going, Henry thought. No doubt he would. It is just what anyone who knew Louise would have expected. "So I wondered if you might be able to include three visits for me to lay some flowers and...and this note, at the graves." She gave him a list, some artificial poppies formed in two wreaths, a small vial, and wax wrapped dried flowers.

"Two of the graves are at Etaples, if you are going there," she said. Lewis and Brian nodded so identically it made her smile. "I thought you might like to see where your father served."

"And where you served as well," Brian added. "Robert wanted to see the place where he was brought after he was wounded."

"There are two graves there," Louise said, her eyes getting wet. "One is of a patient who was my very first case when I started on the Heads Ward at Etaples. His name was Ronald Leaman. Ronnie, we called him. A beautiful boy, but not when he died." She turned her head, Henry handing her a handkerchief and touching her shoulder tenderly. "The other one was my dearest friend from Bart's, Maeve Gallagher. She was an Army nurse, too. Killed in the air raid bombing in May 1918. Dear

286

Maeve." This time the tears flowed as Henry hugged her. "Their names will be in the Register near the gate, Brian," Lewis said quietly. "You can find their graves that way. It is a huge cemetery, apparently. Twelve thousand graves."

"Oh," Brian said, speechless. Twelve thousand graves in one place! It beggared the imagination.

"And these, Louise?" Brian said, looking at the little brass vial and dried, pressed flowers.

"These are for someone who was very special to me once," Louise said, looking at Lewis. "Someone I loved."

"David," Lewis whispered.

"Yes," Louise said. "His name was David Gordon Giles and he was a Lieutenant in the Worcestershires. He is buried at Heilly. Could you just bury these things near his headstone there? Just a little ways down, so they are safe and will stay with him always?"

"Of course, Louise," Brian said, taking her hand. "It will be an honor."

"He was a lot like you in some ways, Brian," Louise said, smiling at Lewis. "Very fine, very easygoing, and very kindhearted." Brian blushed but Lewis added, "Hear! Hear! I suppose that is a tribute to your father, don't you think?"

"Of course, Dad," Brian grinned, embarrassed by the compliments. "I'd better be shoving off now, to pick up Robert and Elizabeth. Any other goods for the car?" He scanned the doorway but saw no servants lurking with additional blankets or flasks.

"Goodbye then, Dad," Brian said, first shaking his father's hand, then hugging him. "We'll be back by Thursday evening."

"Ring for any reason," Lewis said, hugging him tightly. "I can be there by plane in an hour. Godspeed."

"We'll be fine. You'll see," Brian said. "Robert is a strong man and gets stronger every day."

"Go well and safe journey," Henry said, shaking his hand. Louise hugged Brian tightly, already feeling that he was her son. "Thank you," she whispered in his ear. "It gives me a feeling of clearing my heart."

"I'll guard it with my life until it is safe in Heilly," he whispered back.

They watched him drive off, the sky still holding its wet contents. "You've a fine son there, Lewis," Henry said. He turned to Louise. "What were those things you gave him for David? Flowers?"

Louise blushed, then held up her head. "Yes, Henry. They were flowers I kept from Geoffrey's funeral all those years ago. David and Geoffrey were as close as brothers. I wanted him to have something to link them together forever." She choked on the words. "I wrote him a note, too. Silly, isn't it? To leave with him forever." She walked back to the car, Lewis looking sad and confused.

"It's all right, Lewis," Henry said, taking his arm. "She told Eleanor what was in the note. It was about you, really. How she had loved David and missed her chance because of her own fear. That she would not do that with the man she now loves."

"The man she now loves?" Lewis started to smile. "Are you sure it was me and not Robert?"

"Absolutely," he replied, heading toward his car.

"What about a spot of breakfast with your husband to be?" Lewis smiled, elated at Henry's words.

"No, I'm sorry," Louise said. "Poor Rose Henning is going to be on her own for the next few days. I am going to look after her and keep her company."

"Once a nurse, always a nurse," Henry smiled as he pulled up to Lewis. "You do know what you are undertaking by marrying this woman, don't you?"

"Really, Henry," Louise interrupted. "Rose will wonder where we are."

"Of course I do, Henry," Lewis said, putting his head into the car. "These are exactly the reasons I have always wanted to marry her." Louise gave him a silly grin as she waved Henry on before Rose began to worry.

Once everyone was picked up, packed with yet more food and supplies, and tucked into their respective seats, Brian shifted gears as they made their way to Dover. The rain held out, actually clearing as they got toward the coast. Robert sat comfortably in the back, lost in his own thoughts, occasionally commenting on the countryside or the sunrise, which took on so many red and pink hues it seemed as if the sky was alight over the water. Elizabeth sat in front with Brian, talking low about trips to France they had both made as schoolchildren. Brian had made sure that she had a blanket for her knees, although his car had a very efficient heater and radio.

The crossing by ferry was mercifully uneventful, the skies clearing and becoming brighter the closer they got to France. Although there was no rain, it was still very cold and windy. They went on deck. Elizabeth found herself shivering and thought they should go in and get a cup of tea.

"No, you two go ahead," Robert said, leaning on the railing, his hands linked. He was staring straight ahead as Calais came closer and closer. "I'll be in later."

"All right, Robert," Elizabeth said, her face worried. Once inside she said, "Do you think we should leave him on his own like that? I don't like the way he is just standing there, staring at the water."

"You don't think he is going to jump, do you?" Brian smiled, but his nerves were on edge. "He probably wants some time to think by himself, that's all. We have to trust him."

"I suppose," Elizabeth responded, allowing herself to be shepherded to the tiny tea room on an upper deck. "If anything happens to him I would not only lose him, but my mother as well."

"Nothing is going to happen to him," Brian tried to allay her fears. He sat down, taking off his damp hat and laying it next to him. "The poor man has barely had a moment alone his entire adult life. I know I'd want to do some thinking on my own, too, if I were him. We'll have our tea and get one for him. All right?" He said everything with a conviction he did not feel.

"All right," Elizabeth agreed, her smile so dazzling Brian almost forgot about Robert. "You always seem to make me feel better, Brian. Do you always know what to do in every situation?"

He gulped his hot tea too quickly, gasping, while she started to get up to help him. "No, no, it was just a little too hot, that's all," he said, wiping his streaming eyes. "Is that what you think? That I always know what to do?"

"Well," she said, stirring her tea idly, "Whenever I am angry, or worried, there you are – voila! The perfect answer to the situation."

"I suppose if we mean to go on as we start I had better divest you of that idea straightaway," he smiled at her, again caught up by the sparkling lights in her eyes. She was the most beautiful girl he had ever seen. It struck him how lucky he was that she wanted to come along.

"Do we mean to go on?" Elizabeth asked seriously. "Do we?"

"Well,..if...well..." Brian stuttered.

She began giggling. "I'm sorry, Brian. I am sometimes so like Mummy I have to laugh. You do know how she met Robert, don't you?"

"No," he said, not sure he wanted to find out.

"She was biting a sewing machine repairman who tried to have his way with her," Elizabeth laughed, so lightly it sounded like little Christmas bells. "Granddad saved the day and she met Robert. He never asked her out. So she took matters into her own hands, and asked him out. In 1913. Very bold, Mummy." She daintily sipped her tea. "I suppose she meant to go on as she started, too." She stared at Brian.

"Elizabeth, I.." Brian began as the loudspeaker announced that they would soon be landing in Calais and should return to their motorcars and prepare to go through Customs in France.

"We'd better find Robert," Elizabeth said, standing up quickly as the crowd began to disperse toward the lower decks. "We can give him some tea from the flask to warm him up."

"Right," Brian said, chasing after her disappearing figure in the crowd.

A quick search of the decks produced no sign of Robert. Frantically they searched, calling his name as people were running about, shouting for children, gathering up items and getting ready to disembark. Brian felt sick, hoping Elizabeth had not been right and Robert had not jumped overboard.

As they rounded the last point of the deck they saw him, now looking back toward England. He seemed oblivious to the crowds, stepping out of the way as they raced around him. Elizabeth took his sleeve. He turned and smiled at her.

"Is it time to go already?" he said. "It seemed a much longer trip in 1916."

Elizabeth breathed a sigh of relief as she turned to Brian, who was grinning inanely. "What is it?" Robert smiled, confused.

"We're just silly, that's all," Elizabeth said, taking his arm. "We have to get back to the car so we can disembark."

A few hours later they were heading south toward Boulogne, the point where Robert had arrived in France that hot August morning in 1916. The day warmed to the point where Elizabeth opened her window and let the wind rush through her hair. Robert seemed transfixed by the road signs naming points and villages along the way.

They arrived in Boulogne mid-afternoon, stopping for a luncheon along the quay. Robert showed them where he seemed to remember coming ashore, noting how 'civilian' it looked now. "It was full of khaki and lorries and sergeants shouting," he said, staring at the water. "None of us knew what to expect. All I could think of was your mother, Elizabeth. That I had married her and we were man and wife." Elizabeth creased her lips, almost feeling like her mother for a moment.

They drove the short distance to Etaples, Robert seeming to remember every step. "We were packed into trains at Boulogne, thinking we would get a good meal and a rest when we got to 'Eat-Apples.' 'Eight horses or forty men' the sign said in French on the side of the boxcar. I think we were packed double that. They kept telling us about this place called 'The Bull Ring.' That's what it was, too. A proper horror show where we were driven like bulls. My mate Arthur said it was so we'd hate it so much here, behind the lines, we'd be glad to go up to the front line trenches." He shook his head sadly. "I think he was right."

"You weren't allowed to eat or sleep after a night on the ship?" Elizabeth said incredulously. "That was cruel and inhumane torture."

Robert smiled at her. "The whole war was, Elizabeth. The whole blasted war."

The imposing stone pillars that framed the entrance to the Etaples Military Cemetery were imposing enough to make Elizabeth gasp. "Lutyens, the architect who did the Cenotaph..." Brian began.

"And the Thiepval Memorial," Robert added.

"He did the design of this cemetery, too," Brian said. He smiled shyly. "I did a little study about the places we were going to visit. Dad and I spent all day yesterday going over some maps he got, finding out bits." Elizabeth smiled at him. "That is so nice, Brian. I would never have thought to do that."

"My Dad was here at Etaples, too," Brian continued. "He did neurosurgeries here. Louise met him here when she was taking care of Robert, which is how he actually came to do Robert's first operation."

"I don't think I really understood that," Elizabeth said, everyone still looking at the amphitheatre-like structure from the car. "I didn't know."

"A lot of history here, a lot of tragedy," Robert said, getting out of the car and walking unsteadily toward the portals.

"Is he all right?" Elizabeth asked, taking Brian's arm.

"He's fine," Brian said, patting her hand. "Let's get close behind him, just in case." He grinned at her but kept a firm grip on the glass syringe in his other pocket.

"Would Daddy have come to the Bull Ring, too?" Elizabeth asked when suddenly she was struck dumb.

Before her lay thousands and thousands of white gravestones, all uniform, all arcing around as if they were waiting for her to sing a grand aria. It was like looking down from the top steps of the portals to a waiting silent audience who would never hear or see again. As far as her eye could see the stones stretched, her eyes so wide she felt they could no longer see the horrors that the war had wrought.

"Twelve thousand graves," Brian whispered. "Mostly sick and wounded from the hospitals who didn't make it home to England. Nurses and doctors, too. Louise asked me to visit two people for her and asked me to give them some wreaths. I'll just go fetch them from the car and get the grave locations from the Register. I won't be a minute." He left her standing still, staring out over the blurring white of the stones.

"Elizabeth?" she heard Robert's soft voice. "Are you all right?"

"I never understood," she barely whispered. "When we learned something of the War at school, it just seemed, well, like it happened a long time ago and far away. I never imagined something like this. Never." She kept her eyes on the stones as if she thought the people beneath would rise up to greet her.

"All right?" Brian said, two red poppy wreaths in his hands and a scrap of paper stuck between his fingers. "First off, Maeve Gallagher. Louise said she was her best friend from the time they went through nursing school at Bart's. Killed in the big air raid they had here in May 1918. She's closer to the front than the other grave, so let's go see her first, shall we?" Elizabeth nodded numbly as they followed an intrepid Brian, working his way down the tightly packed rows. Without thinking she took Robert's arm, leaning toward him as Brian shouted, "Here she is!"

Brian put the wreath down, wiping the wet grass clippings from the base of the grave. "Mother of God Give our sister rest," Elizabeth read out as Brian got up from the ground. Along with the insignia of the Queen Alexandra Imperial Military Nursing Service, it said that Nurse Maeve Gallagher died on May 23, 1918 at the age of twenty-nine.

"They never talked about women dying in the War," Elizabeth said, still clinging to Robert's arm. "How Louise could stand all this horror I don't know."

"She's an amazing woman," Robert said softly. "I owe her my life."

"Yes," Elizabeth said. "She must not have been all that much older than me when she was here."

" A little bit, I think," Brian smiled. "But still pretty young. Not thirty, certainly."

"Shall we go on to the next one?" Brian said. "It gets dark early here in November and I want to make sure we find our hotel in Boulogne." Etaples was making him nervous and he wanted to go. It felt to him as if some of those poor souls that his Dad operated on wanted to reach out to him. He was trying to be cheerful but the oppression he felt walking among so many people whose suffering seemed to linger here was pushing him to conclude his business and leave.

Ronald's grave was harder to find, closely aligned in one of the curving rows at the right side of the cemetery. Elizabeth bit her lip when she saw his age. Only eighteen. Exactly as old as she was. She automatically put her hand down to see if he had an inscription, but only the official rank, age, and date of death were there with his name.

"Why doesn't he have an inscription like the nurse?" Elizabeth questioned as Brian and Robert were talking quietly.

"They charged the families for it, at first," Brian said, coming over to lay the wreath. "Perhaps his family couldn't afford it at that time." Elizabeth was still on her haunches, her hand running over his name. "May I?" she said, holding her hand out for the wreath. Brian handed it to her and she placed it lovingly in front of his grave. Somehow this boy touched her heart, almost as if she could feel him close to her.

"Louise said he was a beautiful boy," Brian said softly. "They called him Ronnie."

"Hello, Ronnie," Elizabeth whispered. "I'm Elizabeth. I'm eighteen, too." Robert turned away, walking rapidly down the rows. Brian kept a careful eye on him as he heard Elizabeth continue her chat with Ronnie.

"Louise Whiting was your nurse. She has sent you these poppies," she continued. "I hope that you didn't suffer, Ronnie, and that you are happy now." She got up, wiping her hands together, bits of wet grass and mud clinging to them.

"How old would he be now, Brian?" Elizabeth asked, not taking her eyes from Ronnie's grave.

"He was eighteen in 1916, so he would be thirty-seven now," Brian said, glad to see that Robert was walking back toward them.

"Goodbye, Ronnie," she said, kissing her hand and putting it on top of his gravestone. "Sleep well." She walked off with Brian, Robert's worried look making her smile.

"He was just my age when he died," she said. "He might have had a girlfriend like me. Perhaps he was even engaged." As they climbed the steps to go back to the car, she turned once more. "All of them had girls who loved them, probably. Girls like me. Or girls like Mummy." Robert and Brian looked at each other, their eyes locking in understanding.

"Goodbye, Maeve. Goodbye, Ronnie. Louise will never forget you. Neither will I." Elizabeth turned and walked to the car. Brian and Robert stood watching her.

"Well, come on, you two. It is freezing cold here and getting dark. Let's get back to Boulogne in case our navigator cannot find the hotel. I need a hot meal and a hot bath, in that order." She got into the car, both of them looking astonished.

"I'm not sure what she meant," Robert said, referring to her remark about her mother. "I think it was a good sign."

"I'd say a very good sign, Robert," Brian said, quickening his pace as he heard the engine turn over. "We'd better hurry before she leaves us here for the night."

"Not something I'd fancy," Robert said, moving quicker than he thought he could. "Remember, I was almost a permanent resident here myself." He grinned at Brian, who smiled back, amazed by the men of that generation who could make light of such devastating events and still keep their sanity.

293

A good meal of fresh seafood, hot baths, and comfortable, clean beds soon found them all asleep. Brian kept waking up periodically, the pall from Etaples not leaving him. Elizabeth seemed to feel only their spirits, not the miasma of pain and death and suffering. It was almost as if they were alive to her, and she was visiting them, not their graves. She seemed horrified by the waste, touched by it, but did not let it destroy her view of them as individuals. Her voice talking to 'Ronnie' as if he were an eighteen-year old friend and not a long-dead boy from twenty years past lingered with him. Robert's even breathing reassured him. They did not all die like animals, did they? Robert survived, he has his sense of humor, he can love and be loved. Brian's mind was usually so uncluttered and free from worrisome thoughts it surprised him how deeply this day had touched him.

Robert and Elizabeth emerged for breakfast looking fresh and ready for the drive to Albert. Brian's haggard visage elicited a sympathetic look from Elizabeth and an apologetic look from Robert.

"I hope I didn't snore too loudly and keep you awake," he said, a worried look on his face.

"No, no, just had dreams, that's all," Brian said. "Couldn't quite shake the feeling of being at Etaples. Ghastly. The horror of it all. The waste."

"Yet it still goes on, doesn't it?" Elizabeth said. "Germany rearming, that ridiculous dictator they have strutting about and inciting things. Why do men want to kill each other so much? I shall never understand." She bit into a buttery croissant, closing her eyes as she savored the taste.

"Oh, no one would take him seriously," Brian said. "He's a fool, a clown. Like that Mussolini character. They just strut and parade. They're not serious."

"I don't know," Robert said, buttering a crusty roll. "The Kaiser used to strut and parade, too. He had feathers everywhere. Look what happened. I wouldn't discount either of them."

"Not another war, surely," Elizabeth said, her eyes terrified. "How could anyone ever go to war again after what we saw yesterday?"

"Perhaps we should invite all the world leaders to Thiepval," Robert said, sipping his coffee. "We saw those twelve thousand graves at Etaples. Just British graves, mind you. There are 73,000 names of the missing on Thiepval. All British. All missing still. Except me. I've been found." He stared across his coffee cup to the dreary rain outside.

They sat in silence, finishing their breakfast before picking up their packed lunches and departing. Once again they drove past Etaples, Elizabeth noticing Robert bowing his head in meditation as they passed. She sent her thoughts once again to Maeve and Ronnie, who would never know the sweet taste of a buttery croissant, or find love, or drink coffee on a rainy morning. She turned her head away from Brian, whose usually cheerful face seemed solemn and impenetrable this morning.

Once they left Etaples and headed south their mood gradually lightened. Although the weather remained drizzly and grey, it was not so bad as to make driving difficult. Robert got out the maps and asked Brian to take him through some particular villages where he had been billeted: Magnicourt et Comte; Houvign-Houvingeul; Lucheux. Elizabeth found it hard to believe that what they had covered in the car Robert had to walk.

"My Dad...," Robert began.

"Granddad Charlie," Elizabeth said to Brian.

"Right," Robert smiled. "He insisted that he hadn't spent years buying me good shoes to see the Army ruin my feet. Right before I left for the Army, he went out and had bespoke boots made for me. Must have cost him a packet, too. They were the best thing he could have given me, besides what Margery gave me."

"What did Mummy give you?" Elizabeth turned around and asked.

"Do you really want to know?" he grinned wickedly. "I'm not sure you're old enough for this sort of thing."

Elizabeth blushed and Brian thought perhaps Robert was not quite so well as he thought.

"Oh, no, nothing like that," Robert apologized profusely. "No, no. It was very naughty for a 1915 Christmas gift. She bought me woolen drawers so I wouldn't be cold in the trenches. Your Auntie May was scandalized."

The laughter rang out in the car as Elizabeth said, "I can just see Mummy doing that, too."

"Besides the boots, I thanked her every day for that gift," he continued. "We were training in Wiltshire in January. Ever stood outside for hours on the Salisbury Plain in January? She was the most marvelous girl I ever knew. Still is." He got very quiet and Elizabeth asked, "Was she much older than me when she met you?"

"Younger," he replied. "In fact, after we went to the dance..."

"That *she* invited you to go to with her," Elizabeth laughed.

"Right," he smiled. "I was so flattered your Auntie Rose hit me with a broom at work to bring me back to reality."

"She turned eighteen a few weeks after the dance," he said, his mind obviously back there. "That's when I first met May and Harry and had Sunday lunch at their cottage. I knew I loved her then. I just didn't quite know how to say it."

"How old were you?" Brian asked, glad the earlier black mood had dissipated.

"Just nineteen," Robert replied.

"That seems so young," Elizabeth said.

"I suppose it was, too," Robert concurred. "We didn't think so. Your Grandmother kicked up such a row when we got engaged. I was not yet twenty-one, you see. We knew we were meant to be together. Did you ever look inside the ring she wore?"

"No," Elizabeth said. "I thought it was her wedding ring."

"That shows you how much Jack loved her," Robert said, watching Elizabeth closely as he mentioned his brother's name. "He told her she could wear the ring I gave her as her wedding ring. Now that is a huge sacrifice not many men would make for the woman they loved." Elizabeth turned back to the front seat, obviously trying to collate in her mind how Robert could be so fond of the man who tried to kill him.

"We had them engraved," he said. "We walked and walked all around London with no luck until our feet were burning. We were just about to give up when this little shop stood there. I thought it looked dodgy, but she insisted we go in. And you know with Margery, when she insists, you go." He grinned at Elizabeth again as she turned around, nodding her head and sighing deeply.

"We bought the buckle rings and had our names and an inscription put inside," he said. "That was how Louise knew my name was Robert all those years before they found out my surname."

"May I see it?" Elizabeth said, holding out her hand. She had often thought her mother's ring was so pretty. Now a more masculine version slipped into her hand. Holding the ring up to the light from the window she read the inscription out loud: 'Robert and Margery. Joined together in love. Never to be parted'" She handed the ring back to him, her eyes moist.

"That's really nice," Brian said. "I'd like to do something like that when I..I..get engaged," Brian finally finished. "Look. Didn't you say you wanted to stop in Puchevillers? There's the turning right there."

"I spent two weeks there," Robert said, sitting up and holding onto the back of Elizabeth's seat. "It was a casualty clearing station. When we marched in from Houvin we were dead tired, but still behind the lines. We were supposed to find our billets which were in a barn when whoosh – BAM!" he said, illustrating the impact. "This huge shell comes over. None of us had been anywhere near a shell, so we're running like mad. Of course, we got lost and separated from everyone. Had a lovely lunch of egg and chips at some old lady's house. She had chickens everywhere. It was right outside the village toward the casualty clearing station."

Brian pulled into the village, noticing it could be traversed on foot in less than ten minutes. A plain Norman style church, a few shops, some houses, and a café were pretty much the entire place.

"Two weeks here, Robert?" Brian smiled. "I guess shells coming over must have livened it up a bit."

"We didn't get many of those back this far," Robert said soberly. "Let's go out this road and toward the CCS." Brian drove through the village and took an uphill turning. At the top there was a huge open field to the left and a large cemetery to the right.

"The CCS," Robert said pointing to the cemetery, 'and our billets, with barns now missing." His hand swept over to the left. They looked at the cemetery, not as enormous as Etaples, but substantial enough to corroborate the horrors that happened on the Somme..

"I helped out in the CCS, because I had been a fully trained Ambulance man with the St. John Ambulance Brigade before the War," Robert said. "Dad really gave me hell when I didn't join the RAMC. When I signed up, I thought I was going to be a stretcher bearer. Whatever gave me that idea I don't know. Dad spotted it straightaway. Said I'd signed my death warrant. He was almost right, too. He wouldn't let Jack join up. When Jack got conscripted, he told him to go into the Army Service Corps so he wouldn't have to go into the trenches. Jack did and came home intact."

"Not quite intact," Elizabeth turned to him. "He had horrible nightmares. Terrifying for him and for us."

Robert seemed pained by this revelation. "Jack kept everything locked inside," he said, holding his hand over his heart. "I'm not sure why, but I am sure that is why he had the dreams. It was the only way he could get his agony out over the whole thing."

"See that road down there?" Robert pointed out to both of them. "When we marched up, we were marching alongside ambulances and walking wounded. When we got here after our little 'detour,'" he grinned, "and were promptly taken out by our Sergeant, we saw the reality of what war was. I was a shop assistant. Even though I had been in the Ambulance Brigade, nothing in the world prepared me for what I saw when I stood here twenty years ago." He closed his eyes as if he felt that would erase the images from his mind.

"It was an endless stream of ambulances, wounded, unrecognizable things that used to be boys like me," Robert said, staring at the road as if he still saw the wounded there. "When we left two weeks later, don't think those images were not seared in our minds. Every one of us thought, 'Will

I be one of those shapeless, bloody lumps brought back to Puchevillers?' I think I was, actually." Brian was watching him very carefully, afraid that this memory might trigger some sort of seizure. Robert seemed calm and collected, like a narrator on a newsreel.

"Why don't we walk around the village?" Elizabeth said. "Did you do anything much when you were here, to get away from the CCS, or weren't you allowed to?"

"The café was the estaminet, you know, where you could have some weak French beer or cheap white wine," he laughed. "We couldn't afford much else. It was more for the company and conviviality. Sometimes there were girls who would dance with you. I had my twenty-third birthday at this estaminet." They turned left after coming down the hill, the little café on the corner open for business.

"I think it might be nice to have lunch in the place where you had your birthday," Elizabeth said, linking arms with both men. "It smells good, whatever they have on offer."

As soon as they opened the door the memories flooded back to Robert so rapidly he had to blink to keep himself from seeing the past and present together. They were seated quickly, a very young girl coming over to give them an idea of what was on the menu. Brian's French was excellent. They soon ordered fresh soup, omelets, and the house white wine.

"Much nicer than my last visit. At least, the menu is," Robert smiled. "My friends, Arthur and Jim, kept hinting they had done something really special for my birthday. Out here, it was hard to imagine what could be so special. We used to moan about what we really wanted if we could have anything. Besides the usual wanting to get out of here and go home, I used to say all I wanted for my birthday was a hot bath and a bed with real sheets and pillows. That was heaven to me." The young girl brought over their soup and they began to eat.

"They took me out on my birthday, we got a bit legless, no mean feat on the plonk they served," Robert said. Elizabeth looked puzzled and Brian said, "The Tommies couldn't say 'vin blanc' so they said 'plonk.' Right, Robert?"

"Right," Robert winked. "After that, all I wanted to do was go back to the barn and sleep it off. Oh no, Arthur tells me. You have to go upstairs, he says, and they drag me up there. What do I find? A hot bath, soap, towels, the lot. They had arranged for me to sleep in this enormous featherbed for most of the night as well. It was heaven, pure heaven. Except that night the brass hats decided to move us up the line in the middle of the night. Arthur was scrambling up here to get me before I was put on Field punishment. Or, worse yet, shot for desertion."

"That must have been a sight," Brian was laughing so hard he could not finish his soup. "Three legless soldiers running around trying to get themselves up the line. My Dad is pretty straight-laced you know. I doubt he'd ever get legless. He'd probably say he knows the ill effects of alcohol on the brain." His final mimicking of his father's voice made Elizabeth giggle.

"He's a great man, a great surgeon," Robert said, more subdued. "Without him I would not be here. Louise fought for me, but as a woman and a nurse, no one listened. Your father did, and intervened on my behalf."

The young girl served their omelets and they spent another half hour talking about Robert's adventures in Puchevillers. Elizabeth found herself comfortable with him, understanding not only her mother's attraction to him, but how difficult it must have been for her father to live in his shadow. Every once in a while he would strike a pose or expression that reminded her so much of Jack her heart would ache.

"My compliments to the cook, Mademoiselle," Brian said in excellent French. The young lady replied and Brian translated. "She said it is her Grandmother who is the cook and thanks us. She asked if you were a soldier here, Robert. Apparently Granny was running the estaminet then."

"My French is pretty rusty, but..." Robert said that he had been here and wondered if he could see her Grandmother.

A few minutes later an elderly lady came out, her face wreathed in smiles. He stood up, accepting her kisses and her gratitude for saving her village. Brian worked hard to translate the rapid-fire French that obviously had Robert baffled.

They exchanged information, and the words, 'Queen's Royal West Surreys,' 'September 1916' and 'birthday party,' went back and forth. At the mention of the party, the older lady stopped and asked his name. "Robert Morne," he replied, puzzled. She called back, "Yvonne,' motioning them to wait.

A middle-aged dark haired woman, obviously the mother of the girl who had waited on them, came in, listening to her mother, staring at Robert, and then bursting into tears as she came over to him, dropping her towel on the table and kissing him three times in the French fashion.

"She says wait here a minute, she has something of yours," Brian translated, looking puzzled, as if he had not heard her correctly. The old lady stood beaming while the young girl looked at Elizabeth in a puzzled way. Elizabeth smiled back at her. Yvonne came running into the room, something dangling from her hand. She gave the object to Robert, who took it into his hands as his knees buckled and he fell heavily to the chair.

"Steady on, Robert," Brian said, frightened that whatever this woman had handed to Robert would trigger a seizure. Robert had his fingers tightly clenched around whatever she gave him and seemed reluctant to open his hand.

Brian spoke rapidly, first to the older lady, then to the woman known as Yvonne. Elizabeth's schoolgirl French lost them after the first few sentences. It seemed that it had something to do with the infamous birthday party Robert had recounted.

"My Mama," the young girl came over to Elizabeth, smiling and trying out her English, "she like British soldiers. My father was British. He died in War. We make British welcome. Is good for us. For me. Like sisters, you and me."

"Y..yes," Elizabeth said, wondering how true that statement might be. Could Yvonne have slept with Robert? Could this girl really be her sister? Perhaps whatever was in Robert's hand would tell.

"When were you born?" Elizabeth asked, afraid to know.

"1919," the girl said. "War over, but he died anyway." She shrugged her shoulders and cleared the table. Elizabeth let out her breath. Somehow she did not want to think that there was anyone else but her mother in Robert's life.

"It seems that when Robert got up and left in such a hurry, he lost something," Brian said, keeping a wary eye on Robert. "The bath water weakened the string around his neck. His identity discs broke off and Yvonne found them in the bed after he left."

"His identity discs!" Elizabeth said so loudly Robert looked up.

"Yes," Robert said, laying them on the table, his expression bereft. "These two little pressed paper discs were the only thing that would have saved me from twenty years of hell. Twenty years of not knowing who I was and having anyone else know. Just these two little objects."

Elizabeth picked them up, looking at their almost new appearance, except for the frayed, tattered string. Only his number G/7190 Robert James Morne The Queen's CE were engraved upon the surface. Hardly room for anything more. What it carried would have changed the lives of almost everyone in the room.

The two French women looked confused by Robert and Elizabeth's reactions. Brian explained succinctly what had happened to Robert and how the identity discs were missing when he was found.

Yvonne cried out, her tears anguished as she explained to Brian in rapid French that she tried to give the discs to British officers but no one wanted them, saying that the soldier would have new ones by now and she should keep them as a souvenir. She had often wondered if Robert had survived the War. She remembered him very well from his birthday party night. He did not look much different in her eyes.

Yvonne and her mother came to Robert, murmuring incomprehensible Picardy French to him, hugging him, kissing him, and not wanting to let him go. Eventually he stood up and said his au revoirs. They left in silence, Robert holding his discs tightly in his hand.

"I remember what the mother said when we left that night," he smiled grimly. "She said may God bless us poor lambs. The Queen's regimental symbol is the Paschal Lamb. Like lambs to the slaughter, she meant. As bad as my French was, I understood that." He left Puchevillers without looking back.

Chapter Thirty-Seven

Their dinner was solemn that night as they all turned in early. Robert seemed subdued, almost angry, Brian thought as he tried to engage him in conversation. He had to admit he himself was feeling edgy and irritable, as if the injustice of what had happened on this land was tangible enough to infect his brain.

During the night he heard Robert moaning, sitting up suddenly and shouting something unintelligible to the sleepy Brian. "What is it, Robert?" he said, coming over and trying to relax the rigid arms that held something aloft. "Didn't you see something out there, Arthur?" he said, his eyes blank. "I thought I saw something. Didn't you?" Elizabeth appeared in the room, quickly wrapping a silky robe around herself. "What is it, Brian?" she said, her voice so faint she sounded like a little girl. Her face grew into a silent movie-style pantomime of a frightened damsel when she saw Robert's gritted teeth and sweating brow.

"Is it a seizure?" she asked.

"I don't know," Brian said, his heart racing. "I think he is just having a nightmare about when he was here. It has something to do with finding his identity discs again today." He attempted to have Robert sit back in bed, but his rigidity forced him to stop trying.

"I think he is having some form of seizure," Brian said, running a hand through his disheveled hair. "God, I hope not."

Elizabeth came over to the bed and sat next to him. "Let me try to talk to him, Brian. Mummy always managed to make Daddy go back to sleep. Move over." She moved closer to Robert, taking his rigid arms in her hands and began talking to him soothingly.

"Robert," she said softly. "You are safe in your bed in Albert. We are far behind the lines here, very safe. You are not in the trenches now. Lie back and sleep. You need to rest to be fit and well tomorrow." She rubbed his hands gently, her heart leaping when she felt the ring that symbolized so much.

"Margery?" he said, his eyes still blank but his face confused. "Margery, how did you get out here? Go back, go back," he shouted. "You'll get killed out here. There's a shell coming over. Don't you hear it? It's coming this way. Get out! Arthur! Get the hell out! Get out!" He tried to get out of bed and run. Brian caught him as he fell back, exhausted. His pajama top opened slightly, revealing he had mended the torn string and was wearing his identity discs.

"He must have thought you were your mother," Brian said, glad that Robert seemed to be back asleep. "You do sound like her a bit, and you have some of her features as well."

"Poor man," Elizabeth said, stroking his arm which now lie outside the blanket. "It is as bad as it was for Daddy. They must have been very sensitive boys to have been affected so badly."

"From what we have seen so far, I think you could have been made of rock and still been affected," Brian grumbled. "Beyond belief, really."

"He was just a boy, about your age, when he went through all this," Elizabeth said, still running her hand up and down his arm in a patting gesture, like a mother with an infant. "Just your age." She looked at Brian, her eyes quite awake. She is beautiful, Brian thought, so beautiful and kind I just want to be with her always. He leaned over and kissed her, his heart so full he could not restrain himself.

She did not resist and he pulled away, saying a murmured, "Sorry." She stopped patting Robert's arm and took Brian's hand as he started to get off the bed. "Why be sorry?" she said, smiling. "I am not a child, Brian. We have been out together and kissed before."

"But here, alone, sort of," he felt himself grinning, seeing the peaceful, deep sleep of Robert. "Not a good idea."

"You are a real gentleman. I shall be sure that my father knows it," she smiled, getting up. "I think he will be all right now. Goodnight." She moved away from the bed, the fragrance of roses trailing behind her. Before she went into her room, she turned and blew him a kiss.

"Goodnight, dear Brian," she said. "I hope I dream about you, because it will be a long time until I see you again at breakfast."

Brian sat on Robert's bed, feeling confused and exhilarated at the same time. Does that mean she loves me? he pondered. I wish I could wake up old Robert here and ask him how he knew that Margery loved him. Did he feel as confused as I do by what she did and said? Robert was slumbering so soundly it was as if he had never had that nightmare. Brian looked at the identity discs around his neck. Like talismans, he thought. As if he thinks by wearing them he can turn the clock back twenty years.

The next morning brought more miserable weather. Robert seemed none the worse for wear, even being somewhat cheerful. Elizabeth asked him if he had any particular dreams. He said no, he had slept rather well despite everything that had happened in Puchevillers.

"This is our last day here," Brian said as they scuttled into the car to avoid the pelting rain. "I think we want to make for Heilly and then for Thiepval. What do you say, Robert?"

"Whatever you say, Brian," Robert agreed from the back seat. "When I was here I had no idea where I was or in what direction I was going. They just told us to march this way or that way. I do remember Moo Cow Farm." He smiled at the recollection.

"That's just here, near Thiepval," Brian pointed out to Elizabeth on the map. "Heilly is a bit south of there it looks."

"And Heilly was...?" Elizabeth asked.

"Where Louise and Dr. Gibbons, Robert's doctor, were stationed," Brian said. "It is also where her fiancé is buried. She asked me to give him these things." He dug around and handed the pressed flowers and brass vial to Elizabeth.

"What are they?" she said, seeing that the flowers were very fragile and old.

"Apparently there is a note for him from Louise in the vial. The flowers were from her brother's funeral years ago," Brian said, watching for the turnoff to Heilly as he peered through the curtain of rain that was turning into sleet. "She said this fellow and her brother were as close as blood brothers."

"David and Geoffrey," Robert piped up from the back seat. "Her fiancé was called David and her brother, Geoffrey."

"I remember she said that it was her brother's death that made her go into neurological nursing," Elizabeth pondered. "She did call him Geoffrey. He was just a little boy when it happened." She turned the flowers carefully in her hands.

"There it is," Brian said as they pulled into a layby near the cemetery entrance. "I'll go check the register first. You two stay here."

"I'm coming with you, Brian," Robert said, getting out of the car. "I want to see where he is."

Brian shrugged and said, "We'll be right back, Elizabeth. Where's that slip of paper with his name on it?"

"David Giles," Robert said flatly. "Lieutenant." They set off toward the gate, almost disappearing in the sleet.

Elizabeth turned the vial around in her hands. Louise had written her long-dead fiancé a note. What did it say? It was not right to read it. Her curiosity overcame her. She could see David and Robert just getting to the gate, so she twisted off the cap and slipped the note out, unfolding it carefully.

My darling David,

It is nearly twenty years since I saw you at Heilly, your face so twisted with pain and your beautiful body so ripped to pieces I wanted to tear down the vaults of heaven and ask God, "Why?" as I did when Geoffrey was taken. It would have done no good, as it did no good then.

I think of you every day, darling, and want you to know that I meant what I said when I told you I loved you. I was a foolish girl, unable to believe that love could be anything other than passion and romance. I know better now. You would have been all of that to me, I understand that. Soon I will be marrying a man, a fine doctor who is so like you in many ways. I thought I did not love him, either. Then I remembered you, and your voice, and your words. I remembered how I felt. And that is when I knew. I knew that I truly loved you. And I know that I love him.

I will always love you, my darling and never forget you.

With all my heart and love,

Eeze

Elizabeth folded up the paper and put it carefully back in the tube, just sealing it as Brian flung the door open. "It is wretched out there," he said, shaking off the water from his hat and coat. "May I have those things for him, please? He would be nearly at the far end of the cemetery, too. I've got a little trowel here. She wanted me to bury them at his grave." He reached in for the items and was looking for an umbrella when he saw her tear-stained face.

"What is it, Elizabeth?" he said, taking her hand. "What's happened?"

"Nothing," she said, opening her door. "I am just overwhelmed out here, that's all. I want to go to his grave, please. I must."

"All..all right," he said, seeing the determination on her face. "Let me get the umbrella." He ran over to her, covering her quickly as they sloshed their way to the gate where Robert stood waiting.

She trudged along with them, the wind and sleet blowing into their faces. Brian led the way until they reached the right row. "He's down here," Brian said, pointing away from them. "Near the middle somewhere."

Robert went first, his eyes trying not to read the names and ages of all the men who were buried here. It was an overwhelming sea of white mixed with grey, as if the veil of death lay over this cemetery. He stopped suddenly.

"Is this her fiancé?" Elizabeth said, her eyes taking in the stark words chiseled on his stone, the lion of the Worcestershire Regiment boldly staring at them, as if daring them to disturb his charge beneath. She read the details: Lieutenant D G Giles Worcestershire Regiment, 3rd July 1916 Age 26. Her thoughts returned to the heartaching letter Louise had written to him.

"I think we should say a prayer or something for him," Elizabeth said, as Brian knelt down on a piece of cardboard he thought to bring and began to dig a small hole at the base of the grave. "Is there a personal inscription, Brian?"

"Yes," he said, brushing away some dead leaves. "It says, 'Until we see you again you will be ever in our thoughts. Your grieving father, mother and sister." Robert stepped away and turned around, his back to them.

"Just keep an eye on him while I finish this," Brian whispered, worried at the impact all this was having on a fragile man. "Then we can say a prayer and go on." He inserted his trowel, digging about a half foot down, and laid first the flowers, then the vial, into the hole. He covered them up, a few stones showing up in the soil. One seemed to sparkle so he picked it up, its green color making it unusual.

"Let me take that back for Louise," Elizabeth said excitedly. "It looks like an emerald, doesn't it? It would mean so much to her." Brian nodded, feeling a kinship in some way with this David Giles. He wondered if Louise had a photograph of him.

They said a quick prayer, Robert rejoining them, his eyes strained. Elizabeth lingered before they left, then bent down and kissed the headstone, saying, "Louise loved you after all, David. She knows it now. I apologize for reading your note. I hope you don't mind." The sleet had started to dissipate then stopped. She followed the men to the car when a shaft of sunlight broke through over the cemetery.

"Thank God for that," Brian said, shaking off his hat and Robert following suit. "It was getting so bad I thought we might not be able to make Thiepval after all."

"Look, Brian," Elizabeth said. "Isn't that the row where David's grave is? Right there where the sunlight is focused?" Brian shielded his eyes and said, "Yes, I think so. It almost seems to be shining right on his grave, too. Odd, that. Really odd."

Elizabeth smiled as she got into the car. "Thank you for that, David. Thank you." She closed the door, the strange smile still on her face. Brian shook his head, pulling out of the layby to head toward the behemoth known as the Thiepval Memorial.

The sun shone intermittently on the drive to Thiepval, occasional rain and sleet still falling. Brian hoped that the weather would hold for the walk up to the Memorial, glad that Louise and Lewis had suggested they all bring their Wellington boots. The mud was the sucking, sticky variety, full of white clay, just as he had heard about when people talked of the Great War and the mud that killed soldiers by drowning them. After his walk through Heilly today, he understood why.

They came through a small main street, following the signs. The remains of Mouquet Farm lay to their right as they advanced up the road, past a church that was still standing. Robert was silent. It was obvious that every muscle in his being was at attention, taking in the landscape where he spent his last conscious moments before his injury.

"It's over there," Elizabeth said, spotting the red brick edifice through the trees. Trees, Robert thought. There were certainly no trees here twenty years ago. Brian turned left and headed to the parking area in the front of the Memorial.

The sun had disappeared as the got out of the car, the grey skies glowering as small stings of sleet hit their faces. Robert said nothing, just got out and began walking in the opposite direction from the Memorial.

It's over..." Elizabeth began. Brian grabbed her arm.

"Let him go, Elizabeth," Brian said. "I think I know where he is headed."

"Where?" Elizabeth asked, puzzled. "There's nothing but that road and those fields beyond. We can't let him wander around the countryside in this weather."

"He's going toward the jumping off point for the 7th Queen's on the day he was wounded," Brian said. "Look at this map my Dad got for me." He unfolded a complex looking trench map, directing her gaze to the squiggly line and a very faint, '7th Queens' notation underneath. It was just a short distance from where they were standing.

"So on that day he went over the top he was standing about where he is now?" Elizabeth said, watching the slight, dark figure, the sleet hitting him and whipping his coat around his insubstantial frame. "Just a boy, really, wasn't he, when he faced that. I don't know how he did it. I don't know how any of them did it."

"I like to think we would be up for the challenge, too, if it ever came to that," Brian said, his hawk eyes focused on Robert. "I wonder if our generation would be as strong as theirs was."

She leaned into him. "I can't keep the thought out of my mind that he was just your age when he stood in that trench. Just your age. It seems young to me, too young for your life to be taken away in an instant."

"It was," Brian agreed. "Let's hope we never have to do that again to our own children."

Robert stood looking out over the landscape, none of it really familiar. He had looked at Brian's map and saw where the jumping off point for his battalion had been on that day. It was here. As he stood here, it was as if his feet remembered the feel of the earth and his body knew the place. The sleet hit him in the face, stinging his eyes, but he could not turn away from the view over the sloping fields in front of him. In the distance he could see a cemetery atop a hill. The Schwaben Redoubt. The cemetery lay atop the Redoubt. How many of his friends were in that place as well? He kept scanning the vista, wondering if he thought hard enough he could turn back the hands of time and relive that day, changing the outcome. I've got my identity discs on now, God, he shouted in his mind. I won't turn around to look for Arthur. Can we do this again? He smiled at the idiocy of his thoughts.

His hat felt heavy with ice so he thought perhaps he should pay the inevitable visit he dreaded to the Memorial. What names would he find there? Arthur's? Jim's? Sgt Morrison's? He knew his own would be there. That would be the hardest part.

He turned around, seeing the worried looks on Elizabeth's and Brian's faces as he approached them. "Does it look the same?" Brian enquired, searching Robert's face. "I'd never even know where I was if I hadn't looked at your map last night," Robert said, smiling. "Should we go up to the Memorial now?" He led the way as Brian and Elizabeth exchanged looks.

The sight of his slender figure walking into the wind, moving forward with a determined stride, gave Elizabeth pause. He looks no older than he was then, she thought, wondering if the effects of being here the past few days were starting to play tricks with her eyes. His hat seemed flatter, almost like a cap, the water that had melted pouring down the back of his dark overcoat. The sleet had lessened, but little flecks of cold rain still shot at them. Like bullets, she thought, except they wouldn't kill me or render me without my memory for nearly twenty years.

"I can barely keep up with him," Brian puffed, his feet sucking into the wet earth. "The training he had must have stayed with him."

"I think he is driven by something inside himself," Elizabeth replied, her squelching boots providing a harmony to his deeper sounding ones.

"Mummy was worried about him coming back here. She hoped it would not destroy his soul."

Robert reached the steps and climbed them, his legs and back aching and his head full of flashing lights. No damn seizures here, he swore to himself. I have to make it to the top of this monument. I must see the names and pay my homage to my friends. He was carrying flowers he had brought with him, wet and withered looking things now after being subjected to the icy winds. Flowers had seemed a good idea earlier in Albert. Now it hardly mattered, as these names on the Memorial were nothing but withered things like the bouquet.

He oriented himself to the layout, knowing the walls went in order of regimental status. Guards divisions first, of course, he smiled to himself. Then the Royal Scots. Then the Queen's. He did not need a register to find them. The long list, almost too high for him to see the top, stood before him.

He saw Percy Balch's name first, a young, thin boy who had been braver than he thought he would, and who went down before he even got over the wire. Then George English. George was almost a father-figure at thirty-seven years old and he was from Bletchingley, near Upper Marstone. Robert had not known him in civilian life, but George had known of the W.C. Brooke Company. He smiled as he recalled Sgt Morrison's hearty assertion, "You'll be a hell of soldier, English, with a patriotic name like that!" Then Alfred Sprague, a Devon lad who wound up in the Queens. Fred had been amazed at Rob's ability to mimic his West Country accent until Rob told him about his parents' genealogy.

Visions flashed like a photographer's bulb – forming up in the trench; the order to 'Fix bayonets!' echoing as if he had just heard Sgt Morrison over the years; the standing, hands slippery with nerves, bayonets fixed, facing the trench wall; his nervous smile to Arthur Higgins, his best mate, right before the whistle blew; the running into smoke and chaos; the turning around; the shots that hit him and sent him flying upwards, looking at the sky, a warm, blue, peaceful sky. He dropped the flowers, sank to his knees, and bent forward.

"Oh, no," Brian said, bolting up the Memorial stairs two at a time and going over to Robert. Elizabeth ran as fast as she could after him, her heart racing. "Daddy, please don't let him get hurt. Please." Invoking Jack seemed the right thing to do. He had always protected her from every hurt; surely he would protect his own brother here.

Brian grabbed Robert's arm, hoisting him up, as Elizabeth arrived breathlessly and took the other arm. "Oh, Robert, are you all right?" she said, her eyes full of tears. "I was so worried that something happened to you."

He turned to her, his eyes so clear and beautiful Elizabeth thought she had never seen anything quite like them before. He regained his balance, saying, "I don't think Sgt Morrison would appreciate me falling down on the job like this." He grinned at them, but as soon as his eyes returned to the wall of names, he became serious.

"My friends," he said, pointing to the long list of Queens. "There's Percy Balch, and George English, and Fred Sprague. Do you see an 'A Higgins' or a 'J Crombie' there, Brian?" Brian looked up the rows, shaking his head, then his eyes rested on another name: Morne, R J. There was the name of the man who stood next to him, alive.

"What is it, Brian?" Elizabeth said, vainly trying to see where Brian's eyes were looking.

"Morne, R J," Robert replied quietly. "About halfway down."

Brian turned, amazed at the intuition of this man. During the trip he had come to enjoy his company and his stories. He was strong, a fighter, no matter that his almost delicate appearance belied that idea.

Elizabeth could not avert her eyes from his name. Her father's name, engraved on this wall for the past three years, and engraved on her mother's heart for many more than that.

"Do you see Bertie Keeble anywhere, Brian?" Robert asked. Again Brian shook his head no. "I hope that means they are all still alive. If my memory serves me about that day, I doubt it."

He picked up the bouquet he had dropped, trying to freshen up the flowers before placing them at the base of Pier D, Faces 5 and 6. He removed his hat, bowed his head, and remained silent for so long Brian became worried. Elizabeth also bowed her head, standing slightly behind her father. Their resemblance at that moment struck him, from their stance to the angle of their bowed heads.

Robert eventually reached up, touching his own name with his hands, running his fingers over the letters. He turned and smiled at Brian and Elizabeth. "I was just saying goodbye," he said, his eyes full of tears. "Goodbye to my friends I once knew, goodbye to the horror of that day, and especially, goodbye to this boy." Again he turned, touching his own name. "Morne, R J, the boy who came out here, is dead. He died on September 28, 1916 and he will never return in the form he once had. I told your mother, Elizabeth that I would come back and we would start a new life together. So I must leave R J here where he belongs." He gave one last touch to the stone and said, "I think we should go back now. I feel that I have made my peace with my friends." He walked off toward the car, Elizabeth and Brian following behind.

That night Robert seemed more lighthearted and happy than he had during the trip. They ate a scrumptious meal, enjoying the wine before the long trip home the next day. The waiter came to refill their glasses and said to Elizabeth, "For you, M'amselle, and your...." He hesitated, looking at Robert. "My father," Elizabeth replied. She raised her glass to Robert, who could barely see her through his tears.

Chapter Thirty-Eight

The journey home from France was fraught with bad weather and a bumpy crossing, but the goodwill and closeness between the three travelers made it seem almost fun. When they arrived home on Thursday evening, Elizabeth insisted that both Robert and Brian come in to see Margery.

"Oh, darling, I am so pleased to see you!" Margery nearly shouted as Elizabeth burst through the door, calling for her mother. "I've just come home from Rose's cottage myself and the kettle is on the boil." She hugged her daughter tightly, looking at her shining eyes when she noticed Brian and Robert standing by the door, watching the scene with expressions of tenderness.

"Come in, both of you," Margery said, holding out her arms to Robert. He embraced her tightly, his arms holding her in a grip that made it seem he would never let her go. They stood together for a long time, he looking deeply into her eyes, then buried his face in her shoulder.

"Let's go into the kitchen, shall we?" Margery said, when Robert finally let her go. She helped him off with his coat, keeping her eyes on him the entire time, then took his hand and led him to the kitchen.

"The curtains!" he said, surprised. "You've got the curtains from the cottage in Sussex!"

"Yes," Margery said, inviting everyone to sit down and pouring out the tea. "Louise told me she made them. I loved them when I saw them, so asked to take them. And here they are." She sat down, magically producing a plate of biscuits from somewhere.

They recounted their trip in detail, especially the episode at Heilly with David Giles' gravestone being illuminated. Elizabeth appeared animated, even relieved, Margery thought. In fact, it seemed that both Robert and Elizabeth acted as if a great weight had been lifted from them. While she

312

had hoped she would see that in Robert, she did not quite understand why Elizabeth should feel that way.

Brian, however, seemed less ebullient than normal. "I suppose it was very hard to see all those young men buried out there, wasn't it, Brian?" Margery asked carefully, thinking perhaps seeing graves of boys your own age would be unnerving.

"Horrendous," Brian agreed. "At the end of the trip, when we were at Thiepval, I could not help but think of a quotation from Dickens' *A Christmas Carol*. If I remember, it goes something like, 'Spirit, remove me from this place. I can bear it no longer.' That is how I felt being out there." He lowered his head, his brows knit together as he sipped his tea.

"Yes, I can imagine," Margery nodded. "That War lingers with us all, one way or the other, doesn't it, darling?"

Robert smiled at her in response. "It did, darling. It will always be part of me. But I promised you I would start a new life when I came home, and that is exactly what I intend to do. Brian, have you got that little bottle of cognac I bought? I think we could use a warm up in our tea. It's in my coat pocket." Brian went to get it, pouring liberal doses into cups until Margery giggled, 'That's quite enough, Brian. I shall toddle all around the kitchen if I have more."

Robert raised his teacup, looking at the faces around him. "I want to drink a toast to my friends of the 7th Battalion, whose names and faces I will never forget; to my beautiful wife, with whom I am blessed to live the rest of my life, however long that will be; to my lovely daughter, who has given me the greatest gift I could imagine on this trip; and to Brian, one of the finest young men I have ever met. If I ever had to go into the trenches again, Brian, I would want you right by my side." Everyone raised their cups but Robert stopped them. "And one more person. To my brother Jack, who has made this possible. I felt him with us the entire trip and knew he was at my side. I knew him long enough to sense his presence. To Jack."

"To Jack," Brian repeated, as Elizabeth choked out the name. Margery said nothing, just looked at Robert with wonder in her eyes.

"I always said you were nicer than me, Robbie," Margery whispered in his ear. "I was right."

The conversation turned to other news. "I have been spending hours over at Rose's," Margery said, putting more biscuits on the plate from a biscuit tin. "Louise has been staying there, you know, looking after Rose. Rose has not been going on well, poor old dear, but never lets on. It was very lonely here without Elizabeth, so we have been making nice meals for ourselves and I even baked a few cakes." She smiled, patting her tummy. "I think all the food is beginning to show."

"It looks beautiful on you, darling," Robert said, his smile lighting up the kitchen. Elizabeth could understand why her mother had found him so attractive and still did.

"Go on, silly boy," Margery beamed. "Louise and Lewis are getting married next Thursday, can you imagine? Nothing fancy, you know. Just the Registrar's office and a blessing in St. Bartholomew's Church in Leigh. Then a nice party at the house."

"That's quick, isn't it?" Robert said. "Did they want to do it so quickly?"

"No use waiting any longer, is there?" Brian said. "He's known her for donkey's years. Neither of them is particularly religious. Dad said he lost religion when he served on the Western Front. I can see why now."

"But I felt such as sense of...spirituality out there," Elizabeth said. "That is a silly way to put it. It was not just endless horror for me." She looked at Brian, who sat staring into this teacup.

"The point is," Margery continued, her expression worried as she looked at Brian. "Louise wondered if you would be her maid of honor, Elizabeth. She asked me to see if you are willing and let her know."

"Me?" Elizabeth said. "Why not you, since you have obviously become quite good friends with her?"

"No, sweetheart, I am baking the cake!" Margery laughed. "That's because she and Lewis would like Brian as their best man." Brian's head shot up. "Really?" he said. His smile creased slightly. "That would be very nice, then, wouldn't it, Elizabeth? What do you say?"

"You'll get a new dress out of it," Margery smiled at her daughter.

"I'd love to," Elizabeth replied.

"We've been all week planning things out," Margery continued. "It kept my mind off worrying about all of you out there." She took Robert's hand in hers while she spoke, rubbing his fingers and running her hands over his knuckles continuously. It is as if she still does not believe he is real, Elizabeth thought. As if he would disappear any second if she lost physical contact with him.

They discussed the wedding and the trip for an hour when Margery saw that both Robert and Brian looked tired. "You two had better be going," Margery said. "Poor Brian has done so much driving, and he still has a fair way to go home. You are welcome to stay the night, Brian, if you like."

"Thank you, Mrs. Morne, but I am fine," he stifled a yawn. "I think I will have a proper lie in tomorrow."

"Not too long," Elizabeth said. "I will be ringing you up so we can go shopping for our clothes."

"Shopping?" he said in a mock horrified manner. "Not that, surely! What have I done to deserve that?"

"You decided to know me," Elizabeth smiled. "So that is what you get." She yanked on his tie playfully as he put on his coat.

"You don't need to go," Elizabeth said to Robert, holding his coat. "Why not stay?" Margery looked at Robert, the surprise evident in her face.

"I think Rose might be feeling lonely for me," he smiled longingly at Margery, not wanting to admit he could not sleep in the bed where Jack slept. "Soon we will sort things out, won't we, darling?" He put on his coat, reaching into his pocket where he pulled out two little boxes.

"For my best girls," he said, handing one to Elizabeth and Margery. "I bought them in Albert this morning." Inside each package was a necklace. Margery's was an antique setting with a cultured pearl and little diamond like stones. Elizabeth's was a similar necklace with a small emerald in a gold filigree setting.

"Pre-War," he smiled. "I thought they suited each of you."

"Oh, darling," Margery said, putting her arms around him. "I shall wear it to the wedding and everywhere I go."

"In the kitchen, too?" he grinned.

"Silly, silly darling," she smiled at him, both of them lost in each other, unaware of Brian and Elizabeth.

"It's all right if you want to kiss him, Mummy," Elizabeth smiled. "I kissed him in France. Those French ladies kissed him, too. Show her your identity discs, Robert." He opened his shirt buttons, the identity discs still around his neck. "So you see I have a necklace of sorts myself," he laughed. She fingered them, as aware of the part they played in losing him as he was. Somehow the story they had told her earlier of how he got them back seemed more poignant when she saw them. She seemed unable to let them go.

"Louise is going back with you, Brian," Margery said. "She wanted to talk to your father about the upcoming wedding and then he would take her home later."

"Right," Brian said wearily. "I would like a hot bath and my own bed."

"I would, too," Elizabeth said. Robert and Brian stood in the doorway, both reluctant to depart. "Goodnight, Brian," Elizabeth said, kissing him on the cheek. "I'll be chivvying you out of bed bright and early, so be prepared. We'll have a long day ahead of us tomorrow. We want your father and Louise's wedding to be absolutely perfect."

She stepped over to Robert. "Goodnight, Dad," she said, kissing him with such warmth and affection it made him close his eyes. "To me you shall be 'Dad' from here on, if you will allow me. And Daddy, or Jack, will always be Daddy to me." He kissed her back, looking at the perfect little 'oh' that Margery's mouth made.

"War can rent things asunder," Robert said huskily, looking at Margery, "and it can bind things together. We learned a lot about one another out there, didn't we, Elizabeth?" She nodded her head.

"I don't think there is anything in this world that would have made me happier than what I have just seen," Margery said, her eyes full of tears. "Nothing."

"I'm off for a bath and a good night's sleep," Elizabeth said breezily, picking up her bag and heading upstairs. "Be prepared, Mr. Warren. If you thought the trenches were bad, just wait until tomorrow!"

"Yes, Sergeant," Brian saluted smartly, groaning at the prospect of a day full of shopping. "I think I would rather be in the trenches."

"No, no you wouldn't," Robert said seriously. "Even though it is a hard decision. I don't envy you, Brian. At least I am not..."

"And what do you intend to wear to the wedding, Robert?" Margery asked, laughing. "That pin-striped suit is very nice, but you can't wear it for all occasions. Don't you remember how you used to make fun of Jack and your father for wearing the same old black suit everywhere? 'Morne and Son' Undertakers, he used to call them. You used to be such a swank, darling. I think shopping is on the agenda for us, too."

"Well, we're for it, then," Robert grinned at Brian. "Fix bayonets and over the top!" He kissed Margery goodbye and left.

Margery looked at Elizabeth standing on the stairs, her arms crossed and a smile on her face. "Well?" Elizabeth said. "I did a lot of thinking. I felt Daddy out there, too. He wanted me to think about things, I know. I came to the conclusion that Daddy would always be Daddy to me, but that didn't exclude me from loving and having a Dad." She went upstairs, Margery amazed and delighted at her daughter's ultimate acceptance of the irrevocable truth and the man who was her father.

Chapter Thirty-Nine

Thursday, December 6, dawned a clear, crisp winter's day. Louise awoke early, her creamy, ivory suit hanging over the cupboard door. Today was her wedding day, a day she never imagined would come for her, except to Robert Morne. She turned over, looking at her clock and seeing it was not even six o'clock. Sighing, she got up, putting on her robe and going over the past week's events in her mind.

It seemed impossible to her that Margery could have become such a good friend. Something happened between them while Robert was in France with Elizabeth. They both knew they shared the love for the same man, but it went deeper than that. They had both been heartbroken and now had been offered another chance for happiness that they never expected. Somehow that drew them together.

Earlier in the week Elizabeth had come with her mother to deliver the beautifully decorated, rich, fruity wedding cake to the Warren house, where Louise was supervising the decorations for the wedding party. Margery beamed at the compliments. In that moment Louise saw the girl Robert loved. Elizabeth was so excited to be her Maid of Honor, a suggestion made by Margery when Louise told her that Lewis was going to ask Brian to be his best man. Elizabeth took Louise aside and gave her a little green stone, a 'gift,' she said, from David. At first Louise did not understand. As they talked, while Margery was in the kitchen organizing the disposition of the cake, Elizabeth told her of the incident at David's grave, and her great feelings for him and for Ronnie Leaman. She had also gathered several other stones and some soil from David's grave, giving them to Louise in a little package.

"Do you have a picture of David?" she asked sweetly. Louise went up and got the one photograph she had of him, bravely smiling in his uniform. Louise kissed it before going downstairs to show Elizabeth.

"So handsome," Elizabeth said. "He's got lovely, warm eyes. I think eyes tell so much about a man, don't you? I know you must have loved him very much, like Mummy loves ...Dad," she added slowly, looking carefully at Louise.

"Dad?" Louise asked, puzzled.

"Robert," Elizabeth repeated. "I learned much about him when we were together in France. I know why you loved him so much, Louise. I thank you for saving him for Mummy and me." She put her arms around Louise, hugging her tightly. Stunned, Louise put her arms around Elizabeth, holding her and patting her back like a child.

"When we found the green stone at David's grave, I felt he knew everything and was happy. Happy for you that you will be marrying someone as fine as Brian's father. Does that sound silly?" Elizabeth asked.

"No, dear," Louise said, sounding like her Aunt Eleanor. "It sounds just like David, really."

"I wish I had known some of these men. I suppose I do, now that I know Dad," she said.

"I am going to carry this stone on my wedding day," Louise smiled at her. "He will always have a special place in my heart." She looked at Elizabeth sadly.

"In mine, too, Louise," Elizabeth said, kissing her on the cheek before going to find her mother.

David's picture was still lying on her dressing table, his face so young and his eyes full of hope and life. No crying on your wedding day, she reprimanded herself. Just be glad that you did not lose this chance to be with a man you love. 'She who hesitates is lost,' she thought to herself. With every man she loved she had hesitated. Lewis had always been in her heart. She remembered how angry she felt when he told her he was going to marry Constance. It was not just anger; it was jealousy, too. She had loved him then, but would not acknowledge it to him or to herself.

She ran her bath herself, liking the new haircut she had and even seeing a different look in her eyes now. Romance novels and silly stories had never had much appeal for her. Now there was almost a radiance around her. "Tosh," she said to herself, then caught herself smiling as she stepped into the bath.

The ceremony at the Registrar's Office and the blessing at St. Bartholomew's were perfect, Lewis looked splendid in his pin striped trousers and cutaway coat. Brian matched his father, and although taller, looked more like his father today than he ever had. Elizabeth was a picture in a wine-colored dress, carrying a small posy bouquet dotted with red poppies, as Louise requested. Louise decided to wear her emerald pin from David on her dress, as a way to have him at the ceremony. Eleanor cried audibly, joined by Rose, who leaned heavily on her cane and Eleanor's arm. Maisie, however, just beamed, not a tear in sight.

Although Lewis and Louise both disliked parties, Louise had worked very hard to make this an elegant yet comfortable occasion. Eleanor and Margery had added their expertise. The cake took center stage, the addition of the poppies around the sides a lovely touch. "Robbie helped me make those," Margery smiled at Louise in the reception line. "He's far more artistic than I am. They look real." Louise nodded, little pieces of Robert woven into the tapestry of her wedding day.

Robert's beaming smile and warm kiss on her cheek as he held her hand, reluctant to let it go, almost brought her to tears. She could see his eyes were wet, too. "Nothing, nothing I would have wished for more," he whispered in her ear. "He'll be a much better husband than I am. You can check with Margery on that." Her heart ached to hear his voice and feel his breath in her ear. Like David, he would always have a place in her heart that no one could usurp.

The party went on the rest of the afternoon, Robert and Margery showing off the correct way to do the tango amidst much laughter as they occasionally misstepped. "It has been twenty years, you know," he grinned, then executed a perfect turn.

Louise met Lewis's daughters who were cordial but not enthusiastic about their father's new choice. Both beautiful girls, they looked much like Constance. Brian, however, had become very fond of Louise and she of him. He danced with her, whirling her about as she laughed.

"I am an awful dancer," she said. "Your feet will look like raw steak after this."

"I've got good sturdy shoes on," he laughed. "No worries."

"Elizabeth looks lovely, doesn't she?" Louise said. "You should spend more time dancing with her, if only for your feet's sake."

"Oh, I intend to," he said, almost dreamily. "She is a topping girl, the very best."

"I see how much you two like one another," Louise smiled.

"It shows, does it?" he grinned. "I've been neglecting her a bit. Harry and his wife are leaving after Christmas for Dorset. I will be on my own with the business then."

"And no doubt do fine," Louise reassured him.

"You sound like a Mum already," he laughed. "Shall I call you Mum?"

"I don't think your sisters would like it much," Louise grimaced.

319

"Oh, don't worry about them," he said easily. "They will come around once they get to know you. You'll see."

"Do you know your father has never told me much about his family," Louise said. "I know his mother died young of a brain tumor. He told me that long ago. Her death was the cause of him pursuing neurosurgery."

"He was an only child," Brian whirled her dangerously near the punch bowl. "His father was a bank manager in London. They lived in Hampstead. Then his father died when he was a little boy. His mother had some money from her parents, so she sent him to the best schools she could afford, then to medical school. I don't think Dad ever had much love in his life, though. My mother's family was all he had. They are not exactly the affectionate sorts."

"Oh," Louise said, looking at Lewis talking animatedly with Cyril Gibbons and Angela Meade, the former matron at the East Preston Army Hospital. He caught her eye and smiled in such a way her heart leaped.

"This is rather a confession, but I suppose I fell in love with him very early on, when I was still a schoolgirl," she turned to look at him again as they passed by. "I just thought he would never be interested in anyone like me."

"Au contraire, Madam," Brian said, ending the dance. "I think it was only ever you."

"I feel quite undone, my dear," Louise said, smiling. "You are a wonderful dancer. Look at Elizabeth. What a forlorn looking girl she is at present!"

"I suppose I had better rescue her," he grinned. He leaned over and kissed Louise. "I am so happy to have you as my stepmother. Dad is a lucky bloke. I'll make sure he knows it."

"Go on, now," Louise said, blushing slightly. "She's waiting."

Later on they changed clothes for their trip. Lewis said they were going to a surprise location for their honeymoon. Louise normally did not like surprises. Today she felt as if she had emerged from a long and binding chrysalis.

They walked to the car, rice flying that mixed with the light snow that had begun to fall. Louise turned and threw her bouquet, carefully removing the little dried flower from Geoffrey that she had inserted during the ceremony. Her smile of satisfaction matched Margery's as Elizabeth caught the bouquet. The car accelerated as they pulled out of the large carriageway unto the road, the couple waving at everyone until they were out of sight.

"Now, tell me where we are going, Lewis," Louise smiled. "Near? Far?"

"Not too far," he grinned. "Worcestershire, actually."

"Worcestershire?"

"One of my old friends has a lovely house near Evesham. They are in Singapore for the holidays, so told me I could use it. Thought it would be just the sort of place we would like to be for our honeymoon, rather than racing around somewhere." He was silent. "That is all right, isn't it?"

"Yes," Louise agreed. "That is very close to Little Comberton."

"Yes," Lewis replied, the snow falling a little harder now as the windscreen wipers started their rhythmic whoosh-whoosh. "That was the other reason I chose it. I want to see where you grew up, Louise. I want you to take me to Geoffrey's grave. He was the reason I met you. I want to thank that boy."

Louise turned her head, staring out the window at the falling snow, biting her lip. Yes, Geoffrey was the reason she met Lewis. She wished it had been otherwise, and that somehow Lewis would still have come into her life.

After the couple drove off, everyone turned to go back into the house to dance and enjoy themselves a little more when they heard a yell. Rose had slipped on the newly-iced pavement, her cries of pain mingled with exclamations of disbelief.

"Let me through, please," Henry said, followed closely by Cyril Gibbons and Angela Meade. "Oh, dear, Rose. Now what have you done to yourself?"

"Oh, doctor," Rose said, her eyes full of anguish. "It hurts more than I can say. Please help me."

"Let's get an ambulance," Cyril said, asking if there was a board that they could use to lift her and take her into the house. "I'm afraid you will have to go to hospital, Mrs. Henning."

"Oh, Rose!" Margery and Robert appeared close by, "what can we do?"

"Go back in and have fun," she said, her eyes closing.

"Now, Rose, that's silly," Robert said, squeezing her hand. "You know no one will have fun unless you are there."

"Listen to me, boy," she said, sounding as she once had in the draper's shop. "I am eighty-five years old and no one had better ruin a party on my behalf." She leaned back as they found a large board and hoisted her up. The sirens of a distant ambulance sounded as everyone filed back into the house and began gathering their coats.

"I think she's broken her hip again," Henry said as Cyril nodded his head. "I don't know if she will be able to survive this bout."

"Surely they can fix it, Henry?" Eleanor asked, her face pale.

"Oh, yes, they can fix it," Cyril said quietly. "But will she survive it?"

Everyone left rather quickly as Rose was taken to hospital. "Look after Catkins, Robbie," she said as he held her hand all the way to the ambulance. "And my cottage."

"Will do, Rose," he said, giving her a kiss before the doors closed.

"What will you do, darling?" Margery said, holding his hand as they stood watching the ambulance lights fade away in the gathering darkness.

"What?" he asked, looking at her, his mind still on Rose's pained expression.

"You'll be on your own," she said. "I think you should come and stay with Elizabeth and me."

"I have Catkins to think about," he smiled weakly. "I'm under orders."

"Why don't you go stay with Dad at the cottage, Mummy?" Elizabeth said. "I'll be fine on my own."

"No, darling, I wouldn't want to leave you like that," Margery said. She seemed torn about what to do.

"What about Harry and May?" Robert piped in. "May has been feeling pretty tired lately. She might like having Elizabeth around for a few weeks before they leave."

Margery hesitated and turned to Elizabeth. "Perfect!" Elizabeth agreed. "Uncle Harry has been moaning something awful about how difficult it is for Auntie May to get things organized. I'd be happy to help. You can stay with Dad at the cottage."

"If you will be all right," Margery hesitated.

"Oh, Mummy, I am not a baby any longer," Elizabeth grinned at Robert. "Dad needs to be looked after by you, so you had better go there for the time being."

"If you think..." Margery said, looking at their two almost identical faces and knowing she had lost the argument.

"Let's go and fetch your things," Elizabeth said. "I'll just say goodbye to Brian and let him know where I'll be staying." She ran off, her dress flying behind her.

"She's just like you," Robert grinned at her. "Won't take no for an answer."

"I was thinking she was just like you," Margery smiled at him. "So persuasive you don't even know you've agreed to something and there you are."

"I suppose she is just like both of us," Robert shuddered. "A lethal combination. Poor Brian Warren." They looked at their daughter lingering with him, holding his hand.

"Do you place any credence in that catching the bouquet myth?" Robert whispered in Margery's ear.

"Do you mean do I think she will be married soon?" Margery asked, watching the interaction between Elizabeth and Brian. "Certainly not. She is far too young to be married. Far too young."

Robert began chuckling softly until she turned to him, her eyes full of accusation. "And just what has amused you so much, Mr. Morne?" she demanded.

"Oh, just your words and tone of voice," he smiled. "Reminds me of a certain mother I used to know in Upper Marstone. I think her name was Elizabeth Morne."

"I do *not* sound like your mother," Margery retorted. "God forbid."

"Oh, but you do, darling," he said, taking her in his arms. "Exactly like her. I can still hear her when I told her we were engaged. 'You are far too young, Robert. Far too young.' He nuzzled her ear lightly.

"Listen, my sweetest of hearts," she said. "Are you willing to give her away to another man when you have just found each other?"

"If they love one another, I am," he said. "This way we have a son, too. A fine one. I would agree to it in a second if he asks for her hand in marriage. Which I suspect he will one day soon."

"Let's go home," she said. "This will be the very first night we can be together alone and I will not have to go home."

"That I remember, too," he said, kissing her sweetly on her lips. "How we hated to be parted to go to our own homes. And beds."

"Just like them, I suppose," she said, seeing Elizabeth trail her hand behind her as she left Brian. "I suppose they are just as we were then."

"No doubt about it," Robert smiled, understanding completely Elizabeth's expression as she came toward them.

Chapter Forty

The house near Evesham was set close to the Malvern Hills, the location affording a glorious view of the Vale of Evesham. The snow continued during the drive, but it was not so thick as to cause any problems. When they arrived, they were greeted by the pleasant butler, Jenkins, and found the house warm and inviting.

Louise awoke the next morning, at first forgetting where she was, rolling over into Lewis and finding herself surprised. She began to laugh to herself as he grunted, thinking it was not an auspicious way to start her first official day of marriage by bruising her husband! She got up, loving the lightness of the room and the view from the windows in the little rounded alcove. Snow had fallen on the hills during the night, making the vista breathtaking.

"Up already?" Lewis croaked, turning over to look at her. "It is damn bright in here."

"It's beautiful. Come and have a look." He got out of bed, putting on his robe and taking her hand.

"And where is Little Comberton?" he smiled, kissing her hair. "Shall we go over there today while the weather is so nice? Jenkins, the butler, told me it was supposed to be frosty and stormy the next few days."

"Yes, I think I would like that," Louise replied, leaning closer to him. "It has never been easy for me to declare my feelings, Lewis." He nodded, running his hand over her thick hair. "But I want to tell you this. I love you. I think I have always loved you. So many things have happened that have made me realize that. While I do love Robert, I know now it was not the same as I feel for you. And David..."

He stopped her with a kiss, murmuring, "If I had only followed my heart instead of my head, we would be celebrating twenty-five years of marriage now." They went down to breakfast later than they expected.

Dressed for the weather, they set out to make the short drive to Little Comberton. Louise felt excited at first. As they drew closer, the signs pointing the way, she began to feel apprehensive. The last time she had been here was for her father's funeral twelve years earlier. She never expected to see the village again.

The road began to look familiar as they drove toward Little Comberton. First a small farm, then another. As they rounded the turn, St. Peter's Church loomed up on their left, looking exactly the same as it had when she was a girl. No longer could she see Geoffrey's stark stone from the road. The churchyard was filled with new gravestones that occluded her view.

"Shall I stop here, darling?" Lewis asked, concerned for her as she seemed to have gone pale. "Yes, this is fine," Louise responded, the memories of her mother's dislike for her, despite her plea for forgiveness before she died, coming back to her as vividly as if her mother were in the car. Jenkins had thoughtfully included two Christmas wreaths to lay on the graves of the Whiting and Giles families. Lewis opened the boot and took out the wreaths while Louise stood at the churchyard gate, as if afraid she would no longer be admitted to this hallowed ground.

"Fine looking church," Lewis said, taking her arm. "Do you think we can go inside and have a look?"

"I don't see why not," Louise said with more calm than she felt. It was very unsettling to be here again. Everyone she had ever known as a girl was here, except for her sister Sylvia, now in Australia, and David Giles.

"Let's lay the wreaths first, then have a look inside," Lewis suggested, very aware of her nervous manner. He knew her family had been wicked to her as a girl. Eleanor and Henry had told him all about it. "Even though Hetty was my sister," Eleanor had said, "she treated her daughter worse than any brutal prison matron would have. That is why I had to take her away. She would have been crushed beyond recovery." He knew that Henrietta, or Hetty, had begged for Louise's forgiveness before she died in 1914. Still, painful memories die very hard. He wondered if this had been the right thing to do.

"They're here," Louise called, walking directly to the spot where her family lay. "Here is Geoffrey, my mother, and my father." Lewis looked down, seeing the aging gravestone of Geoffrey Bancroft Whiting, 1892-1905. So, Geoff, old man, we meet at last. I wish to God I could have been here when you had your accident. I don't know whether I would have been able to do anything for you, but I would have tried beyond all measure. He brushed some snow away, clearing the stone so the name stood out more prominently.

Louise laid the wreath down, her eyes welling with tears but she did not allow them to spill. Hello, my darling. It has been so long. I swore I would not come back here, because I know you are with me everywhere. I thought you were somehow in Robert, in his ways and manners. I know now Robert is his own man, and the man you would have been will never come to be. I gave David some of the flowers I saved from your funeral, pressed in my Bible. He died in France, you know. He is buried there.

Lewis waited while Louise cleared the snow from the adjoining stones: Henrietta Whiting, 1871-1914 and George Whiting, 1870-1923. Her family. He knew how George Whiting had been a handsome man who had seduced Louise's mother, then was set up in business to keep everyone from knowing of the shame. The shame. That 'shame' was now his wife. He took Louise's arm and held her closer to him.

"I want to see the Giles as well," Louise said, placing her hand on the gravestones in a sign of farewell, lingering longest at Geoffrey's stone. They walked through the snow-covered patches of grass a short distance away to an imposing looking cross. "These were David's parents, Emily and Frederick Giles." Again, they had been relatively young when they died. More than likely the grief of losing their only son contributed to their early deaths.

Lewis gave Louise the wreath, which she lovingly placed on the grave. She opened her handbag and pulled out a little bag. "What is that, darling?" Lewis asked as she began to spread some dirt and rocks at the base of both graves.

"Elizabeth brought this back for me," Louise replied, her voice mottled with tears. "It is dirt and stones from David's grave in France. I wanted to bring David back home in some way. Back to his family." She sprinkled the contents of the bag and lightly buried it into the partially frozen soil.

"Now I feel that in some way he is home again," she smiled at Lewis. "I hate to think of him lying out there in France all alone. His parents were lovely people really, very kind to me most of the time. I tried to give my engagement pin back when David died, but they insisted I keep it. You don't mind if I wear it, do you?" He shook his head and said, "Of course not, Louise. I have very fond memories of their son, too, you know. I know how much he loved you." Louise closed her eyes, willing herself to gather up her emotions. Again she touched their stones in a gesture Lewis found familiar, saying her farewells to them. And to David.

The church was open so they went inside. The small interior was lit brilliantly by the sunshine pouring through the stained glass windows. The entire church smelled of evergreen. The Christmas decorations were tastefully tied with red ribbons and decorated the altar and every pew.

Lewis began to explore, reading inscriptions and looking at wood carvings. Louise went immediately to one side of the church where she remained riveted.

"Quite an old place, isn't it?" Lewis said, coming over to her to see what transfixed her. Then he read the Memorial dedicated to David Gordon Giles of the 10th Battalion, Worcestershire Regiment, who was killed in battle on July 3, 1916. It went on to tell of his bravery and his courage. Louise reached out and touched it, looking at Lewis.

"His father could never stop grieving," Louise said. "It killed him. Margery told me that Robert's father was just the same. How many others?"

"Too many," Lewis nodded. "With all the saber rattling going on in Europe right now, don't think I am not worried about Brian having to go to war."

"Oh, no, surely not," Louise exclaimed. "I feel as if he is my own son."

Lewis smiled. "I think he feels very fond of you as well." The door opened behind them, so quietly it was as if the person opening the door was deliberately trying to avoid being observed. A thin, dark figure came in, almost ready to turn around but Lewis said, "Excuse me. I hope it is all right for us to be in here."

"I..I'm sure the vicar wouldn't mind," the woman said timidly. "If the church was open, everyone is welcome. I've just come to do the greens. I won't disturb you."

"Ivy?" Louise questioned, her eyes large with disbelief. "Ivy, is that you?"

"Sorry?" the woman replied. "I..I don't think I know you."

"Ivy, it is Louise. Louise Whiting." Louise came over as the woman backed up and swayed, as if she would faint. "Steady on," Lewis said, coming to her side and helping her to a chair at the back of the church. "Are you faint?"

Louise looked into a face of a woman wracked with pain and guilt. David's younger sister looked nearly one hundred years old, yet she was younger than Louise, approximately the same age as Louise's sister Sylvia, who was not yet forty. Her bony hands and anorexic frame belied the fact that she was actually alive. Lewis surreptitiously took her pulse while Louise talked to her.

"What are you doing here, Louise?" Ivy said, frightened. "I saw someone had left a wreath for my parents. Was that you?" Louise nodded. "I saw one on your family's graves, too. No one comes anymore, you know. All dead now. Everyone is dead that we knew."

"Sylvia is alive," Louise said gently. "I am, too. This is my husband, Dr. Lewis Warren. We are staying on the other side of Evesham for a few more days. Perhaps we can take you out for dinner and talk about old times."

"No, no," Ivy said, getting up with amazing strength. "I don't go out anymore. Just to do the greens and flowers at church. No reason anymore. None." She began to shuffle away.

"Some friends of mine have recently been to see David's grave in France," Louise said directly. "They brought back some stones and dirt, which I put in your parents' plot. I wanted to bring David home." Ivy's face wrinkled up slowly, but she was unable to cry.

"David has been gone so long," she nearly whispered. "Then Mummy couldn't bear it, so she died when she got 'flu. Then Daddy was so heartbroken he just keeled over. Now I keep hoping I will die, but I never die. I just go on and on for no reason at all." Lewis seemed alarmed as Louise gave him a warning glance and said, "What about your housekeeper, Mrs. Lott? Is she still with you?" Ivy nodded so Louise said, "Listen, Ivy. Lewis and I will take you home, as it has gone quite cold now." Ivy began to shake her head, but Louise put on her best nursing sister's voice and said, "No arguments. Come on. Off we go." Lewis admired her ability to become once again the most professional of St. Bartholomew's graduates when the situation called for it.

As they turned to leave the church, the sun burst through again, directly illuminating the brass on David's memorial plaque. Lewis gave Louise a look of uncertainty, having heard the story about what had happened at David's grave. As Louise took Ivy out to the car, Lewis thought he heard the sound of boyish giggles. He turned quickly, just catching what seemed to be two young boys racing up to the organ loft. He shook his head, the sound of the laughter softer now, but still faint in his ears. No, he said, I don't believe in ghosts or phantoms or anything like that. I am a scientist and one who works with the brain. Not possible. As he pulled the church door shut, he could not get it out of his mind that the two boys he had seen were the ghosts of Geoffrey Whiting and David Giles.

Chapter Forty-One

The week sped by quickly when Louise and Lewis returned to find Rose had taken such a bad turn and was still in hospital. "We've been over there every day," Brian explained, Elizabeth nodding in agreement. Elizabeth had been out for dinner with Brian and they were both sitting in the parlor waiting for the newlyweds to return. "Robert and Margery have stayed at the cottage. Rose seems to be in a very bad way."

"Did she break her hip again?" Lewis asked, concerned.

"Nearly," Brian said, giving his father and Louise a glass of whisky each. "It is just as if she has given up on life."

"I don't know what to do," Elizabeth lamented. "She wants to come home so badly but she can't unless she has care."

"Why not bring her here?" Louise said boldly, Lewis's surprised expression amusing Brian.

"You're not going to nurse her yourself, are you, darling?" Lewis moaned. "I suppose the only way I will ever get any attention from you is if I have a serious injury and need care."

"Of course not, Lewis," Louise replied, ignoring his comments and the suppressed smiles of the others. "There is so much room here we could open a hospital. She could have her own suite. We could hire nurses to look after her until she gets well enough again."

"I don't think she would ever be able to live on her own again in her cottage," Lewis said. "Robert is not going to be living there on his own much longer."

"Was he on his own?" Louise said, alarmed.

"Oh, no," Elizabeth said. "I went to help out my aunt and uncle and stay with them. Mummy went to stay with Dad at the cottage." Louise breathed a sigh of relief. "He really is ever so much better, Louise. He

329

has not had any seizures at all for weeks." Louise did not miss Elizabeth's crossed fingers as she said that.

"The lesson I learned from caring for Robert," Louise continued, "is that being among people who love and care for you, in your own surroundings, helps you get better much quicker. If she no longer needs to be in hospital, but is not well enough to be on her own, we should bring her here. Will you see to it, Lewis?"

"Well, dear, I will ask her family," Lewis smiled. "They do have the first say as to what happens to her, you know. Besides," he continued, "I am not her doctor. I would have to ask him if I could interfere."

"That's all right, Dad," Brian smiled. "Dr. Eaton is her doctor."

"There, that's settled then," Louise said, getting up and going to the telephone. "I'll ring Henry right now. I wanted to talk to them anyway and let them know we are home." Lewis raised his eyebrows and then his glass as Louise marched to the phone.

It was settled very quickly and Rose was brought home to the Warren's home with a private nurse a few days before Christmas. Louise was organizing another Christmas party, "like the ones the Giles used to have before the War," she said, and seemed to be enjoying married life and her new home more than she ever believed possible. Elizabeth loved helping with the decorations and seemed to be at the house more and more with Brian. Not that Louise minded; she found Elizabeth much like her in some ways. Her resemblance to Robert also made her heart remember the man she would never forget.

Christmas Eve came in with a swirling, gusty snowstorm, but it only added to the beautiful effect as the trees glazed over. "Like a fairy wonderland!" Margery exclaimed, sitting in the back seat with Robert as Brian picked them up for the party.

"Would you believe I have even coerced Mummy into buying that new evening dress?" Elizabeth smiled. "I never thought I would have to compete with my own mother for attention. She is smashing in it."

"Oh, darling, you know I am nothing but your old Mum," Margery laughed.

"I wouldn't say that," Robert smiled at her.

"As for you, Mr. 'Butter Wouldn't Melt in Your Mouth' Morne, .."

"You two sound as if you have been married for twenty years," Brian laughed. "Even though officially it has only been a few months."

The house was ablaze and more alive than Brian had seen it since his mother died. They had ordered a tremendous Christmas tree for the hall, its colorful lights and bulbs shining a Christmas spirit into the courtyard through the tall windows. Rose sat comfortably ensconced in her wheelchair, taking coats and hats and greeting all the visitors as they came in.

Lewis had brought a small orchestra from London to accompany the buffet dinner with Christmas carols and games. There were the usual charades and even the dreaded 'Consequences.' The cut glass crystal punch bowl shone in the light of many candles as the smell of mulled wine and evergreen permeated the room.

"You have never looked happier," Robert said to Louise, catching her by the fireplace where a roaring Yule log burned brightly. "I hope Lewis is treating you well?"

Louise smiled. "Do you know what, Robert? I think that I have always loved Lewis. First there was David, of course. I did love him. Let me say that I loved you, and always will. But true love is different, isn't it? It is what you feel for Margery. What I couldn't understand. Now I think I do."

"Then a kiss for Christmas between us," he said, kissing her cheek. "And a thank you again for believing that I was not dead. For believing so much that I could be here tonight that you gave everything for that. There is nothing that can repay that, nothing." He walked away as Louise flushed.

"All right, dear?" Henry said, keeping his eye on Rose Henning wheeling at breakneck speed from one group to the other.

"Yes, Henry," Louise said. "I don't think I have ever been happier in my life."

"As for Lewis," Henry beamed. "Look at him. He has put on weight. He is enjoying himself. He is the happiest man in Surrey, I think."

"Except for Robert Morne," Louise said, slightly wistfully. She looked at Robert talking and laughing in a small group, his arm around Margery.

"Except for Robert Morne," Henry agreed. "Come over here. Eleanor has been telling everyone of your brave adventures in the War." He shepherded her toward a small group where Aunt Eleanor exclaimed a loud greeting.

Around ten o'clock there was a tinkling of glasses, growing louder and louder. Brian's voice attempted to ring out over the party, eventually succeeding in getting their attention.

"Ladies and gentlemen," Brian said, his voice hoarse. "I wanted to take this time to tell as many of my father and stepmother's friends some important news. Since October I have had the privilege of meeting some fine people. I have been accepted into their lives, bought into their business, and now I hope to become part of their family. This gracious lady here," he held Elizabeth's hand, 'has agreed to become my wife. She probably doesn't know what she is in for, but she has said yes."

331

Thunderous applause burst out around the room as Margery looked at Robert.

"Is that why you and Brian sequestered yourselves the other day in the parlor?" Margery said, her eyes flaming. "Why didn't you tell me?"

"He asked me not to," Robert said, smiling. "He wanted it to be a surprise. After all, there would be no wedding if her father withheld his permission, would there?" She smiled at him strangely. He whirled her around and said, "He loves her, darling. He loves her as I love you. How could I say no? You wouldn't have, either."

"I suppose not," she said uncertainly. "Still, she could have told me."

"She didn't know," Robert said. "Not until tonight. It was really up to her to decide. I think she has made a good decision."

Elizabeth ran over, her silvery dress and jewelry giving her the appearance of a Christmas tinsel angel. "Oh, Mummy," she said, coming to hug her, "look at this lovely ring. It is an antique from his mother's family." Margery saw the diamond and gold design resting comfortably on Elizabeth's hand. Brian followed behind sheepishly.

"Mrs. Morne," he began, then interrupted himself, "I mean, Margery. I did so want to tell you first. I was afraid she might turn me down, you know."

"As if I would," Elizabeth said, her face shining in the candlelight.

"He asked Dad for my hand, too," Elizabeth said. "And I asked Daddy, right before I said yes tonight. I almost heard him say, yes, yes, yes! So I said it, too." People came over to the couple, Margery kissing Brian and saying, "Welcome to the family, dear boy. Given the circumstances of our lives lately, I hope you know what you are getting into."

"Feet first," he smiled as Louise and Lewis came over.

"So we shall be related after all," Robert said to them both. "That means that I will always have my neurosurgeon close at hand if I need him, being that he will be my in-law."

"As will your nurse," Lewis grinned.

"I thought you wanted me to give up my nursing sister behaviors," Louise smiled.

"Absolutely," Lewis chuckled. "Except I always thought the uniform was so fetching on you."

"Yes, we will be related now, won't we?" Margery said thoughtfully. "Don't you sometimes wonder if there isn't a bigger plan than we all know?" Everyone stood silently, the individual pillars of how they arrived at this place together tonight standing tall in their minds.

"Well, we'll have to be planning that wedding starting now," Rose wheeled over to the small group, pushing Lewis aside as she did so.

"Dresses to be made, invitations to be sent, flowers to be ordered...." Robert burst out laughing. "What is so funny, then, Robbie?" Rose said, glaring at him.

"You looked just as you did when Mr. Brooke used to make us take the inventory in January," he laughed, joined in by the others.

"This is no laughing matter," she said seriously. "One has to plan months in advance nowadays. Have they set the date yet? I think June. A June wedding is best. Nice weather, everyone can travel, no need for coats."

"And just who is the mother of the bride here?" Margery laughed.

"And the groom?" Louise added.

"Well, I'm an old hand at this. We'll work together and it will go much faster. Nicer, too, if we can make all the dresses. Margery and her sister May are fine seamstresses. Are you good with a needle, Louise?"

"Oh, yes," Margery piped in. "She made my lovely curtains in the kitchen."

"I can manage," Louise said dryly.

"I don't think Elizabeth is much for it," Rose shook her head sadly. "The younger generation is too busy tooling around in motorcars to sit down and sew. No need nowadays with ready-made thing on the racks. Still, we can do it. Something special and unique, just for my little girl." She turned her eyes to her goddaughter, who stood laughing and talking with a group of people.

Rose wheeled over to Elizabeth, the group breathing a sigh of relief. "That woman will not need Henry now until after the wedding," Lewis said, chuckling. "You were right, Louise. All she needed was to feel wanted and loved. She has a purpose now, a goal to achieve."

"She is a remarkable seamstress, although her eyes are weak," Margery added. "Well, Louise, I suppose we should start thinking about a date."

They linked arms, leaving Lewis and Robert alone. "If you haven't had a seizure over all this, Robert, I must pronounce you cured." Robert smiled, his eyes on his girls.

Chapter Forty-Two

After all the excitement in December, January seemed dull and bleak. The feeling intensified when George V died at the end of January, ushering in the new year of 1936 on an even more somber note.

Robert and Margery continued to live at Rose's cottage, while Elizabeth moved from her aunt and uncle's house to the Warren. At first Margery was upset, but Elizabeth assured her it was mostly to be with Rose, to keep her company and help look after her. Margery knew it was also to be close to Brian. With Louise there, she had nothing to worry about and she knew it.

Rose was improving. As Lewis predicted, she would never be able to live on her own again. Louise saw to her care, and with Elizabeth's help, they had Rose nearly able to function normally. They even celebrated her eighty-sixth birthday at the end of January with another party. Louise insisted on inviting Rose's children. None of them showed up or even responded to the invitation. The party went on and was a great success with Rose's newfound family. Louise kept waiting for some sort of apology, but as February turned into March, she had heard nothing from Rose's family, not even an enquiry into her health and progress.

"Never mind," Rose said while Louise was fuming at their bad manners. "I tried to raise them right. Their father was no good. Why do you think I had to work in the drapery trade most of my life? Someone had to feed them. I guess they thought I neglected them or didn't care for them." She seemed sad but not unduly upset.

"I cannot understand how a woman who works as hard as you did for them could be accused of neglecting them," Louise said angrily. "I've a good mind to ring them up and tell them what I think of them." Rose smiled, grabbing her hand.

334

"It's been a long time since I've cared. Outside of my one daughter, who is so ruled by that no-good husband of hers she would never cross him, not one of them cares for me. You, Lewis, Brian, Robbie, Margery, and my little Elizabeth, you're my family. I think of you as my own daughter. No one has ever cared about me and my welfare the way that you do." She got a bit teary-eyed, pulling several handkerchiefs from her bosom and blowing her nose loudly.

"Well, I feel the same, Rose," Louise smiled. She found it easier to smile and accept love from others since she married Lewis. In her heart she wondered why it had taken her so long to find out that loving others, and being loved, was the easiest thing in the world.

"You know we want you to stay with us," Louise said gently, sitting next to Rose. "Rose, Lewis and I are of the opinion that it would not be good for you to live on your own again. Robert and Margery are still looking after your cottage. Margery loves it and so does Robert. Of course there is still Margery's house, and..."

Rose nodded her head. "They love the cottage, do they? I know Robbie is finding it a hard go trying to convince himself he could live in Jack's house. Can't say as I blame him, either."

"I know," Louise said. "Margery said that Jack picked that house out when he decided he wanted to move. She had little to say about it. It is a nice house, but if she had her choice, she would have picked a cottage like yours."

"I know Elizabeth loves that house on Tilburstow Hill," Rose tilted her head, lost in thought. "So it is a muddle, isn't it? Once she's married, well, that will be different."

"And June twenty-seventh is getting closer, isn't it?" Louise smiled. "Margery and Elizabeth went to pick out the fabrics today for the wedding gown and the bridesmaids' dresses. We'll have to make a start on the sewing soon."

"It's only early March," Rose smiled. "I think with the little sewing circle you've arranged we will have them done in no time at all."

"My sewing skills are a little rusty, other than patching things," Louise said. "I hope I can manage."

"I'll keep after you," Rose smiled, nodding off in her wheelchair by the window.

Louise looked out at the unkempt yet once beautiful garden. We will really have to have that sorted as well before the big day, she thought. An idea came to her suddenly. The grass was getting greener and it was now time to start the pruning and clearing up for the spring and summer flowers. She left Rose slumbering and went downstairs to find Lewis.

She found him engrossed in the library, his silvery head bent over some article. He was so deeply engrossed in it he didn't hear her come in. "It's not another issue of *Brain* is it, Lewis?" He looked up and smiled as if he had been caught in an illegal act. "No, no. Actually, I just got a letter from Cyril. Of all things. He's gone and got himself married. Very quickly, he says, in Sussex, so he wanted to apologize for not inviting us."

"Very quickly?" Louise said, her smile wicked looking. "Surely he didn't have to get married, did he?"

"Cyril?" Lewis howled. "Well, I think the bride might be a bit too old for that dilemma. Guess who he married?"

"I have no idea," Louise said, looking puzzled. "Do I know her?"

"Oh, yes indeed. Go on, guess."

"I don't know, Lewis. Tell me." Louise had never liked guessing games, but she was dying to know who Cyril married."

"None other than Sister Meade," he grinned inanely. "Angela Meade is now Angela Gibbons."

Louise sat back in her chair as if the air had been knocked out of her. "They did seem rather fond of each other at our wedding. Do you think we inspired them?"

"Perfectly possible," he laughed, removing his glasses. "Good old Cyril. He always seemed the perfect career Army man to me. Never would have thought it of him. Anyway, he has also asked if we might like to join him and Angela..."

"Oh, I don't think I will ever get used to calling her that," Louise shuddered.

"No doubt, after years of 'Sister Meade," Lewis continued. "Seems there is a neurological conference in Australia in July. Right around Brian's birthday, so I wondered if perhaps he and Elizabeth might not join us and we could go? You could see your sister Sylvia again, and her children. You've never seen them, have you?"

"No," Louise said. "I would love that. I think Aunt Eleanor and Henry might like to see the children as well."

"Henry would find the conference interesting, no doubt," Lewis added.

"As would I," Louise snapped. "Is it just for doctors?"

"I don't know," Lewis smiled. "I am sure it will not be when you get there. I imagine old Angela must have softened a bit to marry Cyril, don't you think?"

"We all have," Louise said. "I suppose one doesn't even realize how hard one becomes doing that sort of work every day. I was just talking to Rose about staying with us. She took it rather well. After the way her family treated her, I think she is well pleased to have a new family of sorts."

"She's a feisty old thing, but that second fall didn't do her any good," Lewis said seriously. "Whatever time she has left she is more than welcome to stay here with us."

"That puts her heart at ease, I know," Louise said. "Mine, too, as I've become very fond of her."

"So have I," Lewis replied. "Is that why you came in here and tried to catch me reading *Brain* on the sly?" He leaned back, smiling in anticipation of her questions.

"The wedding," she said as he groaned. "No, really, Lewis. I was with Rose and after she fell asleep, I was looking out at the garden. Do you have a gardener?"

"I think Hayward gets someone in from the village every spring," Lewis said. "Do you want me to tell him to ring the man?"

"Do you have a contract with him?" she asked.

"I don't think so," Lewis said, rubbing his forehead. "Why?"

"Robert could do the gardening for us," Louise said, the light dawning in Lewis's eyes as she spoke. "He needs a job, something of his own. Now that he has been showing no signs of relapse," she hesitated, the question in the air.

"No signs of relapse," Lewis said. "He has only had a few minor episodes the past few months. Just needed his dosage adjusted. Otherwise, doing quite well."

"So you see," Louise said. "We could hire him as our jobbing gardener. I know he is capable of doing the work. It would look splendid by the wedding. And he would be doing it for his daughter."

"That's a big garden for one man," Lewis said.

"He did the entire hospital grounds himself," Louise said. "If he needs help we can get some boys from the village or something."

"Did you really need to ask me?" Lewis smiled at her. "You've made your mind up, so there it is. My question is: should I be jealous?"

"No, this is not a ploy to get Robert over here every day," she said, her lips curved in a half-smile. "You must know by now that as attractive as I find him, it is you who has stolen my heart after all." She came to the desk, leaning over and kissing him.

"How can I say no after that?" Lewis said. "Put the idea to him. Aren't they coming round tonight to see Rose?"

"Yes," Louise said. "I'll have him take a look at the work and see what he thinks. And Lewis," she smiled, turning around at the door.

"Yes, dear?" he said cautiously, wondering what next.

"If he manages to do well, which I am sure he will, do you think you can recommend him to your friends in the area? His pension isn't much, you know. If he had work of his own, a feeling of being his own man with his own business, I think it would do much to make him happy." She left the room before he could answer.

"Well, Robert," Lewis said aloud. "Once again we have been outmaneuvered by Louise. If she had worked with General Haig, the War would have been over in two weeks." He chuckled to himself, picking up the surreptitious copy of an article on the reoccupation of the Rhineland by German troops he had been reading before Louise came in to talk to him. A bad sign, he thought, praying that there would not be another war that would claim his only son for a soldier.

Chapter Forty-Three

"Just turn the key," Elizabeth said to Robert as they sat in a layby outside of the village. "It's not like the old days, where you had to crank the car to get it started."

"Amazing," Robert murmured. "I want to do this right from the start. Just turn the key," he repeated, moving the key to the furthest position.

"Not all the way to the end, Dad," Elizabeth laughed. "Just until it starts." The engine burst into life. "Right," Robert smiled in relief. "Now, gears and clutch. I remember that. Do you know I actually drove a Rolls? I took Mummy to a posh dance in Caterham for the Ambulance Brigade. Mr. Brooke let me use his car."

"What year was that, Dad?" Elizabeth grinned. "Cars are much different now. Easier to drive, too."

"All right, then," he said. "Let's see how she goes."

After a few false starts and stalls, Robert soon got the hang of it. "I think you were just trying too hard, Dad," Elizabeth said as they sailed along the road, his gear changing getting smoother and his coordination with the clutch becoming almost seamless. "The gears on those old cars really required a lot of muscle to change them. Probably the reason why not as many women drove as they do today."

"There were enough women drivers then," Robert grinned. "I dodged them all the time crossing the High Street."

"No women driver jokes, please," Elizabeth pleaded. "Women can do anything they like now, really. We can vote, we can drive, we can smoke..."

"Very unattractive habit," Robert said. "Especially for women."

"You are so old-fashioned, Dad," Elizabeth said. "It's a new world now for women. If I want to be a doctor, I can be."

"There were women doctors in my day," he said. "Not many, but some."

"Not many, because they made it so hard for them to get into medical school," Elizabeth said. "Watch out for that roundabout." He negotiated the roundabout with little mishap. They carried on toward the next village.

"So you are a suffragette then, are you?" Robert grinned. She groaned again and said, "That is an old term, Dad. I am just a free woman who wants to make her own decisions in life."

"You have told Brian all this, haven't you?" he smiled at her.

"Brian knows I am free," Elizabeth said. "I don't think I have to tell him that. Did you think that Mummy would have let you make all the decisions?" She looked so serious he had to laugh.

"We are talking about your mother here, aren't we?" he laughed again, more heartily this time. "The woman who asked me to the dance? The woman who asked me to marry her?"

"Mummy asked you to marry her?" Elizabeth squealed. "How delicious! How did she do it?" Elizabeth leaned toward him, all ears.

He downshifted as they came into the next village. "Shall we stop and have a cup of tea?"

"How about a pint instead?" Elizabeth said. Robert nodded, pulling the car in front of the Red Lion Pub.

"I suppose I will have to get used to this world of new women," he said gently. "Your granddad never thought women were anything but equal. So did Jack and I. You can be anything you want to be, sweetheart. Anything."

"Thanks, Dad," she said, leaning over to kiss his cheek. "Now, tell me how Mummy asked you to marry her." They went inside, Robert recounting how his indecision led Margery to pop the question before he got around to it himself.

That evening Robert agreed to take on the gardening job for Lewis and Louise, his eyes shining as he saw the finished product in his mind. It was not only the idea of getting out and working that delighted him, but also that he would be doing this for his daughter's wedding, a daughter he had come to love so deeply over the past few months he didn't know how he ever lived without her before.

Spring was fast approaching and Robert was spending nearly every day over at the Warren. The garden was already looking different as his practiced eye and hand made a difference in the overgrown areas. Louise watched him from the window, the dull heartache no longer there, replaced now with a true love for the man he was, and a wish for his great happiness.

Elizabeth drove him over and took him back when he worked. He had acquired a set of tools from Lewis, who intended to make a gift of them to Robert after the job was finished. It was now April. Several of Lewis's friends had commented on his new gardener and where he had found him. Lewis came up behind Louise, grabbing her around the waist and said, "I knew you would be here, lusting after that gardener again. Well, here's something for him. And you." He handed her a sheaf of papers. "What's this?" she asked.

"Have a look," he said. "I think we should start looking into hiring those village boys after all."

The papers were work orders for gardens. At least five large houses had asked Lewis for the name of his gardener and intended to engage him at very substantial rates.

"He can't do it all on his own," Lewis said. "Still, he can tell others how to do the work, no doubt. I see a "Morne, Jobbing Gardener" business in the near future."

"This is wonderful, Lewis," Louise cried. "Did you twist their arms?"

"No, I spiked their drinks," he laughed. "Actually, it was Ted who noticed the garden coming on when he was here last week and asked if I was still using the fellow from the village, as he'd heard he retired. I told him about Robert. He was very keen to have him. Then he told a friend of his, and so on."

"Shall we go tell him?" Louise asked.

"Yes, but I think we had better tell him we would like to invest in his business," Lewis said. "He is going to need tools, a van, the lot. As you say, his pension will only carry him so far. Just a loan, you understand, until he turns a profit. I thought you might tell him. You have that special knack..."

"You mean I am terribly bossy and he rarely refuses me when I tell him what to do," Louise said. "Well, Dr. Warren, I am a changed woman now. No more Sister Whiting, you understand. However, I will do it just this once, since it is such a critical issue."

"Oh, well done, Sister Whiting," Lewis clapped. "I feel much better about it now."

Robert seemed reluctant to accept the loan at first. As Louise explained it to him, she told him it was a good business investment for them. They needed to make their money work, not just lie in the bank. They couldn't think of a better investment than Robert and his gardening. When he saw the requests for his services, the smile on his face nearly lit up the entire garden.

341

When Elizabeth was ready to take him home, he went to the driver's side of the car. "What's this?" Louise asked. "He's been driving and I've been teaching him," Elizabeth laughed. "We make it look as if I'm doing the driving, but he is. It's all right, isn't it, Lewis?" Lewis was dumbfounded and replied, "Well, I suppose it is, I mean..."

"I've never seen you speechless before, Lewis," Robert said. "Thank you for everything. You won't regret it." He put the car in gear smoothly and drove off.

"It is all right for him to drive, isn't it, Lewis?" Louise said, her face worried as she scanned the road until the car was out of sight.

"I probably would have advised against it," Lewis said. "But I can't stop him. He's nearly completely on his own now. Let's just keep our fingers crossed that he never suffers a seizure while driving." They linked arms and went into the house.

As April progressed, the sewing circle met almost every day at the Warren to work on the wedding gown and bridesmaids' dresses. Elizabeth wanted to have a wedding like her mother had wanted, with yellow bridesmaids' dresses and an ivory satin gown. Rose's eyesight was not good, but her fingers still worked nimbly. She was surrounded by yards of creamy satin, French lace, and seed pearls.

May had come back from the south coast, her health much improved. She also missed her family and Upper Marstone. She and Sally Shepherd joined the sewing circle, making the work go faster. Louise found she had lost none of her skill, but the delicate work was best left to May, Sally and Margery.

Elizabeth came in to chat and watch the progress of the work. She complained when she had to be fitted again and again. Secretly she loved being among all her favorite women. The conversations were funny, silly and loving.

"Do you know that in 1923, after my father died, I went on a grand bicycle tour of Surrey?" Louise said, breaking a thread with her teeth. "I didn't want to, but poor Aunt Eleanor broke her wrist and couldn't go, so she volunteered me instead." Everyone laughed, imagining the outrage Louise must have felt. "I was so irritated by the idea. It actually turned out to be a good thing in the end. When Lewis and I were in Upper Marstone the other day, I asked him to take me to St. Nicholas, so I could see the church where Elizabeth was to be married. I remember it so well, especially the War Memorial. When we stopped there on that tour, there was a man standing at the Memorial who was so heartbroken about his son. He said, "That's my boy there," and pointed to the Memorial. I was numb and didn't know what to say." Elizabeth looked at her strangely and said, "I think I remember that day."

"You?" Margery said. "How could you remember that day, darling? You weren't on that bicycle tour, were you?"

"No, Mummy," Elizabeth said. "Don't you remember that group of ladies and all the bicycles parked by the lychgate? Granddad went to the War Memorial because it was the day Dad died, or Granddad thought he had."

"You came up from the churchyard," Louise said. "You had been at your Grandmother's grave..."

"That's right," Elizabeth said. "Remember, Mummy? She told us she was a nurse who took care of sick soldiers."

"Do you have a photograph of your father-in-law, Margery?" Louise said. "I will never forget that man's face as long as I live." Margery nodded, putting down her sewing and reaching for her handbag. She handed a picture to Louise.

"That is my favorite picture of Charlie, taken when Elizabeth was christened," Margery said as Louise stared at a handsome man who looked like a cross between Jack and Robert. He was smiling widely as he held the baby Elizabeth in his arms. Despite the smile, the grief in his eyes was so evident Louise recognized him immediately.

"That's the man," she said, staring at the picture. "Oh, God, if I had only known! To think I was talking to Robert's father! He was so anguished it broke my heart then. And you! I talked to you as well. Oh, dear." She kept staring at the picture, an older, ravaged looking woman standing slightly behind Charlie Morne. "Is that Robert's mother?" Louise asked. Margery nodded. Louise just closed her eyes, handing back the picture to Margery.

"You could not have known," Margery said, taking Louise's arm. "You didn't know his last name."

"No," Louise said quietly. "I wish I could have sensed something. I do remember thinking the little girl, Elizabeth, reminded me of someone. Obviously I know who it was now." She hesitated and said, "And when I looked at you, Margery, there was something about your eyes that I felt I had met you before. It was Robert's drawings of you, but I just didn't make the connection." She sighed deeply.

"Oh, Louise," Elizabeth said, coming over and putting her arms around her, "You brought him back to us, even if it took a long time. I know Granddad understands. I do."

"Not to sound callous, but we can't cry over spilt milk," Rose interrupted. "There's work to be done here, so let's get on ladies."

Margery gave Louise a smile, her heart aching for Charlie. Oh, Charlie, she thought. If you and I had had psychic powers, we could have known who Louise was. That day came back to her, how Charlie had talked of what a fine woman that nurse was to dedicate herself to nursing such severely wounded soldiers with head wounds. It was his son she was caring for and bringing back to them.

The talk turned to more casual topics and the upcoming wedding. "When Billy and I got married," Sally said, "it was right after the War. There wasn't much to be had, really, in the way of fancy materials. And our cake! Ghastly, really. Still I was happy to have him home again and to marry him. Margery was the only bridesmaid. What did you wear, Marge?"

"I think May and I cut down that blue organdy frock I had, didn't we, May?" Margery laughed. "It wasn't like before the War. When Robert and I got engaged..."

"Yes, Mummy," Elizabeth laughed. "Dad told me all about that."

"He did, did he?" Margery said. "And what did he tell you?"

"That you asked him to marry you!" Elizabeth clapped gleefully.

"That's somewhat true," Margery laughed. "I am sure he made it sound as if I begged him to be my husband." Elizabeth nodded. "He was always so indecisive, you know. There we were, me pining for him to ask me, and he going on and on about how he hates to be away from me, hates to go home alone at night." The women all made oohing noises. "So I just calmly said, 'There is a way we can be together all the time, and never have to go home alone again.' It took him a minute to understand. His eyes popped out and he said, "What? You mean, get married?" When I said yes, he hemmed and hawed about money, so a few more persuasive words and he was on his knees and asked me. I said yes, of course, after all that maneuvering!" Everyone clapped and laughed when Robert popped his head in the door.

"That's her version," he laughed. "My eyes didn't pop out, either."

"It's not nice to eavesdrop, Robbie," Rose said. "I'm sure your mother taught you better than that. What are you doing in here, anyway? The garden's out there."

"Just popped in for a quick cup of tea and thought I would see how the sewing was coming on," he smiled and everyone beamed back at him. "Nice material, that. Good quality. Right, Rose?"

"You haven't forgotten your training, Robbie," Rose replied. "Very good cloth. Imported, too. We're almost done with the bridesmaids' dresses. They'll have to come around for a fitting tomorrow."

"That's a nice pale yellow color," he said, eyeing the fabric from afar. "Margery wanted yellow for our wedding, didn't you, darling? I remember that because she told me not long before that yellow was her favorite color. It was going to be more like daffodils, wasn't it?"

"Yes," Margery said. "We planned quite a do, as my former employer, Lady Lyons, offered us the use of her ballroom for our reception."

"In exchange for my Dad's free labor," Robert grumbled.

"Still, it would have been lovely to have a church wedding," Margery sighed. "I even had the date picked out. May 8, 1915. May and I had made a start on my wedding gown. Robert would have been in a morning suit. I never had a church wedding either time, you know. Both marriages in a Registry Office." She kept sewing, her face wistful

"I'm back to the garden where I belong," Robert said. "Enjoy yourselves, ladies." He flashed a brilliant smile and left.

"He's still entirely too handsome for a man who's been through so much," May said. Sally giggled like a girl and added, "I must say he looks very good for his age. Quite fit."

Elizabeth sat cross-legged on the floor near her mother, who was finishing one of the yellow dresses. "Mummy," Elizabeth said, "what about a church wedding? In May?"

"Oh, dear, you can't go changing things now at last minute," Margery said, finishing off the stitches.

"No, not my wedding," Elizabeth said, "*Your* wedding."

"My wedding?" Margery said, confused. "Whatever are you talking about, darling?"

"Why can't you have that May wedding you should have had years ago?" Elizabeth asked. "Who were your bridesmaids then? Sally, no doubt."

"Sally," Margery recounted, "and Janie and Milly. Isn't that right, Sally?"

"Yes," Sally said, excited. "Why not, Marge? It needn't be elaborate. Just the wedding you should have had with Robbie at St. Nicholas."

"Oh, it might be silly, as we are already married," Margery said, her eyes full of hope.

"No, a church wedding is different," May said.

"That's right," Rose added. "Makes a difference to have a church wedding."

"Please, Mummy?" Elizabeth begged. "It would make me so happy."

"We could even invite Janie and Milly," Sally added. "We know where they live."

"There's no time for dresses and such," Margery said. "And the catering..."

345

"I am sure I can organize all that," Louise said. "What was the name of the person? Lady Lyons? How can I reach her?" Their chatter went on as they almost forgot their sewing for the other wedding. By the end of the day they picked the date: May 9, 1936. Fingers were crossed that they could have the church that day.

"That is my birthday," Louise said. "It would be a wonderful gift."

"I suppose we are going to do it, then," Margery laughed, Elizabeth jumping up with a shout and kissing her mother.

"Now you just have to break the news to Dad that he is going to be a bridegroom at last," Elizabeth giggled.

Robert was actually more enthusiastic about it than Margery thought as they all told him at once. As everyone was getting ready to go, Rose motioned to Robert and Margery that she wanted to see them privately.

"What is it, Rose?" Margery said concerned. "Is there something you need?"

"Well, Louise and Lewis had their solicitor come around, just so's I could make sure that when I go, all my affairs are in order," Rose said calmly. "Don't talk like that, Rose," Margery said, but Rose motioned for her to be quiet.

"I don't have much, as you know. My children have been none too kind to me," she said without feeling. "I didn't think it was right that they should descend like vultures on my little home that I have loved for years. Not to mention my poor Catkins. They'd put him out straightaway, if I know them." She coughed slightly and then handed them an envelope.

"I was going to do this before Elizabeth's wedding. As you two are now going to have your own wedding, I want to do it now," she smiled. "I know you both love my cottage..."

"And Catkins," Robert nodded vigorously.

"And Catkins," she added. "So here's a wedding present for you. The cottage is yours."

"What?" Margery gasped. "We couldn't, Rose. No, please. Let us buy it from you." Robert was speechless.

"No, and that's final," Rose said. "What do I need money for? There's more than enough to give me a good funeral when the time comes. I've got no debts, a small pension, and Louise and Lewis are looking after me. I couldn't think of two people I want to see living there more than both of you. Please, as my gift. Robert was always like a son to me. He still is. So this is my gift to my boy." He got up, putting his arms around her and holding her close to him. She could feel him weeping as he held her.

"There, there, sweetheart, don't go on," she said, looking at his face. "It was wicked what those Germans did to you, wicked. Now they're at it again. God forbid that they start another war. You deserve wonderful things and you shall have them. I want you both to have this cottage. Don't upset an old lady by saying no." She leaned back in her wheelchair, content that she had made her point.

"Now, off home with you both," she waved her hand at them. "It is your home as of today. You can see the date on the Deed of Gift. Take good care of it and be happy there." They got up to leave. "And don't go thinking I am going to kick over soon. I have two weddings to attend. I will be at both of them, front and center." They kissed her goodbye, both so stunned they couldn't say anything to each other as Elizabeth drove them home.

Chapter Forty-Four

Louise was as good as her word and made contact with Lady Lyons, explaining the situation and promising to work with her on her various charity causes in return. She is still extracting payment, Louise thought, just as she had from Charlie Morne. Still, the ballroom and all the trimmings would be available. Louise offered to foot the entire catering bill and any other expenses.

Robert and Margery began making the invitation list, Sally helping to address the envelopes and putting special notes in for Janie and Milly advising them to wear something 'yellow' although they would not be wearing formal bridesmaid dresses this time around. May found the original wedding dress they had started making in 1914, deciding to finish it for Margery in an updated style. She even found her own wedding veil that she hoped Margery would wear. It was quite early 20th century, but the lace was still beautiful.

A week before the wedding, Louise stopped by to make sure the final arrangements were what Robert and Margery wanted, from the cake to the meal to the orchestra that would play at Lennox Place. The wedding would be an afternoon one, as the Vicar had to squeeze them in after the morning wedding. There would be a wedding supper, then dancing and a honeymoon for the couple at a later date.

"We were just going over to clear a few more things from Tilburstow Hill Road," Margery said. "Robert is going to drive his new van. Have you seen it?"

"How could we miss it?" Lewis smiled. "That green color is just the thing for a gardener."

"Lovely van, too. Drives beautifully," Robert smiled. "Margery is going to be my partner in this business. Do the business end of it, paperwork, bookkeeping..."

"Yes," Margery agreed. "He gets all the fun and I get the paperwork."
"Fun?" he said incredulously. "Slogging in a garden in the burning sun, shoveling manure onto..."
"All right, darling, let's go fetch more boxes," she laughed.

The house on Tilburstow Hill Road looked lonely and neglected as they drove up. "Wish I could get my hands on that garden," Robert said as they came up the path. "It's a lovely house, but the garden is totally neglected."

"Are you going to sell this house, Margery?" Lewis asked as they stepped inside. Margery flipped on the light and they saw that many personal objects were already gone.

"I'm..I'm not sure," Margery said. "I thought I might keep it in case Elizabeth and Brian want it. She loves this house, you know. It has been her home for years." Margery started up the stairs. "There are some old things in the loft I wanted to get down. We can sort them out at the cottage." They followed her upstairs and then into the loft.

"Let's take these boxes down first," she said, handing a box to each one of them. They put them by the front door when Robert started rummaging through one of them.

"Look at this!" he said, holding up some books. "These are my things! Here are my paints, and some of my old books. I got this little donkey figurine when I was just a lad on holiday in Sidmouth." He took the box to the couch and began rummaging through it.

"His mother packed up his things after she thought he had died," Margery said. "I'd forgotten about that box." She watched the happy expression on Robert's face, glad that the things were still here.

"And my sketchbook!" he exclaimed, holding a dark blue book with gold gilding and an intricate gold design on the cover.

"Robert," Louise said, staring at the book. "Where did you get that book?"

"I don't know," he replied, wondering why she looked upset. "Let's see. I always used to put the dates in my books. Yes, look here. It says, 'Christmas 1905. St. Bartholomew's Hospital. That's right. I broke my femur and was in hospital."

"Do you remember who gave you that book?" Louise persisted.

"It just says, 'From Father Christmas'," he added nervously. "What's the matter, Louise?"

"Was your nurse's name Catherine Webb?" she asked. This time Lewis said, "Catherine?"

"I don't know," Robert said. "Yes, actually, I do remember. Sister Webb. She was lovely. How did you know that?"

"Because she handed you that book and told you that Father Christmas had left it for you," Louise said, her eyes wide. Lewis took her arm, steadying her.

"Y..Yes.." Robert stammered, his eyes confused.

"I bought you that book, Robert," Louise said. "I came to the hospital to meet Lewis," she turned to him, "but first Catherine Webb gave us a tour of the hospital. She was in the orthopedic ward and there was a little boy who seemed so forlorn and scared. When I went home I couldn't get you out of my mind. I bought you this book because she said you liked to paint and draw. You have that femoral scar on your right leg. I met your parents that day. They talked about your brother Jack." She sat down heavily, her face in her hands.

"It's very strange," Lewis said, "almost as if you two were supposed to know each other from the beginning."

"Geoffrey," Louise said. "Geoffrey brought me to the hospital to see you, Lewis. He wanted me to see Robert, too. Geoffrey was looking out for me and he knew what my future would hold." Robert held the book in his hands, staring at it as if it were an enchanted tome.

"Let's get the boxes to the car," Lewis said. "It's beyond belief how this could be true, Louise. We are all inextricably linked somehow."

"Louise," Margery said, taking her arm, "in normal circumstances I would not have known you. You would probably not have known Robert, either. We cannot think of our lives without you and Lewis now. Whatever the reason, and if your brother was responsible, I am glad it has brought us all together. And hope we will all be together for years to come." They gathered up the boxes, turned out the lights, and went to the warm and cozy cottage together.

Chapter Forty-Five

Arthur Higgins sat over breakfast one May morning, reading the local county paper. Inside there was a half-page article on the return of a missing soldier from the Great War, who due to a head injury and subsequent loss of memory, had been unidentified in an Army hospital for nearly twenty years. It went on to say he was finally going to marry his fiancé at St. Nicholas Church, Upper Marstone, at two o'clock on Saturday, May 9, 1936. The soldier's name was Robert Morne.

"Robbie!" he said. "God, it's Robbie!" He got up and shouted to his wife, "Look at this, luv! It's my best mate from the Army! We're going to a wedding in Upper Marstone next week!"

At the same time former sergeant with the 7th Battalion, The Queen's Royal West Surrey Regiment, Ed Morrison, now divorced and living on his own in Surrey, saw the same article. "Robbie," he said, making plans to be at the wedding. John Whitlock, former Lieutenant with the same regiment, was reading his morning paper, stretching out his two prosthetic legs in front of him. His second wife grinned as he tapped into her leg, saying, "We're off to a wedding in Upper Marstone next week. One of my men miraculously back from the dead. I must see him."

Stopping for a cup of tea before finishing the morning farm chores, Jim Crombie read the same article, gasping in disbelief and then delight. Saturday afternoons were not too busy as the farmer's schedule goes. He and his wife could manage to get to Upper Marstone for this event. After all, how many times does someone you considered a brother in that holocaust called the Great War return from the dead?

Saturday, May 9, dawned clear and beautiful, the sky filled with fleecy white clouds and sunshine. Margery awoke in her sister May's house near the church, as she would have if she had married Robert in 1915. May had fussed and fussed over the final fitting of the gown, the fabric more delicate than it had been twenty years earlier, yet its fragility gave it even more beauty.

Billy came over in the early afternoon to get Rob. He was to be the best man, as he would have been years earlier. Or it might have been Jack, Billy thought. Jack, if you have had a hand in all this, I think you have redeemed yourself. He knocked on the door and got no answer. Worried, he opened the door, saying, "Rob? Everything all right?"

He looked around and could not see Rob in the house. What the bloody hell has happened now? Frantically he searched, seeing that the bathtub had just been used and Rob's pajamas were on the bed. Where is he? Billy looked around, going into the kitchen, seeing a half-finished cup of tea and barely touched piece of toast.

Rob was standing in the back garden, looking up at the sky while Catkins ran and played in the garden. He was watching the birds, his expression so blissful Billy hated to interrupt him. He opened the back door and Rob turned around and smiled.

"What are you doing out here?" Billy asked, walking through the beautifully manicured path of flowers.

"Thinking," Rob replied. "Thinking about how lucky I am to be standing here alive. Thinking about how lucky I am to have a woman who loves me like Margery. Thinking about how lucky I am to have a beautiful daughter like Elizabeth. And friends like you, of course." Billy stood next to him, both of them looking up into the sky at a flock of birds.

"No one can say how they feel, really," Billy said. "Just that I think it has reinforced our faith in some higher power to have you back. You know that for some reason you were spared..."

"When Bert and Steve were not," Rob said, turning to Billy. "I've been thinking about them today. They would have been at my wedding in 1915. My parents would have. Jack would have."

Billy shuffled nervously. "They're here, we just can't see them. I was thinking about Jack today. He would have been best man if he was alive and things were different. Somehow I think Jack has had a hand in things. Especially with Elizabeth."

Rob smiled at him, the sun making him squint, showing the lines that hadn't been noticeable in other light. "I think so, too, Billy. I've been thinking about Jack all day. I miss him, despite what happened. He was the only brother I had. We could have made things right with each other. I hope he knows that wherever he is, I thank him for this day." They turned back to the house and went off to church.

Margery stood nervously at the back of the church. Both Millie and Janie were there, considerably older, but dressed in almost identical shades of yellow. "As if we all sensed each other's color," Janie said, her terrible marriage not daunting her silly comments. Milly was sedate and graying, a schoolteacher now. They were so anxious to see Robert they could not contain themselves.

"He's still handsome and charming and has that radiant smile," Sally giggled like the girl she once was.

"Even after having half his head blown away," Janie said sadly.

"He did not have half his head blown away or he wouldn't be standing at the altar," Milly reprimanded her. "Use your own head."

"Mine's all whole, I think," Janie laughed.

"I wonder if it ever was," Milly said sourly.

Margery smiled as the banter reminded her so much of their younger days. It is almost as if it were 1915 again, she smiled. She closed her eyes and heard the organ begin to play. Harry took her arm. "Are you ready?" he grinned. "Glad you two decided to do this before my old flat feet prevented me from walking you down the aisle."

Elizabeth led them off, strewing flower petals along her mother's path, followed by Sally, Milly and Janie. Robert smiled widely at them all, trying not to laugh as Janie's mouth dropped open wide when she saw him. Billy had their buckle rings, specially blessed by the vicar. As Robert scanned the crowd, he saw some familiar faces grinning at him. Arthur, Jim, John Whitlock, and Ed Morrison. Ed who had been his best mate at the hospital in East Preston. Robert now remembered; Ed had been the sergeant who took him, Arthur, and Jim over the top that fateful day. Ed still didn't remember that early afternoon near Thiepval in September 1916, but now Robert did.

Dr. Gibbons stood there with Sister Meade. Louise told him they had got married, of all things! Billy's old Dad was there, Dick Shepherd. Neighbors and friends and people he had once loved, and would love again. Rose was already crying even though the ceremony had just begun. Louise stood dry-eyed, smiling at him, her arm on Lewis's. He smiled back, both of them feeling that bittersweet pang of what might-have-been, knowing that somehow, it had worked out the way it was supposed to have done.

Elizabeth beamed at him, her face so like his own it made his heart jump. The twenty years of hell seemed like nothing when he saw her face. And then Margery. His Margery. His best girl. His everything. She was wearing the dress she would have worn, her veil softly falling over her dark hair. The most beautiful girl in the world, he always thought. She always would be to him.

The ceremony moved him so deeply he thought he was going to have a seizure, then realized it was simply the power of his emotions making his knees buckle. As they slipped their rings on each other's fingers and repeated the sacred, traditional words, the fire of their love burned so brightly it seemed to illuminate their entire beings. The final kiss of the ceremony brought loud bursts of weeping from nearly everyone.

As the afternoon went on, Robert rekindled his friendships with his friends from the Army, who enthralled Brian and Elizabeth with their feats in and out of the trenches. Robert told them about his identity discs and their recent trip to France. Margery pulled him away for a few dances and toasts. Billy's words as best man were so moving that even Margery cried.

Brian danced with Elizabeth, holding her close. She murmured that this was the perfect day, absolutely perfect. "I have one more thing that will make it even more perfect," he said, whirling her outside into the garden.

"What could possibly be more perfect than this day and my parents practically illuminating the entire place?" she laughed.

"I thought as I am doing business in Upper Marstone, we ought to live here," he said conspiratorially.

"That's a good idea," Elizabeth said. "We will."

"With that thought," he continued, "I have bought us a house."

"Oh, you have, have you?" she said. "Without consulting me?"

"Oh, I have a feeling you will like this house," he smiled. "It is 7 Moorcroft Gardens."

"What?" she squealed. "You bought it?"

"Signed it yesterday with your mother at the bank," he laughed, relieved she was happy. "She knows how much you love the place. I do, too. It will always be your father's house."

"Daddy's house," she corrected him. "My house, too."

"Now it shall always be your house," he smiled. "Just an early wedding gift from me to you."

"I don't know what I shall buy you to top that," she laughed. "But I will think of something."

"I don't doubt it," Brian smiled at her.

Bill and Sally went over and put a word in the bandleader's ear. There was a silence and then the leader said, "We have a special request for the bride and groom. A song they always loved and will remember. It was 'their song. He raised his baton and struck up the first notes of 'Meet Me Tonight in Dreamland.'

354

"I thought they were going to play a tango," Robert said, as everyone laughed. He bowed to Margery, she curtseyed, and they fell into each other's arms, dancing as if they were young lovers again.

"I used to dream I was dancing with you to this song," Margery whispered in his ear, no one on the floor but them. "Then I would always wake up and find you not there. Tell me that will not happen, darling. Please tell me that this is real."

"It's real, darling," he whispered. "But I refuse to pinch you in front of so many people to prove it."

"No pinches necessary," she smiled at him, holding him so close to her she almost believed that they could waltz back in time and start over again.

"Do you know where I want to go for a honeymoon?" she said to him. "To France, as we once planned. Not now, but when we are ready. To Paris."

"To Paris," he repeated.

They clung to each other, the room seeming empty of anyone else but them. The music played on as they held each other, the dreams they had now lying before them, just waiting for them to make them come true.

*****

About the Author

Cynthia Mills has lived in England and currently resides in Mentor, Ohio. Her avid interest in the Great War and its aftermath inspired her to write a trilogy about this era. **Missing, Believed Killed** was the first book in the series, followed by **Bring the Dead to Life**. Cynthia is currently at work on a mystery series set in England during the Great War and post-war years. Please visit her website at www.cynthiamills.com to read more about her work and this fascinating time period.